BE AMAZING

Also available from **mental_floss**

CONDENSED KNOWLEDGE

FORBIDDEN KNOWLEDGE

COCKTAIL PARTY CHEAT SHEETS

WHAT'S THE DIFFERENCE?

SCATTERBRAINED

GENIUS INSTRUCTION MANUAL

IN THE BEGINNING

THE MENTAL FLOSS HISTORY OF THE WORLD

mental_floss *presents*

BE AMAZING

GLOW IN THE DARK • CONTROL THE WEATHER
PERFORM YOUR OWN SURGERY • GET OUT OF JURY DUTY
IDENTIFY A WITCH • COLONIZE A NATION • IMPRESS A GIRL
MAKE A ZOMBIE • START YOUR OWN RELIGION

By MAGGIE KOERTH-BAKER

with WILL PEARSON *and* MANGESH HATTIKUDUR

COLLINS
An Imprint of HarperCollins*Publishers*

BE AMAZING. Copyright © 2009 by Mental Floss LLC. All rights reserved. Printed in the United States. No part of this book may be used or reproduced in any manner whatsoever without written permission except in the case of brief quotations embodied in critical articles and reviews. For information, address HarperCollins Publishers, 10 East 53rd Street, New York, NY 10022.

HarperCollins books may be purchased for educational, business, or sales promotional use. For information, please write: Special Markets Department, HarperCollins Publishers, 10 East 53rd Street, New York, NY 10022.

FIRST EDITION
Illustrations by Mike Rogalski
Interior designed by Susan Van Horn

Library of Congress Cataloging-in-Publication Data

Koerth, Maggie.
Mental floss presents Be amazing / Maggie Koerth, with the editors of Mental floss.—1st ed.
p. cm.
ISBN 978-0-06-125148-1
1. Handbooks, vade-mecums, etc. 2. Curiosities and wonders. I. Mental floss (Durham, N.C.) II. Title. III. Title: Be amazing.

AG106.K625 2008
031.02—dc22

2007050186

09 10 11 12 13 ID/RRD 10 9 8 7 6 5 4 3 2 1

To Christopher Baker, for all his support, compassion, and love. —MK

Contents

FULFILL YOUR YOUTHFUL DREAMS

Find Buried Treasure 2
Run Away and Join the Circus 4
Learn to Walk 6
Colonize a Nation 7
Change Your Name 8
Live Underwater 10
Be Raised by Wolves 11
Impress a Girl 12
Ski in the Desert 14
Talk to the Animals 15
Mooch 17
Hunt a Whale 18
Find America 20
Drink Like a Caveman 22
Be One of the Guys 24
Start an Urban Legend 26
Be a Teen Idol 27
Finally Get Your Own Hoverboard 29
Not Get Married 30
Make Love, Not War 31

IGNORE THE NAYSAYERS

Move a Whole Town 34
Glow in the Dark 35
Be Invisible 36
Search for Atlantis 37
Illustrate the Land Before Time 39
Cross the Atlantic by Train 40
Sink a Battleship 42
Outrun Molasses 44
Live Without an Immune System 46
Get Well 47
Visit North Korea 48
Get Rescued from a Desert Island 50
Capture a Giant Squid 51
Be Killed by Soda Water 52
Be Two People at Once 54

BE A TYCOON

Succeed in Business 56
Print Your Own Money 57
Use All of Your Brain 58
Own the World's Tallest Building 59
Fool All of the People All of the Time 61
Buy the Moon 63
Live a Better Life 64
Have Greatness Thrust upon You 65
Make a Fortune Gambling 66
Lose It All 67
Leave Your Worries Behind 69
Beat City Hall 70
Own Your Mistakes 72
Sell Out 73
Be Worth It 74
Get Away from It All 75

AMASS LAURELS

Get in the Guinness Book 78

Get a New Word in the Dictionary 79

Leave Your Mark on History 81

Be the World's Oldest Athlete 83

Curb an Outbreak 84

Be the Center of the Universe 85

Invent a Language 86

Have the World's Most Dangerous Job 87

Have the World's Greatest Memory 88

Stop Global Warming 89

Save Holland 91

Die Young and Leave a Squeaky Clean Corpse 92

Be Like Mike 93

Circumnavigate the Globe 95

Train a Cat 97

Save a Life 98

Change the Face of America 99

CHARM SOCIETY

Be Discovered 102

Win a Duel 104

Taste Wine 105

Visit the Queen 107

Be an American Icon 109

Plan a Party 110

Improve Foreign Relations 111

Be King 113

Be an Artiste 115

Find Your Roots 117

Pick the Perfect Mate 119

Spread a Rumor 120

Upgrade Your Spouse 121

Grease the Wheels 123

Get back to Nature 125

Preserve Your Legacy 126

Have a Classy Obituary 127

IMPRESS YOUR MOTHER-IN-LAW

Be a Man 130

Crack an Unsolved Murder 132

Be a Late Bloomer 133

See Without Eyes 135

Fuel Your Car with Thanksgiving Leftovers 136

Boil Water . . . Naturally! 137

Build Your Dream Home 139

Be an Astronaut 141

Quit Smoking 143

Get a Better Job 144

Brew a Lifesaving Cuppa Joe 146

Don't Get Lost 147

Fight the Law . . . and Win 149

IMITATE AN ACTION HERO

Live through Anything 152

Become a Ninja 154

Become a Pirate 156

Gain Superpowers 157

Thwart a Bioterrorist Attack 159

Drive a Tank 160

Be an Army of One 162

Survive an Asteroid Impact 164

Dodge Bullets 166

Be a Spy 167
Break out of Prison 169
Survive the Witness Protection Program 171
Blow Stuff Up 172
Wrestle an Alligator 174
Be MacGyver 175

BEND THE LAWS OF SCIENCE

Time Travel 178
Live on Mars 179
Find a Unicorn 181
Believe in Fairies 183
Find a New Planet (or Lose an Old One) 184
Become a Mom . . . and a Dad 186
Change Your Child's DNA 187
Slow down Time 189
Fly 190
Grow Meat 192
Teleport 194
Power Your Interstellar Spacecraft 195
Develop Multiple Personalities 196

MASTER THE SUPERNATURAL

Start Your Own Religion 200
Weigh the Human Soul 202
Shapeshift 203
Walk on Fire 205
Revive the Really, Really Dead 206
Get Excommunicated 207
Perform an Exorcism 209
Make a Zombie 210
Commune with the Dead 212
Don't Get Left out of the Bible 214
Know Everything 215
Identify a Witch 216
Live Forever 217

FLIRT WITH THE DARK SIDE

Become a Cyborg 220
Destroy the Earth 221
Get out of Jury Duty 222
Shrink a Human Head 224
Be a Hacker (Without a Computer) 225
Destroy Tokyo 226
Be a Ladies' Man 228
Escape from Death Row 229
Travel to the Center of the Earth 231
Control the Weather 232
Rule with an Iron Fist 234
Fight a Land War in Asia 235
Build a Nuclear Bomb 236
Build a Dynasty 238
Convince Others to Do Your Bidding 240
Feed an Army 242
Go Insane 244

LET LIFE HAND YOU SOME LEMONS . . .

Get Stranded on a Desert Island 246
Drive an Animal to Extinction 247
Plagiarize 248
Sell a Kidney on the Black Market 250
Write a Really Bad Book 252
Sell Your Younger Siblings 253
Cause an International Crisis 255

Host a Roman Bacchanalia........................257
Join the Amish........................259
Destroy History........................261
Start a Riot........................262
Build an Inland Sea........................264
Perform Your Own Surgery........................265
Marry Your Cousin........................266
Get Electrocuted........................268
Spontaneously Combust........................270
Speak Your Mind........................271
Ask a Lady Her Age........................272
Be Unlucky........................274

. . . THEN MAKE LEMONADE

Be a Loveable Eccentric........................276
Eat Cannon Fodder........................278
Don't Mow Your Grass........................279
Avoid a Fate Worse than Death........................280
Get by with a Little Help from Your Friends........................281
Don't Let it Get You Down........................282
Get out of the Frying Pan and into the Fire........................284
Get Detained at Customs........................286
Run around like a Chicken with Its Head Cut Off........................288
Be Close, But Get No Cigar........................289
Shiver Your Way to Greatness........................290
Crawl out of Quicksand........................292
Avoid Dangerous Animals........................293
Be Wrong........................294
Squander Your Genius........................296
Be Misquoted........................298
Become Obsolete........................299
Start Over Someplace New........................300
Die Laughing........................302

Dear Reader,

We know you're tired of sitting on the couch and watching the world go by. We, too, once daydreamed of greatness, not knowing where to begin. (Although we had tons of ideas for what to do once we actually ruled the world.)

No more. Today is the day you start adding salsa to your life, not your chips. Today, we welcome you to our course in amazing-osity. This will be your guide to transforming your schlubby self into a paragon of virtue, success, and (yes) mind-boggling coolness. Before you begin, please read these handy instructions:

Step 1: Accept that you can be more amazing and that achieving that goal doesn't mean wearing spandex or a cape. At least, not necessarily.

Step 2: Look for amazing mentors. These are the people who will inspire you to greater heights of awesomeness. Luckily, this book provides a wealth of amazing biographies. Read them. Use them. And soon people will be writing about you.

Step 3: Familiarize yourself with amazing moments in history, science, literature, and politics. It turns out that this book does that for you as well. Isn't that handy?

Step 4: Make your mistakes spectacular. Nobody said "amazing" had to equal "nice." Plus, there are valuable things to be learned from the world's most amazing evil-doers. Somehow, this book covers those too.

Step 5: Actually, why don't you just read this book before you do anything else? If you still aren't amazing when you're done, we'll talk.

Sincerely,
Your Amazing Teachers

Fulfill Your Youthful Dreams

Find Buried Treasure

YOU WILL NEED

- A reliable guide (emphasis on "reliable")
- Tenacity
- A shovel

Tip #1: *LOOK IN PLACES YOU WOULDN'T EXPECT*

In other words, don't head straight for the Caribbean. Instead, try looking somewhere new, somewhere exotic—like, say, New Jersey. Turns out, the Garden State harbored a lot more piracy than you'd think. Most famously, the state (then a sparsely populated colony) was one of the last places notorious privateer-turned-pirate William Kidd visited before he was captured in 1700. Kidd was hanged in England, swearing to the end that he'd buried a fortune and would happily trade it for his life. No one was willing to take him up on his offer, possibly because a cache of gold worth roughly $2.4 million in today's currency had already been found near Long Island shortly after his arrest. But Kidd claimed that another $7.2 million worth of gold was left for the repillaging. If he wasn't lying, then it's still buried. Where? A story published in Issue 14 of the magazine Weird New Jersey suggests that the most likely spot is the Garden States Raritan Bay, where Kidd is known to have anchored and where 17th century gold coins have been found in two different locations. Further proof: Two of Kidd's former crewmen later turned up nearby—living significantly reformed (and, reportedly, well-financed) lives.

Tip #2: *LOOK FOR OBJECTS YOU HADN'T IMAGINED*

It's true, all the glitters isn't gold—sometimes, it's space rocks. In 2005, a professional meteorite hunter named Steve Arnold started leasing tracts of western Kansas farmland and scouring them for the metal lumps known as pallasites, extremely rare meteorites made up of iron and laced with hunks of crystal. Arnold's search was the result of an extensive study of pallasites found strewn over one Kansas county since 1900—all of which were leftover bits from a much larger meteorite that entered Earth's atmosphere somewhere around 10,000 to 20,000 years ago. By Arnold's calculations, there were still tons of pallasites left to be discovered and in October 2005, he was proven right. More than 5 feet beneath the farm field, he discovered the largest pallasite on record, a 1,430-pound behemoth. And, thanks to a rollicking collector market, *Wired* magazine estimated in January 2007 that the rock is worth more than $1 million. In fact, smaller pallasites Arnold has found have sold as yuppie objets d'art for anywhere from $40,000 and up.

Tip #3: *LOOK FOR TREASURES BIGGER THAN A BREADBOX*

You'd hate to miss the forest for the little wooden chests. After all, one of the greatest missing treasures in all of Europe is—literally—the size of a room. Originally given to the Russian Czar Peter the Great as a sign of friendship with Prussia, the Amber Room was just what it sounds like: An 11-square-foot room where just about every inch was covered in precious, intricately carved amber. Today, it would be worth $142 million—that is, if anyone knew where it was. Despite the Russians' valiant attempts to disguise the room behind wallpaper, the Nazis ended up finding and dismantling it during World War II. What happened next is all speculation. Various first-and-second person accounts have placed it in an abandoned German mine, in a torpedoed Nazi steamboat at the bottom of the Bering Sea, and—most ironically—burnt to cinders by the Allies during an air raid. Whatever the case, most historians don't expect the room to ever turn up intact. In 1997, however, German police did bust a man for trying to sell a jasper and onyx mosaic that had once been part of the Amber Room. The lead wasn't particularly useful, though. It turned out that the man's father had been part of the escort that brought the room from Russia nearly 60 years before and had swiped the piece then as a personal trophy. In April of 1997, the mosaic was returned to Russia.

Run Away and Join the Circus

Tame a Lion

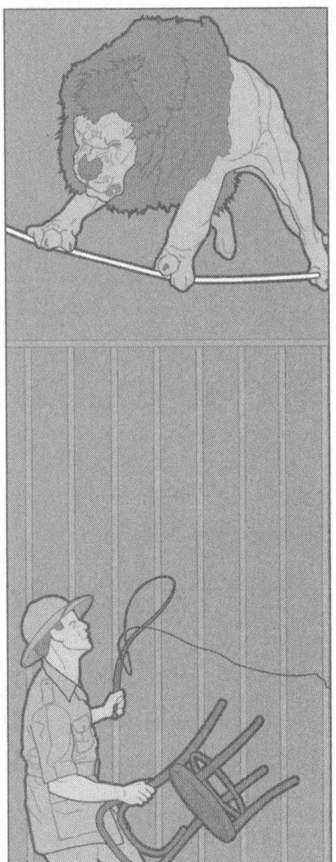

Method A: ***TOUGH, LIKE ISAAC VAN AMBURGH:*** The man who popularized big-cat acts in America, Van Amburgh got his not-exactly-auspicious start in 1833 when his boss was apparently eaten by the feline co-stars. So it's not surprising that Van Amburgh's "training" "techniques" had all the compassion of a Charles Bronson revenge film. Clad in a toga and quoting biblical passages about man having dominion over the animals, Van Amburgh became famous beating lions, tigers, leopards, and panthers into submission with whips and a crowbar.

Method B: ***TENDER, LIKE GUNTHER GEBEL-WILLIAMS:*** Von Amburgh's example ruled the animal-taming business until Gebel-Williams came along. In 1947, when he was 13, Gebel-Williams's mother abandoned him, leaving the boy with a circus. Understandably mistrustful of people, Gebel-Williams developed a special bond with animals, particularly big cats, which he hand-raised using positive reinforcement, rather than threats, to train them. However, this method wasn't without danger. During the course of his life, the cats knocked out all Gebel-Williams' real teeth (and two sets of replacements).

Walk a tightrope

According to Jean François Gravelet

YOU WILL NEED

- A good sense of balance
- Discipline
- An omelet pan

Step 1: ***LEARN THE TRICKS OF THE TRADE . . . WHETHER YOU WANT TO OR NOT***

The real key to circus acrobatics is finding your center of gravity and getting accustomed to heights. Normally, this takes years of specialized training to achieve, but Jean François Gravelet (better known as world-famous tightrope walker Charles Blondin) learned his trade in a mere six months. His secret: regular beatings. In 1829, at five years old, Blondin was sent to the École de Gymnase, an acrobatic training school that chose its "apprentices" from France's sweatshops and orphanages, forcing them to perform increasingly dangerous stunts at fairs and exhibitions.

Step 2: ***GET A GIMMICK IF YOU WANNA GET AHEAD***

But though his childhood reads like a particularly bizarre Dickens novel, Blondin eventually became the greatest tightrope walker who ever lived, famous for performing at death-defying heights without a net. In 1859, he crossed Niagara Falls on a tightrope for the first time, a feat he repeated over the years with various theatrical additions—blindfolded, in a sack, and and even while cooking an omelet.

Swallow a sword

YOU WILL NEED

- A sword
- A severely repressed gag reflex
- Good insurance

Tip #1: ***FIND A PATIENT, FATHERLY INSTRUCTOR***

We associate it with circus folk, but sword swallowing originated about 4000 years ago among deeply religious Sufis in India who wanted to demonstrate their faith in the gods. It wasn't until the first millennium C.E., when the Romans and the Japanese picked up the practice, that sword swallowing became theater. In fact, in the Indian state of Andhra Pradesh, the religious tradition still survives. The swallowers there pass (carefully, we presume) the art on from father to son.

Tip #2: ***STRIVE FOR PERFECTION (OR DIE!)***

There's no such thing as a mediocre sword swallower. With 10 organs sitting in harm's way, even the slightest mistake could puncture something important and kill you.

Tip #3: ***KEEP ON THE STRAIGHT AND NARROW***

Dangerous as it is, sword swallowing is a lot easier with a straight sword. There are fewer than five performers in the entire world who can swallow a sword with any curve to it at all—the best being American performers Dai Andrews and Brad Byers, who are both capable of getting down a 90-degree curve.

Learn to Walk

The Wedding March

The Movement: Left foot, feet together. Right foot, feet together. Repeat until you get to the minister.

The Music: Play whatever you like, see if we care. But at real classy weddings they play Richard Wagner's "Bridal Chorus." However, there is an exception. Members of the Lutheran Church, particularly the Missouri Synod branch, shun this song (better known as "Here Comes the Bride") because the "bride" in question was originally the heroine of Wagner's decidedly pagan opera Lohengrin.

Racewalking

The Movement: Is more difficult than mall walkers make it look. To qualify for Olympic-level racewalking, you must never (repeat NEVER) let both your feet leave the ground, however briefly. It's also against the rules to bend your knees.

Wait. Olympic-level Racewalking?: Yes, it's true. You can racewalk your way to a gold medal: But if, and only if, you follow the stringent rules. Walkers who get too close to running are disqualified. In 2000, at the Sydney Olympics, the three front-runners in the women's 20K event were all ejected within sight of the finish line. The reason: illegal walking styles.

Goose Stepping

The Movement: A ceremonial military march that somehow manages to impart fear while simultaneously making participants look like a particularly fascist troop of can-can girls.

The History: Invented by the Prussians, who ruled what is now Germany from the 16th to the 18th centuries, it's most commonly associated with their governmental descendants, the Nazis. Either way, the march is meant to convey that these particular soldiers are both well organized and in very good shape. I.e., you and your puny little girly army should be afraid.

Colonize a Nation

YOU WILL NEED:

- **1 nation—preferably with a weak government**
- **1 invading force**
- **1 ceremonial brass band (optional)**
- **Plenty of moxie**

Step 1: *PICK A TARGET*

Let's face it, this used to be easier back in the days when it was open season on any landmass—no matter how large—provided you had guns, and the other guy didn't. Nowadays, you're probably going to have to stick to colonizing tiny nations that can't fight back. Luckily, the Pacific Ocean is home to plenty of these. In fact, it's estimated that there are more than 20,000 islands in the Pacific and many are just ripe for colonization. Case in point: the Republic of Minerva, a would-be libertarian paradise established in 1972 by Nevada businessman Michael Oliver. According to a *New York Times* article from that year, Minerva was to have no income taxes—opting instead for a system that gave business and individuals special incentives for contributing to the government (sort of like a high-stakes version of the PBS pledge drive). However, the wise colonizer will note that this also means they had no standing army.

Step #2: *MAKE A GOOD FIRST IMPRESSION*

If you really clinch this step, you might not have to even fire a shot. Just ask Taufa'ahau Tupou IV, the King of Tonga, a nation located about 260 to 270 miles east of The Republic of Minerva. About five months after Michael

Oliver founded Minerva, King Tupou arrived to greet—and invade—his new neighbor. Reports on the invasion force vary, but it apparently involved one or more of the following: a military gunboat, a convict work detail, and a rowboat manned by the king and his ceremonial brass band. At any rate, the invasion was successful and on June 21, 1972, the Minervan flag was hauled down and the atoll became part of the Kingdom of Tonga.

Step 3: *IF AT FIRST YOU DON'T SUCCEED . . . WELL, YOU KNOW WHAT TO DO*

Unfortunately for Tonga, that brass band wasn't enough to intimidate away all other would-be conqueror-come-latelies. A gang of Americans showed up in 1982 and held the island for three weeks before Tonga had to send troops to chase them off. And a more legit claim was made by Fiji in 2005; one that made it all the way to the International Seabed Authority, where the atoll's ownership is still in dispute. Of slightly less concern is the claim made on the land by "Prince Calvin," a Charleston, South Carolina man who declared the atoll his principality in 2003.

Change Your Name

So you've finally decided that you no longer want to go through life burdened by the horrible name your parents gave you. Great! But you're still going to have to explain that decision to dear old Mom and Dad. And, unless you really like awkward family holidays, it's best you have an excuse other than, "You guys suck!" In the interest of your continued familial bliss, we provide the following controversy-free reasons for your moniker switch:

BECAUSE THE GOVERNMENT'S MAKING YOU

Naming your baby Brooklynn, America, or Lindsee might be acceptable (if mockable) in the good ol' U.S. of A., but don't try a stunt like that in Denmark. Of all the European laws regulating baby names, Denmark's are the strictest. Danish parents must choose from a state-approved list of 7,000 names, which seems like a lot, until you fall in love with a name that isn't on there. And bucking the system means months of slogging through a bureaucratic process to get your chosen moniker individually approved by the Names Investigation Department and the Ministry of Ecclesiastical Affairs. Each year, the organizations reject 15 to 20 percent of the names they review—all in the, well, "name" of protecting the baby's dignity.

BECAUSE YOU AREN'T AS RELIGIOUS AS YOUR PARENTS

Forget the hippies, the award for #1 crazy-baby-name subculture absolutely has to go to the Puritans. Well known for burning eccentric neighbors, forcing adulterers to wear colorful letterman jackets, and condemning the concept of "fun" in general, Puritan culture was basically a big ball of repressed wackiness looking for an outlet. Thus, did little Silence, Humiliation, and Mene Mene Tekel Upharsin (i.e. the writing on the wall from the Book of Daniel) pay the price for their parents' self-flagellation. Some, however, later rebelled. Sometime before 1660, a preacher's son-turned doctor changed his name from Hath Christ Not Died For Thee Thou Wouldst Be Damned Barebone to the more sensible Nicholas Barbon.

FOR THE SAKE OF A LITTLE PUBLICITY

Between 1965 and 1979, San Francisco painting contractor Bill Holland changed his name no fewer than three times. But Holland's odyssey wasn't part of some New Age attempt to find himself. Rather, according to the brief write-up Holland warranted in *Time* magazine, his capricious name-hopping was a purely Capitalist scheme. In order to become easily identifiable as the "last name in the phone book" Holland took on the professional pseudonym of Zachary Zzzra. Over the next 15 years, he had to periodically add some "z's" as first a "Zelda Zzzwramp" and then a "Vladimir Zzzzzzabokov" moved to town. By 1979, Holland's painting contract business could be found under the unwieldy moniker of Zachary Zzzzzzzzzra.

Live Underwater

Life may be better down where it's wetter, but you'll still run into problems unless you do these three things:

Step 1: ***LEARN THE VALUE OF STRONG WALLS***

In order to keep out that nosy neighbor, Billions of Gallons of Ocean Water, your home has to be airtight. But airtight objects are very buoyant. So unless you want to end up living on top of the water, the structure's weight has to be greater than the buoyant force acting on it. Meanwhile, the pressurized air inside will be trying to force your roof upward. So your new house will have to be both very heavy and very strong if it—and you—are going to survive.

Step 2: ***MAKE YOUR NEW ABODE LAND-MAMMAL FRIENDLY***

Humans can only live three minutes without oxygen—so it's a bit important you get some. Traditionally, underwater habitats have either pumped air from the surface or used chemical-based filters to clean air on site. But, in April 2007, several Australias began living in BioSUB, the world's first fully self-sustaining, self-sufficient underwater habitat, using plants such as algae to recycle oxygen.

Step 3: ***KEEP YOURSELF IN THE UNDERWATER LIFESTYLE TO WHICH YOU'VE BECOME ACCUSTOMED***

For that, you'll need a comfy supply of cash. When Jacques Cousteau launched the first underwater habitat project, Conshelf, in 1963, he got funding from the French government and French oil companies—both of which were very interested in a system that could allow man to make use of natural resources deep beneath the ocean. A later underwater habitat, called Tektite, got its funding from NASA because the survival systems needed for underwater living are very similar to those needed in space. Air filtration methods, food production systems, and waste processing units can all be tested and perfected underwater, for far less expense than in space. Of course, if federal grant writing isn't your thing, don't lose hope—you can always open a hotel. The world's first underwater hotel, Jules's Undersea Lodge, opened in 1986 off the coast of Key Largo, Florida. Today, rooms rooms rent for about $350 per person, per night.

Be Raised by Wolves

If you're reading this, it's probably a bit too late for you to play Mowgli in real life. But, for those of you who'd like to make your fantasies that much more realistic, we offer the following advice:

YOU WILL NEED

- Wolves
- To move on all fours
- A few drinks when this is all over

YOU WILL *NOT* NEED

- Clothing
- Human social or verbal skills

FIRST, GET BACK TO NATURE

In 1920, a missionary in India named Joseph Singh received an unusual request from his parishioners—banish the evil dog spirits from the nearby jungle. Singh, an educated man, opted instead to have the villagers show him said demons before he went through the trouble of an exorcism. Accompanied by a cadre of armed men, Singh visited a certain clearing in the dead of night, where an abandoned termite mound was supposed to be the locus of demonic activity. There, he watched agog as a mother wolf emerged from the mound—followed by two humans who walked eerily on all fours and peered at the world through their matted hair. A few days later, he returned, determined to capture the humans and return them to civilization. This required shooting the snarling female wolf who stepped in to protect her "cubs." The humans turned out to be two girls, age roughly 8 and 18 months. Definitely a weird and uncommon situation, but not one without precedent. Records of children raised by animals date back to the 1300s. And in modern times, researchers have seen several well-documented cases of abandoned children who were, at least temporarily, cared for by animals. These incidents are particularly common in Russia, where an economic collapse in the late 1990s left millions of children homeless, though only a few of those ended up feral. India also had factors that made wolf-raised children more likely, particularly a tradition of leaving babies on the edges of jungle-ringed agricultural fields while their mothers worked. This tendency made it easy for wolves to grab babies, both for food and, occasionally, for rearing.

THEN, GET BACK TO CIVILIZATION

This step can be much, much harder, depending on the length of time away from human socialization and the age at which the child began living in the wild. The issue appears to be that while human beings are wired by nature to learn language, we also have a narrow window of time when we can be nurtured into achieving our full language potential. There are several documented examples of children who spent their formative years without human contact and, despite huge amounts of effort, were never able to become fluent in any language. Among them are the little girls that Reverend Singh found. Named Kamala and Amala, they appeared to have no concept of human social behavior: eating only raw meat, refusing to wear clothing, and communicating only through grunts, howls, and snarls. They were even unable to walk upright, their calf muscles having tightened into a position fit only for movement on all fours. Amala died from disease shortly after being taken in by the Singh family, but the older one lived with them for nearly 10 years. During that time, she learned (painfully) to walk on two legs and started wearing dresses. But she still shied from being touched and, even at her peak of progress, was still limited to a vocabulary of some 40 poorly pronounced words—none of which she could string into a sentence. Autopsies and brain scans done on children like Kamala display signs of mental retardation, but whether the damage is a result of their confinement away from society or a precursor to it is anyone's guess. However, children who learned to talk before they disappeared into the wild have been more successful. In fact, John Ssebunya, a Ugandan boy who lived with vervet monkeys from ages 4 to 6, recently toured England with a youth choir—his ability to speak and socialize completely restored.

Impress a Girl

According To Shah Jahan, builder of the Taj Mahal

YOU WILL NEED

- **1 girl (Jahan, of course, had more. But only the one was really important.)**
- **A whole lotta money**

Step 1: *MAKE A GOOD FIRST IMPRESSION*

Khurram was just a simple, unbelievably wealthy prince of the Mughal Dynasty—a family of Muslim Persians who ruled the Indian subcontinent for much of the 14th and 15th centuries. But, humble though he was, he certainly knew how to catch a lady's eye. In 1607, the teenage- Khurram met the daughter of his father's prime minister at a royal bazaar. Although he was already married (twice over, in fact), Khurram took an immediate liking to Arjumand Banu Begum and bought the girl a 10,000-rupee diamond. We have no idea what that translates to in modern, American engagement rings, but we're assuming it was a big 'un because Arjumand agreed to marry him then and there.

Step 2: *MAKE HER FEEL SPECIAL*

Unfortunately for the pair, it was another five years before they could be married. (*Titanic* fans, take note.) After their wedding, Khurram also picked out a romantic moniker for his new bride. From here on out, she was known as Mumtaz Mahal—"Beloved Jewel of the Palace." Although she was the Prince's third wife, he made sure she clearly had top billing. He took her advice on affairs of state, and even brought her along with him on military campaigns. And, as if the other two wives weren't jealous enough, Mumtaz Mahal also bore all his children. In the meantime, Khurram would become king in 1628, taking the name Shah Jahan or "King of the World."

Step 3: *MAKE SURE EVERYONE REMEMBERS HER JUST AS YOU DO*

Shah Jahan certainly thought Mumtaz Mahal was beautiful. After all, history claims that "the moon hid its face in shame before her." But, despite the glowing accounts and numerous portraits labeled "Mumtaz Mahal," we actually have no idea of what the woman looked like. Under the Mughal's interpretation of Islam, high-born women like Mumtaz didn't sit for royal portraits. In fact, they were under obligation to completely hide their faces from public view. But, it's probably safe to say she was pretty darn stunning, considering that, shortly before she died in 1631 she managed to convince her husband to not only build her the most beautiful mausoleum ever, but also to never marry again. He laid the foundation for the Taj Mahal six months after she died and pretty much gave up paying attention to anything but its construction and his own grief. In fact, Shah Jahan was so wrapped up in the Taj Mahal that he didn't notice his own son plotting against him. In 1658, Prince Aurangzeb (who was clearly not as broken up about his mother's death) overthrew Shah Jahan. The former king was locked in a prison tower and lived out the last few years of his life behind bars.

Ski in the Desert

Once a backwater, the United Arab Emirates and particularly the city of Dubai, have become some of the world's top luxury tourist destinations. What's driving this influx of wealthy vacationers? We think it might have something to do with:

ROBOT JOCKEYS

Why are they cool? Because they're jockeys that are robots. What more do you need? Of course, there's also the fact that they're making the UAE a safer, more human-rights friendly sort of place. Up until 2005, the quest for smaller, lighter camel jocks had led many racing camel owners to purchase small children on the black market. The 35-pound robotic version introduced by a Swiss company promises to put an end to child slavery (yeah!) without compromising the wonderful world of forced camel labor (yeah?).

MAN-MADE ISLANDS

This is almost a whole sub-industry in and of itself. Wealthy visitors can book resort accommodations (or buy their own land) in one of several carefully constructed island chains, each with it's own theme. Like poetry? You can stay at the Palm Islands, an atoll that's formed in the shape of a giant palm tree surrounded by smaller islands which are shaped into Arabic verse. Dreams of grandeur? Buy into the World Islands, a chain of islands shaped like the seven continents.

INDOOR SKI MOUNTAINS

Geography isn't an issue for alpine-loving Emiratis. Since 2005, they've been able to hit the slopes at a 242,000-square-foot indoor ski facility attached to the country's largest mall. Ski Dubai features a constant 30°F temperature and more than 6,000 tons of artificially produced snow. Now all that's needed is a Winter Olympics team!

THE WORLD'S CHIC-EST HOTEL

Ostensibly the only 7-star hotel on earth, the Burj al Arab features 202 two-story suites that can be rented out for as little as $1,000 a night or as much as $28,000—depending on the room. In fact, the hotel is so fancy, they even charge people to look around. A tour costs about $55.

Talk to the Animals

YOU WILL NEED

- Some animals
- A psychology degree
- A robot dog (optional)

Step 1: *FORGET WHAT YOU THINK YOU KNOW*

Yes, yes, we know. Mr. Scratches is just like one of the family and you know exactly what he's trying to tell you. Unfortunately, you're probably wrong. Humans have an innate tendency to anthropomorphize. We like to attribute human thoughts and emotions to instinctual animal behavior—and nowhere is this more apparent than in human-house pet relations. Dog behavior, in particular, can largely be explained via instinctual social cues that date back to the days when your Pomeranian's ancestors ran with the wolf pack. For instance, you know how your dog always rolls over for a belly rub when you get home? That looks like unconditional love, but in reality he's just trying to clarify that you're the pack leader, and even though you've been away, he's still subservient to you. That's also the point he's trying to make when he licks your face. In the wild, wolf puppies lick the faces of their parents to get the older wolves to regurgitate food for them to eat. After they grow up and join the hunt, they then lick the dominant wolf's face to demonstrate their dependence on him. So basically, while your puppy does think you're #1, it's not really in the way that you think.

Step 2: *GET IN TOUCH WITH THEIR EMOTIONS*

While it's probably unreasonable to assume your dog has a deep inner life, he does have distinct emotions. In 2001, a Japanese company introduced a robot called Bow-Lingual that uses a collar-attached microphone to pick up your dog's barks, growls, and other sundry noises. The computer then runs those sounds through a database and connects the noise to one of six ostensible canine emotions: frustration, alarm, self-expression, happiness, sadness, and desire. Besides displaying these immediate feelings, the Bow-Lingual also stores up to 24-hours-worth of barks and compiles them into a journal of sorts—using preprogrammed phrases to sum up what your dog "thought" about that day. Examples range from the predictable, "So many fun things today. What an ultra-happy day," to the guilt-inducing, "I'm arf-ullly lonely. Please play with me more."

Step 3: *BE CAREFUL, YOU MIGHT GET PLAYED*

Often, when we think we've taught an animal to communicate what we've actually done is taught ourselves to fetch. One prime example: The "education" of Nim Chimpsky. In 1973, researchers at Columbia University attempted to teach human language to a baby chimpanzee. The goal was to disprove the theories of linguist Naom Chomsky, who believed that sophisticated language is something only the human brain could grasp. The researchers thought that if they raised a baby chimp in the same learning-heavy environment baby humans are raised in, then the chimp would learn language the same way humans do. Over the next 44 months, Nim learned 125 sign language words and could combine them in various ways—but he didn't seem to be able to progress from there. The experiment was judged a failure. However, when the researchers later viewed tapes of Nim, they realized that something important had happened—rather than learning language, Nim had learned how to manipulate humans. For instance, the sign for "dirty" stood in for "bathroom." All teaching stopped and Nim was hauled off to the potty. Watching the videos, the researchers noticed that, very often, Nim didn't actually need to use the bathroom—he would sign "dirty" just to get a break. Nim had learned that certain signs (like the one for "orange") elicited certain responses (like getting an orange). Today, researchers aren't sure whether Nim understood what the signs meant, only that he knew what he got for using them.

Mooch

Think this type of behavior isn't a virtue? You're in the minority. Of all the animals on earth, scientists estimate that parasites outnumber non-parasites by a ratio of four to one. So get with the program, sucker! Remember, if you aren't a mooch-er, you're the mooch-ee.

GET HOOKED UP WITH A GOOD ENABLER

Like many animal-loving parasites, the filarial worm owes much of its success to its buddy, the mosquito. Baby filarial worms are born in the lymphatic systems of human or animal hosts. After birth, these larvae quickly migrate to the circulatory system where they spend their formative years bumming around the bloodstream. But, there's a method to their loitering. During the day, almost all the larvae can be found hanging out in the lungs, but at night, particularly between the hours of 10 p.m. and 2 a.m., these little buggers head out into the blood vessels that serve their host's limbs—knowing that this is the time when they're most likely to get sucked up by a passing 'skeeter. Pretty crafty, no? For the filarial worm, getting into a mosquito is sort of like getting into a good college: It's the place where they mature and, without it, they aren't likely to have a good shot at a pleasant adulthood. In addition, the mosquito is also a handy transportation system, allowing the now older and wiser worms to get inside a new host. Of course, the host has little to thank the mosquito for. Once inside, filarial worms stage a hostile takeover of the host's lymphatic system, turning what should be an important component of the mammalian ability to fight off disease into a totally trashed crash pad. This results in often horrendous symptoms like elephantiasis, when the host's limbs and genitalia end up grotesquely swollen, with thickened, pebbly looking skin. More than 120 million people worldwide carry the worm and, of those, 40 million suffer the debilitating side effects.

CONVINCE YOUR NEW "FRIEND" THAT YOU KNOW WHAT'S BEST FOR THEM

And, trust us, what's best for them is always what's best for you. Take the sacculina—one parasite that really knows how to get what it wants. Actually a barnacle with a parasitic bent, the sacculina starts out life as a weensy free-floating organism, swimming around the seas. Although she spends her early life footloose and fancy-free, what the female sacculina really wants is to meet a nice crab and settle down. What the crab wants never really factors into the equation. Once she finds a crab, the sacculina swims around to its belly and, using a sharp hollow point on her exoskeleton, injects herself into the crab's flesh, leaving behind an empty husk. Inside the crab, the sacculina begins to take over, burrowing long, nutrient sucking tendrils into every part of the crab's anatomy, from the eyestalks to the claws. As she does this, the sacculina also changes the crab's behavior, effectively neutering it, preventing it from growing and winnowing down its once-vast list of interests to a single hobby: Eating. And, after the sacculina picks up a male or two, the crab will even spend what little energy resources it has helping to tend her baby parasites and giving them a good start in the world. Now entirely under her control, the crab ends up living only to serve the sacculina—no matter what his crab buddies try to do to help him out.

Hunt a Whale

According to the Japanese

YOU WILL NEED

- **A loose national definition of "scientific research"**
- **A growing group of supporters who may or may not be on the take**
- **Harpoons**

First: *FIND A LOOPHOLE IN INTERNATIONAL LAW*

In 1986, the International Whaling Commission took a decisive step toward saving some of the Earth's most unique creatures. For the first time in human history, whale hunting became illegal. But there was a loophole. The Commission decided that some whales could be killed each year for scientific purposes and, into this loop, the nation of Japan slipped its entire whaling industry. For 20 years, the Japanese government has headed out to sea every season, bringing back hundreds of dead whales, ostensibly to study the animals' ages and eating habits. Once this incredibly important research is done, all those whale carcasses end up in fancy restaurants and gourmet bellies.

Second: ***KEEP YOUR CITIZENS INTERESTED***

This is harder than it sounds. Although Japan has a long history of whale hunting, the Japanese people aren't exactly clamoring for whale steak these days. Right after World War II, many Japanese subsisted basically on whale—and were happy to exchange diets once the country's economy improved. Today, older Japanese still associate whale meat with poverty, while the youngsters blow it off in favor of beef, salmon, and trendy Western fast foods. But the government, which has now staged an epic protest in the name of eating whale, has an interest in keeping the public on board. In 2005, they took their case to the youngest Japanese, introducing whale meat on school lunch menus in the coastal state of Wakayama. There, the school board is hoping that breaded, fried whale patties and minced whale burgers will get children interested in their whaling heritage and their country's two-decade battle to protect it.

Third: ***NEVER GIVE UP***

In 2006, after decades of ineffectual protest votes, Japan managed to win a (very slim) pro-whaling majority in the IWC. The vote won't repeal the ban (to do that they'd need to win by two-thirds) but it was definitely seen as a sign of growing support. Anti-whalers, on the other hand, are quick to point out that most of the countries that have suddenly joined Japan's fight are small, undeveloped ones that receive aid from the Asian nation.

Find America

YOU WILL NEED

- Bravery
- A certain amount of craziness
- At least a modicum of evidence if you expect us to take you seriously

Explorer: ***SIBERIAN HUNTER-GATHERERS***

Arrived: Between 20,000 to 12,000 years ago, via a land bridge across the Bering Strait.

Evidence: Plenty, namely their descendants, who were scattered across North and South America long before anybody else is even rumored to have arrived. Interestingly, current genetic research now suggests that of the many hundreds of people who crossed the Bering Strait, only 70 left a genetic impact that continues to this day.

Likelihood It's for Real: We'll go out on a limb here and call this one a sure thing.

Explorer: ***VIKINGS***

Arrived: 1000 C.E., at various spots along the northeastern coast of North America.

Evidence: Beginning around 1000 C.E., Viking sagas claim Greenlanders began exploring and attempting to settle a land they called "Vinland the Good," in honor of its not being quite as frigid and desolate as Greenland. The sagas were largely written off as fiction until 1960, when Norwegian archaeologists uncovered remains of a Viking settlement at L'Anse aux Meadows in Newfoundland. Since then, most everyone has identified Newfoundland as Vinland, but that doesn't quite add up. The Viking sagas reported finding wild grapes, thus the "Vinland" part of the name. To find those, they'd have had to sail at least as far south as Rhode Island.

Likelihood It's for Real: Certain, at least at the Newfoundland site. Other remnants of Viking exploration have yet to be found.

Explorer: ***MERCHANT FISHERMEN FROM BRISTOL, ENGLAND***

Arrived: Between the 1480s and 1490s, along the coast of Newfoundland.

Evidence: A number of old records from the Bristol, England port authority and a letter sent to Christopher Columbus. The port records give a tantalizing hint that something fishy was going on. Over a period of several years, certain Bristol sailors would set out during fishing season, ostensibly to Ireland. They'd sail off to the west and later return, loaded down not with fine Irish goods, but with tons of salt cod and hides. Weirder still, they were always gone far longer than it should have taken to get to and from Ireland. At the time, many suspected that the men had a secret fishing ground. Then in 1961, historian David Quinn published the first record of a letter sent to Columbus around 1498. Referring to Newfoundland, then in the news for its recent "discovery" by John Cabot, the writer told Columbus that it was likely this was the same land previously found by . . . yes . . . fishermen from Bristol.

Likelihood It's for Real: Fairly high, but since they apparently didn't spend much time on shore, it's difficult to prove for certain.

Explorer: ***JAPANESE***

Arrived: About 5,000 years ago, near the coastal Ecuadorian city of Valdivia.

Evidence: Largely centered on a collection of pottery fragments uncovered in the 1950s. According to supporters of this theory, the designs and style of this pottery are nearly identical to that found in Japanese pottery of the same period. In fact, prior to this sudden outbreak of clay work, Ecuador seems to have no pottery at all. Since the discovery, many people have speculated how the Japanese-style pottery could have ended up in South America. The most popular theory is that a boatload of fishermen were blown off course and caught in the Japan Current, which pushed them around the Northern Pacific and down the coast of the Americas. Why stop in Ecuador? Nobody knows.

Likelihood It's for Real: Slim. There's no corroborating evidence of a Japanese presence in this hemisphere and plenty of other evidence that pottery was being made elsewhere in South America before 5,000 years ago. As for the similarities between the pottery styles, most archaeologists believe they're just that—similarities.

Drink Like a Caveman

YOU WILL NEED

- Rice
- Honey
- Yeast
- Wild berries
- A hardy palate

Step 1: *FIND YOUR BREW*

Patrick McGovern, an archaeological chemist, found his at the office, stuck to a collection of 9,000-year-old pot-shards stored at the University of Pennsylvania Museum of Archaeology and Anthropology. The shards had actually been unearthed at a site in Jiahu, China, and catalogued back in the 1980s, but until McGovern came along, no one had really given them much thought. In a November 2005, article in *Discover* magazine, McGovern explained how he was able to determine that the clay jars had probably held an alcoholic beverage and how he figured out what the beverage had been made from. Given all the time that had past, all traces of alcohol and sugar had long since disappeared. But, the jars were found at a burial site and McGovern guessed that they probably had held a ceremonial fermented beverage. He put his theory to the test. First he soaked the shards in a mixture of methanol and chloroform—a process that pulled the tiny leftover specs of compounds that had once made up the drink off the shards. Then, all he had to do was evaporate off the methanol/chloroform mixture, leaving behind a thin layer that contained the chemical signatures of whatever it was the ancient Chinese had been drinking. Then he analyzed the sediment with a spectrometer and a chromatograph, devices that measure the light absorption levels of organic materials. The results from these experiments were then matched to the known absorption levels of various potential ingredients. He found matches for rice, beeswax, and some sort of fruit containing tartaric acid—all of which add up to a high likelihood that the residents of Jiahu were brewing the world's oldest known alcoholic drink.

Step 2: *IMPROVISE*

Unfortunately, the results of McGovern's test weren't exactly a neatly typed recipe. To re-create the Jiahu drink, he needed more than a little creativity. First off, the tartaric acid seemed to indicate that grapes were involved, but, as far as anyone knew at the time, the ancient Chinese weren't using wild grapes or cultivating domesticated ones. Instead, McGovern settled on the hawthorn berry, a fruit that was and still is commonly used in Chinese cooking. But hawthorn berries are hard to come by in the U.S., so he had to settle for using an imported dried, powdered version. As for the rice, McGovern knew it would have to be brown, since 9,000 years ago nobody had developed the technology to make white rice. However, the type of rice the ancient Chinese used hadn't been grown in 5,000 years, so again he had to settle, using a modern domesticated version instead. But the biggest difference between McGovern's brew and the original is barley. Ancient China had yet to be introduced to the plant, but the Bureau of Alcohol, Tobacco, and Firearms requires that breweries brew only beer—defined as a drink having at least 25 percent barley malt. To meet this requirement, McGovern's team used the lightest barley malt they could find.

Step 3: *TRACK DOWN A DISTRIBUTOR*

This is actually easier than you might think. In the last few years, a surprising number of brewing companies have produced beers based on ancient recipes. The trend was started back in 1989 by Anchor Steam Brewing Company, which based its back-in-time beer on an actual recipe from an ancient Sumerian text devoted to Ninkasi, the goddess of brewing. Other companies have based brews off ancient remains found in Egypt and at English Druid sites. McGovern worked with the Dogfish Head Brewing Company, which had previous experience in the field of archaeological alcohol. The company had already created a drink designed to mimic food and drink remains found in a 2,700-year-old burial from Turkey. That drink's claim to fame: The burial was that of the ancient king who probably inspired the legend of King Midas. In 2005, the pair released Château Jiahu, the final result of McGovern's tinkering. The drink is peach-colored, frothy, and, apparently, tastes nothing like beer.

Step 4: *RECREATE ANCIENT HEADACHE MEDICINE*

Be One of the Guys

IN THE ARMY

Hundreds of women disguised themselves as the opposite gender to fight in the Civil War, getting through standard medical examinations largely because standard medical examinations weren't particularly thorough. With the need for new soldiers pressing, army surgeons often did nothing more than give new recruits a cursory (and clothed) once over before sending them into the field. Once there, women could maintain their disguises— partly because sanitary conditions in military camp restrooms made peeing alone in the bushes a fairly common choice and partly because, thanks to Victorian mores, nobody really knew what a woman looked like in pants. According to De Anne Blanton and Lauren Cook, authors of *They Fought Like Demons*, the very idea of women trying to join up was so foreign that soldiers often never thought to question the presence of a high-pitched, lightly built, smooth-cheeked recruit in their unit. Other girls had biology, and a history of farm life, on their side. When Melverina Elverina Peppercorn (yes, really) joined the Confederate army at 16, she was over 6 feet tall and a crack shot with a rifle.

YOU WILL NEED

- **To wear the pants . . . and maybe pad them a bit for verisimilitude**

IN THE CHURCH

The Monk Marinos (aka the Nun Maria) was awarded Orthodox sainthood for his/her exceptional piety and obedience. And this AFTER her sex switcheroo was discovered. The story goes that around the beginning of the 6th century, a widower named Eugene left his home in Asia Minor to join a monastery. At the time, becoming a hermit for religious reasons was a fairly popular pastime, as many believed it was the only way to truly gain a spiritual connection with God. So, it's not so surprising that when Eugene headed off to be a monk, his young daughter insisted on going with him. Disguising herself as a boy, the newly rechristened Marinos quickly stood out as a pillar of ascetic virtue. (S)he was even said to have gained the power of healing. But then, on a trip with several other monks, Marinos spent the night in an inn. A few months later, the innkeeper's daughter turned up pregnant. In a panic, she accused the young monk as her seducer. Oh, the irony. Unwilling to defend himself (for obvious reasons) Marinos was thrown out of the monastery. Instead, he began living an even holier life at the wall of his former home. When the innkeeper showed up to drop off the illegitimate baby with its "father," Marinos willingly accepted and raised it. This persuaded the monks to accept Marinos back into the fold, but with punishments—which, of course, Marinos gladly accepted. It wasn't until years later, when Marinos died, that her true sex (and innocence) came to light. Amazed at her virtue in the face of unjust suffering, the Church canonized her. You can celebrate her saintly day on February 12.

IN THE MUSIC BUSINESS

Jazz halls were no place for ladies in the 1930s, but Dorothy Tipton could think of no place she'd rather be. Beginning in 1933, when she was 19, Dorothy began passing herself off as pianist Billy Tipton. The ruse not only worked, it got "Billy" a touring show, a record deal, and three (count 'em) ex-wives. Dorothy lived as Billy for more than 50 years, with only a few close musician friends in on the secret (note that we didn't say anything about the wives). At age 74, Billy collapsed from heart failure in "his" trailer and his youngest (adopted) son called the paramedics. It was only when they undressed Billy to try to revive him that Billy's son discovered that the bandages wrapped around his "father's" chest weren't there to protect an old rib cage wound after all. The discovery helped explain why Billy Tipton died in obscurity. In 1958, he'd been offered a deal to have his trio become the house band for a new, swanky Las Vegas casino. The job would likely have been the start of a brilliant big-name career. But, more exposure would have likely meant eventual outing. Instead, Billy dropped out of the band, moved to Washington State, and started working as a booking agent. He'd died almost broke, all so he could protect the secret of his true sex.

Start an Urban Legend

You've heard this before—the story of the unlucky hunter who didn't shoot anything out in the woods and then hit a deer with his truck on the way home. Not wanting to return empty handed, he loads the deer into his truck and heads off down the road, happy as a clam. That is, until the deer wakes up and starts breaking windows and generally causing havoc. The hunter tries to hit the deer with a tire iron, misses and hits his own dog—which returns the favor by biting him. Thoroughly freaked out and being pursued by the now-furious dog, the hunter seeks shelter in a phone booth, where he calls 911. Naturally, the dispatchers have a laugh at his expense and the whole story really did happen—to a friend of your cousin's buddy. But just because the story is legendary now doesn't mean it doesn't have roots in reality. Urban legend expert Jan Harold Brunvand traced this story back to its source in his book, *The Truth Never Stands in the Way of a Good Story . . .* !

First: *START WITH A REAL STORY*

In February 1974, a Poughkeepsie, New York police officer named Allen Clouser takes an emergency call on the city's pre-911 call system. The caller explains, in a panicked, expletive-laced way, that he's trapped in a phone booth after a deer started tearing apart his car and his dog went psycho on him. The man describes his general location and police head out to look for him—but never find any sign of a man vs. deer vs. dog struggle. The call might have been a hoax.

Second: *TAMPER WITH THE "EVIDENCE"*

At some point after the Poughkeepsie incident a tape, allegedly of the emergency call, begins circulating among police and 911 dispatchers. Along the way, the tape, which might have been the real thing to begin with, gets doctored to make the story funnier and new, improved versions are created.

Third: *BASK IN IMMORTALITY*

By the 1990s, when it was first researched by a St. Louis newspaper reporter, the Poughkeepsie incident had grown into a fully fleshed tale that had supposedly happened in just about every state in the Union.

Be a Teen Idol

According to Tutankhamen and David Cassidy

Though separated by time, space, and a whole lot of hair gel, those guys on the cover of *Tiger Beat* aren't so different from their 3,000-year-old counterparts. In fact, between teen god-king Tutankhamen and teen TV-dream David Cassidy, teen idols haven't changed much at all.

Step 1: *BE YOUNG AND DESIRABLE*

Based on cranial analysis that showed wisdom teeth still firmly buried in his jaw, archaeologists suspect that Tutankhamen was around 18 years old when he died. That means that Tut's whole reign happened in his teen and preteen years, after he took the throne at age 9.

David Cassidy got his start a little later than Tut. His first professional acting gigs began in childhood. Bit parts on *Bonanza* and *The Mod Squad* followed, but Cassidy didn't really get his big break until he was 20. A year later, in 1971, he was one of the world's highest paid performers.

Step 2: *REALIZE THERE IS NO SHAME IN LEANING ON FAMILY CONNECTIONS*

We know from inscriptions that King Tut was the "beloved son" of a king. But which king? The records aren't that clear. Most likely, he was the son of Akhenaten, a renegade pharaoh who abolished traditional polytheistic Egyptian religion, replacing it with one that worshipped a singular sun god. Needless to say, a lot of people weren't happy about the change. In fact, if Tutankhamen is Akhenaten's son, then he was quite the little rebel—reversing all of his father's monotheist reforms to the point of changing his own name from Tutankhaten.

Did we say one famous family? Heck, Cassidy had two. His parents were both actors. So was his stepmom, a lady named Shirley Jones, who ended up playing Cassidy's mother on *The Partridge Family*. Based very loosely on a couple of real-life all-family bands, *The Partridge Family* made Cassidy more than a little famous. Within a few years, he had a bigger fan club than both Elvis and the Beatles.

Step 3: *DATE YOUR SISTER*

Tut's main squeeze was Ankhesenamun, who was (efficiently) both his wife and his half-sister. (Think of the money you'd save on birthday cards!) Tut didn't live long enough to amass a plethora of wives, but papa Akhenaten wasn't so misfortunate. He had six daughters, counting Ankhesenamun, with his chief wife Nefertiti. Tut's mother, meanwhile, was most likely a lesser wife called Kiya.

There was no shortage of girls flocking to Cassidy in his heyday, from his often-underage fans to TV "sister" Susan Dey. But all the attention became significantly less fun in 1974, when a 14-year-old died when a pack of rabid fans rushed the stage during a concert in England. After that, Cassidy dropped out of sight, taking a 3-year sabbatical from both *The Partridge Family* and his burgeoning music career.

Finally Get Your Own Hoverboard

YOU WILL NEED

- 1 childhood dream
- The technology to fulfill it

Tip: *DON'T BE FOOLED BY IMPOSTERS*

Frankly, we're still bitter at Robert Zemeckis. Not only did his 1989 movie, *Back to the Future Part II*, taunt us with its totally awesome hoverboard chase scenes, but the director himself went on to encourage rumors that the floating object of lust really did exist. Press interviews from the time record him answering questions about special effects with, "What do you mean, how did we do it? It's a real hoverboard. It flies. Michael [J. Fox] just practiced a lot." But Zemeckis's cruel teasing didn't end there. When the 3-movie DVD set came out in 2002, it included a mock behind-the-scenes documentary detailing how Zemickis had ostensibly gotten real hoverboards from Mattel and featured scenes of movie crewmen "testing" the boards out in a field.

Tip: *VISIT AN AUCTION*

According to Ketzer.com, a movie memorabilia Web site, one of the main hoverboard props used in *Back to the Future Part II* was sold at a Christie's auction in 1991. Although on display for many years at the Planet Hollywood restaurant in Beverly Hills, the board was auctioned again in 2000, this time to a private collector.

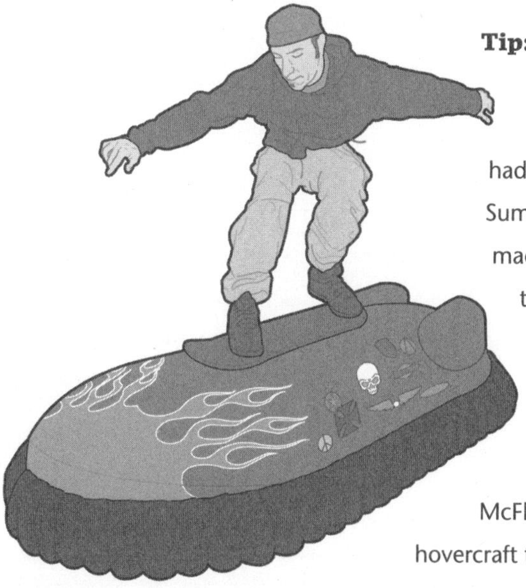

Tip: *TURN TO SCIENCE*

Owning a real-life personal hovercraft is not an impossible dream. In fact, one such device actually had a cameo in the opening ceremonies of the 2000 Summer Olympic Games. Called the Airboard, this machine is (unfortunately) much larger and clunkier than a hoverboard—really more the size of a small scooter. Another company, called Future Horizons, sells a hovering device that actually has the size and look of a hoverboard. In both cases, however, the principles at work aren't really very Marty McFly-esque. Instead, the machines are based on basic hovercraft technology, using small motors and fans to force air into a bag beneath the vehicle. The whole contraption floats on the air trapped between the bag and the ground. This means that any hoverboard you can buy today won't be able to "fly" more than 2 or 3 inches high. Another downside: They're expensive. The Future Horizons model, for instance, retails for $9,000, although you can buy a set of detailed plans that show you how to build one yourself for $50.

Not Get Married

Oh sure, the obvious method would be to . . . wait for it . . . just not get hitched. But, frankly, why settle for that uncreative solution when you can have all the benefits of wedded bliss without that whole "wedded" part?

GET MARRIED, BUT ONLY KINDA-SORTA

Want to get married, but just don't have the money (or, perhaps, the level of devotion) necessary? If you're Muslim, you could try a "misyar." Traditional Middle Eastern marriages require men to pay for a ceremony, a dowry to the bride's family, and a home. Those costs can add up pretty fast, particularly in wealthy Saudi Arabia. Misyar marriages, on the other hand, are technically legal, but lack some of the requirements of regular weddings. In a misyar, men don't have to provide financially for women or buy them a house. The couple just agrees to meet up periodically at wherever they both already live. It sounds like a great deal, but some Islamic critics say that it's often used in less honorable ways. For instance, a man who wants a second wife, but doesn't want his first wife to know about it, can get a misyar marriage. Ditto for couples who just want to fool around without any serious commitment.

GET MARRIED TO A PRINCE WITHOUT PERMISSION

Maria Anne Fitzherbert was a rich, twice-widowed (and therefore, by the standards of the time, seductive) older woman who wooed the English Crown Prince George in the late 18th century. By all accounts, the two were deeply in love, but Mrs. Fitzherbert's status as a) Catholic and b) not pre-approved by the Prince's father, knocked her out of the running for queen. Nevertheless, a marriage—validated by the church, but still technically illegal—did happen in December of 1785. After that, the trick was keeping it quiet. While certain members of society and even the Royal Family were apparently aware, and approved of, the marriage, everybody knew that the high-rolling, frequently-in-debt prince was likely to get cut off from the family bank account if his father found out. This little issue came to a head about 10 years later, when Prince George was informed that his latest debts wouldn't be paid off unless he married his first cousin. He took the offer and ditched Mrs. Fitzherbert, but, shockingly, this second marriage didn't exactly pan out. By 1797, Prince George and his cousin were permanently separated. Over the course of the next decade, George and Maria Anne had an on-again, off-again and remarkably public relationship, finally breaking up for good sometime between 1809 and 1811 when the stress of being the Prince's (Not) Wife finally got the better of the good Mrs. Fitzherbert.

Make Love, Not War

According to the very loving, very peaceful Citizens of Freetown Christiania

YOU WILL NEED

- Creativity
- An abandoned military instillation

In 1971, a group of Dutch hippies busted their way into an abandoned Copenhagen military barracks as part of a protest. And they've never left. Today, Freetown Christiania is an independently governed city-within-a-city and houses about 750 adults, 200 children, and no cars (they're illegal here). Although originally a motley band of squatters, the citizens of Christiania have evolved into an extremely organized group that pays for their utilities and land taxes. As you can imagine, though, the cost of living is still ridiculously low, particularly for canal-front property in crowded Copenhagen. The *Copenhagen Post* reports that Christianians only pay about $155 dollars per adult per month, which the city uses to pay for taxes and improvements, like a bridge they built across the canal. There's a kindergarten, a grocery store, and—up until 2004 when it was raided by Danish authorities—an open-air marijuana market (harder drugs having been banned by village consensus in the early 1980s). Unfortunately, Christiania may be in its death throes. Since Denmark's conservative party took control in 2001, it's been cracking down on the village and in 2006, the *Post* reported that the national parliament had voted to turn much of the land (which it still, technically, owns) into condos.

Ignore the Naysayers

Move a Whole Town

According to the residents of Hibbing, Minnesota

Hibbing, Minnesota, was a mining town. Established in 1893, it quickly became the largest of several cities built on the Mesabi Range iron-ore deposits. Known as the "richest village in the world," the town grew to a population of 20,000 by 1915 and boasted opulent hotels, decorative Victorian banks, and all the cultural amenities of "big city" life. But, in 1912, a geologic survey revealed that Hibbing was actually closer to the iron ore than any of its founders had anticipated—as in, right on top of it. Clearly, something had to give, and in an area where iron was king that something was obviously going to be the city of Hibbing. Lust for iron aside, the locals weren't quite ready to raze the town and start over from scratch. Balancing greed with thriftiness, they simply decided to reuse what they already had—moving the bulk of the town two miles to the south and out of the way of the strip mining machines. Amazingly, for an era when heavy construction equipment was still just a twinkle in a foreman's eye, this plan actually worked. Hibbing survived and the awkwardly placed iron mine, now known as the Hull-Rust, is the largest open-pit mine in the world today, covering 2,291 acres and producing 1.4 billion tons of ore. Granted, your hometown might not sit on top of a veritable gold mine of, well, iron, but if you don't try moving it you'll never know for sure.

YOU WILL NEED

- A town
- Horses
- Logs
- Chains
- A very understanding citizenry

Step 1: *LOSE THE FOUNDATION.* It was just holding you down anyway! Mary Jane Finsand's book, *The Town That Moved*, explains how the citizens of Hibbing slowly jacked up their public buildings and homes high enough that they were no longer connected to the foundations beneath.

Step 2: *GET ON A ROLL.* Giant trees from the nearby forest were felled and stripped to become rollers, which were laid one after another beneath each building. Chains attached the building to a team of horses. As it moved across the line of rollers, workmen would bring the end log around to the front. Hey, we just said the process worked . . . not that it was fast! Moving began in 1919, but the final building didn't make the journey until the 1960s.

Step 3: ***BE SAFE.*** The people of Hibbing trusted the movers not just with their possessions but also with their lives. Many houses were actually moved with all the furniture and residents riding inside. Lucky for them, the movers had a pretty solid success rate. Of the 200 buildings moved, only one didn't survive the trip.

Glow in the Dark

YOU WILL NEED

- **1 hand (your own, preferably attached)**
- **1 set of fingernails (see above)**
- **1 powerful photon counter (check your local university research laboratory)**
- **Photons (don't sweat it, you've already got those)**

Do It Because: ***IT'S ALREADY THERE***

Some kids want to be princesses or mermaids. But we always thought it'd be fun to be a firefly. (Not the "hey, your tush is blinking on and off" part, mind you, more just the general glowing.) Turns out, we've always been closer to our dream than we realized. In 2005, researchers at Japan's Hamamatsu Photonics Central Research Laboratory revealed that humans already do glow in the dark. Our hands, feet, and foreheads all shine, thanks to photons—tiny, energized packets of light emitted by our skin. According to a *Discovery News* article on the study, researchers say that fingernails release the most photons, possibly because the material they're made of can function like a prism, scattering light far and wide. So how's it work? The researchers aren't entirely sure. However, using some hand models and a photon counter, they figured out that warm temperatures, increased oxygen, and mineral oil all increase the photon output—making it likely that the glow is caused by chemiluminescence (a fancy word that simply means "light caused by chemical reactions"). Coincidentally, this is same process that makes those firefly fannies flicker.

Use It To: ***ATTRACT POTENTIAL MATES, ENTERTAIN YOUR FRIENDS . . . AND HELP OUT YOUR DOCTOR***

Besides grade-school wish fulfillment and some serious potential for party tricks, there are actually some practical benefits to this knowledge. Both the Japanese researchers and a second team in Germany say that disease and illness may affect the glow. The Japanese say that sick people emit a dimmer light, while German studies on multiple sclerosis patients revealed that the disease seemed to change the rhythm at which the photon light pulsed. The teams hope that one day their discovery could be used to help doctors diagnose specific disorders in a less invasive way.

Be Invisible

If you have several billion dollars and a defense department contract: You may be able to get invisible, thanks to a new technology based off the Fantastic Four. According to comic-book mythology, the Invisible Woman pulls off her shtick by bending light waves around her body with a force field—so instead of seeing a blond chick in spandex, supervillans see whatever happens to be behind her. So far, this skill is strictly for fictional hotties, but researchers at St. Andrews University in Scotland think that, in the near future, those of us not genetically altered by radioactive rays from space may be able to do something similar. The concept works like this: We see objects because they reflect light back to our eyes. So if an object were able to curve light around itself like water flowing around a river stone, it would be effectively invisible. We'd see all the things around and behind it that reflected the light instead. To be invisible, a person or object would have to be concealed behind a shield made of metamaterials, highly engineered man-made solids that can bend waves of energy. So far, the metamaterials are still theoretical, but scientists agree that they're coming soon. Both the researchers at St. Andrews and a different group at the Pentagon have predicted that successful metamaterials capable of hiding objects from radar or electromagnetic waves (though, sadly, not from the human eye) could debut as early as 2008.

If you have a couple of million and airfare to Japan: You can be transparent right now, though people may accuse you of cheating. Tachi Laboratories at the University of Tokyo has developed a sort of virtual invisibility cloak made of a luminescent material, similar to a movie screen or

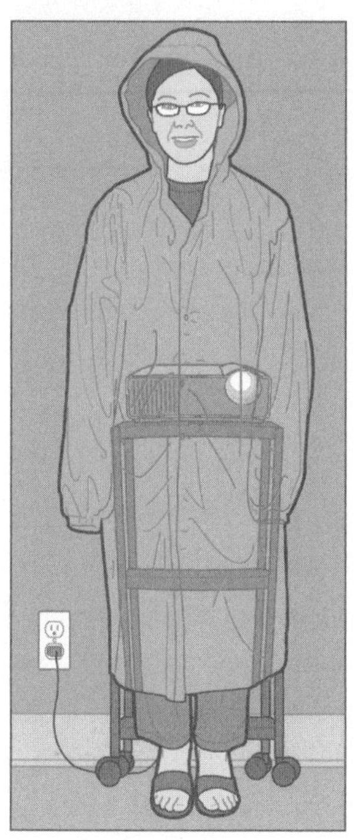

stop sign paint. Using a digital camera linked to a powerful computer, researchers can project live images and video from behind the cloak onto its front, making it blend in, chameleon-style, with the background. The effect isn't all that realistic; you won't be using this cloak to walk into a bank and rob it undetected. However, the technology promises to be very useful to surgeons, who could use it to "see" through their own hands for a better view of their patient's innards.

If you're on a budget: You can't be invisible, but your Pyrex® glassware can. Turns out, Pyrex and Wesson oil reflect light at almost the exact same angle—so if you immerse a rod of Pyrex in a jar of cooking oil, the submerged glass will appear to vanish.

Search for Atlantis

YOU WILL NEED

- A goofy and/or offensive theory
- Evidence (doesn't need to be good)
- A very stretchy imagination

Tip #1: *RULE OUT SWEDEN*

Somebody's already tried that and it didn't go very well. Olof Rudbeck, a legit scientist who is credited with the discovery of the lymphatic system in 1651, squandered most of his once-grand reputation by spending the last 30 years of his life attempting to prove that Atlantis lay in his home country of Sweden. Yes, that Sweden. What started as a simple recognition of certain similarities between Swedish runes and ancient Greek quickly blossomed into a nationalistic quest to prove Sweden's innate cultural superiority. According to historian David King, Rudbeck thought that Sweden was where Jason and Argonauts searched for the Golden Fleece, Uppsala was the city of Atlantis, and the Greek gods were really just mythologized versions of actual ancient Swedish kings. Yes, if Rudbeck was to be believed, pretty much every aspect of Western classical culture was shipped out of the North like so many boxes of Ikea furniture. And it didn't stop there. In 1699, by which point he'd basically lost all academic credibility,

Rudbeck was claiming that the Buddha had been based on a medieval Norse hero named Buda.

Tip #2: *CHECK YOUR MOTIVES*

Think you've found Atlantis? Just to be on the safe side, perhaps you should take a step back and examine your reasoning from an objective standpoint. For instance, is your claim of discovery based solely in racism? Someone really should have tossed that question out to Leo Frobenius in 1911, when the German explorer and ethnographer announced that he'd discovered "irrefutable" evidence of the lost city on the coast of Africa, in what is now southwestern Nigeria. This evidence? A bronze bust that Frobenius believed could not possibly have been produced by the local Yoruba people. Why? Frobenius said that the bust was too well made and the person it depicted wasn't (according to then-current theories on race and physical features) African. Thus, by his calculations, it had to be Atlantean in origin. As offensive as they were illogical, Frobenius's claims still managed to garner a lot of press (even in the *New York Times*, no less) before (thankfully) fizzling away.

Tip #3: *TRY YOUR BEST TO SOUND PLAUSIBLE*

In 2003, a researcher named Robert Sarmast announced that he'd found the remains of Atlantis off the coast of the island of Cyprus in the Mediterranean. According to Sarmast, Cyprus had once been a giant peninsula, connected by land bridge to Syria and Lebanon, and was the place where all the classical ancient civilizations—from Egypt to Greece—had their beginnings. Sarmast's research was based on earlier discoveries of an underwater landmass by Israeli and Russian scientists and he used state-of-the-art sonar to map the area and, according to him, match its features to 48 of Plato's 50 descriptive details of Atlantis. Of course, Plato also said that Atlantis was surrounded by a 600-foot-wide moat, the length of which would have hemmed in an area larger than the whole country of Greece. So maybe Plato should be taken with a grain of salt. Worse yet, second-opinion research conducted for a 2007 History Channel documentary showed that Sarmast's sunken city is actually more likely to be piles of sea floor sediment. But hey, it certainly sounded good on paper.

Illustrate the Land Before Time

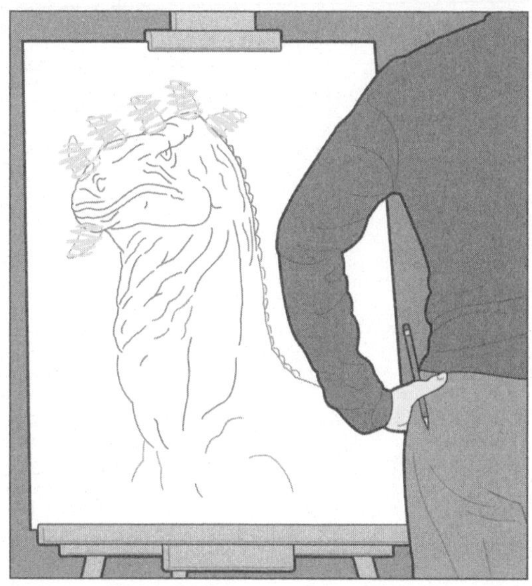

How do you draw something nobody's ever seen? In the 18th century, the earliest paleontologists answered that question by turning to the long-standing tradition of biblical illustration. Soon, artists who'd cut their teeth on the Creation were diligently (and, as it turned out, ironically) fleshing out dinosaurs and wooly mammoths. Today, most major museums employ artists who specialize in illustrating the bodies, environments, and behaviors of creatures long since dead. Needless to say, this isn't the easiest job in the world. But, if you're determined to color your parachute diplodochus red, here's what you'll need to know:

YOU WILL NEED

- **Dead things (the more leftovers the better)**
- **Art supplies**
- **A working knowledge of diverse anatomy**
- **A good imagination**

FIRST, GET AS INTIMATE AS POSSIBLE WITH YOUR SUBJECT: And, we can all agree, it doesn't get much more intimate than bone structure. Unfortunately, after several million years of decomposition, flooding, geological upheaval, and general lying about in dirt, most fossil animals don't have a complete skeleton left. In fact, it's pretty common, particularly with newly discovered species, to end up working from some very random bits and pieces—like, say, a jaw, a leg, and a big toe. That can lead to some pretty awkward misunderstandings. For instance, back in 1825, gentleman archaeologist Gideon Mantell discovered the first known herbivorous dinosaur, a creature he named "iguanadon." Among iguanadon's remains was a long, pointy spine, which Mantell promptly decided belonged, unicorn-like, on the dinosaur's snout. And there it remained, until years later when another scientist discovered the first complete iguanadon skeleton and everybody realized that the "horn" was actually one of four thumb spurs.

That said, fossil analysis has also led to some really amazing discoveries—like the fact that dinosaurs probably weren't cold-blooded. In the 1960s and 70s, paleontologist Robert Bakker studied as many dino hip joints has he could get his hands on, discovering that the thunder lizards probably didn't walk like lizards at all. Reptiles like alligators, move via a sort of bow-legged waddle, which looks silly, but is actually really energy-efficient— perfect for cold-blooded bodies. Dinosaurs, however, most likely had legs that moved forward-to-back; a lot like ours do. So why would gigantic, ostensibly cold-blooded dinosaurs waste their precious energy on mammal-like movement? It just didn't make sense—unless the dinos were warm-blooded. You can thank Bakker (and Occam's Razor) for invalidating everything you learned in kindergarten.

THEN, MEET ITS RELATIVES

In an attempt to prevent a repetition of the iguanadon fiasco, modern illustrators have crafted a careful process that allows them to fill in the fossil gaps, without resorting to pure, ridiculous whimsy (at least, not very often). Today, the key step to recreating any long-dead creature is careful study of its relatives—both living and long gone. From this, illustrators pick up invaluable hints that can help them make educated guesses about an extinct animal's diet, environment, and even color. This is most important for recreating the bits that don't fossilize; soft tissues like ears, fins, and scales. For instance, in 2006, Slate.com described how paleontologists had decided that the 30-million-year-old fish, Dunkleosteus, had had a Jaws-worthy dorsal fin when no such appendage had survived the fish's millennia-long sojourn underground. Turns out, Dunkle is an uncle to the modern shark.

Cross the Atlantic by Train

YOU WILL NEED

- **Technology that already exists**
- **A big honkin' wad of cash**

Step 1: *DON'T DISCOUNT THE IDEA JUST BECAUSE IT SOUNDS RIDICULOUS*

After all, so did the Chunnel between England and France back in the day, and that turned out to be successful and safe. Not convinced? Did we mention that the transatlantic tunnel's biggest promoter is the same guy who got the ball rolling on the Chunnel back in 1956? Frank Davidson, a lawyer specializing in engineering and public policy, put together the design team that came up with the first technical specifications that eventually led the Chunnel out of the realm of fantasy. What's more, according to an article in the Summer 2002 issue of the *Harvard Law Bulletin*, Davidson's not the first prescient science

visionary to think a tunnel under the ocean is a good idea. Jules Verne brought the idea to the table in 1895 and Robert Goddard, the father of rocketry, worked out detailed enough plans for a transatlantic tunnel that he ended up taking out a couple of patents on it in the early 20th century.

Step 2: *MAKE IT WORK*

Truth be told, this ain't that hard. We already possess all the technology needed to bring a transatlantic tunnel into fruition. It would just be on a scale (and a budget) larger than anything humanity has previously used that technology for. For instance, watertight tunnels aren't a big deal. And we wouldn't even need to worry about digging beneath the surface of the ocean, as Davidson's plan calls for the tube to float about 150 feet beneath the waves, harnessed to the bottom by giant anchors. Of course, it will be outrageously long—3,100 miles, to be exact—a fact which has led people to speculate that the project could cost anywhere between $30 billion and several trillion dollars and take decades to construct. If anything sinks Davidson's plan permanently, it'll probably be these factors.

Step 3: *MAKE IT COMFORTABLE*

What's the point of dropping a couple of trillion if people can't travel in style? To cross the Atlantic super fast, Davidson has proposed running magnetic trains through a vacuum, which would make it possible to move at speeds upwards of 5,000 mph. To combat the G-forces produced, proponents have suggested building special seats for passengers and sealing each train car up as if the train is a chain of space ships.

Sink a Battleship

The German Way

YOU WILL NEED

- **1 battleship of your own (naturally it is superior to those of your enemies)**

Step 1: *BUILD A BETTER BATTLESHIP*

Shortly before the opening volleys of World War II, Germany launched what promised to be the most sophisticated and heavily armed battleship on the high seas. Named for a ruthless 19th-century military leader, the *Bismarck* was meant to be the ultimate blockade ship, a massive floating fortress that would stop or sink any liner bringing supplies to England from across the Atlantic. Nearly a sixth of a mile long, the Bismarck boasted 36 guns, 13-inch-thick armor plating, and a squadron of six planes that could be launched from its deck via catapult. In fact, the boat was so much better than its peers that it was, technically, illegal. After World War I, Germany had signed a treaty promising not to build any ships that weighed more than 35,000 tons—the *Bismarck* clocked in at 42,000. But by 1939, when the *Bismarck* was formally launched, Germany wasn't exactly worried about getting invited to the League of Nations Christmas party. They simply lied about the *Bismarck*'s weight.

Step 2: *USE YOUR BATTLESHIP TO SINK YOUR ENEMIES'*

This is a pretty straightforward plan, but then the Germans are nothing if not efficient. On May 18, 1941, the *Bismarck* embarked on its maiden voyage. Six days later, it made its first kill—the *Hood*, formerly the pride of the British Navy. Although well armed and vaunted in the press as the "fastest ship in the world," the *Hood* was flimsily built. A few well-placed German artillery shells went right through the ship's deck, sinking it in less than 20 minutes.

The British Way

YOU WILL NEED

- **Pluck . . . and**
- **8 battleships**
- **2 aircraft carriers**
- **4 heavy cruisers**
- **7 light cruisers**
- **21 destroyers**
- **6 submarines**

Step 1: *HOPE FOR SOME HUBRIS ON THE PART OF YOUR ENEMY*

Luckily for England, all that efficiency made the Germans a little cocky. When the *Bismarck* set out for the Atlantic on May 18, its captain showed an almost zero sense of secrecy. The difficult-to-miss ship sailed through narrow Norwegian straights in broad daylight, giving English reconnaissance plenty of time to photograph it, map its trajectory, and ready an opposing force. The Germans also had a bit too much faith in the *Bismarck*'s supposed unsinkability—particularly considering the fact that this belief was largely based on a system of watertight chambers in the hull, similar to those on the *Titanic*.

Step 2: *IF AT FIRST YOU DON'T SUCCEED . . .*

Just try not to bomb your own boat on the next try. After the *Bismarck* sunk the *Hood*, the English turned to their second line of defense, aka throwing everything they had at the *Bismarck* and hoping that something would sink it. Between May 24 and 27, the Bismarck played cat and mouse with the English ships, disappearing into the fog for large stretches of time as it tried to make its way to the safety of occupied France. Along its journey, the English sent three waves of airborne bombers after the Bismarck. Initially, this wasn't much of a success. The first round of bombers missed their target. The second round mistook an English ship, the *Sheffield*, for the *Bismarck* and bombed it instead. Finally, the third set of bombers managed to do something right, knocking out the *Bismarck*'s rudder and steering compartment.

Step 3: *CELEBRATE! (MAYBE)*

With no way to maneuver to the coast, the *Bismarck* became a sitting duck and was quickly surrounded by dozens of British ships. But this wasn't the end. For two hours, the British Navy attacked the *Bismarck* without managing to sink it. Down to their last two torpedoes and the tail end of their fuel supply, the troops decided to take one last shot at the German battleship before giving up and heading home. It was those final torpedoes that managed to do the trick, sending the *Bismarck* (and all but 115 of its 2,400-man crew) to a watery grave. Although much hearty British-on-British back-patting followed, research done on the *Bismarck*'s remains in 1989 has shown that the English may not have actually been responsible for the battleship's demise. Judging from the wreckage, it looks as though the *Bismarck*'s captain may have flooded his own ship, to prevent it from falling into enemy hands. While still technically a victory for England, this new evidence definitely takes a little wind out of their "We sunk your battleship!" campaign.

Advantage: *GERMANY* (Beers all around!)

Outrun Molasses

Don't think you'll ever need this skill? Yeah . . . neither did the residents of Boston.

FIRST, TRY MOVING TO A BETTER NEIGHBORHOOD

Boston's North End was a sardine can of tenements and poor immigrant families in 1919. Needless to say, none of these people were really in any position to resist when the powerful Purity Distilling Company had built a massive molasses storage tank there four years previously. At the time, Purity and its parent company, United States Industrial Alcohol, had supplied the alcohol distilled from the molasses to the government for munitions. After the war ended, the 2.3-million-gallon capacity tank remained, turning its attention to serving the rum industry.

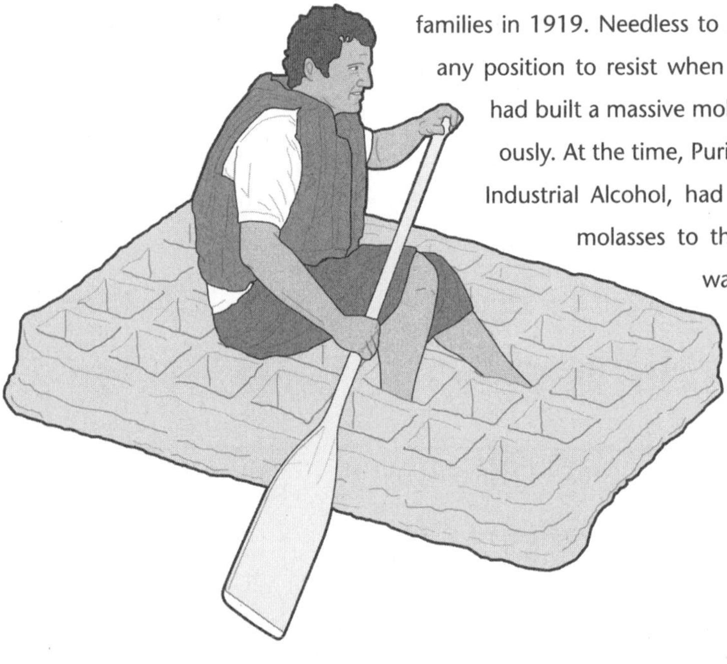

THINK AS FAST AS MOLASSES MOVES (IN THIS CASE: ABOUT 35 MILES PER HOUR)

Then came the specter of Prohibition. In January of 1919, USIA filled the North End tank to capacity. According to some sources, the company was hoping to hedge its bets and sell as much rum molasses as possible before Prohibition became law, while others say it was anticipating an increased demand for "industrial" alcohol. Either way, on the morning of January 15, the tank was packed full to the brim. Perhaps, in retrospect, a bit too full. Around 12:30 p.m. that day, the 50-foot-high wall of the tank burst open, releasing a tsunami of syrup that was clocked at close to 35 miles per hour. Twenty-one people died, hundreds were injured, and a number of wooden buildings in the path of the deluge were ripped apart. Worse, as the molasses cooled in the January chill it inhibited rescue efforts, slowing would-be saviors in hip-high sticky glop. On the plus side, the ambulances got there almost immediately. According to an article in *Smithsonian* in 1983, a policeman making a call into his station saw the wall of molasses advancing toward him and was able to sound the alarm before he had to swim for his life.

WHEN ALL ELSE FAILS, SUE

The ensuing lawsuits ended up involving 3,000 witnesses and lasting six years. USIA reportedly spent more than $500,000 in today's currency trying to prove that an anarchist bomb had been to blame. They lost. In a landmark decision for the time, the judge ruled that the company had been negligent on safety. Between out-of-court settlements and ordered restitutions, USIA ended up paying the equivalent of somewhere around $5 million to $11 million.

Live Without an Immune System

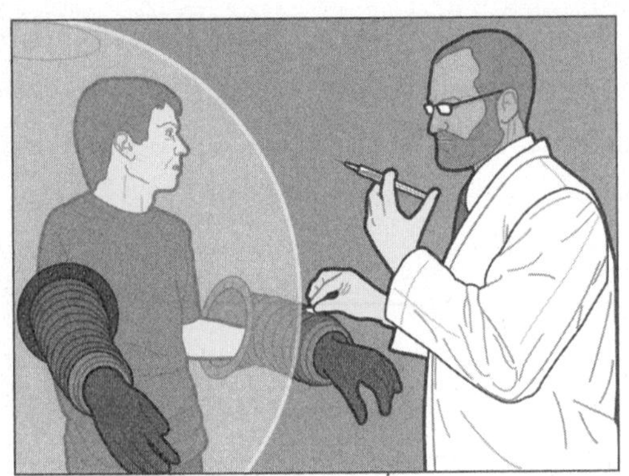

YOU WILL NEED

- Bravery
- Luck
- Good health insurance

Method 1: *A GIANT PLASTIC BUBBLE*

Oh sure, you probably think bubble boys are funny, but before living in a plastic poof became a punchline, it was an incredibly effective treatment. Back in 1971, when David Vetter was born, there wasn't a reliable way to physically treat Severe Combined Immunodeficiency Syndrome, a genetic disease that prevents the body from fighting any and all infections. But, instead of writing little David off as a lost cause, doctors at Texas Children's Hospital decided that, if they couldn't fix the boy, maybe they could fix the environment he lived in. Shortly after birth, David was placed in a sealed, sterilized isolation chamber where bacteria and viruses couldn't touch him. As he grew, the bubble grew with him, eventually taking up most of a room. With a little help from NASA, he was even able to go outside in a specially designed "spacesuit." At the time, most people with SCIDs died within a few months of birth, but, safe in his bubble, David was able to survive for almost 13 years.

Method 2: *GENE THERAPY*

Over the last 20 years, SCIDs treatment has improved to the point that almost all babies born with the disease can expect a normal life span. The key lies in the patient's own blood. As soon as a baby is diagnosed with SCIDs, some of its blood is drawn and sent to a lab. There, scientists can isolate the defective cells that cause the immune system disorder and change the DNA of those cells to make them like those of a healthy baby. Those cells are then injected back into the patient where they grow and divide and eventually replace the supply of genetically damaged cells. This treatment has had the most success with newborns, whose altered cells came from their cord blood—essentially a form of stem-cell therapy. And, thanks to a blood test for SCIDs developed especially for newborns in 2005, more and more babies will soon have access to the cord blood treatment. Does it work? You bet. Of babies who get gene therapy before they're 4 months old, a full 95 percent successfully develop working immune systems.

Get Well

According to Medieval medicine and Richard Zacks's brilliant tome An Underground Education

YOU WILL NEED

- To be brave
- To ignore empirical evidence
- To close your eyes and think of England . . . anesthesia isn't on the table just yet

Method 1: *THE GREEK WAY*

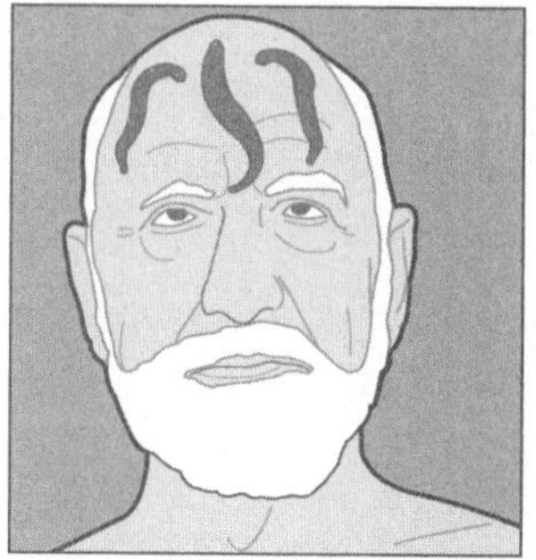

Beginning in the Golden Age of Greece, medicine languished under the theory of humors. Coincidentally funny, humors were supposed to be four bodily fluids that corresponded to the four (*sic*) earth elements: water (black bile), air (yellow bile), earth (phlegm), and fire (blood). Given the phlegm (not to mention all those biles), this already sounds a little off-putting, but the theory gets odder. Proto-doctors believed that illness was caused by too much or too little of these humors and good health was all about balancing. This meant that if you were, say, coughing up phlegm you'd need to cut down on your cold, earth humor by eating a lot of spicy food. Likewise, if you had a fever, you obviously had too much fire humor and needed to be bled, which is where all those leeches you've heard so much about come into the picture.

Method 2: *THE ARABIAN WAY*

If you had the misfortune to get sick in medieval times, your best, if not only, hope was to find an Arabian doctor. While Western medicine went various places in a hand basket during the middle ages, Middle Eastern doctors preserved the more logical aspects of Greek and Roman scholarship and built on them, eventually putting together a superior, and largely accurate, medical theory. One 12th century account of how a European and an Arab doctor treated a patient with tuberculosis shows how great this gulf really was. The Arab doctor prescribed a cleansing diet and fresh air, while the European doctor declared that there was a devil in the patient's brain. He then cut her hair and when that didn't cure her, he cut open her head and rubbed her brain with salt, killing her instantly. On the plus side, no more tuberculosis!

Method 3: *THE WAY YOU SHOULD PROBABLY AVOID*

Uneasy lies the head that wears the crown, especially when the doctor is in the castle. Before the advent of modern medicine, money could only buy more remedies, not better ones. In 1685, Charles II of England suffered a massive stroke. His Royal Physician, Dr. Scarburgh, prescribed, among other things, the following treatments: one pint of blood bled from right arm; one enema containing rock salt, mallow leaves, beets, fennel, cinnamon, and linseed; shaving and blistering for the king's head; a plaster of pitch and pigeon dung applied to his feet; and finally (Charles died shortly afterward) an elixir of pearl and ammonia poured down his throat.

Visit North Korea

Visit beautiful North Korea—because this way, somebody might actually be interested in your vacation slide show. And by "somebody," of course, we mean the U.S. State Department! Despite (and partially because of) the nearly 60 years of oppressive and increasingly crazy totalitarian leadership, the "other" Korea does have some fascinating tourist attractions—from the natural glory Mt. Paektu, a 9000-foot-tall inactive volcano, to creepy-but-impressive Mass Games, a sort-of communist half-time show extravaganza with a cast of thousands. But to see any of North Korea's sights successfully (i.e., not in a gulag), there are a few tips you'll need to remember.

YOU WILL NEED

- A love of adventure
- A desire to experience new cultures
- A way to figure out whether or not your room has been bugged

Tip 1: *PRETEND TO BE CANADIAN*

Granted, it's best not to lie on your official entry applications—we don't want to get anyone branded a spy. But, as you may have noticed, the United States and North Korea don't really have the best relationship right now and this animosity spills over into practical areas, like currency exchange. North Korea is one of the few countries in the world where flashing greenbacks will get you nowhere. Instead, you'll need to trade your dollars for euros before you get in country. Even then, don't expect to be able to trade euros for souvenir-quality North Korean wan; the government is touchy about letting foreigners have access to local currency.

Tip 2: *GET PERSONAL WITH YOUR PROPAGANDISTS*

Tour guides are mandatory in North Korea. Every group of visitors must have two state-authorized guides with them at all times. And while it's handy to have a couple of Korean-speaking locals around to keep you from getting lost, they'll also be keeping you from a few other things—like ever having any contact with an average North Korean. The guides are there to make sure you stick to the Kim Jong Il–approved paths. For instance, they'll undoubtedly take you down to see the capital city's immaculate, art-filled subway . . . but you'll only ride from the Puhung station to the Yongwang station. In fact, since 1973, this one-way trip is all most visitors have ever seen, inspiring rumors that the rest of the system is dilapidated and abandoned. However, there are ways to charm your guides into complacency. Reportedly, they're big fans of chocolate and American souvenirs.

Tip 3: *CATCH UP ON YOUR SLEEP*

If you like the nightlife, baby, North Korea may not be the place for you. There are, according to *Lonely Planet* guidebooks, a grand total of 3 nightclubs in the whole country, and these are reserved for the small group of foreigners who live and work in Pyongyang. No casual tourists allowed. This fact probably doesn't bother most North Koreans, however, as they're not allowed out that late anyway. Citizens have compulsory political education classes every night after work and only get Sundays off. By the time the propaganda schools shut down for the night, curfew has already kicked in.

Get Rescued from a Desert Island

YOU WILL NEED

- 1 unstoppable will to live
- Patience
- Possibly a good warm coat

Tip #1: *ACCEPT THAT YOU MAY HAVE TO WAIT AWHILE . . . AND IT MAY SUCK*

If there's one thing you can say about most desert island strandings it's that, at the very least, the weather is nice. There are certainly worse islands to be trapped on, thousands of miles from civilization, than a tropical paradise. Antarctica for instance. Unfortunately, that's exactly what happened to a group of explorers in the fall of 1915. Part of the team helping Ernest Shackleton attempt to cross the Antarctic continent, the group had landed on the opposite coast from their leader, in order to lay supply depots for the second half of his journey. Unfortunately, the job ended up being harder than they thought. Food supplies ran low, everyone got frostbite, and then their ship was swept out to sea, stranding them. The men tried to complete their job, but they lost several of their number and had to eat all their sled dogs. They ended up being stuck—surviving on a diet of seal and more seal—for two years before Shackleton (who hadn't fared much better on the other side of the continent) showed up with a boat to rescue them.

Tip #2: *THINK OF YOUR RESCUE AS A NEW BEGINNING*

You've just survived an amazing ordeal, why go back to exactly the way life was before? Instead, take a tip from Manjiro Nakahama, a young Japanese fisherman who turned a desert island rescue into a lucrative opportunity for travel, education, and career advancement. In 1841, when he was about 14, Nakahama and several of his coworkers were wrecked on a tiny island far from home and eventually rescued by an American whaling ship. While the others elected to get dropped off at the nearest port, Nakahama asked to stay aboard and go to America. With the help of patrons, he enrolled in school, learned English, navigation, and barrel making, and went on to first join a whaling ship and then make a small fortune in the California Gold Rush before making his way back to Japan. There, with his knowledge of foreign language and culture, the former fisherman became a valuable asset to the Japanese national government. He eventually became a respected translator and naval strategist and was made a *hatamoto*, sort of the Japanese version of a knighthood.

Capture a Giant Squid

As the name implies, giant squid are carnivorous mollusks the size of a school bus with a beaklike mouth that can cut through steel cable. So you think they'd be hard to miss. However, the squid tend toward the deepest water and are so seldom seen that, before the 1860s—when a French ship brought back a chunk of one—they were thought to be merely a myth. But don't let that get you down, there's more than one way to skin a sea monster. . . .

Method 1: *FORGET THE NET*

You might have more luck "capturing" a squid on film. In September 2004, Japanese researchers took the first photos of a live giant squid in its natural habitat when they sent cameras attached to barbed bait hooks (the bait: smaller squids) nearly 3,000 feet below the Pacific Ocean. Before long, a 26-foot squid attempted to eat his scrawnier brethren and hooked himself on the barbs, allowing researchers to take some 500 photos before he could escape.

Method 2: *OFFER A TASTY TREAT*

If your preferred squid looks hungry, try luring it with an oil tanker. During the course of the 1930s, the Norwegian tanker the *Brunswick* was attacked not once, not twice, but three times by giant squid. Metal boats don't sound delicious, but scientists think that squid mistake the large gray objects for whales—a decidedly yummy entrée giant squid have been known to dine on. Unfortunately, the steel hull of a tanker is more difficult to get a good grip on than the pliable hide of a whale. When the squid tried to put the *Brunswick* in a choke hold, its tentacles would slip and the squid would make a fatal slide into the ship's propellers.

Method 3: *JUST GO HAVE A BEER AND WAIT FOR THE SQUID TO COME TO YOU*

This is the time-tested, classic method. (Not to mention the most relaxing.) In fact, the largest squid ever measured was discovered washed ashore on November 2, 1878, by two Canadian fishermen from Timble Tickle, New

Brunswick. Although technically on the lookout for smaller aquatic creatures, the fishermen gladly accepted what the sea gave them, hauling the giant beast further onto shore and tying it to a tree. After it was dead, they measured it and found that, from the tip of its tail to the end of its tentacles, the squid was more than 50 feet long.

Be Killed by Soda Water

YOU WILL NEED

- A really unfortunate series of geological events

Step 1: *LIVE NEAR AN EXTINCT VOLCANO IN THE TROPICS*

If *Super Size Me* is to be believed, drinking carbonated beverages will kill you eventually, but carbonated water can (and has) caused fatalities of a much more immediate nature. The problem is the gas that makes the water so delightfully bubbly, carbon dioxide, is extremely deadly in large, free-floating doses. Luckily, the gas doesn't get a chance to go out roaming around on its own like that very often. But, under specific geological circumstances, such a disaster is possible. It works like this: volcanoes, even ones that aren't erupting any more, are still constantly releasing a veritable Long Island Ice Tea of gases, most prominently carbon dioxide. If a lake forms in the crater of one of these ex-exploders, carbon dioxide that drifts up from the below ground magma chamber will filter into the water. In most crater lakes, this isn't a problem because either the lake water is stirred up often enough to keep the CO_2 from accumulating or because the gas vents are close enough to the surface that the result is a harmless, bubbly soda spring. But, in certain tropical regions, lake waters don't move a whole lot. In these situations, carbon dioxide filters into the water at the lake bottom and stays there, building up for years, even decades. These CO_2 reservoirs are essentially waterlogged time bombs.

Step 2: *TRIGGER AN ERUPTION*

Denser than regular water, the carbonated water stays put on the lake bottom until something forces it to move. This might happen as the result of a landslide or an earthquake that stirs the bottom water to the top—or it could

be caused by the CO_2 reaching a level of 100 percent saturation, making the gas suddenly lighter than the water above it. Either way, the gas then rises out of the water with a powerful force, like a giant, exploding soda can. Released from its watery prison, the gas is then free to travel along the ground, evicting almost all oxygen wherever it goes. Thus, any oxygen-breathing creature in its path is in danger of almost instantaneous suffocation.

Step 3: *CHANGE YOUR MIND ABOUT THAT WHOLE "BEING KILLED" THING*

Luckily for flip-floppers like yourself, the death-by-soda-water scenario isn't very common. In recorded history, it's only happened twice. In 1984 and 1986, two lakes in a mountainous region of Cameroon, Africa, released carbon dioxide bubbles. The 1986 event ended up killing almost 2,000 people as well as countless animals and is estimated to have involved more than 300 million cubic feet of gas. Since then, geologists have identified only one other lake, also in Africa, where carbon dioxide buildup is a problem. However, *Smithsonian* magazine has recorded accounts of myths and legends from the area that suggest the bubbles are regular occurrences. Meanwhile, scientists say there's also physical evidence that gas bubbles have killed before, at roughly 1,000-year intervals. Both facts have prompted local governments to take evasive action against all three lakes. Today, pipes attached to floating platforms serve as artificial artesian wells, sucking up carbonated water from the lake bottoms and throwing it high into the air where the CO_2 can harmlessly float away in small amounts. The tactic keeps the gas from building up on the bottom and has been running successfully since 2001.

Be Two People at Once

First: *GET THAT MEDDLING SIBLING OUT OF YOUR WAY*

Imagine you're a fertilized egg, just a few days old. There you are, floating around the womb and minding your own business when, bam! You run smack into another just like you. Well, not just like you. But close enough to be a threat. The choice is yours: You can roll over and let yourself be born just another fraternal twin or you can stand up for your individuality and absorb that interloper. Naturally, you do the smart thing, and nine months later your parents take home one healthy baby.

Then: *DISCOVER THAT THEY AREN'T AS DEAD AS YOU THOUGHT*

YOU WILL NEED

- A twin (preferably of the same sex as you)
- To be one tough zygote

Like a horror-movie villain locked into a three-picture contract, your twin never really goes away. Instead, she'll end up hiding in plain sight—within your very cells—rendering you a chimera, a single human who carries the genetic makeup of two different people. Yes, it's far out. And yes, it's rare. But it's not as rare as you might expect, particularly as increased use of fertility drugs raises the chances of having twins to absorb. In fact, it's likely that most chimeras don't realize they are chimeras. If the twin you absorbed was the same sex you are, there usually aren't any outward signs that your body is harboring a stowaway. Take Karen Keegan, for example, who discovered her chimera-ness at age 52. When needing a kidney transplant, she and her children underwent DNA testing that showed the two of them weren't related to her. The case confounded doctors for over two years until, in 2000, the docs finally realized that Karen's blood cells carried different genes than the cells in her ovaries—genes from a long-ago-absorbed twin. Of course, chimeras that incorporate two different sexes have it a bit rougher. In 1998, Scottish doctors reported treating a teenage boy for an undescended testicle, only to discover an ovary and fallopian tube where the missing testicle should have been.

Be a Tycoon

Succeed in Business

According to David Sarnoff

YOU WILL NEED

- Savvy business acumen
- A certain amount of comfort with moral grey areas

First: ***INDULGE IN SOME SHAMELESS SELF-PROMOTION***

As the president of RCA during its formative years in the 1930s to the 1960s (and, arguably, one of the most famous businessmen in history), you'd think David Sarnoff wouldn't have had to embellish on his personal biography. But, apparently, reality was never quite good enough for Sarnoff—he wanted to be a legend. Case in point: while in his early 20s, Sarnoff was a telegraph operator in New York City and happened to be on duty the night the *Titanic* sank. That alone is a pretty good story. But, in later years, Sarnoff would embellish it, claiming to be the first telegraph operator to receive the distress call and, in some versions of the tale, the only operator to work straight through the night.

Then: ***CRUSH YOUR ENEMIES***

Without a doubt, Sarnoff was a business genius, foreseeing the need for a common household radio, color TV, and even the VCR. But he also excelled at grinding his enemies into dust. One former friend, E. A. Armstrong, learned this the hard way. In 1933, Armstrong invented FM radio and tried to convince his pal Sarnoff to adopt the technology. But Sarnoff wasn't biting. And when Armstrong went off to found his own FM station, Sarnoff used his considerable financial muscle to push the FCC into limiting the use of FM. The two ended up in a legal battle, which Sarnoff dragged out over six years, so utterly destroying his former friend's finances and psyche that Armstrong ended up committing suicide.

Finally: ***IF IT LOOKS GOOD—TAKE IT!***

When it came to patents, Sarnoff believed strongly that RCA should never have to pay copyright fees, only collect them. In pursuit of this ideal, he wasn't above sending his researchers to "visit" the labs of competitors and patent the pilfered technology before the actual inventors got the chance, using RCA's vast wealth to beat down any legal challenges. In fact, this is exactly how RCA ended up being able to sell television sets without paying the machine's true creator Philo T. Farnsworth a single cent.

Print Your Own Money

Here are three home-grown monetary systems you should avoid copying too closely.

THE RAAM

Although best known for his contribution to the spiritual lives of the Beatles, Yogi Maharishi Mahesh and his Transcendental Meditation movement recently got into another business: International financing. In 2001 or 2002, (reports differ) the Maharishi's so-called spiritual nation, the Global Country of World Peace, began issuing its own legal tender. Called the "Raam" and adorned with Indian-style art, the bills are currently only in use in TM–associated communities, like Vedic City, Iowa, and some areas of the Netherlands, where their exchange rate reportedly rests at $10 or 10 Euros per 1 Raam.

THE REAL DOLLAR

The Midwest apparently attracts a lot of people dissatisfied with the dollar. Just down the interstate from Vedic City, Iowa, you'll find Lawrence, Kansas, a mid-size college town that began printing its own currency in 2000. Meant to encourage people and businesses to buy locally, REAL (Realizing Economic Alternatives in Lawrence) Dollars were printed in denominations of $1, $3, and $10 and featured images of home-town heroes like Langston Hughes and William S. Burroughs. Unfortunately, their creation managed to coincide with the rise of the cashless society. Today, of the $65,000 worth of REAL Dollars printed, only $5000 remain in circulation—much of that in the hands of out-of-state collectors.

THE COMPANY-STORE TOKEN

Think your job's the pits? Trust us, it could be worse— at least you're paid in U.S. greenbacks. For blue-collar workers in America and England during the 19th and early 20th centuries, payday often meant pay in non-exchangeable tokens, which could only be used at stores owned by their bosses. You see the problem? Of course, there was some logic to this. Many factories and most mines were far from established cities, so owners built housing, stores, churches, and schools for workers' families, making it more convenient than traveling all the way to a non-company town just to go shopping. Still, without competition, company stores were free to over-charge and mistreat customers, who, until the labor reforms of the 20th century, had little recourse.

Use All of Your Brain

Step 1: *BE ALIVE*

Actually, that's pretty much all you have to do. Despite what the Uri Gellers of the world would have you believe, you're already using all of your brain. The myth that you only use 10 percent most likely originated from some of the early and very rough experiments in neuroscience, which showed that stimulating certain parts of the brain produced an instant, and obvious, physical response. But, when electrodes were applied to other parts, there seemed to be no effect at all. Scientists called these areas "the silent cortex." By the 1930s, stories of these cranial dead zones had morphed into the oft-repeated "factoid" that quickly became a favorite of advertising writers, self-help salesmen, and paranormal power hucksters—all of whom claimed to have the secret to unlocking that ostensibly unused 90 percent. It didn't help matters much that respected scientific figures such as Margaret Mead and Albert Einstein (say it ain't so!) thought nothing of stepping well outside their own realm of scientific knowledge to repeat the 10 percent claim as if it were truth. But, just because some of the 20th century's greatest minds were suckers for an urban legend doesn't mean you have to be.

Step 2: *KNOCK SOME LOGIC INTO YOUR FRIENDS*

The "silent cortex" zones that neuroscientists discovered in the 19th century later turned out to be running some very important functions—like language and abstract thought. Personally, we'd rather not live without those, thanks. Modern brain-imaging systems clearly show that there aren't any vast swaths of useless cerebral cortex lying around. Although we don't use every part of our brain constantly, we do use just about all of it at some point throughout the course of a given day.

Think of it this way: nobody ever signed up for a lobotomy expecting to think the same (or better) afterward. If we truly did only use 10 percent of our brains, we would be able to remove big chunks of the gray stuff and not have it matter much at all. But that isn't the case. Take away 90 percent of human brain's volume, and you're left with something roughly akin to the size of a sheep's brain.

Own the World's Tallest Building

All you have to do is find the current tallest building and go just a wee bit higher, right? Wrong. The rankings for World's Tallest Anything are so in dispute that an international governing body, the Council on Tall Buildings and Urban Habitat, had to step in to arbitrate in the 1990s. And, even with their help, there's still an awful lot of fudging going on. Technically, the Taipei 101 Tower in Taiwan is the official record holder, but several other structures also claim the title and not totally without reason. If you want your tower to be number one, there are a couple things you can do to make a semilegitimate claim.

1. *QUESTION THE DEFINITION OF "BUILDING"*

What's in a name, anyway? Most of the time, we think of the World's Tallest Building as an office tower in a big city. That's what the Taipei 101 is and so are most of its closest competitors. But, while the height to the architectural top of Taipei 101 is a staggering 1,671 feet, there are several structures that are much taller. The CN Tower in Toronto, Canada, is 1,816 feet tall and the Petronius Platform in the Gulf of Mexico tops out at 2,001 feet. Meanwhile, in the middle of a North Dakota farm field, the 2,063-foot-tall KLVY television tower broadcasts signals to an area larger than District of Columbia, Hawaii, Massachusetts, New Jersey, and Connecticut, combined with a force strong enough to make your fillings hurt. So what's wrong with them? Why don't they count? The answer: Mostly because they're unoccupiable. The CN Tower is a glorified observation platform for tourists and, while the KLVY tower does have an elevator, it's basically a big antenna, not something people live or work in. The Petronius Platform, however, gets a bum deal. A massive oil drilling rig, it really is home and office to huge crew of workmen. Instead, it gets knocked off the list because most of its height is below water and it's supported by buoyancy.

2. *QUESTION THE DEFINITION OF "TOP"*

Ever since 1996, there have actually been multiple Worlds' Tallest Buildings, based on several different measurement standards ordained by the Council of Tall Buildings and Urban Habitat. The Taipei 101 gets cited as the tallest today because it wins in three categories: ground to architectural top, ground to highest occupied floor, and ground to top of the roof. The other category, ground to top of the pinnacle, was added after a major dispute between fans of Chicago's Sears Tower and those of the Petronas Twin Towers in Malaysia. By pre-1996 standards, the tallest building was only measured by ground to the architectural top. Spires or other decorations meant to stay attached to the building counted, but antennas didn't. That's equivalent to measuring someone's height and counting their beehive—but not their cowboy hat. Under the previous system, the Sears Tower could be 1,729 feet to top of its massive, functionally immobile antennas, but still lose out to the Petronas Towers, whose spindly architectural spires reached 1,483 feet.

Fool All of the People All of the Time

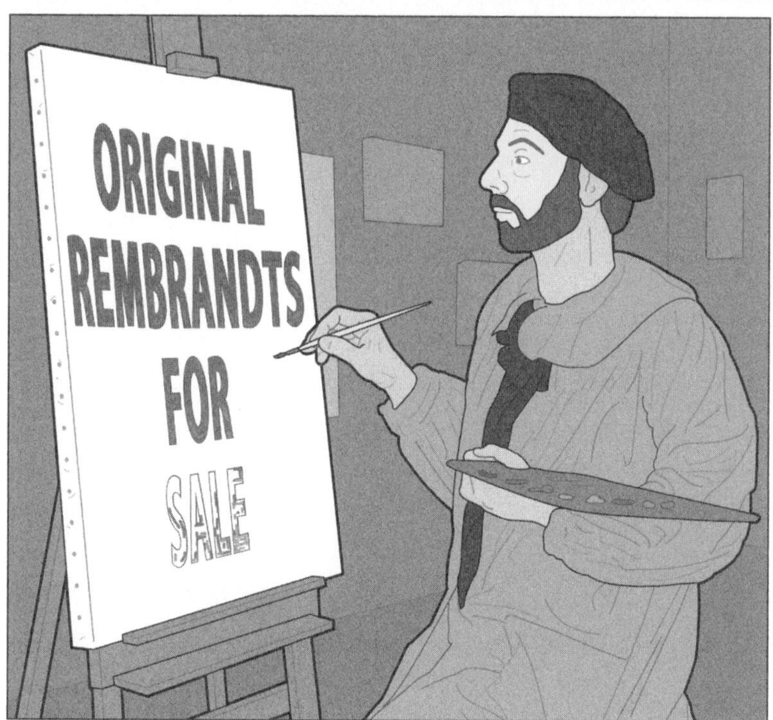

FOOL THE ART WORLD

For years, Dutch painter Han van Meegeren toiled on realistic, Rembrandt-influenced portraits that completely failed to take the art world by storm. His mistake: being born a few hundred years too late. By the time van Meegeren began his career in the 1920s and 30s, nobody was into straight portraiture. For a while, he accepted his fate, but when a critic decried him as "lacking originality," van Meegeren decided the time had come to prove his worth—and if he could make his foes look like idiots at the same time, all the better. Van Meegeren hatched a plan: He would forge a Renaissance-style painting and make it the talk of the art world. Then, once he'd suckered his enemies, he'd reveal himself as the artist, thus exposing his critics as the real frauds. To add insult to injury, van Meegeren decided that the forged painting would not be a copy of well-known work; instead, he would paint an entirely new image in his own oft-mocked style, but with the hallmarks and signature of Dutch master Jan Vermeer.

YOU WILL NEED

- **Historically accurate paints**
- **Talent**
- **Years of pent-up professional bitterness**
- **A plan to save your hide when your hoax gets away from you**

FOOL YOURSELF

To pull off the deception, van Meegeren learned how to mix Renaissance-era paints, prepare canvases the way Vermeer would have, and artificially age his paintings. The result was a never-before-seen work of art, called *The Disciples at Emmaus*, which quickly captured the attention of art collectors across Europe. Van Meegeren spent most of 1936 basking in his critics' warm praise, as they lavished compliment after compliment on the new

"Vermeer." *The Disciples at Emmaus* even ended up in a gallery retrospective chronicling the best of 400 years of European art—quite the coup for an unknown artist. In fact, the flood of praise ended up overwhelming van Meegeren's morals. Instead of outing himself, he sold *Emmaus* for about $300,000 (equal to $4 million today) and began working on another forgery. Over the next 5 years, van Meegeren sold the equivalent of $60 million worth of forged art. Sadly, he also developed booze and morphine addictions on his rise to being the secret darling of the art world.

FOOL THE NAZIS AND BECOME A HERO!

The long con finally came to an end in 1945, when the Allied forces discovered an unknown Vermeer hidden in a salt mine along with piles of other Nazi-pilfered artworks. From the Third Reich's well-organized record books, the authorities discovered that Field Marshall Herman Goering had bought the painting, *Christ and the Adulteress*, from a Dutch art dealer named Han van Meegeren. But when they questioned him, van Meegeren refused to tell them who the painting's rightful owners were. Instead, he was sent to prison on charges of treason, a crime potentially punishable by death. It was only after six weeks of imprisonment (and, presumably, six weeks of going cold-turkey off morphine) that van Meegeren finally cracked, screaming from his cell, "Fools . . . ! There was no Vermeer, I painted it myself!" Awkwardly, nobody believed him. But the Allies made him a deal. If he could paint another forged Vermeer, they'd drop the charges. Supplied with painting supplies, court-appointed witnesses, and liberal quantities of intoxicating substances, van Meegeren turned out one final "Vermeer." The painting's versimilitude shocked both jailers and art critics and turned van Meegeren into a public hero—a crafty fox who outwitted the Nazis. Better yet, he was acquitted of treason and sentenced to a mere one year in jail for profiting off forgery.

Buy the Moon

YOU WILL NEED

- A checkbook
- A dream
- Some help figuring out lunar property taxes

Step 1: *FIND LOOPHOLES IN INTERNATIONAL LAW*

A quick look at the 1967 Outer Space Treaty (signed by the U.S., Britain, and the Soviet Union) will tell you that countries aren't allowed to own space land. However, the treaty says nothing about the rights of individuals. On the other hand, the 1979 Moon Treaty does ban individual lunar real estate investment—but the United States never signed it. So, technically an American could claim that it doesn't apply to him or her.

Step 2: *FIND A REALTOR*

May we suggest Californian Dennis Hope, if for no other reason than the fact that, back in 1980, he publicly claimed ownership of the whole moon and has been selling it off piecemeal ever since. You might say, he has the most experience in this sort of real estate transaction. Hope issues deeds through his company, Lunar Embassy, which, to date, has brought in more than $1.6 million selling lunar plots for about $27 per acre. Alternately, you could opt to get yourself in on the ground floor of the moon's first subdivisions. The British owners of Moon Estates purchased a large block of land from Dennis Hope several years ago and are now selling it at one acre for 16.75 Pounds, or about $33. For your piece of mind, both companies assure that moon property lines are registered and mapped on a computer system so that no acre can be sold twice.

Live a Better Life

YOU WILL NEED

- To quit your day job
- In fact, just go ahead and quit everything

Step 1: *HUNT*

Step 2: *GATHER*

Pop quiz: In the game of life, who's better off? A farmer or a hunter-gatherer? Being the descendants (and dependants) of farmers ourselves, we're prone to guessing that the former has a better existence. After all, it was farmers who broke out during the Neolithic Revolution to produce cities, science, art, technology, and all the trappings of our modern world. In fact, you might even assume, as philosopher Thomas Hobbes did, that hunter-gatherers are stuck with lives that are "nasty, brutish, and short." And, up until the 1960s, scientists probably would have agreed with you. But, in 1966, anthropologist Marshall Sahlins turned those ideas on their head with a paper called "The Original Affluent Society." The basic gist is that, far from being malnourished, haggard, and pitiable, hunter-gatherers actually enjoy a pretty decent lifestyle in which as little as 15 hours a week might be spent finding food (compare that to 40 + overtime). Hunter-gatherers generally take more daytime naps than we do and have plenty of time for hobbies and crafts. Even more surprising, more recent research recorded by sociologist Jared Diamond has shown that they actually have better nutrition and longer lifespans when compared to non-industrial farmers. For instance, before ancient Greeks took up the plow, the average height for a guy was about 5 foot 9 inches. After agriculture, however, this plummeted to a mere 5 foot 3 inches. Greeks didn't regain their lost height until the last couple of centuries. And, today in central Africa, a group of pygmy hunter-gatherers called the !Kung often take in more than 2,000 calories a day—far more than neighboring farmers can hope to consume. In fact, the !Kungs' diet is actually more varied (and healthier) than that of the local farmers as well, largely because small-scale farmers focus on one or two carbohydrate-heavy crops. So, if the hunt-and-gather lifestyle was so great, why'd we ever switch? Both Sahlins and Diamond theorize that agriculture became popular because it allowed families to support more members. Essentially, the theory is that we sacrificed quality for quantity.

Have Greatness Thrust upon You

According to a President and a Heavy Metal God

LIKE JOHN TYLER

With his tendency to vote in favor of proslavery causes, John Tyler wasn't the least divisive (or most ethically sound) guy to ever wield the power of the American presidency. In fact, he wasn't really meant to be president at all. The Whig party only chose him as William Henry Harrison's 1840 running mate in a last-ditch effort to appeal to Southern voters. It worked. Unfortunately, Harrison died of pneumonia a month after taking office. Tyler, who'd been intended to spend four years as a support-generating figurehead, was informed of his new role while on his hands and knees, playing marbles with his young sons.

LIKE TIM OWENS

Once upon a time, Ohio salesman Tim Owens was the lead singer of a Judas Priest cover band called British Steel. Although pretty good as cover bands go, it was the sort of hobby that, after a certain age, mothers and various other females start bugging a guy to give up. Luckily for Owens, he didn't listen. In 1996, British Steel played a show at a small bar in Erie, Pennsylvania, unaware that two friends of Judas Priest's actual drummer was in the audience. Equally unbeknownst to Owens, those friends so impressed with his vocals that they taped the Erie performance and sent the video to Judas Priest. At the time, the Priest had been on hiatus for several years after their original lead singer had bailed. In Owens, they saw a suitable replacement and a path back to the charts. Like a mythical chariot from the stars, drawn by skull-headed horses and manned by Thor, the band swooped down and plucked their biggest fan to be the their new lead singer.

Make a Fortune Gambling

According to old West legend Poker Alice Ivers and one-win wonder Ashley Revell

YOUR TEACHERS:

"POKER" ALICE IVERS

Like most women born in the 1850s, Alice Ivers had planned on being a housewife. She fell in love in Colorado and married a mining engineer. And because gambling was to 19th century mining towns what Monday night football is to the modern suburb, Alice actually ended up spending a lot of time hanging out with her hubby at the local saloons, watching him play poker. Turns out, osmosis learning does work—at least, it did for Alice. Before long, she was sitting in on her husband's games . . . and beating him. When he died in a mining accident, she became a poker dealer. Eventually, she was pulling in upwards of six grand a night. That's the equivalent of about $100,000 today. She later supported her second husband and their family of seven all on poker winnings.

YOU WILL NEED

- A fistful of dollars
- A catchy nickname
- A backup plan

ASHLEY REVELL

In 2004, the 32-year-old Londoner boggled British reality show viewers when he bet $135,000 on a Vegas roulette wheel and won, doubling his pot to $270,600.

THE LESSONS:

1) *IF YOU FEEL LUCKY, YOU ARE LUCKY*

It's tempting to mock someone for claiming that their smelly, moldy tube socks will help them strike it rich, but sometimes little rituals can make a big difference—at least, psychologically. Poker Alice, for instance, may have been a professional gambler, but she stuck to her religious guns by refusing to work (i.e., play poker) on a Sunday. Revell, meanwhile, had originally intended to bet his money on "black" but switched to "red" at the urging of his TV viewers—apparently believing that the combined force of people hoping for that color would help him out.

2) *THROW CAUTION TO THE WIND*

Betting 100 grand on a roulette spin is a little distinctive, but, in the grand scheme of Las Vegas history, it's hardly unique. So, what made Ashley Revell stand out? How about the fact that he was wearing his only belongings at the time? Revell sold and pawned all of his worldly possessions, including clothing, to come up with the $135,000. In fact, of what he was wearing at the roulette table, only the underpants were his. He'd rented a tux. Then, surrounded by friends, family, and the crew of a reality show called *Double or Nothing*, he bet everything he owned.

3) *KNOW WHEN TO FOLD 'EM*

Luckily, Revell won. But you can't always rely on pure fate. A true professional always has a backup plan. For Poker Alice, it was booze. When the elderly champ finally retired, she moved to Sturgis, South Dakota, and made a killing running a speakeasy and brothel.

Lose It All

According to John Law, 17th century economist

THE MAN:

John Law's public career didn't exactly get off to an auspicious start. At 23, the aristocratic Scottish playboy was forced to leave England after he killed a more important aristocrat in a duel. He spent the next few years bouncing around Europe and the colonies, living off what he could win at the gambling table and what he could charm out of wealthy ladies. But, unlike your average lothario, he also had quite a way with numbers and, during his travels he managed to publish what would later become highly influential papers on the mechanisms of credit.

THE PLAN:

In 1714, King Louis XIV hired Law to help get France out of debt (and help get the increasingly angry French populace out of an exorbitantly high tax bracket).

THE PATH TO DESTRUCTION:

Step 1: *CREATE THE FIRST PAPER-MONEY BANKING SYSTEM*

In 1716, Law convinced the French government to bet the ferme on his Banque Generale, which was to issue paper currency supported by stockpiles of gold and silver.

Step 2: *ESTABLISH A GLOBAL MONOPOLY*

A year later, Law organized the Company of the West, a private corporation that was given exclusive trading rights to the French colonies in America. Over the course of 1718 and 1719, he bought exclusive trade rights to Africa, China, and the East Indies. By 1720, Law's company was printing France's primary currency, issuing the only currency that could be used to pay taxes, and holding much of the country's debt.

Step 3: *ENCOURAGE INSANE INVESTING*

As the Company of the West became more profitable, more and more Europeans wanted a chunk of the action and Law's stock price flew like a deranged eagle. In 1719 alone, shares increased in value from 5,000 livre to more than 20,000. More and more people bought shares of the Company on credit, many of them borrowing the money from Law's own Banque Generale.

Step 4: *PANIC*

In January 1720, investors began to cash out and the company's stock price began to fall. Law tried to slow the sell-off by making all payments to investors in paper money, rather than gold. But, unfortunately, the sudden influx of cash kick-started inflation. More people sold their stock for cash to cope with rising prices and inflation got worse. When the company finally tanked, it took the economy of France, the Banque General, and the savings of hundreds of Europeans with it. The economic depression that followed played a huge role in setting the stage for the French Revolution. Even today, most French financial institutions are known as "credites" to avoid any unsavory association with Law's "*banque*."

Leave Your Worries Behind

Psychiatry: You've come a long way, baby. Time was, controlling one's depression or other mental malfunction wasn't as simple (or as pleasant) as popping a Prozac. So how would your mental illness have been treated in the dark days before the pharmaceutical revolution?

Method 1: *LOCK YOU UP*

One of the first "treatments" developed for mental patients was simply to keep them locked up and separated from the rest of society until they either recovered or, eventually, died. Sometimes, this was a voluntary imprisonment. For instance, around the year 1475, Flemish painter Hugo van der Goes got himself to a monk-ery, entering the Red Cloister, a monastery near Brussels, Belgium. Apparently afflicted with what we'd diagnose today as severe depression, van der Goes was convinced of his own inherent vileness and had to be restrained from killing himself at least once. Van der Goes received treatment from the other monks, most notably a form of musical therapy based on the biblical story of how David's harp playing calmed crazy King Saul. Eventually, the artist was able to rejoin society. However, not all stories of confinement are as idyllic as that. England started carting its mentally ill citizens off (often by force) to Bethlehem Hospital around 1400. Here, patients were frequently chained up and basically treated like prisoners, receiving poor rations and getting little light or fresh air. It's no wonder, then, that the patients made such a ruckus that "Bedlam," as the locals pronounced it, became synonymous with a high-volume version of madness.

Method 2: *SHOCK YOU UP*

The next big leap in psychiatric treatment didn't occur until the early 1900s when an Austrian doctor named Julius Wagner Jauregg noticed that there seemed to be a connection between high fevers and improved mental health. Although not the first person to make this connection (it goes all the way back to ancient Greece), Jauregg was the first to set up a scien-

tific trial that fully established a link between fever and decreased madness. In 1917, he tested his theory scientifically—if somewhat unethically—by shooting up several dementia patients with malarial blood. Of the nine patients/victims, four recovered from their dementia completely and two showed some serious improvement. As for Jauregg, he won the Nobel Prize. Later research built on his work and showed that the improvements were the result of seizures in the brain. Amazingly, we still don't know why brain seizures can improve the health of people with schizophrenia, severe depression, and other illnesses. But this lack of knowledge didn't stop the therapy from becoming very popular. Throughout the next 40 years, doctors induced seizures with overdoses of insulin, chemical compounds, and (most notoriously) electric shock. Although the improvements were real, so were the dangers. Electric shock, at least as it was practiced in the 1930s and 40s, could break a patient's bones or even kill them.

Beat City Hall

According to Alfred Ely Beach, underground genius

YOU WILL NEED

- **To disregard the corrupt political system**
- **To be sneaky**

Step 1: ***BE A PROPHET IN YOUR OWN HOMETOWN***

Of course, we all know how successful that usually is. In the mid 1800s, New York City was suffering from an immigration-fueled transportation crisis. Enter Alfred Ely Beach, an inventor who'd previously come up with a typewriter for the blind and the cable railway, had a plan for the city. To him, the future lay below ground, in a series of subterranean tunnels where people could travel safely from one place to another via pneumatic trains. (OK, so his foresight was only half right.) In 1867, he ran a mockup of said train at the American Institute Fair to great success. Encouraged, he applied for a permit from City Hall to build a real-life version. He was promptly denied. Why? According to subway historian Stan Fischler, famously corrupt mayor "Boss"

Tweed earned (and we use that term loosely) a great deal of cash from the trolley, streetcar, and elevated railway companies; cash that would have dwindled if those companies had to deal with a real competitor.

Step 2: *FIGHT THE MAN—UNDERGROUND*

But Beach wasn't the sort of guy who gave up easily. According to some sources, he next went to the state legislature and, feigning disinterest in his old scheme, requested—and received— permission to build a pneumatic mail delivery system that was, significantly, too small to carry people. In other versions of the story, he simply ignored the long arm of the law altogether and started digging under cover of darkness. Either way, Beach got his way. In a rented-out basement, using a hydraulic boring machine of his own invention, he completed a block-long subway tunnel by February of 1870. It was definitely meant for people moving, decked out with a be-fountained waiting platform and a florid, velvet-seated train car. By some accounts, the station even featured its own fish tank.

Step 3: *STILL LOSE, BUT BE HONORED BY HISTORY*

On February 26, the Broadway Underground Railway opened for business, carrying hundreds of curious passengers up and down the tunnel for 25 cents a head. (About $3.65 today.) Beach submitted a proposal to continue the line for five miles to Central Park past both houses of the state legislature, but despite overwhelming enthusiasm, the tunnel never expanded past a block. The governor, under the thumb of Boss Tweed, vetoed the bill. Beach kept trying to bring his vision to fruition and nearly succeeded again in 1873, after Tweed and his cronies had been ousted. Unfortunately, a major financial depression set in the same year and the railway was moved, permanently, to the back burner. Beach died in 1896. His tunnel, sealed under the city, was forgotten. In 1904, New York got an electric-powered subway system. Amazingly, though, the Beach line did briefly reappear a few years later, when a group of subway construction workers stumbled upon it while digging out a new line. Reportedly, they found the opulent platform still largely intact, though the wooden car had mostly rotted. Nobody knows exactly what happened to the Beach line, but most likely it was incorporated into the City Hall subway station and the tunnels that now occupy roughly the same spot.

Own Your Mistakes

If you want to be a financial big shot, you're going to have to learn fess up when you screw up and there's no better way to learn than by practice. So go ahead, make a poor financial decision. Go crazy! (But, if we were you, we'd keep it on the small side.)

Step 1: *USE A CEREAL COMPANY AS YOUR REALTOR*

Back in the Golden Days of Radio, Quaker Oats sponsored a program called *The Challenge of the Yukon.* Essentially the sort of story that Dudley Do-Right would later mock, *Challenge* revolved around the adventures of a brave and true Mountie and his thematically named dog, Yukon King. But, with the advent of television, ratings for the show began to slump. Hoping a change of venue would do a world of good, Quaker ponied up the cash to transfer the show to television. Along the way, they decided that they needed a way to make kids care about the Klondike again. Their solution: pint-size plots of real estate.

Step 2: *STAKE YOUR (SQUARE INCH) CLAIM*

In 1955, Quaker executives decided that the best way to drum up press for *The Challenge of the Yukon* would be to actually give away bits of said Yukon to cereal customers. Certainly a far better prize than your average cheap, plastic thingamabob, deeds to square-inch tracts of Yukon Territory land could be found in every box of Quaker Puffed Rice and Puffed Wheat cereals. The company actually sent a contingent of suited execs up to Canada to buy a 19-acre plot of moose pasture. (Along the way, one of the businessmen reportedly got frostbite.) Quaker divvied up the land and, because binding deeds would have been too much of a pain for the Canadian government, printed up pseudo-deeds in the name of the Klondike Big Inch Land Company.

Step 3: *FALL BEHIND ON YOUR PAYMENTS*

The promotion, and subsequently the show, was a major hit. Thousands of boxes of cereal flew off the shelves and children across America became landowners. However, once the campaign ended, it became clear that nobody knew what to do with the land. Sure, plenty of kids wrote to Quaker asking about making improvements (one reportedly even sent a toothpick fence he wanted erected around his portion), but there's really not a lot you can do with a square inch. Eventually, Quaker just stopped paying the taxes on the land and the Canadian government claimed all 19 acres for a little more than the equivalent of $251. By contrast, you could probably sell a Big Inch Land Company deed to a collector today for more than $50, some have even fetched upwards of $90.

Sell Out

Yes, Mr. Ramen Noodle, we know you're above such things. But just think about it, OK? That pathetic Dickensian cough isn't getting any better and, frankly, you'd be in good company. All you have to do is decide when and how . . .

Sooner: *LIKE ANYONE WHO EVER WENT ON* ED SULLIVAN

Variety shows aren't exactly hip these days. But once upon a time, they could make or break an entertainment career—and none more so than *The Ed Sullivan Show*, which dominated America's Sunday nights for 23 years. These days it might seem a little schizophrenic for a single show to feature acts like ballet and Broadway snippets alongside puppet shows, rock and roll, and ludicrous vaudeville acts like plate-spinning, but by appealing to nearly every demographic under the sun, the show was able to pull in an average of 50 million viewers a week in its heyday. Of course, along the way, much of the rock music got heavily sanitized. For the sake of exposure, a surprising number of bands were willing to briefly de-hippiefy themselves. Among the sell-outs: the Jefferson Airplane, who agreed to sing an obscure ditty called *Crown of Creation* when their hit *White Rabbit* was deemed un-family-friendly. Other bands got to sing their hits, but with slight alterations. Anyone who saw the Rolling Stones

perform in early 1967 was treated to the sight of Mick Jagger crankily mumbling "let's spend some time together," rather than singing his better known lyrics, which implied illicit hanky panky. Artistically shameful though it was, the switch did get the Stones invited back for a repeat performance. However, on that show, they endured another indignity: Sullivan had them cleaned and primped to look less "freaky" for the folks in Peoria.

Later: ***LIKE BOB DYLAN***

Yes, Virginia, it's true. After 50-odd years of mostly unblemished artistic integrity, Dylan (*THE* Dylan) finally sold out. Or did he? Many of the troubadour's long-time fans were annoyed (and/or deeply confused) when he showed up on TV, leering his way through a particularly obtuse Victoria's Secret ad in 2004. What was the deal? Had he just gone senile? Turns out, Dylan's turn in the advertising industry may have actually been the punchline to a decades-old joke. Way back in December of 1965, the notoriously media-shy Dylan gave what is most likely his first and last televised press conference. As with today's young, idealistic, upcoming musicians, the talk quickly turned to when and if he would ever sell out. What force, reporters wondered, could possibly make this youth messiah tarnish his glowing reputation? Dylan's response: "Ladies' undergarments."

Be Worth It*

*And by "it" we mean "lots of money"

YOU WILL NEED

- **One captivating body part**
- **An unimaginative PR agent**
- **The phone number for the Lloyd's America insurance office**

Step 1: ***MAKE YOUR CHOSEN BODY PART AT LEAST SOMEWHAT IMPORTANT***

Most of the time, when somebody insures a body part for a lotta money, they want you to notice. For instance, according to the India Times, Heidi Klum got her legs insured as part of her contract to promote a new hair-removal product. And Slate.com reported that a supermarket chain was able to pull in a ton of publicity after they took out a policy on the taste-buds of their head wine buyer. That's why the insured-body-part thing has remained popular since the 1920s when wacky silent film star Ben Turpin insured his crossed eyes for $20,000. Other showpersons ponied up for insurance they probably didn't need include Bette Davis ($28,000 on her waistline) and Dolly Parton ($600,000 on her breasts).

Step 2: *CALL LLOYD'S OF LONDON*

The British insurance firm is the undisputed king of what's known in the biz as "surplus lines," insurance policies covering any number of eclectic objects, including body parts. In fact, while it's often PR buzz, body-part insurance does have some practical purposes. For some people, the part they insure really does have a major impact on their livelihood. Dancer Fred Astaire, for instance, insured his legs and singers like Bruce Springsteen and Rod Stewart have policies on their voices. Meanwhile, the award for the most logical and yet most unexpected policy should definitely go to Poh, a transsexual lounge singer from Thailand. According to the *Irish Examiner*, Poh got her breast implants insured for $500,000 after she was warned that the high altitudes on a flight to a show in England might rupture them.

Get Away from It All

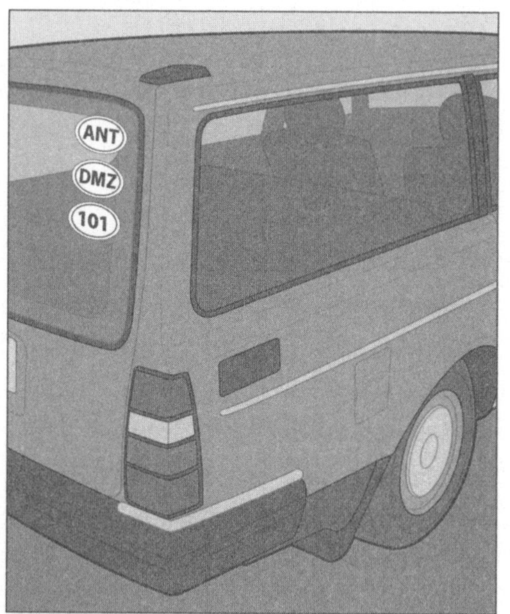

ALL ABOARD FOR ANTARCTICA!

Get Away From: Stupid people. Without any permanent residents, the only folks you're likely to encounter are the 4,000-odd scientists who live in the continent's 40 year-round permanent research stations.

Also Left Behind: Your clock. Antarctica lacks a standard time zone system. Instead, the various research stations use their home country's time, the time on the nearest landmass, or Greenwich Mean Time. In Antarctica, it's always 5 o'clock somewhere.

VISIT BEAUTIFUL DEMILITARIZED ZONE!

Get Away From: Civilians. The Demilitarized Zone is a 2.5-mile-wide demarcation line between North and

South Korea. Other than tourists (and a very small population living in dueling North/South propaganda villages) the only people around are soldiers.

Don't Forget: Your sense of adventure. After all, the DMZ is home to the World's Most Dangerous Golf Course—a single par 3 hole where the "rough" is actually a live minefield.

ZDRAVSTVUJ *FROM THE 101ST KILOMETER!*

That Means: "Hello" in Russian. For some reason it's not as common in the American vocabulary as *Do Svidanya* ("goodbye").

Get Away From: All the "good" communists. Back during the heyday of the Soviet Union, dissidents (actual and otherwise) were shipped off to the gulag prison camps in Siberia. The lucky few who survived that ordeal returned home to find they couldn't actually return home. To keep former prisoners culturally silent, Soviet law stipulated that they weren't allowed to settle in cities. Instead, they had to live at least 100 kilometers (62 miles) away—leading to the creation of 101st kilometer towns where nearly every resident was a "reformed" dissident.

Amass
Laurels

Get in the Guinness Book

According to: The Guys Who Claim to Have the Most Records

Today, settling a drunken trivia dispute requires nothing more difficult than whipping out your wireless-capable PDA. (Trust us, we're experts.) But 50 years ago it was a bit more complicated. Just ask Sir Hugh Beaver, managing director of the Guinness Brewing Company. Beaver managed to overcome the considerable handicap of his own name and went on to achieve greatness, but in 1951, he was faced with a question that left him stumped: "What is the fastest game bird in all of Europe?" Although he and his drinking buddies safely ruled out the unladen European Barn Swallow, they couldn't come up with a real answer. Three years later, on a different pub night, Beaver and his friends got into the exact same argument, thereby proving that the English aristocracy really needed something better to do with its time. For Beaver, that turned out to be going into the trivia book business. In 1954, he hired a fact-checking company to produce a series of annual record books perfect for home or bar. But how can you become a part of such record-holding history? First, get a gimmick; then listen to these guys.

The Contender: ***PAUL SAHLI***

Day Job: Mechanic

Specialty: Juggling, he's probably best known for juggling a billiard ball with his feet. Sahli's feet also often feature prominently in his records, thanks to his long career as an amateur soccer player.

Current Number of Records Held: He claims 64.

The Contender: ***ASHRITA FURMAN***

Day Job: Health food store manager

Specialty: Ridiculous, yet physically strenuous, stunts—think underwater pogo stick jumping and somersaulting the entire length of Paul Revere's ride. Furman is a big Eastern-philosophy buff and breaks records on the advice of his yogi, Sri Chinmoy, apparently in an attempt to demonstrate the limitless powers of the human body.

Current Number of Records Held: 57, as of April 2007.

Claim to Fame: Being the guy the Guinness Book says has the most world's records; inventing many fun (and we use the term loosely) hobbies, including: landrowing (i.e., attaching wheels to an indoor rowing machine) and underwater juggling.

The Contender: ***JIM MOUTH***

Day Job: Comedian, Internet radio show host

Specialty: Putting things in his mouth, naturally. Mouth holds lots of records for simultaneous smoking, including: most pipes (41), most cigars (41), and most cigarettes (159). The best part is that his stunts are done for a good cause. Mouth uses his record breaking as a way to raise money for charities like the American Lung Association.

Current Number of Records: 21, which seems paltry compared to the other two, but even Mouth admits that he's only the "self-proclaimed" greatest record breaker.

Advantage: Furman. We aren't going to argue with the guys at the Guinness Book.

Get a New Word in the Dictionary

New words pop up in the dictionary all the time, thanks to a handy—and almost maniacally extensive—editorial system. If you want your word to make into the big books, you'll need to slip it past the gatekeepers.

Step 1: *INVENT A WORD AND, MORE IMPORTANT, GET IT IN PRINT*

Over at the Oxford English Dictionary, they'll tell you that the the life of a new word starts out in their Reading Programme department, where about 50 people spend their 9-to-5s gobbling up all the printed material they can get their hands on: novels, television transcripts, song lyrics, newspapers, magazines . . . anything. They're on the lookout for new words (or innovative uses of old, mundane words). New discoveries end up on a searchable electronic database that Oxford calls its "Incomings."

Step 2: *BUTTER UP YOUR EDITOR*

In our experience, this is pretty much "Step 2" in any creative undertaking. And it's no different in the world of words. Each new word under consideration is assigned to a specific editor, who then begins tracking its use and popularity in the long-term. How long-term? Try 5 years. The rule of thumb at Oxford is that a word can't be included in the dictionary until it's appeared 5 times, in 5 different sources, over a period of 5 years. We don't know for certain, but if we were word editors, we'd be a lot more likely to notice that all-important fifth usage if there was a bottle of 12-year-old Scotch left on our desk. Just sayin'.

Step 3: *STAY POPULAR OR PERISH*

Yes, the dictionary is just like junior high. Dictionaries are meant to record English as a living language, not a museum showpiece. So when a word falls out of use, it can kiss its spot on the all-dictionary cheerleading squad good-bye. In 2003, the *San Francisco Chronicle* reported that the good folks at Merriam-Webster opened the doors for 10,000 up-and-coming new words and usages, including: "phat," "Frankenfood," and "cheesed off." (This should give you hope for your favorite word. Whatever it is, it's gotta be better than "cheesed off.") But, that same year, several hundred words got the ax. Among them, "snollygoster," which once (back when your grandma had all her teeth) referred to an unscrupulous politician, and "Vitamin G," which hasn't technically disappeared but is now called "riboflavin."

Leave Your Mark on History

Like the Irish

Claim to Fame: ***INVENTED THE SURNAME***

Prior to the 10th century, Europeans didn't really have last names. Sure, you might be known as "Bob, son of Jim," but your son would be "Larry, son of Bob." The award for first recorded, fixed surname in Europe goes to Tighernach Ua Cleirigh, who died in 916 CE. Ua Cleirigh's name literally translates to "grandson of Cleirigh" and is probably better recognized today as "O'Clery." Other common Irish surnames also have identifiable beginnings. For instance, around the start of the 11th century, Brian, high king of the Irish, died. In his memory, his grandson took the name Ua Brian . . . a name carried by his descendants, up to and including a guy named Conan.

Like William Banting

Claim to Fame: ***FIRST FAD DIET ENTHUSIAST***

William Banting began the year 1863 in very bad shape. Losing his eyesight and hearing, unable to walk down stairs without knee pain, and suffering from a bad case of what we will only describe as butt boils, Banting blamed his condition on fat. And he had lots of it to go around. By the end of 1863, however, Banting (eyes, ears, knees, and butt) was on the road to recovery. What changed? His diet. That year, Banting's ear doctor, William Harvey, made Banting a guinea pig for a radical new diet that cut out potatoes, bread, sugar, milk, and beer. If that sounds familiar, it's because Banting's Diet (as it came to be known) was basically identical to the cutting-edge diet introduced by Dr. Robert Atkins in 1972.

Like the Victorians

Claim to Fame: ***CHRISTENED THE FIRST "DUDES"***

Neither surfer nor cowpoke (nor even Jeff Bridges in a bathrobe), the first dude was actually a dandy. Originating around the 19th century, "dude" is possibly a play off the word "dud," another Victorian-era slang term, meaning "clothes"—although the *Oxford English Dictionary* suggests that it might have origins in the German word for "fool." Dudes were high-society (but low-life) young men who led lives of fashion-obsessed wantonness. Think Oscar Wilde . . . or, better yet, Dorian Gray (Oscar wasn't quite enough of a himbo). Around the turn of the century, the word became attached to fancy dressed city slickers visiting cowboy country (thus, the "dude ranch"). Its modern definition took shape beginning in the dancehalls of the 1930s.

Like Joaquin Hernandez

Claim to Fame: ***JUMPING-BEAN ENTREPRENEUR***

Maybe our parents were just cheap, but they tried to pass a lot of so-called "toys" off on us: like sticks, our imaginations, and, of course, the jumping bean—those little brown shells that roll (not jump) back and forth under their own power. Or, rather, under the power of hyperactive moth larvae. Every spring the aptly named Jumping-Bean Moth lays its eggs on the equally aptly named Mexican Jumping-Bean Shrub. After they hatch, the larvae eat their way into the soft, immature seed pods and continue munching from the inside as the pods ripen, fall from the shrub, and split into three sections. In order to move the shells, which weigh about as much as they do, larvae spin silk webbing inside and use it to create leverage, grasping the silk with their forearms and then throwing their bodies against the shell. While not so exciting on your kitchen table, thousands of seedpods moving about in their natural environment are pretty cool, and the best place to see that is Alamos, Mexico—the "Jumping Bean Capital of the World." Alamos got its status thanks to Joaquin Hernandez, who, at the age of 12, realized he could make a killing off Americans' fondness for novelty items. With more than 60 years experience, Hernandez is the undisputed Jumping-Bean King and exports as many as 20 million of the things each year.

Be the World's Oldest Athlete

YOU WILL NEED

- Determination
- Good genes
- A vat or two of Ben-Gay

DON'T LET ANYTHING STAND IN YOUR WAY

At 88, Mary Stroebe isn't quite old enough to vie for the title of oldest athlete, but she's certainly in the running for most resilient. Besides numerous shorter races, the Wisconsin great-grandma has run 12 triathlons, never once finishing last. But since her late 60s, Stroebe has also been hit by a car, survived breast cancer, fractured her leg in a skiing accident, broken her hip while bike riding, and sustained a cut on her hand that required stitches—stitches she put off getting until several hours later when she finished the triathlon she was running at the time. Reportedly answering to the name "Lucky," Mary Strobe plans to keep running until age catches up with her.

OUTPLAY. OUTWIT. OUTLIVE.

Before he died in April 2005, 105-year-old John S. Whittemore was the oldest athlete registered with the United States Track and Field Association. He was also the world's oldest world-record holder—setting the pace in the shot put event, 104-year-old division, with a throw just a hair shorter than 6 feet long. Part of Whittemore's secret lay in the fact that he'd outlived the competition. Prior to him, USA Track and Field's age divisions topped out at 95. From that point on, Whittemore was usually alone in his events. Which, given the usual track and field time constraints, was probably for the best. At his last track meet in October 2004, Whittemore took 45 minutes to walk the 100 yards from his car to the competition area.

MAKE FRIENDS WITH MODIFIERS

If you're getting antsy, there's really no need to wait for senility to set in; all you need to do is make your goal more specific. Think of it this way: only one person can be the world's oldest athlete—but there's still plenty of room for you to be, say, the world's oldest dodgeball champion in the Pacific Northwest. Just ask enterprising Canadian Duff Gibson. Before

1998, Duff was just a generic bobsled teammate. But that year, he switched sports to the one-man skeleton sled and qualified for the 2002 Canadian Olympic team. Four years later, at the Turin Winter Games, Duff took the gold—becoming (at the truly ripe age of 39 years, 150 days) the oldest athlete in the history of the Winter Olympics to win a gold medal in an individual event. See how it works?

Curb an Outbreak

Between 1918 and 1919, a fifth of the world's population caught the flu bug and nearly 50 million people died. In fact, that outbreak of the flu killed more people in 24 weeks than the AIDS virus killed in 24 years. Public health officials around the globe had to learn to combat the virus from scratch. You, however, have this handy list to help guide your local populace to good health.

YOU WILL NEED

- Catchy slogans: **It's no use coming up with preventative measures if the public doesn't remember them. During the flu pandemic, officials spread safety tips via rhymes written on posters and taught them to schoolchildren. To remind people to shut their windows, try: I had a little bird/ It's name was Enza/ I opened the window/ And in-flu-enza. Or encourage the use of protective face masks with: Obey the laws/ And wear the gauze/ Protect your jaws/ From septic paws.**

- Authoritarian measures: **If rhymes don't work, jail time will. In December of 1918, when the Committee of American Public Health Association decreed that saloons, dance halls, and cinemas should be closed during the pandemic, cities across the nation agreed—leveling hefty fines on businesses that didn't comply. For a time, even public funerals were banned.**

- The ability to snort stuff up your nose: **In 1918, doctors were just realizing that influenza was transmitted through the respiratory tract. That new knowledge gave them a great idea—clean out the nose and you'll clear out the virus. Patients were encouraged to sniff or spray a variety of solutions up their schnozzes, including various combinations of carbolic acid, quinine, sodium bicarbonate, boric acid, and carbonated soda.**

Be the Center of the Universe

Option 1: *YOU DON'T NEED TO DO ANYTHING, BECAUSE YOU'RE ALREADY SMACK DAB IN THE UNIVERSE'S CENTER!*

At least, that's how it would appear to you if you were observing space from a powerful telescope. Unfortunately, there's an equally narcissistic being on a planet somewhere in the Crab Nebula who's looking in a telescope and thinking the exact same thing. No matter where you choose to observe the universe from, it'll appear that you are in the center. It's a win-win situation for every man, woman, and four-eyed swamp beast in the galaxy!

Option 2: *BASK IN* SCHADENFREUDE

Turns out, the universe technically has no center. Which means that, while you can't be the big central honcho, neither can anybody else. So there. Of course, that just brings up another question. If the universe has no center, then where did the Big Bang happen? Most people think of the Big Bang as if it were a bomb that went off in a house, sending glass, insulation, and various house pets flying away from the point where it once stood. But that isn't very accurate. Instead, when the Big Bang went, well, bang . . . it did so everywhere, all at once. It was an explosion of space, not an explosion in space. Thus, while the universe is expanding, it's not really an outward expansion. Instead, everything is constantly moving away from everything else. And with no actual center to the expansion, the faux-center just appears to be wherever you're standing.

Option 3: *JUST CHANGE YOUR NAME TO CENTER-OF-THE-UNIVERSE SMITH*

Is it cheating? Um, maybe. But does Center-of-the-Universe Smith have to care? We think not. For help with changing your name, check out page 8.

Invent a Language

In its own language, *esperanto* means "one who hopes." That's a pretty good nom de plume for a dialect intent on uniting the world. The fact is a logical, easy-to-learn, universal language has been the great, unfulfilled dream of Western philosophy, dating back to the 17th century writings of René Descartes and Francis Bacon. So it's no wonder that when Polish linguist Ludwik Lejzer Zamenhof introduced his Esperanto language to the public in 1887, it became immediately popular. Cultured people in Europe and the U.S. clamored to learn the speech of the future, international organizations used it to record their minutes, and within 30 years Esperanto had made its way to the League of Nations. Unfortunately, what could have been an important step in Esperanto's global acceptance became its undoing. The League voted on whether to make Esperanto its official language in 1920, but couldn't reach the necessary unanimous conclusion. Of the 11 delegates, 10 favored the proposal. The lone, stubborn "nay" came from France, which saw Esperanto as a threat to the then-supremacy of French as global lingua franca. Aaahhh, hindsight. The final blow, however, came during World War II, when knowing Esperanto became a great way to get killed. Adolf Hitler called Esperanto a plot to unite the Jewish diaspora, and he imprisoned its supporters as antinationalist. Meanwhile, in Russia, Josef Stalin executed a fair share of Esperanto speakers himself, declaring it the "language of spies." With its largest fan base decimated, Esperanto became more of curiosity than a viable language. However, it's as logical a language as you could hope to find. If you want invent your own would-be mother tongue it can't hurt to understand what made Esperanto so great.

YOU WILL NEED

- **1 lightbulb moment:** Before inventing Esperanto, Zamenhof struggled with the number of vocabulary words most modern languages required you to memorize. But one day, while taking a walk, he found his inspiration in two Polish store signs: *svejcarskaja* and *konditorskaja*. They meant "place of the porter" and "place of sweets." Zamenhof realized that he could make vocab simpler by basing it off of an easily memorized system of roots and suffixes.

- **3 to 5 current languages:** Esperanto's vocabulary is largely culled from a cross-section of European languages, a fact that makes it both easier to invent and easier to learn (provided, of course, that you started off speaking an Indo-European language). About 75 percent of the vocabulary is influenced by Romance languages like French and Spanish, 20 percent comes from Germanic languages like English, and the rest is made up of Slavic and Greek influences.

- 1 easy-to-understand system of grammar

Hate the irregular verb forms and "exceptions" to grammar rules that clutter up English? So did Zamenhof. Esperanto is phonetic, so there aren't any of those dreaded "silent" letters. And the rules of verb conjugation are fixed, so there's no guesswork.

Have the World's Most Dangerous Job

YOU WILL NEED

- A career track that affords many opportunities for accidental injury and death
- Statistics to compare your dangerous job to that of others

YOU MAY HAVE ALREADY "WON"

Turns out, there are a lot of occupations that, despite causing enough horrible deaths to make the Bureau of Labor Statistics' list of the top 10 most dangerous jobs, don't really get credit for their death-defying nature. That's right. You may be flaunting your survival-of-the-fittest prowess (and/or risking your neck) every single day and not even know it. Every year, the bureau releases a list of the jobs that caused the most fatalities per 100,000 American workers. And, while the top three spots are largely given over to an unsurprising annual shoving match between commercial fishing, the logging industry, and pilots, numbers 4 through 10 are often a lot more unpredictable. For instance, according to the list released in 2003, the award for fifth most dangerous job in America went to "driver-sales workers," a category which includes people like the UPS man, vending-machine repairpersons, and even pizza delivery dudes. For that year anyway, your laid-back cousin who passes out pepperoni for a living was actually tempting the fates more than construction laborers, truck drivers, or supposed risk-takers like police and firefighters (who didn't even make the top 10). By the time the 2005 list came out in 2006, driver-sales workers had fallen to number eight, but the number five slot remained a dark horse. Instead of delivery boys, that spot is now occupied by garbage and recycling collectors, who, amazingly, managed to best even such ostensibly risky professions as power

line installer. But don't get complacent just because you work in a cubicle. Business and professional services might not kill enough people to get anywhere near the top 10, but 3.2 deaths per 100,000 workers is still pretty amazing considering the most dangerous objects around are sharp (and apparently deadly) paper corners.

Have the World's Greatest Memory

According to the winners of the World Memory Championships

PERFECT THE 30-SECOND CARD DECK

Founded in 1991, the World Memory Championships test the abilities of hundreds of well-prepared minds. Many contestants spend up to 6 hours a day practicing their memorization skills with the hope of breezing through challenges like memorizing a series of names and faces and then recalling them in 30 minutes. But that's not even the most difficult event. In the final game of the championship, contestants must shuffle and then memorize a deck of cards in 5 minutes, set them aside, and then arrange a different deck in exactly the same order. Believe it or not, some people can memorize the entire stack in less than a minute. But, so far, no one has ever been able to do it in 30 seconds or less. Rest assured, the first person to pull this off will be crowned king of the memory nerds.

THINK DIFFERENT

Interestingly, some scientists think that the grand masters of memory don't necessarily have inherently better brains, they've just learned how to use them differently. In 2006, researchers at the University College London ran MRI scans on memory game contestants and regular folks. They found that, when given familiar memory games to play, the contestants used the sectors of their brains that control visual memory and spatial navigation, something the average Joe's didn't do. This is because memory masters are also masters of the visual mnemonic device. For instance, a common tactic for memorizing a pack of cards involves assigning specific mental images of people, things, and actions to all 52 cards. Then, while sorting, contestants separate the stack into three-card sets. Each set makes a sentence—subject, verb, and object. Thus the deck becomes a series of stories and is easier to remember.

LISTEN TO YOUR ELDERS

And we mean way elder. According to Harvard memory researcher Daniel L. Schacter, the father of modern-day memory games was an ancient Greek named Simonides. It's this fellow who's credited with inventing the visual/organizational memory technique—supposedly in response to a 477 B.C.E. dinner party tragedy. As the story goes, Simonides was invited to a party, during which the roof of the house collapsed, leaving him the only survivor. The other, less fortunate, guests were mangled beyond identification, but Simonides was able to save the day (relatively speaking) by visualizing the dinner table and remembering who was sitting where.

Stop Global Warming

Oh, sure. You could always reduce your energy consumption. But we're talking big picture here. In the past century, Earth's temperature has risen about 1.4 degrees, enough to start melting polar ice caps (bad) and start messing with climate patterns worldwide (worse). At this point, we need something bigger to grind the whole dang process to a halt. With that in mind, mental_floss.com is providing a handy guide:

YOU WILL NEED

- **To have big dreams and deep pockets. Reversing global destruction ain't gonna be cheap. We recommend being a major world leader or an uncharacteristically benevolent Bond villain.**

Step 1: *FIND SOME MAD SCIENTISTS*

Hey, outside-the-box thinking takes outside-the-box solutions. But where to find them now that Miskatonic University has closed its doors? We recommend starting in Kenya. In November 2006, that country played host to the United Nations Climate Change Conference, which became one of the first major conferences to take extreme anti-global-warming proposals seriously. That same weekend, NASA's Ames Research Center in California hosted a closed-door session to discuss "geoengineering" ideas, aka the

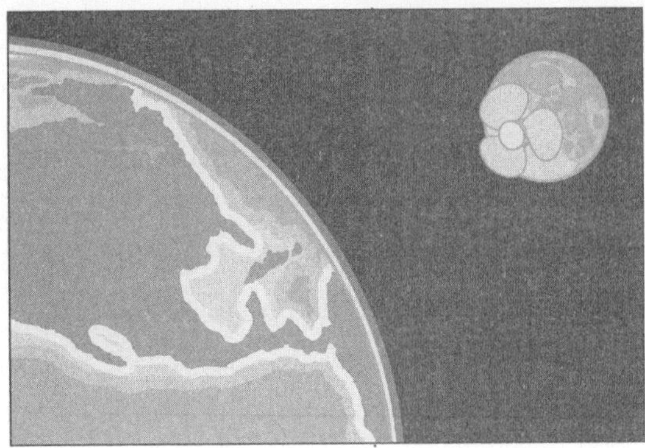

theoretical (for now) practice of artificially manipulating the Earth to ward off the effects of global warming. Long-ignored and/or openly mocked, geoengineering is starting to earn some big-name supporters today, including Edward Teller, father of the hydrogen bomb, and Paul Crutzen, a German scientist who won the Nobel for showing how industrial gasses damage the ozone layer.

Step 2: *BRAINSTORM*

In fact, brainmonsoon. And don't throw away any ideas, no matter how crazy they might sound. One of the most popular geoengineering schemes floating around is a plan, devised by Paul Crutzen, wherein the people of Earth would fight pollution with pollution. According to his research, we might be able to help cool the planet by injecting sulfur into the stratosphere. The process would increase acid rain, but not appreciably compared to the amounts of sulfur dioxide we release into the air every year from factories. And, in the meantime, the sulfur would form a protective shield that would temporarily reflect more of the sun's heat away from Earth, thus offsetting the effects of heat-trapping gasses like carbon dioxide. Another idea (this one the brainchild of an astronomer at the University of Arizona) proposes to reflect those heat rays using trillions of ultra-light, two-foot-wide mirrors, launched into synchronized orbit around the planet.

Step 3: *IGNORE THE NAYSAYERS*

Sure, injecting sulfur dioxide into the stratosphere will take a fleet of jet planes and cost upwards of $50 billion, but that's small potatoes. In fact, that 50 large only makes up about 5 percent of the world's annual military spending. As for the people who think you might be going a little overboard, well, that's a common complaint proponents of geoengineering hear. But, as they're quick to point out, we already have plenty of less-radical solutions that people and nations can't seem to implement. Geoengineering, extreme as it is, is a necessary topic of discussion. After all, it'd be great to have a backup plan to save humanity just in case everything else falls through.

Save Holland

YOU WILL NEED

- Dikes
- Windmills and/or water pumping systems
- A well-organized populace willing to go head-to-head with mother nature

Tip 1: *START EARLY, SAVE OFTEN*

With about half the Netherland's land area sitting firmly below sea level (on the edge of a sea, no less) it's no wonder that the locals started experimenting with impressive flood-protection schemes pretty early in their history. Basic dyke-and-canal schemes started popping up during the Middle Ages and by the late 1500s, the Dutch had progressed from mere defensive measures against the sea to offensive attacks designed to turn water into dry land.

Tip 2: *KNOW WHEN TO POLD 'EM*

Polders are areas of land that have been "reclaimed" from the sea, drained of their H_2O and turned into farmland (and, increasingly, urban centers). To build a polder, the Dutch first ring a tidal-flood plain, peat-bog swamp, or area of shallow sea with tall dikes to block out the water. Once protected, the fenced-off region is drained. Sixteenth-century Dutch pumped the water out with windmills. Today, they use more efficient mechanized pumps. Either way, left behind is a blank slate of newly created land, a fact which put the Dutch several hundred years ahead of the rest of their European peers in the field of urban planning.

Tip 3: *THINK BIG (AND ANAL-RETENTIVE)*

Polders were one of the first places where land was parceled out and cities were planned according to a neat and tidy grid system, as opposed to the, shall we say, somewhat haphazard style of Western cities up until the late 1700s. Because of this, the Netherlands' oldest large-scale polder, known as the Beemster, was designated a United Nations Educational, Scientific and Cultural Organization World Heritage Site in 1999. Constructed between 1608 and 1612 on the site of a former lake, the Beemster's planners organized the 28 square miles along the "ideal of the straight line," with orderly square and rectangular plots separated by a grid of main access roads lined with poplar trees and paralleled by canals. (And you wondered why these folks had a reputation for being hyper-organized.) But lest you think all the polder building is in the past, be advised. The largest polder ever built became the province of Flevoland in 1986. It covers more than 500 square miles and is home to more than 300,000 people.

Die Young and Leave a Squeaky Clean Corpse

She may be called the "Soap Lady," but we wouldn't recommend trying to wash your hands with her. A 200-year-old mummy housed at Philadelphia's Mutter Museum of Medical Curiosities, the Soap Lady's body is actually made up of adipocere, a grainy blue-black substance similar to candle wax. Anna Dhody, the Museum's curator, says that the lady might have died in an epidemic that swept through Philadelphia in the late 1700s, but her manner of death had nothing to do with her current state of being. Instead, after her burial, a chemical/bacterial reaction turned her body into adipocere before it had the chance to rot away. If you're thinking that this is all pretty gross . . . well, you're right. But don't get too high and mighty there, Pollyanna. There's a good chance that, when you die, you could end up preserved in adipocere as well.

YOU WILL NEED

- Body fat
- Alkaline soil
- Water
- Protection against fresh air and bugs

Step 1: *DIE*

Step 2: *BE BURIED IN THE RIGHT PLACE*

Somewhere airtight and damp will do the trick. Underwater is good, but so is your average modern casket. Basically, anywhere that will keep your body protected from flies, animals, and other flesh-eating grubs while still providing enough water to serve as a catalyst for the process. If your burial area is highly alkaline, so much the better.

Step 3: *LET YOUR BACTERIA DO THEIR THING*

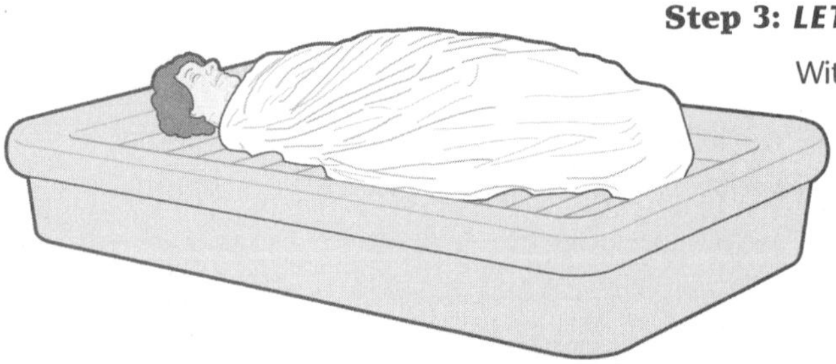

With those three factors in place, your body can get through the initial stages of decomposition without losing too much mass—and fat—to predators. Now your only friends are the millions of bacteria who were already living inside of you before you passed away and who thrive in wet, alkaline, airless environments. Here, they'll start to nibble on you, digesting out adipocere for every bite of body fat they take in. Because airtight caskets often provide the right environment, it's likely that nearly everybody you know will end up with at least some adipocere on them, the cremated folks aside.

Be Like Mike

BE FEISTY, LIKE MICHAEL CAERULARIUS

Of the wide variety of things Michael Caerularius's contemporaries might have been tempted to call him, "easily cowed" was almost certainly not on the list. Named Patriarch of the Christian Church in Constantinople in 1043, Michael immediately set about alienating the church in Rome. To be fair, this was probably justifiable, considering the fact that the Roman clergy had been working overtime on the alienation game themselves: declaring Rome's authority over all the other churches and then unilaterally making changes to official doctrine and ritual details. When Michael C. arrived on the scene, he struck back. First, he refused to help the Roman church in its fight against the Normans. Then, he started going after individual churches in his jurisdiction, demanding that they all use Greek, instead of Latin, as the official liturgical language—any church that refused was shut down. Finally, Pope Leo IX in Rome realized that he needed to improve relations with Constantinople, or, failing that, at least turn the heat down from boiling to a low, hateful simmer. In 1054, he sent a team of cardinals to negotiate with Michael Caerularius. But, when they arrived, they didn't exactly receive a hearty welcome. In fact, they received no welcome at all—Michael refused to meet with them. After four months of non-negotiations, Pope Leo suddenly died and one of his envoys in Constantinople, Cardinal Humbert, decided that the Pope's death was the perfect opportunity to get some frustration off his chest. On July 16, 1054, Humbert excommunicated Michael Caerularius, all of Michael's priestly followers, and—by extension—every Christian who followed the Constantinople Church. If he expected the action to make Michael contrite, well, then he was very silly. Instead, the patriarch retaliated by excommunicating Humbert, and for good measure, the entire Church of Rome. The rift was never mended. July 16 ended up going down in history as the day the Roman Catholic Church and the Eastern Orthodox Church split from one another. However, on a happy note, the excommunications were eventually rescinded. During the Second Vatican Council in 1965, Pope Paul VI and Patriarch Athenagoras shook hands and agreed no longer to condemn each other to hell.

BE ECLECTIC, LIKE MIKE WALLACE

How do you get into the news business and end up one of the most respected reporters in history? If you follow the career of "60 Minutes" newsman Myron "Mike" Wallace, you'll know that the answer isn't to find one thing and stick with it. Unlike most of his journalistic peers, Wallace began his career in 1939 as an announcer for radio programs, covering everything from commercials to action-adventure serials like *The Green Hornet* to soap operas like *The Guiding Light*. Yes, *Guiding Light*. His first foray into TV wasn't much newsier and, in fact, managed to be even more off-beat. From 1950-1953, Wallace starred with his wife in the talk show *Mike and Buff* and its spin-off *All Around Town*, in which Mike and Buff wandered around New York City, visiting tourist attractions and interviewing everyone from celebrities to average Joes on the street. In the early '50s, he also became host to no fewer than two game shows. Finally, in 1956, he dipped a toe in the waters of investigative journalism with *Night Beat*, where he became famous for scathing, skewering interviews of everyone from Salvador Dali to Thurgood Marshall. Still, it wasn't until 1963 that Mike, in his own words, decided to "go straight" with the news. In the meantime, he worked as a quizmaster, a chat-show host, and a spokesman for cigarettes.

HAVE DADDY ISSUES, LIKE MICHELANGELO

You'd think being one of the greatest artists of the Renaissance would be enough to please Pops—but no. Not if your father was Lodovico di

Leonardo Buonarroti Simoni. James Beck, author of *The Three Worlds of Michelangelo,* records how from the moment Ludovico's second son, Michelangelo, announced that he wanted to be a painter, the elder Buonarroti wanted none of it and tried to force the boy into a more lucrative career, like becoming a merchant or lawyer. Fortunately, Michelangelo managed to lure the attention of a wealthy patron, who paid for his training. Judging from later letters between father and son, Ludovico never really forgave Michelangelo for going over his head. Years later, even after Michelangelo had produced some of his most acclaimed and enduring works, Ludovico still wrote manipulative, anti-art tirades to his son. A sample quote: "Not a single one of you [his five sons] is in a position to help me with so much as a glass of water though I am now fifty-six years old . . . When I have a headache, all I can do is scratch my balls." To be charitable, Ludovico was, according to Beck, actually referring to his kidneys, there. Not that it makes more sense. Several times, when the letters got too hurtful or distracting, Michelangelo had to ask his father not to write him anymore. And yet, at the same time, the great master seemed helpless in his need to win his father's approval. "All the difficulties I have undergone," he once wrote. "I always did them for your love."

Circumnavigate the Globe

Itching to see exotic locales? Dying for a much-needed vacation? Just really like going around in circles? Do we have an adventure for you . . . What's your pleasure?

By Sea

The Traveler: ***JOSHUA SLOCUM***

The Year: 1895 to 1898

Claim to Fame: First person to sail around the world alone. Slocum was a life-long sailor, having first gone out to sea as a 14-year-old runaway/cook in 1858. Thirty-seven years later, the old salt still wasn't quite ready to retire, instead opting to begin a round-the-world voyage at the age of 51. The journey took Slocum 3 years, but he returned a hero. His 1900 book detailing his adventures, *Sailing Alone Around the World*, became a classic of the early 20th century, of which the British journalist Arthur Ransome once claimed that boys who did not like it "ought to be drowned at once."

By Land

The Traveler: ***SERGE GIRARD***

The Year: 1997 to 2006

Claim to Fame: Ran across 6 of the 7 continents. And, while he did indulge in breaks between runs during his continent crossings, Girard refused to take a single day off. According to his personal Web site, the 51-year-old Frenchman stays in shape by running an average of 6,215 miles each year. While on his big runs, Girard frequently ate as much as 8,000 calories each day. Between 1997 and 2006, he used some 150 tubes of blister cream.

By Air

The Traveler: ***STEVE FOSSETT***

The Year: 2002

Claim to Fame: First person to fly around the world solo (and nonstop) in a hot air balloon. That's a lot of qualifiers for a world record, but don't write the trip off as a walk in the park. Fossett's cabin on the balloon was no larger than an average closet. He got no more than 4 hours of sleep a day—in 45-minute mini-naps. And, high in the atmosphere, the temperature inside said closet was below freezing.

Train a Cat

HUMPHREY, THE CAT WHO LAUNCHED A POLITICAL SCANDAL

Named the Prime Minister's Official Mouser in 1988, former stray Humphrey quickly became a fixture at 10 Downing Street, overseeing feline issues for Margaret Thatcher and John Major. But, when Tony Blair became prime minister in a landslide in 1997, Humphrey's position quickly became threatened. Rumors flew through the British press that Blair's wife hated cats and wanted Humphrey gone. When the aging cat was shipped off to a undisclosed retirement home a few months later, Blair's political opponents actually accused him of having Humphrey killed. Blair ended up having to bring political journalists to Humphrey's new home and allow them to photograph the cat—hostage style—with copies of that day's newspaper. The scandal is still remembered as the first major challenge of Blair's administration, a fact which we imagine Blair must find completely insane.

YOU WILL NEED

- **To give your cat some good role models, such as . . .**

TOWSER, THE WORLD'S GREATEST MOUSER

Her position verified by the Guinness Book of World Records, it's fitting that Towser spent her 24 years surrounded by booze. The former official mouser to Scotland's oldest working distillery, Towser killed a reported 28,899 mice during her lifetime, earning both the Guinness mention and a commemorative bronze sculpture, which was dedicated at the factory after her death in 1987. However, Towser's official number of kills is not entirely accurate. Instead, it was an average worked out by Guinness officials after observing her work over a period of days.

UNSINKABLE SAM, WORLD WAR II VETERAN

When the British Navy sunk the German battleship Bismarck in 1941, the ship's cat (then named Oskar) was among the 115 rescued by the British. Oskar was taken aboard the destroyer Cossack and lived there for five months, before that ship, too, was sunk. Oskar survived again. Transferred for a third time to the aircraft carrier *Ark Royal*, Oskar was on board (and survived) when the Royal was sunk a mere three weeks later. Rechristened "Unsinkable Sam," Oskar was sent to live out the rest of his life in a home for sailors, curtailing the career of what we can only imagine was one of Germany's most successful naval spies.

Save a Life

According to the Death Adder Snake

It's one of the world's most poisonous animals, but Australia's Death Adder snake has probably saved more lives than it's taken. How? The snake's venom is a key ingredient in recipes for antivenom. At the Australian Reptile Park near Sydney, 200 snakes, including 40–60 adders, are "milked" every two weeks to collect their venom, which is shipped to the country's Commonwealth Serum Laboratories. Antivenom is made by injecting the venom in small, but increasing amounts into horses. The horses aren't harmed but, after a year of the treatment, their blood plasma is filled with antibodies that can fight off the poison in other animals . . . like humans.

According to Harrison Ford

Want to be rescued by Indiana Jones and/or Han Solo? Then we recommend getting yourself lost somewhere in rural Wyoming. Out there, Harrison Ford, action-movie actor, is also a real-life hero as well. Whenever he's vacationing on his ranch in Wyoming, Ford, who doubles as an amateur helicopter pilot, offers his services free-of-charge to the local emergency rescue crews. In 2000 and again in 2001, he was instrumental in saving hikers in trouble. The first time, the rescuee was a twentysomething mountain climber; the second was a 13-year-old boy who'd gotten lost during a camp-out.

According to Viagra

It's probably been euphemistically called a lifesaver, but the erectile dysfunction drug Viagra really saved a life in August 2006. British newborn Lewis Goodfellow weighed only a pound and a half at birth and his lungs were unable to get enough oxygen to get into his bloodstream. After trying several other options, doctors gave little Lewis a dose of Viagra as a last resort. The drug succeeded where others had failed at opening up his teeny, tiny blood vessels and allowing Lewis to breathe. Way to go, Viagra!

Change the Face of America

According to William Levitt

YOU WILL NEED

- **Little boxes**
- **A hillside**

Step 1: *LOOK BACK TO GO FORWARD*

It's a misnomer that suburbia is an invention of the 1950s. Ancient clay tablets from Persia describe people living in residential areas "just outside" the city of Ur as early as 539 B.C.E. and Americans were already living in ever-growing suburban enclaves at the turn of the 20th century. But it was the 1950s—and specifically, the work of William Levitt—that really created and cemented the image of the suburb as we know it today. Miles upon miles of relatively inexpensive, nearly identical houses situated around an interstate—that's all 100 percent Levitt.

Step 2: *KNOW AN OPPORTUNITY WHEN YOU SEE IT*

At any other time in history, who knows whether Levitt's vision would have proven to be so popular. Before going off to World War II, he'd bought a large plot of land on Long Island, which he meant to develop into housing, but it wasn't until he returned from the war that the nature of the development really formulated itself in his brain. At the time, America, and particularly the northeast, was caught in the middle of a housing crisis. With thousands of ex-soldiers armed with low-interest G.I. Bill home loans, there simply weren't enough houses to fill their demand. Young married couples were trapped sharing apartments with their parents. One couple in New York actually camped out in a department store window in protest. Because of this, Levitt could be fairly certain of recouping his investment on each of the 17,000 houses he built in what came to be known as Levittown.

Step 3: *HUSTLE, TEAM. HUSTLE.*

Up until Levitt, home developers relied on skilled carpenters and finished maybe five houses each year. Levitt realized that the construction process was grossly inefficient and set out to organize it into a simple, step-by-step process—no special skill required. To make his housing assembly line, he broke the process down into 27 individual tasks, moving specialized teams of workers down the street, from one house to another. This way, Levitt could turn out 36 houses a day, making them, for the first time, affordable for the working class. The first Levittown houses were sold in 1947 for $7,990—the equivalent to a little more than $74,000 today. With a kitchen, living room, two bedrooms and a bath, the mortgages were often as low as $56 a month ($558 today).

Charm
Society

Be Discovered

According to a not-quite-extinct fish and one giant chimpanzee

Step 1: *BE GLORIOUSLY BEAUTIFUL*

Beauty, is of course, in the eye of the beholder. And when the beholder in question is an extremely excited zoologist or ichthyologist, just about anything can be beautiful—provided it marks a great scientific breakthrough. Two animals whose 20th century discoveries catapulted them to the spotlight are the Coelacanth and the Bondo Mystery Ape. Of the two, the Coelacanth is better known, having been widely hailed as the greatest biological discovery of the last century. Why? Because, technically speaking, it shouldn't have been alive. Coelacanths are large, carnivorous fish native to the tropical waters of the Indian Ocean. Or, at any rate, that's what we know about them now. Prior to their (re)discovery in 1938, Coelacanths were believed to exist only as fossils. Everyone thought they had died out 65 million years ago in the same cataclysm that wiped out the dinosaurs. In fact, when they reappeared in the 1930s, scientists were at first unable to identify them because no one had seen what the creature's exterior looked like. Turns out, the 5-foot-long, wide-mouthed fish comes in a lovely shade of iridescent blue speckled with gray.

As for the Bondo Ape, they're also on the photogenic side. No living specimen has been captured yet, but based on photographic and anecdotal evidence and the size of the creatures' nests and tools, these animals look like chimpanzees, but can be upwards of 6 feet tall, roughly twice the size (and heft!) of your average chimp.

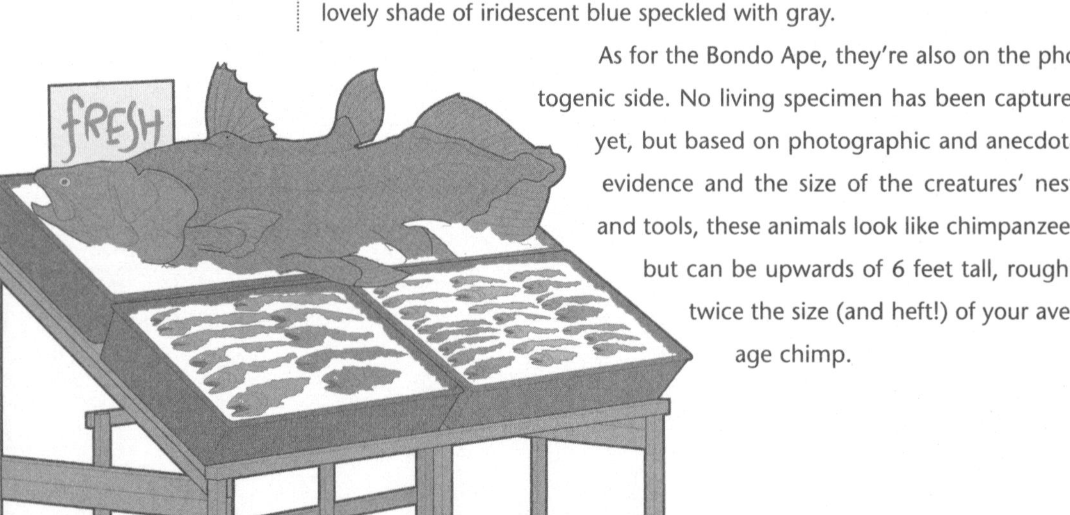

Step 2: ***BE IN THE RIGHT PLACE AT THE RIGHT TIME***

For the Coelacanth, that place was the shores of South Africa in late December of 1938. It was there that scientist and museum curator Marjorie Courtenay-Latimer found the world's first living (or, rather, fresh) Coelacanth buried under a pile of more mundane seafood being shown her by local fishermen. Courtenay-Latimer regularly bought exciting specimens from the fishers to stuff and mount in her museum and she knew right away that the Coelacanth was a keeper—even if she didn't know exactly what it was. After bundling the huge, smelly fish home in a taxi, Coutenay-Latimer contacted several local experts in ichthyology who finally ID'ed it as a living fossil. Unfortunately, by that time, her staff had already gutted and stuffed the fish. Scientists were eager to find another, fresher specimen, but this proved more difficult. It would take 14 years, and several thousand wanted posters, before another Coelacanth cropped up.

Hard as the Coelacanth is to pin down, the Bondo Ape makes it look positively camera-happy. Native to the dense jungles in the northern Democratic Republic of Congo, the Bondo Ape first surfaced in 1908, when two specimens were shot by Belgian explorers. Based on their size and their skull shape, they were originally identified as a subspecies of gorilla. Nothing else was learned about the beasts until a wildlife photographer began studying them in the late 1990s. And even he has yet to examine a live one. Instead, most of our information about them comes from a few photos taken with timed cameras, images of apes shot by hunters, and evidence of their behavior discovered by the photographer, Karl Ammann. From this, we know about its size. Additionally, we know that, instead of sleeping in trees like most chimpanzees, it appears to build nests on the ground, like gorillas do. But, we also know that it isn't a gorilla. In 2003, Amman collected hair and fecal samples from the ape's nests and sent them off for DNA tests. The results revealed that, skull shape and behavior patterns aside, the Bondo Ape has the mitochondrial DNA of a chimpanzee. That means that its maternal line is all chimp. Nobody knows where the ape's paternal line is, however, and, according to a 2005 *Time* magazine article, this has led a minority of scientists to speculate that the Bondo might actually be a chimp/gorilla hybrid.

Win a Duel

It's not as simple as just being able to count to three paces. Take it from Edward Sackville, Earl of Dorset; a duelist who followed every fine tradition that accompanied killing someone over a bruised ego, came away a winner (i.e., alive), and still managed to end up with a bit of egg on his face.

YOU WILL NEED

- Petty rivalry
- Quick tempers
- Just a pinch of aristocratic inbreeding (we assume)

First: *GET EMBROILED IN A LOVE TRIANGLE*

Lord Edward Bruce loved Venetia Stanley. So did Edward Sackville, Earl of Dorset. This being 1613, the disagreement quickly turned to impassioned slapping, which was, of course, an invitation to duel to the death.

Second: *EVADE THE WRATH OF YOUR KING*

Besides commissioning a translation of the Bible, England's King James I is also well known for disliking the "barbaric" tradition of dueling. In fact, he banned it from England, so when Lord Bruce and the Earl of Dorset wanted to duel, they had to take their grudge match to Holland.

Third: *DIE WITH DIGNITY*

The duel turned out to be pretty evenly matched, with both men severely wounding the other. Finally, though, the earl managed stab Bruce straight through twice. With Bruce pretty much done for, the fight broke up so both sides could seek medical attention. But, while the Earl was busy with his wounds, Bruce's doctor attacked him from behind. Of course, at the time, doctors were thought little better of than maids and Bruce couldn't bear to be avenged by someone so low on the social totem pole. From his deathbed, he demanded that the "rascal" doctor halt his attack and, thus, died in an honorable way.

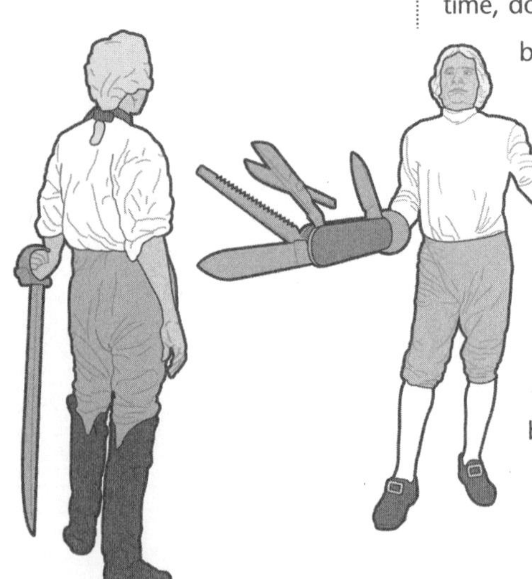

Fourth: *SURVIVE, BUT END UP LOOKING LIKE KIND OF AN IDIOT*

Victorious, the Earl of Dorset headed back to England to claim his lady love . . . Only to find out that, while he and Bruce had been busy paying attention to each other, Venetia Stanley had gone off and married somebody else.

Other Noteworthy Duels

1792—LADY ALMERIA BRADDOCK VS. MRS. ELPHINSTONE

Place: London

Cause: An argument over Lady Braddock's correct age.

LATE 1700S—LORD RICHARD MARTIN VS. MORE THAN 100 PEOPLE

Place: Various locations throughout England and Ireland

Cause: Martin frequently took the law into his own hands to battle animal abusers. He was also instrumental in passing the first animal protection act through Parliament in 1822 and in founding the Royal Society for the Prevention of Cruelty to Animals, acts which earned him the hilarious nickname "Humanity Dick."

2002—SADDAM HUSSEIN VS. GEORGE W. BUSH (PROPOSED)

Place: A neutral location to be chosen by Kofi Annan, who would also serve as referee.

Cause: Prior to the invasion of Iraq, one creative Iraqi vice president offered to solve the dispute between his country and the U.S. by arranging a duel between leaders Hussein and Bush. Surprisingly, no one took him up on his offer.

Taste Wine

The Hard Way: ***BY SOMMELIER***

Pronounced "So-Mel-Yea" (or, if you prefer "Wine-Wai-Ter"), a sommelier is primarily recognized for his or her ability to come up with the implausible variety of flavors we are supposed to be able to taste in wine. But there's a lot more to the job than simply explaining how fermented grapes taste of "butter" or "grass." Sommeliers are also responsible for stocking their home restaurant's wine cellar, pairing wine with specific foods, and recommending wines that meet a diner's taste and budget. And for that, you'll need some book learnin'. Becoming a Master Sommelier is no easy task. In the 37 years since testing began, only 124 people have passed the exams. That's right, "exams" plural: There's an Introductory Exam, a Certificate Exam, an Advanced Exam, and, finally, a Masters Exam. To even sit the Masters Exam, you have to be specially invited. And with the questions including stumpers like, "Name all 13 Anbaugebiet wine regions in Germany," it's no wonder that the pass rate is an abysmally low 4 percent. Now, knowing that, you might assume that just becoming a Master Sommelier is all the exclusivity one person can handle. But remember, the profession is dominated by the French and thus there's still one more level of sommelier success to break through. The World's Best Sommelier competition is hosted every three years by the Association de la Sommellerie Internationale. Competitors are chosen by their national sommelier organizations and are basically subjected to an even more advanced version of the Masters Exam. If you're looking to win, it apparently helps to be French or Italian. Since 1969, all but two winners have been from those countries, with France holding a solid 7-to-3 lead.

The Easy Way: *BY ROBOT*

Leave it to the Japanese to put the French out of a job. In September 2006, a team of researchers from NEC System Technologies and Japan's Mie University announced that they had developed a robo-sommelier. Also known as the winebot, the two-foot-tall appliance/adorable plastic companion can analyze wine using infrared lights. A sensor on the winebot's arm fires light through a liquid sample and then, based on the wavelengths of light that the sample absorbs, determines what type of wine it is—reporting its findings in human speech. While being able to tell one wine from another is only part of a sommelier's job, the bot's creators claim it will one day be programmed to know what foods go best with what wine and even be personalized to recommend wines to suit its owners' tastes.

Currently, one wine-bot costs about as much as a small car. The scientists want to bring the price down to something more reasonable—say, $1,000 or so—before they put it on the market.

Visit the Queen

For a Victorian lady in America, nothing mattered more than social position. It determined whom you could marry, and if you didn't marry well, you were sunk. However, it would be a mistake to think that said position was based solely (or, in fact, at all) on how much bacon your Pops brought home. Much more important was the fatback supplied by Grandpa, Great-Grandpa, and Great-Great-Great-Great Grandpa. After all, "new money" girls were unwelcome at the high-society debutante balls where marriageable young women were presented to potential husbands. There was, however, a loophole, as Karal Ann Marling explains in her book *Debutante*. The ultimate Get Out of Social Purgatory Free card: Make your deb debut before the Queen of England.

YOU WILL NEED:

- Social climbing smarts
- A big budget for fashion
- Infinite patience for jumping through hoops

Step 1: *SNAG AN INVITATION*

Not as easy as it sounds. Remember, the Queen of England wasn't going around opening shopping malls in those days. There were basically only two ways to make the guest list: being friends with the American Ambassador or bribery. The first option worked best for ladies whose fathers had Washington political ties. For them, the Ambassador or his wife might be persuaded to plead the girl's case to the Prime Minister. Others were forced to go through so-called "social brokers," aristocratic British women of reduced financial means who would agree to sponsor unconnected young American women with high ambitions—in exchange for a tidy fee, of course. However, neither way was a guaranteed success. There was an informal quota on how many Americans could be presented to the Queen each year—a fact that Marling says inspired innumerable backroom deals.

Step 2: *ATTIRE YOURSELF PROPERLY*

You couldn't just wear any old dress. Or just any new dress, either. The invitation came with a list of detailed dressmaker instructions—covering everything from the height of the neckline, to the style of the sleeve, to the type and position of headwear. New York tailoring firm Farquharson & Wheelock made a fortune during the period, thanks to their inside-the-palace connections that ensured they knew the years' rules long before anyone else. Hair was also closely regulated and had to be done by a court-approved stylist.

Step 3: *BE PREPARED FOR A POSSIBLE LET DOWN*

After months of work, the young lady's dream day would finally arrive. But even then, visiting the Queen wasn't as simple as just walking in the front door. Beginning early in the morning, women were herded from room to room through the palace on their way to the court. The process took so long that food, card tables, and even books were provided to keep the ladies occupied. Finally, when her name was called, the young woman (in all her carefully prepared finery) would sweep into the courtroom, curtsey to the Queen, and sweep back out again. And that was it. Seriously.

But, anticlimactic as it was, a queenly presentation was often effective. Consuelo Vanderbilt, whose father was regarded by New York society as a "simple" railroad man, managed to move her family on up to the Eastside (socially speaking) after her 1895 debut. Through the court, she met and married a duke, thus making her family officially respectable and greatly inflating the bank account of the previously down-on-his-luck duke. You might say it was a mutually beneficial relationship.

Be an American Icon

Step 1: *EARN AMERICA'S RESPECT AND LOVE*

For Samuel Wilson, a butcher from upstate New York, Step 1 was accomplished via copious shipments of beef. During the War of 1812, Wilson won a military contract to supply meat to American troops. Apparently, he did a pretty good job and, their stomachs satiated, soldiers everywhere began to welcome Wilson into their hearts. The relationship intensified when fighting men who'd grown up near Wilson's hometown began joking that the "U.S." stamped on the meat barrels actually stood for "Uncle Sam" rather than "United States." The nickname stuck and, before long, even civilians were talking about the Uncle who was feeding the troops.

YOU WILL NEED

- An inroad to the public consciousness
- To not worry too much if they take liberties with your appearance

Step 2: *MAKE THE JUMP TO METAPHOR*

Somewhere around the 1830's, "Uncle Sam" came to refer less to Wilson himself and more to a nebulous concept of the federal government as friendly caretaker. Symbolic-Sam made his print debut in 1838 in a political cartoon, where he was depicted as a clean-shaven gentleman in a red stocking cap. But he wasn't alone. Also appearing in the cartoon was a much older metaphorical figure, called Brother Jonathan.

Step 3: *KNOCK OUT THE COMPETITION*

An icon since America's earliest days, Brother Jonathan represented the individualistic spirit of the Republic. Further, as a trickster and a spinner of witty, homespun tales, he also embodied the common man. For many years, he and Uncle Sam lived peaceably as roommates on the nation's editorial pages. But during the Civil War, Jonathan's symbolism—and his fate—changed. As Sam became more identified with a strong, unified federal government, Jonathan came to represent the rebellious South. When the North won the war, so did Uncle Sam. It only took a couple of decades for Brother Jonathan to disappear completely.

Step 4: *ESTABLISH YOUR LEGACY*

It wasn't long before Uncle Sam took on the appearance of America's unifier—Abraham Lincoln. Illustrator Thomas Nast (of Santa Claus fame) widely promoted this version of Sam and the image was later solidified in our collective imagination by James Montgomery Flagg's "I WANT YOU" recruitment posters from World War I. Ironically, Flagg's model for those posters was none other than Flagg, himself. Too cheap to hire a model, he based the image on a self-portrait, instead.

Plan a Party

According to the ancient inhabitants of the Kalahari Desert

Archaeologists had believed that the world's first religious rituals—and thus its first parties—were held in Europe around 40,000 years ago. But the theory was blown away in November 2006, when, according to a press release issued by the Research Council of Norway, evidence of get-togethers, dating back 70,000 years, was discovered in a region of the Kalahari Desert in what is now Botswana. Here, worshipers of the python deity held mankind's first celebrations, a tradition that would eventually (and, perhaps depressingly) culminate in "Animal House."

YOU WILL NEED

- A good reason to get funky

Step 1: *PICK THE RIGHT LOCATION*

If you're holding a themed shindig (and we say "python god" counts as a theme), you'll want the locale to match. After all, you wouldn't have a Cinco de Mayo party down at the local German Brewhaus. The ancient Kalaharians found their perfect place in the Tsodilo Hills—where they took an already serpent-shaped hunk of rock and decorated it with a carved snakeskin pattern. Extremely difficult to reach (the Research Council says that archaeologists didn't find it until the 1990s), the natural geography essentially did double duty as a permanent bouncer. Better yet, a VIP room hidden in the wall, behind the python rock itself, allowed the local shaman to add sound effects and issue divine declarations—Wizard of Oz-like—as though they were coming from the python god itself.

Step 2: *ARRANGE ENTERTAINMENT*

Every good host knows that the party is over when the participants get bored.

But apparently, ritual goers at the python rock didn't need to worry about the experience going stale. Excavations uncovered more than 13,000 relics. In fact, many of them were distinctive red spearheads, brought from rock sources hundreds of miles away, and ceremoniously burned at the site. Firelight provided another key entertainment source. Carvings in the python rock managed to catch flickering light off the campfire such that the "serpent" appeared to move for the crowds. Taken together, the evidence from Tsodilo Hills indicates more than a good party—it shows that human beings were capable of organization and abstract thinking far earlier than anyone realized.

Improve Foreign Relations

A little cultural understanding goes a long way toward making you a welcome guest. Just like knowing how to surf will get you in with Californians and a deep understanding of the Cubs' starting lineup will ingratiate you to the citizens of Chicago, demonstrating your knowledge of these cultural touchstones should help you fit in around the world.

Europe: Wife Carrying

YOU WILL NEED

- **1 woman (not necessarily your wife)**
- **A lot of stamina**

When Finnish bandit Ronkainen the Robber started making prospective gang members carry heavy flour sacks through an obstacle course in the late 19th century, he had no idea that his test of strength would become a 21st-century sport. Drawing on Ronkainen and older Viking traditions of courtship-via-kidnapping, today's Wife Carrying World Championship in Sonkajärvi, Finland, is northern Europe's most popular home-grown sporting event. To win, contestants must carry a woman (not necessarily their own wife) over hurdles, through water traps, and around obstacles. The first place finisher receives his "wife's" weight in beer and various product placements, such as Pepsi. Despite being a Finnish innovation, the sport is largely dominated by Estonians, who've developed a high-tech wife-carrying maneuver. In the Estonian style, the woman hangs upside down, facing the man's back with her legs over his shoulders, giving him a better sense of balance to get through the race.

Middle East: Goat Dragging

YOU WILL NEED

- **1 goat or calf, dead**
- **1 horse, live**
- **24 of your closest friends**
- **A firearm—just in case**

If X-treme sports and Ultimate Fighting just doesn't give you the thrill you're looking for, get a gander of Afghanistan's *chapandazan*. The skilled horsemen play a game known as *buzkashi*—an equestrian free-for-all where two teams of 10-to-12 players each vie for control of a headless goat or calf carcass. "Rules" in *buzkashi* are sort of a casual affair, but traditional etiquette usually prevents players from biting, pulling hair, or using weapons on the field. Off the field, on the other hand, the sport can get a little violent. In order to win, players have to pull the carcass far enough away from the others to claim it as their own. Of course, given that there are often more than 20 horsemen on the field at any given time, achieving this goal is a lot harder than it sounds. This problem is further complicated by the fact that most *buzkashi* matches have an implicit political importance; winning the match is often taken as a demonstration of a warlord's ability to maintain control over his home region. And with the political climate of northern Afghanistan shifting more often than the San Andreas, a bad call by a referee is often considered "fightin' words."

South America: Cacerolazo-ing

YOU WILL NEED

- **Some pots and pans**
- **A regime in need of change**

Sometimes, you've got to make a little noise to make a difference. In 2001, Argentina's economy tanked and in an ill-advised attempt to slow the free-fall, the government put a nation-wide freeze on bank accounts. The move was meant to keep citizens from swamping a bank en masse and withdrawing all their money, but it ended up making life extremely difficult for middle class families who needed access to their cash just to survive. Unfortunately, everyone pretty much ignored their plight. That is, until the people made a racket. In Buenos Aires and other large cities, mobs began to spontaneously take to the streets, banging their significantly empty cookware (*cacerola* is Spanish for "stew pot") in protest of the bank freeze. The protests ended up being so successful that today cacerolazos are commonly organized by political action groups all over Latin America, as a surefire way to draw attention to a cause.

Africa: Internet Scamming

YOU WILL NEED

- Web access
- A good cover letter

Nigeria is known worldwide for a genre of spam in which supposed African heirs and heiresses ask Americans to help them access a fortune stored in a sealed bank account. In return, the American is promised a hefty cut of the dough; all they have to do is provide some basic identity information and/or send thousands of dollars to help cover the cost of fees and bribes. If love is blind, then greed must be functionally retarded, because hundreds of Americans fall for this every year. In fact, in Nigeria, where regular employment is often hard to come by, the scam is such a popular career choice that it's even inspired a hit song—2005's "I Go Chop Your Dollar," in which the singer Osofia raps about greedy white people and how "I take your money and disappear . . . You be the fool, I be the master."

Be King

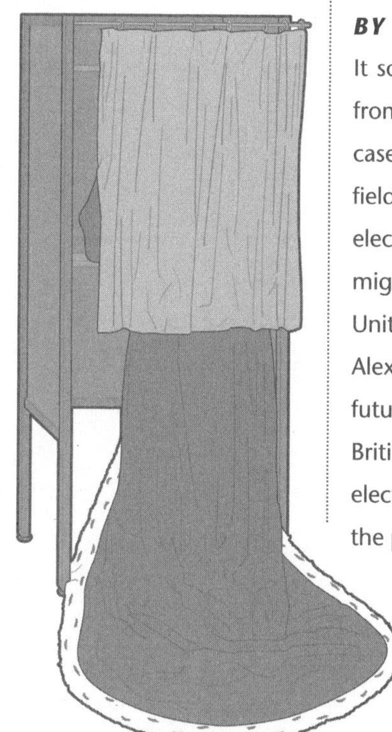

BY ELECTION

It sounds a little incongruous, but a surprising number of royal leaders—from Cambodia to Saudi Arabia—are actually chosen by vote. In most cases, advisors and other aristocratic figures choose the new king from a field of potential candidates within the royal family—so while there are elections, we're still not talking about democracy. One place where you might have had more of a chance to be an elected king, however, was the United States of America—at least, in the version imagined by statesman Alexander Hamilton. At the Constitutional Convention in June of 1787, the future secretary of the treasury presented his plan for America. Calling the British model of government "the best in the world," Hamilton proposed electing the president as well as senators for life and giving the president the power to appoint state governors and veto any law. Essentially, his plan would have made the United States into a slightly less stringent monarchy, a fact Hamilton as much as admitted in a letter to George Washington written later that summer. The people were now "willing to accept something not very remote from that which they have lately quitted," Hamilton wrote. However, his optimism was short-lived. His eloquent five-hour-long speech in praise of elected monarchy failed to make an impression with the Constitutional Congress.

BY INHERITANCE

Time to pull out that family tree and start digging around! Sure, your chances of being an unknown relative of the British monarchy are pretty slim, but there are loads of other countries out there and even if they don't have a monarchy now, most of them did at one point. Lack of a modern monarchy hasn't stopped otherwise average people all over Europe from putting in a claim to their country's now-nonexistent throne, so why should it stop you? Take Henri d'Orléans, who, until his death in 1999, steadfastly claimed to be the true King of France. Henri traced his family lineage (and considerable fortune) to Louis-Philippe, the last monarch from the 900-year-old French royal family of Bourbon-Orleans. But while most people might write off such a connection as a neat genealogical factoid suitable for small talk, Henri saw it as destiny. With his family banished from France by the 1886 Law of Exile, Henri grew up in Morocco and Belgium and basically lived his entire life as though he might re-inherit the throne tomorrow. He held no job, married his cousin, and arranged suitable marriages (to other countries' royalty-in-exile) for his 11 children. After the Law of Exile was repealed in 1950, he moved to Paris and began publishing a monthly newsletter called *The Information Bulletin* from the Political Office of the Monseigneur the Count of Paris, through which he kept his 20,000 subscribers up-to-date on his kingly views of political, economic, and social problems. Although Henri seemed to be fully dedicated to keeping the dream alive, it's questionable what future he saw for his children. After his death, it was discovered that the family was nearly bankrupt and one of Henri's sons claimed his father depleted the fortune on purpose to force the heirs into a different line of work.

BY MARRIAGE

If you can't be born to greatness, you can always try marrying into it. And hopefully, your attempt at wooing royalty will go better than that of Eric XIV, crown prince of Sweden and would-be king of England. According to the version recorded by Geoff Tibballs in the book *Dumbology*, Eric began courting Elizabeth I of England in 1558, originally at the behest of his father who thought the arrangement would be good for Sweden's trading position. Unfortunately, his suit was rejected with Elizabeth politely claiming that she'd love to marry Eric, but (wouldn't you know it?) God had just given her such a desire for celibacy that she couldn't possibly allow herself to be diverted from that holy path. Elizabeth's stock excuse may have worked on other princes, but not Eric. He was smitten and unwilling to give up, declaring his love for Elizabeth (despite the fact that they had never met), thus leading her to repeat the refusal a bit more forcefully 6 months later. Eric then tried sending his brother to plead with the queen, but, not surprisingly, this failed as well. Over the next two to three years, Eric tried every increasingly stupid trick in the book. He wrote her love letters in Latin, contemplated having her favorite boy-toy Robert Dudley killed, and even tried to make the queen jealous by opening marriage negotiations with her hated cousin, Mary, Queen of Scots—all without so much as a response. Eventually, it became clear that Eric was probably more crazy than lovelorn. In 1568, after he executed two of his guards for being annoying, Eric was declared mad and forced to abdicate in favor of his brother.

Be an Artiste

YOU WILL NEED

- **To do anything for art**

TRY POISONING YOURSELF

All you art-school wannabes should consider the Goya way: poisoning for professional reasons. Until he was 46, Francisco Goya was a talented, but dull, painter of pretty portraits and landscapes. But, following a near-fatal illness in 1792, this 18th-century Thomas Kinkade took a turn down a darker path, producing a series of grotesque etchings featuring witches, demons, and hefty chunks of anti-Church social commentary. The new direction made Goya famous and touched off a centuries-long debate over what had caused his stylistic evolution. Over the years, art historians have suggested everything from schizophrenia to that reliable old stand-by, syphilis. But in the 1970s, Dr. William Niederland published a solution to the puzzle—Goya had hand-mixed large amounts of white paint made from lead. And as Niederland pointed out, the painter's symptoms (partial paralysis, speech impairment, dizziness, hallucinations, paranoia) were all consistent with lead poisoning.

DEVELOP AN OUTSIZED PERSONA

Of course, you won't get anywhere in the art world with a meek, forgettable personality. Just ask Caravaggio, an early 17th-century Italian painter, best known for creating the technique of tenebrism, or dramatic, selective illumination. But while his professional life influenced the work of artistic giants like Rembrandt and Velázquez, Caravaggio's personal life is likely to influence no one, except, perhaps, Russell Crowe. Known for getting drunk and starting fights all over Rome, Caravaggio had a rap sheet a mile long. His offenses included the mundane (attacking another artist, 1600), the comical (throwing a plate of artichokes in the face of a waiter, 1604), and the just plain dumb (killing a man over either a disputed tennis score or the disputed affections of a hooker, depending on whom you ask, 1606).

WRITE OFF FAME BEFORE IT HAPPENS

Success, smucksess. You know darn well it won't happen to you. So why bother making art for The Man, anyway? In 1921, Simon Rodia began building a sculpture in his south-central Los Angeles backyard, piecing together random chunks of scrap, including bottle caps, broken china and bicycle parts. Thirty-three years later, Watts Towers, a sprawling, spired monstrosity, was finished. Then, Rodia gave his property to a neighbor and moved away. Though Watts Towers became famous enough to land Rodia a spot on the cover of *Sgt. Pepper's Lonely Hearts Club Band* and beloved enough to be left untouched by the 1965 Watts Riots, Rodia never saw it again. Telling people that part of his life was over, Rodia spent his final years living in obscurity more than 300 miles away from his masterpiece.

Find Your Roots

For Men

YOU WILL NEED

- **A DNA sample**
- **A reality TV show**
- **High-tech science gadgetry**
- **A shovel to scoop your jaw off the floor when the results come in**

Roughly 9,000 years ago, near what is now the village of Cheddar in southwest England, a stone-age hunter met an untimely and tragic end. Nobody really knows what happened to him, but when his remains were discovered in a cave in 1903, his skull had been bashed in with a blunt object. Clearly, "Cheddar Man" had enemies. But, science has shown that he had allies as well, relatives who survived him and went on to give birth, raise their children to adulthood, and have grandchildren. Wash, rinse, repeat several thousand times, and you have the modern, unwitting relatives of one very ancient skeleton.

In 1997, Oxford geneticist Bryan Sykes took the first successful DNA extraction from Cheddar Man, England's oldest known human. Previous attempts had failed because standard DNA from the nucleus of a cell doesn't survive well over vast stretches of time. Further, no one had ever been able to find enough intact DNA left in a skeleton Cheddar Man's age. Sykes, however, took a different approach to the hunt, choosing instead to go after mitochondrial (Mt) DNA, a specific type of genetic coding found in the energy producing parts of cells. and passed from mother to daughter. Previous research had shown that, unlike nuclear DNA, mitochondrial DNA only mutated an average of once every 10,000 years. So, besides being an old broad, Mt DNA is also tough, able to survive conditions and time spans nuclear DNA can't. Deep inside one of Cheddar Man's molars, Sykes and his team found exactly what they were looking for—residual Mt DNA, in large enough quantities that it could be processed and read. For sciencey folk, that news would have been exciting enough. But Sykes and his team were being filmed for a BBC TV show aimed at a general audience. Naturally, that meant they needed something to punch their research up a bit.

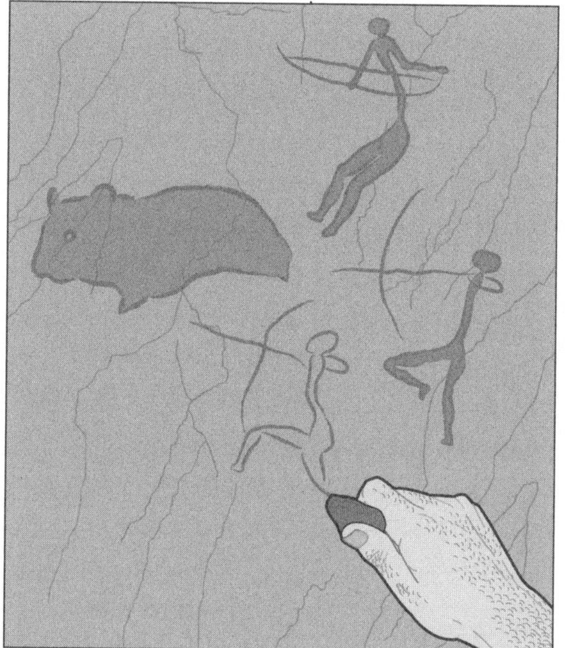

Their solution: Take DNA samples from current residents of Cheddar and see if The Man had any living relatives. Twenty volunteers from a local school were tested and, to everyone's surprise, not one, but three turned out to be Cheddar Man's relatives. Two of the relations actually had DNA markers that were identical to the ancient dead guy, but they were both young children whose parents wanted them out of the public eye. The Cheddar-relative who ended up in the press was fourty-something history teacher Adrian Targett. Although Targett wasn't an exact match with Cheddar Man, the two had a shared female relative some 10,000 years ago, Targett was lauded as the Man's distant cousin, a connection made all the more exciting by the fact that Targett lived only about a half-mile from the cave where Cheddar Man's body had originally been found.

For Mice

YOU WILL NEED

- **To actually be a hamster, rather than a mouse**
- **To be willing to overlook a little inaccuracy for the sake of a good thematic element**

While distantly related to mice, hamsters are widely relegated to filling the role of pet/tortured prisoner in laboratories and grade schools worldwide. But, in the scientific world, they're also well known for being one of the few animals with a traceable genetic history. Other than a brief and failed interlude in the 19th century, hamsters were a strictly wild and mostly unknown species all the way up until April 12, 1930, when a British zoologist managed to capture a female and her 11 babes while on vacation in Syria. At first, things didn't go smoothly for the little hamster family. Apparently, Mama Hamster went on a bit of a cannibalistic rampage, killing several babies before the scientists killed her. Then, a few more babies died of disease and two enterprising fellows escaped. The final three baby hamsters were raised to adulthood and later successfully bred—their offspring quickly earning the dubious honor of being the most sought-after lab animals in all the British Empire. In 1945, things got a little brighter when hamsters were introduced to the pet market, thus securing a marginally safer environment at the grubby hands of nine-year-olds. Today, almost all hamsters—whether in the store or the scientific workforce—are descendants of that same Syrian hamster family.

Pick the Perfect Mate

It's the skill your mother always wanted you to have! Little did she know, it's mostly biological.

YOU WILL NEED

- A million years of ingrained biological imperative
- A new hairstyle, already! And would it kill you to lose some weight?

Step 1: ***KNOW WHAT YOU REALLY WANT, THEN GRAB IT***

We know (believe us, we know), that whole "knowing what you want" thing can be harder than it sounds. But, when you're looking for a date, nothing is more important. Why? Because what you really want determines the type of person you're going to gravitate toward—evolutionarily speaking. According to a December 2006 study, published in the journal *Personal Relationships*, women want different types of men for different relationship roles. In the study, subjects viewed pictures of men who's masculine traits had been artificially exaggerated or diminished (thank you, Photoshop!) and were then asked to describe what they thought those men would be like. Physical traits like chiseled jaws and prominent brow ridges were linked to behaviors like infidelity, competitiveness, and aggressiveness—according the study, the sort of men that women want to have flings with. Softer features, on the other hand, were connected to better childrearing skills and fidelity, coincidentally representing the guys gals want to marry.

Step 2: ***TO MAKE BABIES—CHEAT!***

Testosterone does more than just make dudes into men. Higher levels of testosterone produce a stronger immune system, which, in turn, leads to a healthier body. So, when women start looking for someone to have a baby with, it's no wonder that they'd gravitate toward the men who appear most testosterone-heavy—even when that man isn't their husband. A study published in 2007 in the journal *Hormones and Behavior* found that women were more likely to cheat while they were ovulating and, more importantly, they were more likely to cheat with men who displayed high testosterone levels, healthy bodies, and presumably healthy genes. What's more, a different study published in the journal *Animal Behavior* in 1993 found that women having just such an affair have more orgasms than they do with their regular partner, a factor that makes them more likely to conceive.

Spread a Rumor

So you've always wanted to be a rumor monger, but never had good tales to tell? Never fear. We'll get you started with three tantalizing tidbits about the oh-so-secret lifestyles of the rich and famous.

YOU WILL NEED

- **To have a juicy secret**
- **To keep your voice down, for gosh sakes**
- **To come sit over here by us**

BEETHOVEN WAS A PEEPING TOM

The composer had a famously horrid love life, proposing no fewer than six times to as many women and being turned down by each and every one. In 1809, after yet another disastrous break-up, he soothed his wounded soul by literally moving into a brothel. Besides presumably driving his ex-girlfriends mad with jealousy (and/or hysterical laughter) Beethoven's choice in roommates also lent credence to modern (unconfirmed) theories that his later hearing loss was caused by a nasty case of syphilis. And yet, this still wasn't the low point of his romantic career. That came over a decade later, in 1820, when Vienna police arrested Beethoven after he was caught peering through windows. Granted, in some versions of this story, the composer was merely lost, not perverted. But that sounds like an excuse to us.

EZRA POUND HAD THREE WIVES

OK, we're fudging a little. Technically speaking, Pound was only married to one of them. But you can't really expect an unconventional writer to be a conventional husband. Throughout his marriage, it turns out that Pound was carrying on an affair with a Russian violinist. For more than 20 years, he lived happily as a two-woman man. That is, until the 1950s, when, while being held in a U.S. prison on treason charges (he'd supported Mussolini's fascist government during World War II), Pound met and fell in love with yet another woman whom he referred to as his "personal secretary."

LOUIS XIV WAS BALD

What can we say, it ran in the family. In fact, his predecessor, Louis XIII, had started losing hair at age 23. In those dark days before the Hair Club for Men, the only way to combat the loss was to cover it up. Louis XIV began wearing large, long wigs and flatly refused to let anyone see him without one—going so far as to have his wig passed through closed bed curtains every morning. But, being king, Louis's shame quickly became public fashion. By 1660, large white wigs were all the rage in France. For many years, demand was so high that thieves would tackle teenage boys in the street and forcibly cut off their hair to sell to wigmakers.

Upgrade Your Spouse

Cause we've all thought about it from time to time...

IN THE FERTILE CRESCENT

The oldest official records of divorce date to ancient Mesopotamia, where the world's first divorce laws were part of one of the world's first legal codes. While the Code of Hammurabi is well known for its rather draconian punishments (false accusers were put to death, striking a man of higher rank got you whipped, and architects who's houses collapsed were killed), divorce Hammurabi-style was relatively lenient, compared with other laws of the time. Sure, adulteresses were to be drowned while adulterers got off scot-free, but many of the other divorce decrees were actually quite fair to women. For instance, if a man was captured in war and there was a food shortage in his household, his wife could leave and go marry someone else. And if he ditched out on her and later came back, she wasn't obliged to move back in with him. In addition, men who asked for a divorce for reasons other than wifely infidelity had to provide support to their former spouses. If she'd had children, for instance, he had to give her some of his land and money. If not, he had to give her back her dowry in full. Besides the generic legal details described in the code, archaeologists have found clay tablets with writing describing individual divorce cases. The State University of New York at Stony Brook recently translated a case where a man wanted to divorce his wife for being a nag, proving that times really haven't changed.

WHENEVER YOU WANT TO

Getting divorced was a relatively easy feat . . . right up until the fall of the Roman Empire. From that point on, however, the Christian church held sway over just about everything in European life. Marriage ceased to be a legal issue and became a spiritual one. Annulment—i.e., getting the Pope to agree that your marriage never actually happened—was the only way to end it (other than, you know, death). And annulments weren't easy to come by, being expensive and largely reserved for things like failure to consummate. The Protestant revolution changed all that. Although guys like Calvin and Luther weren't particularly prodivorce, they were virulently anti-Catholic and during the first few years of their rebellion, any and all Catholic doctrine was under suspicion. Despite the fact that Calvinists aren't known for their free-wheeling ways, the basically Calvinist-run city of Zurich had started to give divorce (even for extra-biblical reasons) the thumbs up by 1531. Meanwhile, the Puritans allowed divorce from the start in New England—this being one area where they drew their belief not from the scripture, but from secular Dutch tradition. As for the first no-fault divorce laws, those cropped up in 1792, enabling postrevolution French-persons to split up for no greater reason than irreconcilable differences. South Carolina, on the other hand, was less hospitable to sparring spouses. Divorce was legalized in 1868, outlawed again in 1878, and not relegalized until 1950.

IN RENO

Reno, Nevada, began life as a bridge crossing and later turned into a train depot. But it's location as a busy hub for guys living in the largely female-less wilds quickly made it a center for prostitution and drinking. It's this combination, we suspect, that led the city fathers to set one of the 19th century's shortest divorce waiting periods—a mere 6 months. In fact, it was this shortened waiting period that led to Reno's first celebrity divorce. Way back in 1906, a business tycoon's wife ditched her low-down dirty cheat of a man in a (relatively) quickie manner.

The ensuing scandal was widely publicized and Reno began to slowly develop a new industry. The high point came around the late 1920s, when Nevada lowered it's waiting period first to 3 months and then to 6 weeks. Coinciding with the rise of Hollywood, Reno's divorce economy boomed as celebrities and wealthy Americans flocked to the city to vacation away their waiting period at luxury spas known as "divorce ranches." But just how booming was it? Consider the numbers: between 1929 and 1939, the local county courthouse granted more than 30,000 divorces.

Grease the Wheels

AT ANY TIME

Bribery hasn't always been frowned upon like it is today. In fact, if you were to look at global legal records up until modern times, more people were convicted of witchcraft than bribery. From medieval Catholics bribing their way out of purgatory to Saddam Hussein's attempt to bribe a U.N. Weapons inspector, bribery has been a constant throughout history. For all you wacky historians and larcenous time travelers out there, we, with the help of John T. Noonan and his book, *Bribes*, provide the following handy guide:

Year	Place	Bribee	Suggested "Donation" *(Based on Actual Events)*
74 B.C.E.	Rome	Senator	40,000 sesterces
1204 C.E.	Rome	Pope	100 Silver Pounds
1618	London	Chancellor	50 to 1,000 British Pounds
1795	Georgia	State Legislator	$600 to $1,000 US
1868	Washington, D.C.	President	$25,000
1965	Netherlands	Prince	$1 Million
1970	Korea	President	$3 Million
2006	Washington, D.C.	Congressman	$100,000

FOR ANY REASON

Bribery, it's not just for bad guys anymore. In fact, in some Latin American countries, bribes (known, in these cases, by the less prickly name of "conditional cash transfers") are being used are being used for good—helping poor families to stay healthy and keep their children in school. The concept works like this: In order to really break the stranglehold of poverty, parents need to invest in their children's education and in the health of the whole family. But, for most extremely poor families, that just isn't possible. They don't have the extra cash for check-ups or school supplies, and they can't afford to lose the income their kids could be making if they weren't in class. Conditional cash transfers solve that problem by paying parents for each child they have in school and by providing free health care when problems arise in exchange for the family attending regular check ups or classes on ways to prevent illness. The most successful of these programs, which has run under the names Progresa and Oportunidades since 1997, is in Mexico. Here, one in four families benefit in some way from conditional cash transfers and officials have seen some seriously positive results—including poverty rates that fell even while the country was mired in a recession. Not too shabby. In fact, the cash transfer program has worked out so well in Mexico that other countries are showing interest in it as well, including the United States, where New York City Mayor Michael Bloomberg has been funding a feasibility study that may lead to New Yorkers getting their own good-for-you bribes.

Get back to Nature

According to Henry David Thoreau

First: *CHOOSE YOUR "WILDERNESS" CAREFULLY*

You'd hate to end up communing with the Earth someplace far removed from human civilization. Of course, that certainly wasn't a problem for Henry David Thoreau. Despite the impression reading *Walden* might have given you, *Walden* had more in common with Central Park than with Yellowstone. For one thing, Walden Pond was on land owned by Thoreau's close friend Ralph Waldo Emerson, and when Thoreau claimed in the introduction that he lived a "mile from any neighbor," he meant that quite literally. The Emersons lived just up the hill, exactly a mile away. From his cabin, Thoreau could see a major highway and hear the train that ran along the opposite side of the pond. In fact, Concord Village was close enough that he visited it nearly every day.

YOU WILL NEED

- A secluded cabin within earshot of your best friend's dinner bell
- A lonesome life complete with house parties
- A painfully handicapped sense of irony

Second: *DON'T LET YOURSELF GET BORED*

Turns out, there's plenty of room in the vast wilds for all of your friends and acquaintances to visit. Besides regular weekly visits from his mother and sisters (who brought baked goods and premade meals, lest Thoreau be forced do something drastic, like hunt and gather) and frequent sojourns to the Emersons', Thoreau's idyllic, natural lifestyle also included numerous house parties: He hosted galas for political groups, dinners for luminaries like Nathaniel Hawthorne and Bronson Alcott, and once managed to pack 25 people into his one-room, hand-built cabin.

Preserve Your Legacy

IN A MUSEUM

For inspiration, turn to Comanche, famous survivor of the Battle of the Little Bighorn and one well-preserved horse. In 1876, when the rest of the cavalry arrived a little too late to help their friends, Comanche was the only United States "soldier" left alive on the field. When he died at Fort Riley, Kansas in 1890, his fans in the U.S. military had him stuffed and mounted (which kind of makes you wonder what happens to dead generals . . .). Three years later, the new and improved Comanche visited the 1893 Chicago World's Fair and has lived out the rest of his afterlife behind glass at the University of Kansas's Dyche Museum of Natural History.

ACCIDENTALLY

Elmer McCurdy was a two-bit con with no plans for postmortem lionization. But, when McCurdy was shot in a failed 1911 train robbery, fate (or, rather, an entrepreneurial mortician) intervened. Mummified, McCurdy spent the next 65 years being displayed to the public in sideshows—and as a movie prop in exploitation films like *Narcotic.* At some point, however, the people in charge of McCurdy's body forgot that it was a real body. In 1976, during filming for an episode of *The Six Million Dollar Man,* McCurdy's arm fell off. Revealed as a non-mannequin, the would-be robber was finally laid to rest.

BETTER THAN ANYONE ELSE

Forget King Tut already! The boy king's just roadside taxidermy when compared with the Lady of Dai. It's true, this Chinese queen's immaculately preserved body was discovered in 1971, and more than 2,000 years after her death, the lady has the kind of soft skin, lustrous hair, and fully-working joints that many living people haven't quite achieved (let alone most mummies). In fact, when found, the lady still had blood in her veins. To this day, no one knows exactly how she was preserved, but scientists guess it probably had something to do with both her airtight, multichambered casket and the mercury-based solution her body was immersed in.

Have a Classy Obituary

Don't: ***DIE IRONICALLY***

If you want people to respect you in the event of your untimely demise, you might want to make sure that you don't croak in the middle of some comically incongruous scenario. Case in point: The tragic tale of animal rights activist Timothy Treadwell. Treadwell dedicated his life to improving relationships between humans and wild bears, downplaying bearanoia by "proving" that the animals were really very friendly. Treadwell was known for hanging out in bear country with no means of protection and interacting with bears in in-your-face ways that would have made the Crocodile Hunter blush—including sidling up to the beasts to chant "I loooove you," in a high-pitched sing-song voice. Unfortunately for Treadwell, it turned out that the bears did not reciprocate those feelings. In 2003, he was killed and eaten by Alaskan brown bears, which some people call grizzlies. An equally ironic death is attributed to noted ancient Greek philosopher Chrysippus. A proponent of Stoicism, which praised emotional detachment and clear, level-headed thinking, Chysippus apparently died from laughter while watching a drunken donkey eat a plate of figs.

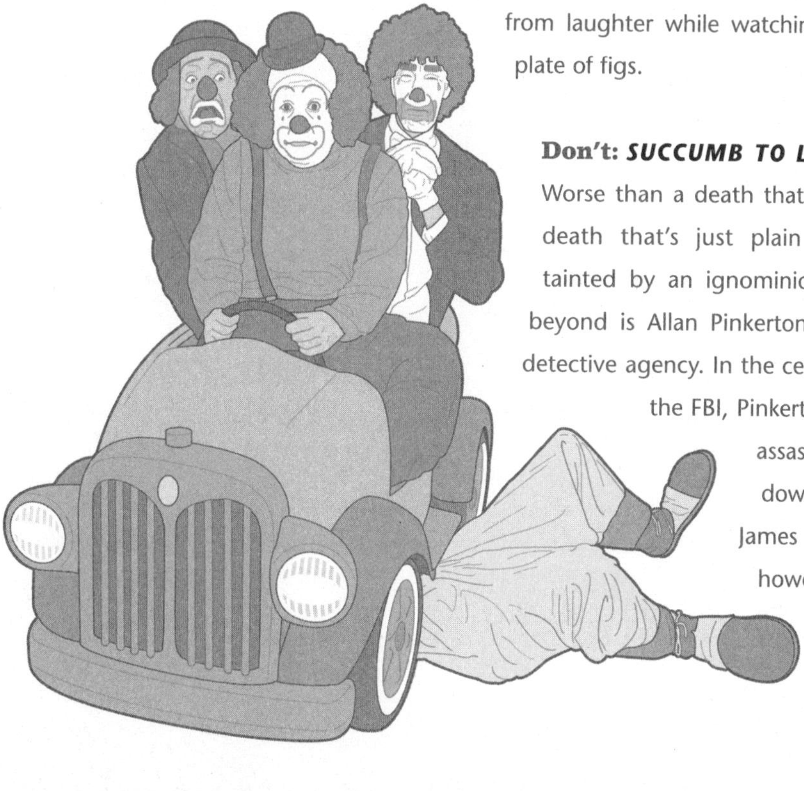

Don't: ***SUCCUMB TO LAUGHABLE CAUSES***

Worse than a death that mocks your life's work is a death that's just plain mockable. Among those tainted by an ignominious send-off into the great beyond is Allan Pinkerton, founder of the American detective agency. In the century before the creation of the FBI, Pinkerton's men foiled presidential assassination plots and tracked down famous criminals like the James Gang. His cause of death, however, is less well known. And with good reason. In 1884, Pinkerton slipped on a Chicago sidewalk and bit his tongue. Rather than just hurting like a @&#^@, Pinkerton's tongue bite managed to turn gangrenous. He died a few days after his fall.

Do: *DIE AS YOU LIVED*

For opera singers, that would mean dying in as theatrical, and melodramatic a way as possible. Congratulations, then, are in order for tenor Richard Versalle who managed to die on stage in a suitably thematic performance. Versalle succumbed to a well-timed (and ironic) heart attack in 1996, while performing an opera about the secret to eternal life at New York's Metropolitan Opera House. His even-better-timed last line: "Too bad you can only live so long."

Impress Your Mother-in-Law

Be a Man

YOU WILL NEED

- **To reach puberty**
- **To be willing to put up with whatever older people say you have to do (even when they're snickering from behind their hands)**

Method #1: *HAVE A PARTY*

Nobody knows how to party like the Japanese, who's national Coming of Age Day celebrates the official maturity of every person who turned 20 the previous year. This party, however, is the celebratory descendant of the decidedly more exclusive *genpuku* ceremony. Dating back to Japan's feudal era, *genpuku* marked the coming-of-age for aristocratic boys, who were given their fist adult clothing and hairstyles and fitted with elaborate ceremonial headdresses. Depending on how rich your parents were and where they stood on the social ladder, your *genpuku* might have happened at any point between your 15th and 17th birthdays. Long-standing tradition though it was, *genpuku* went the way of the dodo after Japan's nobility was dissolved at the end of World War II. Instead, the new constitution provided a replacement holiday that could be enjoyed by commoners and wealthy alike: Coming of Age Day. Since 1948, the January celebration has been used to honor young Japanese who could now drink, smoke, and vote legally. Depending on how much your parents are willing to shell out for the event, your Coming of Age Day can be celebrated anywhere from the local village square to Tokyo Disneyland.

Method #2: *TAKE A TEST*

In our spry, modern democracy (which is actually more of a republic, but why quibble), becoming a man is as easy as turning 18. With that birthday, you're officially considered an adult—blessed with citizenship, the right to smoke legally, and a friendly reminder to register for the draft. But back in the days of Athenian democracy,coming of age—and becoming a true citizen—were much more complicated. For one thing, not everybody could partake in the citizenship-based right of passage—only those who could prove that both their parents had been citizens. And girls weren't eligible at all, beyond the documentation necessary to prove the citizenship of their sons. The road toward citizenship technically began shortly after birth and continued through 10 to 13 years of schooling. But, as Athenian boys neared their 20th year, any of them seeking the title of citizen had to prove their worth via a test called the *dokimasia*. Essentially a trial, the *dokimasia* publicly established your parentage and whether you were fit for military service. If you passed, you were officially an adult citizen and could do things like vote and own property. If you failed, you still got to be a free adult, but a much more limited one. Of course, appeals were permitted. But to discourage frivolous claims to citizenship, anyone who lost a *dokimasia* appeal was sold into slavery.

Method #3: *SURVIVE THE FEATS OF STRENGTH*

Proving you're tough enough to be an adult is a common theme running through many of the world's coming-of-age rituals. In fact, the feats are often acted out in days-long ceremonies where youth suffer severe physical hardship under the close eye of a trained elder. For much of the 19th and 20th centuries, events like these were suppressed in many countries by colonial law, but in recent decades there's been a big push to bring back these traditions—albeit in a slightly different form. In South Africa, boys used to be inducted into manhood by tribal elders near their home village. But today, with people from all across the country flocking to large cities where different cultures mix and mingle, intertribal initiation schools have become the norm. Led by an elder who has a working knowledge of several different tribal customs, initiation schools are three-month-long excursions into the wild. Sort of like Boy Scout camp . . . if the Boy Scouts gave badges for enduring a tin-can lid circumcision. Besides that ordeal, boys might also have to hunt and gather their own food, sleep in makeshift hand-built shelters, and climb 20-foot-tall poles with just their hands and feet. Of course, they do learn traditional customs and legends along the way—lessons that are just as important to becoming a man as the pain is.

Crack an Unsolved Murder

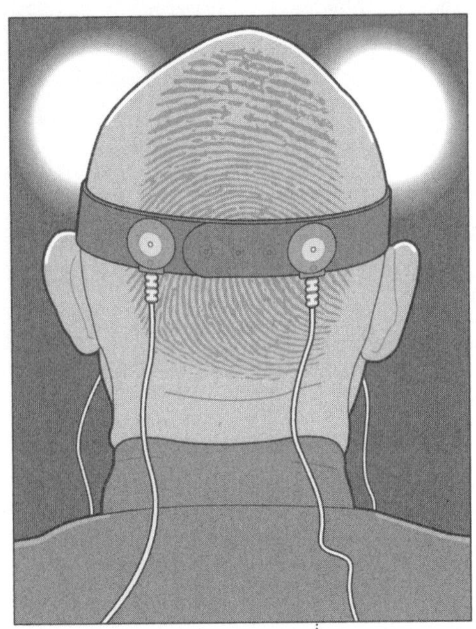

Step 1: ***JUST USE YOUR BRAIN . . . OR SOMEONE ELSE'S***

Scientist Lawrence Farwell was just trying to help the disabled. But, in the mid 1980s, while working on a technology that would have enabled the vocally impaired to speak, Farwell stumbled upon something completely different—involuntary response signals that light up the brain whenever a person encounters something that they consider significant. Called a P300 MERMER (Memory and Encoding Related Multi-facet Electronic Response), this spike of brain activity corresponds to information that a person is intimately familiar with; images, sounds, or words that were important enough to get burned into their memory. Scientists have known about these waves for years, but Farwell was the first to realize that P300s could be used as a sort of fingerprint, a way of positively ID'ing a suspect at a crime scene.

Step 2: ***PUT ON A THINKING CAP***

To test someone's brain fingerprints, Farwell first fits them with a headband covered in electrodes. The headband is connected to a laptop, which records and analyzes the brainwave information. Farwell then shows the suspect a series of words or pictures. These probes are chosen carefully to be a mix of things the subject knows, things he doesn't know, and things he may or may not know. Some are related to crime and some aren't. This variety gives Farwell a solid amount of information that he can turn into an easy-to-read line graph tracking the subject's responses. There are only three lines. One shows what happens when the subject sees information he knows, another tracks his response to unknown information. The third line shows how the subject responded to information about the crime that only someone present at the scene could have known. If it matches up with his "unknown information" line, then chances are, he's innocent. But, if the third line matches the "known information" pattern, it shows the suspect has an intimate connection to the activity. In other words, "Busted!" Unlike a standard polygraph exam, there's no way for a suspect to bluff the brain-wave machine. And, unlike physical fingerprints or DNA evidence, which only turn up in usable amounts in about 1 percent of all criminal cases, nearly every crime leaves brain fingerprints that can be positively traced.

Step 3: *TAKE IT TO COURT*

It's still a pretty new technology, but brain fingerprinting has been used in a couple of real-life cases already. In 2003, Terry Harrington, an Iowa man who'd been in prison for 25 years, was freed when his brain fingerprints showed he had no special knowledge of the 1978 murder he was supposed to have committed. On the other side of the coin, Missourian J.B. Grinder confessed to raping and killing a woman after a 1999 brain fingerprinting revealed that he did, in fact, know significant unpublished details about the 15-year-old crime. He's now serving a life sentence and ended up confessing to several other unsolved murders as well. Even more interesting, brain fingerprinting might get used in the War on Terror. The CIA provided more than $1 million in funding for brain fingerprint research and one of Farwell's business partners, a former FBI agent, has talked about how the technology could be used to pinpoint whether a person is a member of a specific organization (namely, by presenting the subject with that organization's terminology and code words). Neither Farwell nor the government will confirm or deny whether the technology has been used in counterterrorism, but Farwell does say the response in the intelligence community "has been positive."

Be a Late Bloomer

According to two women who were at their best late in life

YOU WILL NEED

- Grey hair
- An attitude

IN ART

Anna Mary Robertson Moses wasn't really an artist. She'd spent her whole life as a frugal and hard-working farmwife, and when she took up painting in 1935, in her mid-70s, it was only to pass the time after arthritis had left her unable to hold an embroidery needle. The first showing of her work was at an upstate New York county fair, where her jams won prizes and her paintings were ignored. But that was all about to change. In 1938, an art collector spotted some of her work at a small-town drugstore. In 1940, Anna Mary, now known as "Grandma," Moses was in an exhibition at the Galerie St. Etienne in New York City. Her nostalgic paintings of country winters and farm chores were both realistic and also oddly surreal—Grandma never had any formal training, so her people didn't have shadows and her depth was off. But that was the charm. By the time she died at the age of 101, she'd painted more than 1,000 pieces and amassed a fortune worth more than $3 million in today's currency. Her paintings, which she originally sold for the modern equivalent of $60, are now, according to Galerie St. Etienne, believed to be worth as much as $100,000 in some cases.

IN POLITICS

Maggie Kuhn was always a liberated woman, starting her career in 1926, back when most people thought women belonged in the home. Beginning in 1950, she happily worked for 20 years for the Presbyterian Church's national Social Education and Action office and would have stayed there for another 20 had she not been forced out by mandatory retirement at the age of 65. But this was 1970, and activist-minded Maggie wasn't going to take a glaring case of ageism lying down. Instead, she started a group—later nicknamed the Gray Panthers—dedicated to wiping out discrimination against the elderly and making a place for aging within American society. She appeared on Johnny Carson and worked alongside Ralph Nader and other political organizers. She also made people squirm with her willingness to talk about one of the great conversational taboos: old people having sex. She once quipped that "Sex should end when the rigor-mortis sets in," and publicly advocated elderly women turning to lesbianism as shorter-lived men died off.

See Without Eyes

According to Ben Underwood of Sacramento, California

Step 1: *CLICK*

Ben Underwood lost his sight—and his eyeballs—at the age of 3 to retinal cancer. Eleven years later, however, he gets around just fine, and he does it without a cane, a seeing eye dog, or any other external device. Instead Underwood clicks. A lot. In fact, when he's on the move, he produces an almost steady stream of clicking sounds. Using this, he's able to skateboard, dance, and even once chased down a classmate who tried to sucker-punch him.

Step 2: *LISTEN*

It sounds an awful lot like a superpower, but Underwood really isn't doing anything new or anything that you couldn't do, too. His technique is called echolocation—essentially, he's making a noise and then listening to hear where and what the sound bounces off of. Yup, just like bats and dolphins. Scientists have been studying this ability since 1749, when, according to an article published by Slate.com in 2006, Denis Diderot published his "Letter on the Blind." Diderot was appropriately impressed that the sightless people he studied still seemed to be able to move around without constantly smacking into things. However, in an era where radar wasn't even a blip on the screen of human knowledge, he mistakenly attributed this ability to a heightened sense of touch that allowed the blind to "feel" objects from a foot or two away. It took a really long time to clear up this misconception—roughly 213 years, to be exact. In 1962, a psychologist named Winthrop Kellogg grabbed the attention of scientists (and blind people) worldwide with a then-revolutionary theory: What if the blind were hearing obstacles? Kellogg successfully tested this idea with what might have been one of history's most comical-looking studies. Subjects were blindfolded and told to make some sort of repetitive sound, while Kellogg held random objects up in front of them. True to his theory, most subjects knew when there was something there.

Fuel Your Car with Thanksgiving Leftovers

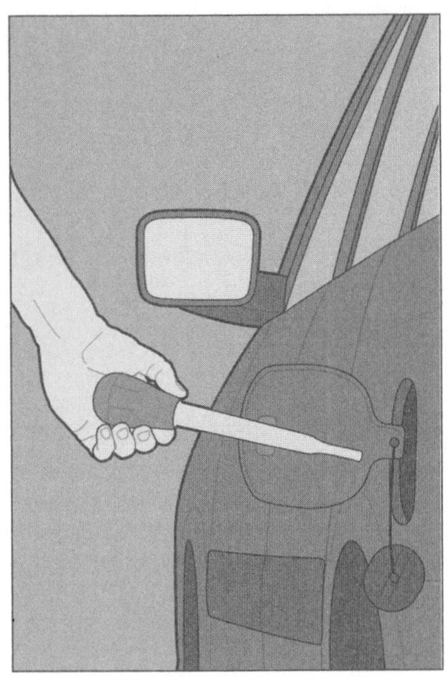

If you're reading this, you're probably hip to the concept that Americans (and pretty much everybody else in world) have a bit of an oil addiction. Of course, unlike some things you could get yourself addicted to, the supplies aren't limitless. So, wouldn't it be great if we could make oil ourselves? Produce it just like the Earth does—through pressure and heat—only faster? It turns out that DIY oil is not only possible, it's a reality! In fact, as you read this, a factory near Carthage, Missouri, is turning tons of waste from a nearby turkey slaughterhouse into diesel fuel and fertilizer. How? A little thing called thermal depolymerization.

See, oil is made naturally when carbon (usually in the form of dead plants and animals) gets buried under tons of earth and is then crushed and heated by the movement of tectonic plates. Needless to say, this takes a while. But, in 2003, a company called Changing World Technologies, which had perfected a way to duplicate this process in a factory in a fraction of the time—as little as 15 minutes in some cases—set up a plant in Carthage. Better yet, because of the way the process works its far more energy efficient than any other available method of producing biofuel, yielding 100 British Thermal Units of energy for every 15 BTUs spent in production. But wait, it gets better! Not only can thermal depolymerization turn turkey into black gold, it can do the same thing with just about any carbon-containing substance—from raw sewage, to old car tires, to cast-off computers. And, what doesn't get made into oil ends up as other handy products, such as the aforementioned fertilizer or useful industrial chemicals. The downside: So far, there doesn't seem to be one.

So why haven't you heard of this? Frankly, we have no idea. Part of the problem, is that when Congress drew up regulations to give biofuel-producing companies a tax credit in 2004, they wrote the legislation in a way that inadvertently excludes thermal depolymerization. This makes it difficult both to get investors and to compete with the tax-break advantaged. Nevertheless, we love the idea of thermal depolymerization—with every fiber of our gizmo-loving, tree-hugging being—and we're hoping that if we explain more about it, that you'll start producing some oil for us.

YOU WILL NEED

- Pressure
- Heat
- Water
- Some sort of carbon-based waste material

Step 1: ***GRIND IT UP***

Whatever you're starting with, whether it's computer parts or turkey giblets, needs to be chopped and churned into a fine, grainy mess.

Step 2: ***ADD WATER***

According to a May 2003 *Discover* article, this is the step that makes Changing World Technology's version of thermal depolymerization unique. Other attempts to recreate the process tried to siphon water away from the waste. CWT figured out that if they add more, then they don't have to heat or pressurize the sludgy glop nearly as much as they would for dry materials—the water helps spread the effect of the heat more efficiently.

Step 3: ***DEPRESSURIZE***

By quickly pumping the heated, pressurized slop into a depressurization chamber, CWT makes most of the water instantly evaporate, a necessary step that would take a lot longer and a lot more energy to do by boiling. If you're making oil from turkey, this is the point where powdery fertilizer, chock full of minerals from the bones, settles out.

Step 4: ***KEEP IT HOT, HOT, HOT***

The remaining liquid is heated to about 900° F. and sent through a series of distillers that separate it into natural gas, two different qualities of oil, and powdered carbon. The gas is used to fuel the process and the rest goes up for sale. For about 200 tons of turkey bits, the whole shebang takes less than 24 hours.

Boil Water . . . Naturally!

YOU WILL NEED

- A geyser

Don't: ***EXPECT IT TO HAPPEN VERY OFTEN***

Fountains of super-heated water and steam erupting from the earth, geysers are impressively cool and, as a result, end up on film quit a bit. So often, in fact, that it's easy to forget how rare a phenomenon they really are. In reality, there are only about 1,000 geysers on the entire planet. And, while nearly half of those are located in Yellowstone National Park in the state of Wyoming, even going on a visit there isn't a guarantee of experiencing a geyser eruption. Old Faithful and its roughly 45-minute intervals aside, most of these founts aren't particularly predictable. Some can sit dormant for years before erupting. Others might let off steam more regularly, but still stick to intervals lasting from five hours to several weeks.

Don't: *TRY TO FROLIC IN THE FOUNTAIN*

Geyser water is hot. We mean really, really hot. Essentially, geysers form when underground springs encounter a volcanic magma chamber, which heats the water, causing it to expand and move upward. At the same time, the boiling water dissolves bits of the surrounding rock. These minerals can later form plugs that constrict the flow of water to the surface. Trapped behind a plug, the water builds up pressure and gets hotter until it finally breaks through and erupts. The water coming out of geysers could literally boil you alive. Ditto with the hot springs that sit nearby and often share the same plumbing. In fact, Yellowstone's hot springs have killed 19 people. But only one, David Kirwan, was love-stricken enough to intentionally jump in. In 1981, Kirwan was driving through a thermal area in Yellowstone when his friend's dog fell into a pool of + 200° F. water. Kirwan dove in after it. By the time his friends managed to pull him out, he was blind and his skin was peeling off. He died the next day.

Do: *BE A LITTLE SUSPICIOUS*

Between all the super-hot water and the underground magma chamber feeding it, you've gotta ask: What's up with Yellowstone? Turns out, nearly half the park's 3,472 square miles lie inside the caldera, or crater, formed from the most recent of three massive volcanic eruptions, some 650,000 years ago. But, while there is clearly still magma beneath the park, scientists with the United States Geological Survey say another eruption of that magnitude isn't likely. Although Yellowstone's volcanic activity is monitored, the probability of an eruption is about .00014% a year.

Build Your Dream Home

Loosely Modeled after the Three Little Pigs

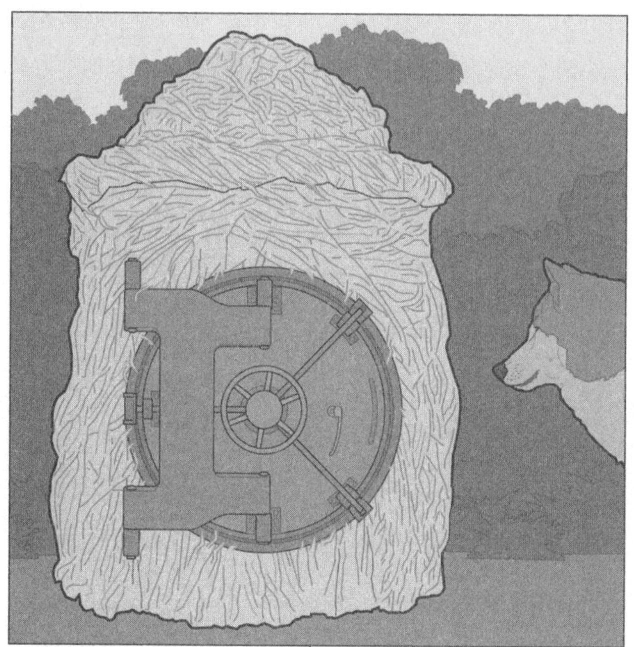

Material: *PAPER*

Pig-Emulating Builder: Elis Stenman, a Massachusetts engineer who, during the 1920s, built a summer cabin entirely out of newsprint. OK, that's not entirely true. The house does have traditional wood framing, a wooden floor, and an altogether average shingled roof. In truth, Stenman only began layering newspaper and varnish on the walls as an attempt to cut down on the cost of insulation. The original plan was to eventually install wooden siding on the outside, but, for some reason, Stenman never got around to that. Instead, he apparently decided to take the paper theme and run with it. And when we say "run," we mean the analogic equivalent of the Boston Marathon. By the time the house was finished in 1924, Stenman had built up hundreds of sheets into a paper wall an inch thick. Even more impressive, he'd decorated with paper as well. All the furniture in the house, from a grandfather clock (which features mastheads from the capital city papers of 48 states) to the fireplace mantel are constructed from tiny rolled paper "logs." The lone exception: a piano, which, unable to construct completely from paper, Stenman opted to coat in a layer of decorative shellac and newsprint.

YOU WILL NEED

- An obsessive personality
- A little bit too much time and/or money

Material: *ONE BIG SANDSTONE OUTCROPPING AND A LOT OF KNICKNACKS*

Pig-Emulating Builder: Alex Jordan—Wisconsinite, designer of "House on the Rock," collector of random crap. According to several sources, Jordan began his odd experiment with building design on a southeastern Wisconsin rock formation in the early 1940s, partly out of familial revenge against architect Frank Lloyd Wright. When Jordan was a boy, his father, a professional architect, had shown a series of building plans to the much more famous Wright. To which, Wright had apparently replied, "I wouldn't hire you to design a cheese crate or a chicken coop." Still cranky about this incident 20 years later, the younger Jordan opted to design his summer retreat as a nose-thumbing mockery of Wright's trademark Japanese-influenced style. But, where Wright preached the gospel of minimalism and taste, Jordan filled the sprawling home with all manner of tacky jumble—from the world's largest carousel, to a room filled with and built from pipe organ parts, to the "Infinity Room," a glass-enclosed corridor that juts out, cantilevered some 300 feet above the neighboring valley.

Material: *CONCRETE*

Pig-Emulating Builder: Civil War veteran, third-party politician, and all-around eccentric Samuel Dinsmoor. After retiring from a life of Populist Party politics and school teaching, Dinsmoor moved to Lucas, Kansas, in 1891. Sixteen years later, he began building a homestead/allegorical masterpiece—which involved several hundred tons of concrete. First off, there was the house, 11 rooms carved from limestone to resemble a log cabin. Surrounding it stands a concrete sculpture garden, the Garden of Eden, with 40-foot trees dripping with vines, giant folk-art figures, and tableaus ripped from the Bible, political cartoons, and Dinsmoor's own mind. Of the latter, some of the most impressive include a crucified "Labor," surrounded by approving figures of a doctor, lawyer, and banker; an octopus-like caricature of a corporate monopoly terrorizing civilians; and Adam and Eve. But, perhaps the most surprising attraction is Dinsmoor himself. Before his death in 1932 he arranged to have his body preserved and encased in glass within a concrete mausoleum—where he can still be seen today.

Be an Astronaut

YOU WILL NEED

- Deodorant
- A barf bag
- To get over any "privacy" issues you might have

WASH YOUR HAIR—VERY CAREFULLY

Hygiene is, shall we say, "difficult" in zero gravity. Baths are a laugh and showers nonexistent—the water would just ball up and float away. Instead, each person on the International Space Station is rationed one pre-moistened wet towel, a couple of dry towels, and several wet-wipes each day. These invaluable supplies are used to give yourself what basically amounts to a sponge bath. As for hair, well, it's not so easy. Anousheh Ansari, who went into space as a tourist with Russian cosmonauts in the fall of 2006, says that space shampoo is dry and rinsing it out of your hair means carefully gathering a ball of floating water around your head inside a plastic bag.

DRINK YOUR FRIEND'S SWEAT

Water is a precious commodity on the International Space Station and every drop is recycled via the station's water conduction unit. And when we say every drop, we mean "every" drop. When astronauts are done exercising each day, they leave their damp towels to float around the station, where the sweat can evaporate, be collected by the conduction unit, and turned into drinking water.

LEARN A NEW LANGUAGE

With missions stretching as long as six months at a time, astronauts on the International Space Station learn a lot about each other, including how to speak in their partners' native language. In fact, most veteran

American astronauts can speak Russian and most veteran cosmonauts can speak English.

TAKE YOUR ASPIRIN

Here's the secret they don't tell you about space travel: It hurts. Spacesickness is common, particularly for first-timers and anybody who launches into a bunch of fancy somersaults before they've had time to get acclimated. As much fun as bathing in space is, you can probably guess how enjoyable it is to hurl. Worse, the effects of weightlessness can really do a number on your body. One symptom is lower back pain. Headaches are another major issue. Without gravity, it's harder for your heart to do its job. Blood pressure drops and your blood doesn't reach your feet as reliably. Instead, it flows to your head, turning your face puffy and red and giving you a headache, just as if you'd been hanging upside down on the monkey bars.

DON'T KISS AND TELL

That's the official NASA stance on whether anyone's ever had sex in space. We may never know for certain whether astronauts and/or their international peers are hooking up up there, but we do know that, if they are, it comes with some less-than-sexy challenges. For one thing, there's no natural convection in zero gravity, so any heat you work up stays with you. At the same time, however, you also tend to sweat more in zero G, making outer space sex both hotter and wetter than that on Earth—and not in a good way. Another problem is that, in zero G, you naturally push away from anything you touch. That means anybody wanting to have sex in space would probably need to be strapped down and strapped together. Oh, and that drop in blood pressure we already mentioned? That would have dire effects on male "egos" galaxy wide.

ENJOY A DRINK, IF YOU ARE RUSSIAN

Alcohol—in small, non-mission-threatening quantities—was always welcome in the old Soviet space station Mir. But, when the Ruskies joined the crew of the ISS they found that American prudery reigned supreme over the heavens. From it's opening in 2000, the ISS was, officially, dry. Predictably, this sort of thing didn't sit well with the hard-working cosmonauts and in

January of 2006, they managed to talk Russian mission control into changing their rules. Good cognac—to be drunk by the thimbleful, as alcohol packs a bigger wallop in space—returned to Russian supply kits. Americans, however, had no such luck. Officially, they're supposed to just watch in jealous sobriety when their Russian pals break out the happy juice.

Quit Smoking

According to the citizens of Nabila, Fiji

YOU WILL NEED

- **Ancient traditions**
- **A new menace**
- **1 pitcher of mildly hallucinogenic punch**

It wasn't until 1986 that the village of Nabila got its first taste of modern health care, but it came along just in time. Within 4 years of opening a new public health clinic, the medical staff realized they had a major crisis on their hands. According to the book *Dying to Quit*, by Janet Brigham, more than 1/3 of all the 238 people on Nabila smoked. In fact, smoking rates had doubled between 1986 and 1990 and hypertension was now running rampant through the islanders. The medical staff pulled out their trusty American Cancer Society posters, but, somehow, the motivational artwork failed to make an appropriate impact. So, what's a dedicated staff to do? Turn to a higher power, of course—the village elders. Informed of the health risk, the elders hit on a sensible solution: Everybody in the entire village would have to stop smoking—effective immediately. And while the whole scheme sounds entirely improbable, the Nabila elders had an ace up their grass skirts. South Pacific island culture has a long-standing tradition, known as *tabu*, by which certain objects, foods, and actions are made spiritually unclean. In the past, *tabu* was usually applied temporarily to a certain group of people, such as forbidding warriors from touching the ladies until after a battle. But, in Nabila, cigarettes were about to become *tabu* permanently for everyone in town. The first step in the ritual involved requiring village puffers to chain-smoke until they got sick. Then came the drinking. But, unlike the average Western pre-cold-turkey binge, this chug-a-lug had some serious symbolic meaning. The beverage of choice was kava, which, unlike anything made in Milwaukee, is actually a mild hallucinogen. And, in South Pacific tradition, this brew also has magical properties. For instance, if you swear an oath with on a swig of kava, you're bound to your promise—on pain of unpleasant circumstances. Nabila's backsliders found this out firsthand. In the four reported cases of relapse, one man tripped and cut himself, another was attacked by a dog, a third ended up with a swollen testicle, and the fourth briefly passed out after mixing tobacco and kava—all of which were attributed to supernatural punishment. Nabila's stop-smoking campaign quickly became a media phenomenon in Fiji, prompting a number of people who didn't even live in the village to join them in *tabu*. In a nearby village, three-fourths of the young people quit smoking in solidarity. Nine months later, Nabila was still smoke-free. And a full two years after that, the only smokers in town were a couple of elderly people who were given a special dispensation and one visiting teenager. In 2006, Nabila received a World No Tobacco Day Award from the World Health Organization, in honor of its continued success.

Get a Better Job

YOU WILL NEED

- **A dream**
- **Another, better, dream**
- **The inspiration and drive to shift from one dream to another**

ACCORDING TO RICHARD PRYOR

You probably wouldn't guess that the comedian best known for scathing, profanity laced (and deeply hilarious) tirades originally set out to market himself as a Bill Cosby-ish nice-guy jokester. Richard Pryor's comedic career actually began in high school, when a teacher made a deal intended to calm down Pryor's class cutup routine. If the budding funny man agreed to behave he was free to stage an in-class performance once a week. Later, these early stabs at comedy blossomed into a full-blown career, just not the one Pryor really wanted. For much of the 1960s, he had a popular routine—playing clubs in classy joints like New York City and Las Vegas, but the Cosby comparisons and the constant string of G-rated one-liners started to wear thin. In 1967, Pryor had a bona-fide road-to-Damascus moment, realizing during a Vegas routine that he hated his jokes and hated the direction his career was heading. So much so, in fact, that he simply walked off stage (and out of the theater) before his set was over. According the Museum of Broadcast Communications, Pryor spent the next two years getting political—he read the works of Malcolm X, hung out with Berkeley intellectuals, and got back in touch with the rougher side of life. More importantly, he found that politics, race, and the seamy underbelly of America could make for a really funny comedy routine. When Pryor re-emerged, nobody but nobody would mistake him for Bill Cosby. By 1975, he had a hit comedy record ("Is It Something I Said?") and was well on his way to f#&@^#!! superstardom.

ACCORDING TO ANDY WARHOL

Andrew Warhola, the son of a Slovak immigrant construction worker, had already changed a lot of things about himself when he made the move from his hometown of Pittsburgh, Pennsylvania, to fabulous New York City in 1949. While attending art school in Pittsburgh, he'd experimented with adopting the name Andre (which didn't stick) and had unceremoniously dropped the "a" from the end of his surname (which did). But, rather than immediately taking the art world by storm, Warhol began his New York career as a lowly freelance graphic designer, illustrating advertisements for things like women's shoes and providing drawings to go along with articles in magazines like *McCalls'* and the *Ladies' Home Journal*. This work, far from being unconnected to his later success as an auteur, actually provided much of the inspiration for it. After all, there's not such a huge leap between drawing women's shoes and drawing cans of Campbell's soup. Another major inspiration: a round-the-world vacation that Warhol took in 1956. Somewhere along the way, the budding artisan decided to drop his traditional "career." When he finally returned to New York, he started pouring his energy into pure artistic pursuits, most of which involved taking the advertising and pop culture icons he'd been illustrating and changing their context, or removing it altogether, to produce an image that was less salesman than statement. One thing Warhol didn't drop from his past life: his mother. Known for her distinct calligraphy style, "Andy Warhol's Mother" was frequently credited (just like that) for her assistance on her son's early work. In fact, from 1952 until her death in 1971, she actually lived with Warhol and was a part of the trendy art scene/ cult he built around himself.

Brew a Lifesaving Cuppa Joe

YOU WILL NEED

- **Coffee beans**
- **A French press, campfire percolator, or some other "Mad Max" style coffeemaker**

JUST AVOID DECAF

That's all there is to it. (And heck, you were probably doing that already anyway.) In 1999, scientists at India's Bhabha Atomic Research Centre put caffeine to the test and discovered that there is a major link between caffeine intake and the body's ability to fight off the effects of radiation. In the study, 471 test mice received injections containing varying amounts of the delicious morning drug, while 196 of their squeaky brethren went cold turkey. Then, all the mice were exposed to gamma radiation, the type of radiation that causes illness, death, and general bad stuff in the wake of a nuclear bomb explosion. The dose was enough to kill a mouse and, in the case of the 196 noncaffeinated mice, it did just that. Of the caffeine-exposed mice, however, 70 percent lived. That's one heck of a causal relationship. The caffeine inoculation works because the drug reacts with hydroxyl radicals, the dangerous molecules that are produced when living cells are exposed to radiation. Instead of raping and pillaging the body's cells and shutting down internal organs, the radicals become basically impotent. So exactly how much coffee should you start throwing back to prepare for a possible nuclear event? Let's just say that Folgers stands to make a killing off this discovery. To protect themselves as successfully as the mice, a 154-pound person would have to drink upwards of 100 consecutive cups of java.

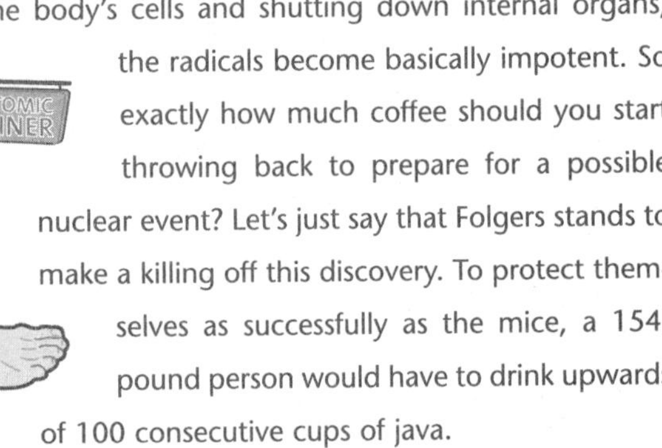

Don't Get Lost

Of course, *you* don't really need a map. You're a navigational god. But, you know, in case you wanted to put one together for the benefit of your less awesome friends and family, we thought we'd offer a few tips.

YOU WILL NEED

- To invent the map

MAKE IT

Illustrating the extent and layout of civilization is a hobby that's almost as old as civilization itself. The oldest drawing believed by many scientists to be a map is a cave painting found in Asia Minor near the modern Turkish city of Ankara. Called Catal Hyuk, this ancient village was depicted two-dimensionally around 6200 BCE in a drawing that included markings for streets, buildings, and landmarks—like the massive volcano that sat right outside of town. Good to know that's there. But, to be fair, researchers are still arguing over whether the drawing from Catal Hyuk represents a real map or merely a painting. To be judicious about this, we'll just say that the earliest definite maps were those that came out of the ancient civilization of Babylon and other societies centered around Mesopotamia. Made between about 2300 and 1500 BCE, these maps also depict city grids and the sites of useful resources like water supplies, farm fields, and hunting grounds.

MAKE IT PORTABLE

Written on clay tablets, the Mesopotamian maps were also the world's first carry-on maps. But, as ahead of their time as the Mesopotamians were, the residents of Micronesia later did them one better by creating lightweight maps that could be easily transported and referred to during ocean voyages. While most Polynesian navigators relied on the stars or virtual maps that had been orally passed down, Micronesians made physical representations of ocean currents and island locations using twigs and shells lashed together with long leaves of grass. No word on whether or not they were difficult to fold.

MAKE IT ACCURATE

Although the earliest maps were certainly innovative, they were lacking somewhat in what you might call "correct detail." Rather than trying to compare them to the work of Rand McNally, you might do better to think of them as the quick directions you'd sketch out on a cocktail napkin. Naturally, the Greeks, Romans, and Chinese were the first groups to really put an emphasis on accuracy when it came to map-making. In fact, by as early as 350 BCE, it was common knowledge in Greece that the Earth was, in fact, round. When the scraggly vestiges of the Roman Empire drifted into the Dark Ages, this tradition was kept alive by Arab scholars—who were helpfully keeping track of what the world really looked like when European cartographers were still putting their energy into picking the right place to draw in the Garden of Eden. Thankfully, some of the worst excesses of the medieval mapmakers are more myth than reality. For instance, despite its inclusion on nearly every faux early C.E. map we can think of, the phrase "Here be dragons" only appears once in real-life, on a 16th century globe, in Latin ("*hic sunt dracones*"), just off the coast of East Asia. For all we know, the cartographers were referring to the presence of mythological beasties in Chinese legend, never intending that anyone would take them seriously.

MAKE IT USEFUL

As maps became more accurate they gained increased political importance. One of the earliest military uses came in England in 1745, after a major coup attempt during which the Scots tried to re-instate the relatives of a deposed king onto the throne. In the wake of this, British Major General William Roy was saddled with the task of mapping Scotland in detail, in the hopes that the maps would help the military better quell any future uprising. To us, this sounds like a job that would be either utterly boring or uncomfortably dangerous (you know how those Scots can get), but Roy came through in the clutch, creating a set of maps so good that they were used for decades. In fact, the Ancient Woodland Inventory of Scotland still swears by the things even today and the techniques Roy pioneered are directly linked to the creation of the Ordnance Survey, one of the largest map-making companies in the world.

Fight the Law . . . and Win

You might think it's futile, but The Man can be bested. You just need to be a quick thinker, like Englishwoman Mary Broad was. In 1767, Mary accosted a rich farm wife on a highway and stole the woman's jewelry and silk bonnet. The haul doesn't seem like much, but this was 18th-century England where capital punishment was very much "in." In fact, Mary's crime was enough to get her sentenced to death, and the only way off the gallows was to agree to ship out for Australia with the first batch of English prisoners being sent there. Mary, along with several hundred other incarcerated women, got sent to Australia to keep the male prisoners (and unmarried guards) "entertained." With no other option, Mary agreed to the deal—but she didn't plan to abide by it.

YOU WILL NEED

- A boat
- Sympathy points

Step 1: *GET MARRIED—FAST*

When the fleet landed in Australia, most of the women drifted into an impromptu "brothel" camp. But not Mary. Instead, she shrewdly hooked up (in the good and legal way) with William Bryant, a prisoner who got special privileges for serving as the prison's head fisherman.

Step 2: *VOTE YOURSELF OFF THE ISLAND*

Despite their position, Mary and William quickly got tired of the prison colony's poor food and deadly animal population. When William was whipped for selling extra fish to other prisoners, the Bryants decided it was time to go. On a moonless night in 1791, William, Mary, their two children, and seven other convicts stole the governor's sailboat and headed for the Dutch-controlled Timor, 3,600 miles away. Amazingly, they made it and for a while lived happily, passing themselves off as shipwreck survivors—until William drunkenly blew their cover.

Step 3: *MAKE THE BEST OF A BAD SITUATION*

The convicts were quickly recaptured and shipped back to England for trial. Along the way, William and both the children died. Depressing events, sure. But when the English press published the story of the brave young mother, the course of Mary's trial took an unexpected turn—her case was picked up by James Boswell. Between his defense, and Mary's rising public popularity, she was granted a full pardon for both the escape and her original crime!

Imitate an Action Hero

Live through Anything

And who better to teach you the basics of survival than nature's supreme survival experts: Bacteria! (Seriously, these things are so survivalist-minded, they might as well have their own militia.)

YOU WILL NEED

- **A foe who underestimates your abilities**
- **Basic survival skills (i.e., ability to light a fire, tie a knot, evolve)**

Step 1: *FIND AN APPROPRIATE TROJAN HORSE*

At first bacteria were afraid, nay, petrified. They kept thinking they could never live when antibiotics were on our side. But now, increasingly, it's looking like they will survive—and it's all our fault. When the first antibacterial drug, penicillin, was introduced to the market in the 1940s, it was hailed as a super-powered cure-all. Naturally, over the years it's been joined by a veritable justice league of equally strong medications. In fact, by the dawn of the 21st century, doctors were able to choose from hundreds of different antibiotics and the public had come to expect a certain level of Howard Hughes-esque cleanliness from their world as heavily promoted by the sale of "anti-bacterial" everything (soaps, hand sanitizers, etc.). As it turns out, this may not have been such a good idea. Why? A little thing called "natural selection."

Step 2: *DO WHAT COMES NATURALLY*

Basically, it works like this. When an antibiotic finds bacteria, it's supposed to kill them. But, sometimes, one of the individual bacterium may have a mutation that makes it just a little stronger. If this happens, that one bacterium can go off and multiply itself into many, many baby bacteria—some of which will have the same resistance factor as its parent. When the group encounters that same antibiotic, far fewer will be killed, leaving behind an even stronger third generation. Eventually, the result is an entire population that's completely unaffected by the antibiotic. It's terrifying, but this scenario becomes more of a reality every time we take antibiotics prescribed for someone else, try to use them to treat a virus like a cold, or take them preventatively when we aren't sick. All these things give bacteria a better chance to evolve just a little bit faster and to build resistance to antibiotics they might not have otherwise encountered. The result: After 50 years of regular antibiotic use, people are once again starting to die from infections like tuberculosis, which we thought we'd conquered. By 2000, there were at least three deadly infections that were resistant to every single antibiotic available.

Step 3: *LOOK BACK AND THINK AHEAD*

Amazingly, bacteria does have some natural predators that can destroy them: viruses known as bacteriophages. Each bacteriophage is specialized to eliminate a specific type or group of bacteria. Once injected into a human, the viruses track down their target bacteria and do their job, which, for a virus, means taking control of the bacteria cell and forcing it to become a zombie-like virus factory until it bursts open and dies, releasing tons of newborn viruses that start the deadly cycle anew. Eventually, these viruses will wipe out the entire bacteria population. It's brutal, but scientists think it might be our best hope against resistant bacteria. Although not yet approved for use on humans by the FDA, bacteriophages are nothing new. Before the advent of antibiotics, they were the cutting edge in health technology and in the former Soviet Union, they remained in regular use long after the rest of the world had switched to penicillin.

OTHER SURVIVORS TO EMULATE:

COCKROACHES

According to a study conducted at the Free University of Brussels in Belgium, cockroaches' millennia-spanning success may be the result of some serious cooperation skills. In 2006, Animal Planet News reported that cockroach society functions rather like a small, disgusting democracy, with large groups of bugs working together to share food and shelter, communicating their intentions via a complicated system involving both touch and scent. .

CHER

Among humans, there's possibly no better example of how adaptation is key to survival—particularly adaptation of one's name. Heck, it's not even entirely clear what Cher's birth name was: some sources reporting it as Cheryl Sarkisian and others as Cheryl LaPiere. Somewhere along the way, Cheryl became Cherylin and, by the time she started recording with future husband Sonny Bono, it was just plain Cher. In keeping with the theme, however, "Sonny & Cher" weren't their original stage names. When the duo first started performing in 1964, they were known as Caesar & Cleo.

Become a Ninja

Q. A ninja:

a) Is a deadly assassin

b) Is a martial arts master with super-cool powers

c) Looks good in black

d) Is not as cool as a pirate, but still pretty darn neat

If you answered anything other than "d," you're going to have spend some time in ninja remedial school. Sadly, most of the things we think we know about ninja come not from reality, but rather from 50 years of really good P.R. The ninja craze was touched off in the 1960s, by the twin forces of Japanese comics and James Bond. Heavily embellished ninja legends had become a staple of early anime, launching a national obsession in Japan that was still going strong when Ian Fleming showed up in Tokyo to do research for his 1964 book, *You Only Live Twice*. Naturally, the assassins appeared in Fleming's finished manuscript and their role was later pumped up by ninja-lovin' screenwriter Roald Dahl for the 1967 film version. From that point on, the whole thing just snowballed into decades of increasingly preposterous film exploits and Internet fad cameos. The truth, Virginia, is that ninjas weren't nearly as cool or as successful as you've been led to believe.

YOU WILL NEED

- Women's clothing

Turns out, Eddie Izzard might have made a pretty good ninja. The earliest ninja-esque legend, dating back to the 8th century C.E., tells the story of Prince Yamato who snuck into a rival's dinner party dressed as a young girl. Some serious flirting and a lot of sake later, Yamato caught the ruler off-guard and killed him with a concealed sword. This may be the first and last time a ninja successfully killed anybody.

- Hand sickle

Back when ninja-ing was in full swing, it was illegal in Japan for anyone other than a samurai to carry a weapon. Thus, real ninja probably weren't going around with a Bat-Belt full of ammunition strapped to their waist. Instead, they likely carried a hand sickle, or kama, a small farming tool that wouldn't have looked out of place on the average village street, but would have provided a practical amount of defense.

- **Pink Slip**

The end of the shogun rivalries in the 17th century brought a new era of peace to Japan—and a new era of unemployment to ninjas. Largely Samurai-style soldiers who engaged in espionage for particular warlords, ninjas were faced with a crisis when the need for spies dried up.

- **Eggs**

Real ninja didn't have super powers. Instead, they had sophomoric practical jokes. The famous ninja ability to disappear is most likely traced to metsubushi, or sight-removing techniques, like filling an eggshell with a mixture of pepper spray, gunpowder, and small explosives. When thrown, the smoky, irritating egg-bombs gave ninjas plenty of time to make a sneaky escape.

YOU WILL *NOT* NEED

- **"I Heart China" banner**

Ninja are often said to have originated in magical Chinese secret societies. But their real origins are a lot more pedestrian. *The Art of War*, written by Chinese general Sun Tzu around the 5th century B.C.E., was history's first military textbook and contained a useful chapter on espionage. Centuries later, Japanese Samurai would put some of Sun Tzu's ideas into practice, combining them with innovations of their own. Essentially, the real ninja's job description was pretty close to that of an FBI agent, including mostly information gathering and infiltration of enemy fortresses.

- **All-black outfit**

Black pajamas scream "I'm a ninja!" So, logically, they probably aren't the best thing to wear when you're actually trying to be sneaky. Real ninjas usually blended in with the groups they were trying to infiltrate, often wearing replicas of the opposing army's uniform and colors. The ninja goth garb can actually be traced to Kabuki theater, where ninja were popular characters in the 1700s. Kabuki stagehands had long worn black outfits to signify that the audience should ignore them. When directors wanted the audience to pretend that ninja characters were also invisible, they dressed those actors in the stagehands' black uniform.

- Notches on your "Assasination Belt"

By all accounts, ninja were pretty good spies and were great at spreading fear and intimidation in the name of their employer. They were not, however, particularly good assassins. While there are tons of plays and stories that praise the ninjas' murderous skill, there's barely any historical evidence of them pulling off a single successful assassination. Embarrassing, unsuccessful attempts, on the other hand, are legion. For instance, according to legend, a group of ninja tried to kill General Oda Nobunaga with a cannon at point-blank range. They missed.

Become a Pirate

We're not talking about becoming just any old pirate, here. That task can be easily accomplished by celebrating International Talk Like a Pirate Day (September 19, tell yer mateys). Instead, we're discussing piracy as entrepreneurship: how to turn your love of rum, swords, theft, and not bathing into a multimillion dollar empire. It's like *What Color Is Your Parachute?* for people with a flexible moral compass. Your guide on this voyage is Cheng I Sao, history's most financially successful pirate.

YOU WILL NEED

- 1 face (preferably the sort that can inspire thousands of grimy, dangerous men into action)
- The will to whip them into shape when your face doesn't do the trick
- Business acumen
- 1 husband to leave you his empire in his will

First: *QUIT YOUR CURRENT JOB.* For Cheng I Sao, that was prostitution. She gave her two-weeks notice in 1801 after marrying Cheng, a pirate captain who worked the South China Sea. For her new career, Cheng I Sao negotiated one heck of a good contract. She agreed to the marriage on one condition: that she share equally in her new husband's power and be allowed to help him gain more wealth. Add to that her legendary beauty and there was no way the captain could say no.

Second: *DEMONSTRATE YOUR LEADERSHIP SKILLS.* Cheng I Sao worked alongside her husband for 6 years and when he died in 1807, she refused to fade into the background like a "proper" widow. She did, however, demonstrate a keen ability to delegate. Her first act as leader was to appoint her husband's second-in-command, Chang Pao Tsai, official Captain of the Fleet. Meanwhile, she focused on business, military strategy, and the enormous task of governing a growing body of ruffians.

Third: *INNOVATE OR DIE.* In the years after her husband's death, Cheng I Sao expanded his Red Flag Fleet until she controlled almost all the piracy in the region and employed more men than most countries' navies. She branched out from simple attack-and-pillage jobs to blackmail, extortion, and protection schemes and forged economic alliances with mainland farmers to make sure her crews were well fed. She also made sure they were well behaved. Her code of conduct prescribed beheading for a disobeyed order. She also protected female prisoners. Ugly women were to be returned to shore at no cost to their families. And while pretty captives were auctioned off to the crew, their purchase was considered a binding marriage—if a pirate cheated on his new bride, Cheng I Sao had him killed.

Finally: *RETIRE IN STYLE.* Unlike many an ill-fated male pirate, Cheng I Sao evaded Chinese, British, and Portuguese authorities so successfully that they eventually just gave up. In 1810, the Chinese government gave her a pardon in exchange for peace. Fewer than 400 of her several thousand men received any punishment at all, and a mere 126 were executed. The rest kept their booty AND were offered military jobs.Cheng I Sao married Chang Pao and opened a gambling house. She died in her sleep in 1844, a 69-year-old grandma.

Gain Superpowers

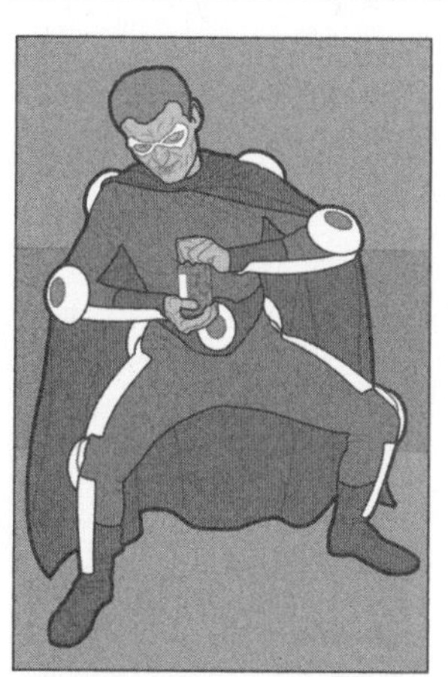

GAIN SUPER STRENGTH

If Japanese robotics expert Yoshiyuki Sankai has his way, super strength will soon be just a bionic exoskeleton away. Sankai is the inventor of a system designed to give the injured, paralyzed, or simply wimpy a chance to move in ways they never thought possible. The system consists of a mechanical suit that straps onto the wearer's limbs and a computer system housed in a small fanny pack. (Hey, nobody ever claimed science was fashion conscious.) Sensors in the suit pick up bio-electrical impulses, telltale signals that the brain has just asked the body to do something. The suit then moves with, or, in some cases, for the wearer's body, allowing them to walk with ease and lift objects heavier than they'd be able to do on their own. Sankai introduced the suit at the 2005 World Expo in Aichi, Japan, where it drew rave reviews and got people buzzing about when they'd be able to buy one for themselves. When it does hit shelves, Sankai's invention is expected to cost between $14,000–$19,000. In fact, the only thing wrong with the suit is the name Sankai gave it: the Hybrid Assistive Limb, or HAL for short. So while the suit will be making the elderly and disabled very happy, it's also likely to make some Stanley Kubrick fans very nervous.

HAVE X-RAY VISION

Like many former readers of comic books, we were intrigued by the promises of the X-ray Spex in our youth. And, while they didn't work exactly as advertised (we never did see anybody's underpants) they were nifty in their own right. Instead of actually allowing us to see through things, the glasses gave the illusion of seeing through things. The "lenses" were actually two pieces of cardboard with a feather sandwiched between them. When you hold your hand up to the light and looked through the hole punched in the center, you'd see the darker image of the feather superimposed on your body—creating the illusion of seeing bones. So yeah, great way to freak out your friends (particularly the gullible and/or drunk ones). Another way to blow their minds: Introduce them to Natasha Deminka. In 1997, the then 10-year-old Russian began claiming to see people's insides. It wasn't exactly X-ray vision; Deminka claimed that her powers gave her the ability to identify illness or injury inside the bodies of anyone she looked at. Naturally, Europe's supermarket checkout tabloids fell in love with her. Since 2004, despite numerous debunkings, she's toured the continent and America diagnosing (whether correctly or not) illnesses as she goes.

Thwart a Bioterrorist Attack

YOU WILL NEED

- Some llamas

Step 1: *RECOGNIZE THE AWESOMENESS THAT IS THE LLAMA*

Push those vile stereotypes out of your mind. Llamas are more than just South American walking sweaters. For one thing, they jump high enough to warrant a competitive circuit. They also make excellent guard animals for smaller beasts, like alpacas and sheep, and, if the citizens of South America are to be believed, they make a pretty good steak, too.

Step 2: *GET YOUR LLAMA TO SUBMIT TO A BLOOD TEST*

Granted, this will probably get you spit on (they do that when they're cranky), but, according to some scientists at the U.S. Naval Research Laboratory in Washington, D.C., that blood sample may be worth going through a roll or two of extra-absorbent paper towels. As it turns out, llama blood contains molecules that may one day be able to help soldiers, scientists, and city officials set up an early warning system against the tiniest weapons of terror—biological agents like anthrax or small pox. Currently, if one of these diseases were to be let loose, it would be difficult for the authorities to know anything was wrong until innocent people started turning up sick. But, there might be a better way to catch these predators—and it's in the llama blood.

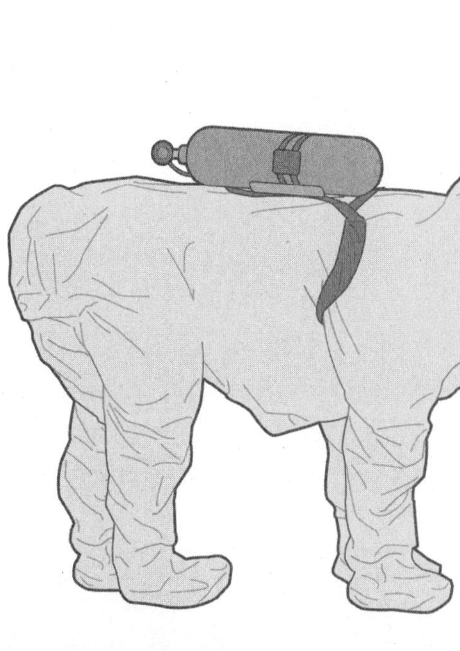

Step 3: *CONVERT THE BLOOD INTO A BIOWEAPON DEFENSE SYSTEM*

The secret: antibodies, tiny molecules that float around in the bloodstreams of almost all animals. On an average day, these antibodies can be found putting in hours as a major player in your immune system. Thanks to antibodies, your body (or, hypothetically, the body of a bird, bat, or llama) can keep a "memory" of the diseases, allergens, and other intruders it encounters. Then, if the same infiltrator shows up again, it will match up to the record stored by the antibodies and your body will immediately know how to fight it. For a while now, scientists have used genetically altered antibodies to help identify and fight specific diseases. But these treatments always ran into a common problem: Antibodies were just too delicate to be of much use outside a hospital. Enter the llama. A December 2006 report by LiveScience described how, along with sharks and camels, llamas have extraordinarily tough and hardy antibodies, capable of sustaining exposure to temperatures as high as 200° F. This discovery has given the U.S. naval researchers hope of perfecting antibody-based sensors that could be distributed around cities and successfully identify the first signs of biochemical warfare.

Drive a Tank

Driving a tank is every destructive little child's personal goal. But with age comes maturity, and with maturity comes the realization that getting a hold of one of these puppies is going to be a little difficult. For all those tankophiles who just aren't ready to make a personal commitment to the military, we offer the following tips for getting yourself behind the wheel:

CHECK YOUR NEIGHBORS' MAIL

It may seem a bit hopeless, but the key is to not be fooled by misleading labels. After all, what are the chances that the Johnsons are really getting a 3,500-ton package of Belgian chocolates? This lesson would have come in mighty handy to the German army in 1915, when the first British tanks were shipped over to join the World War I combat in France. Developed by the British and originally christened "land ships,"

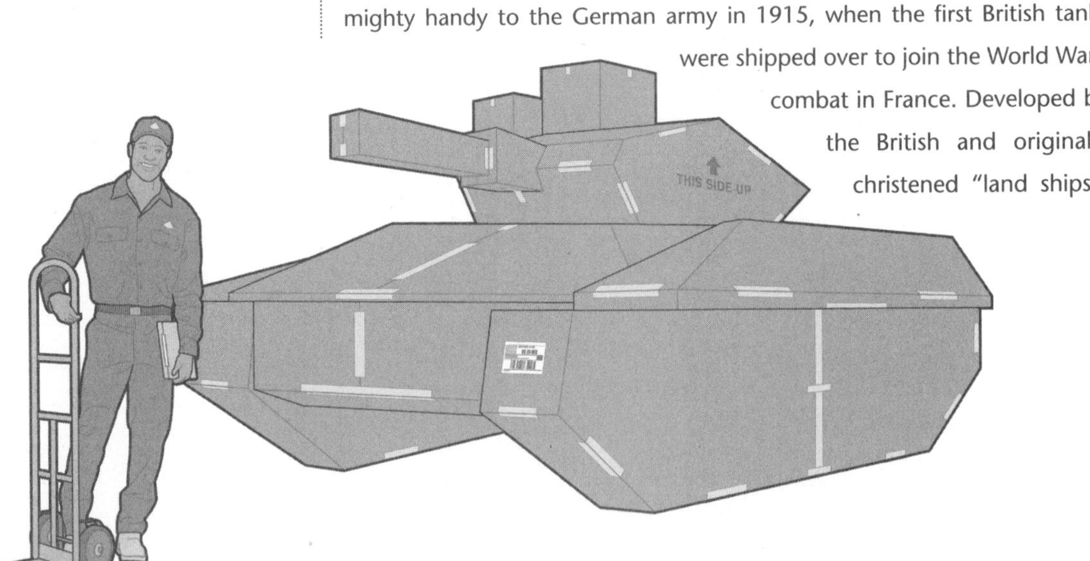

the new weapons were sent by train to the front lines. Fearing those trains might fall into enemy hands, the British military changed the name from the too-accurate "landship" to "tank," a name that implied the shipment of weapons actually contained water cisterns. Very sneaky. In fact, the British turned out to be too sneaky for their own good. Because of the secrecy surrounding the tank's development, the men leading the Army infantry divisions that were actually supposed to work with the tanks didn't know what to do with them or how to use them in battle. During the tank's first few battles, these early tanks would end up cut off from their foot soldiers, resulting in both man and machine being easily defeated.

TRY AMAZON.COM

Say you wanted to combine the thrill of tank driving with the social experience of a really good kegger, then what? In 2002, a California design firm came up with the perfect solution: the JL421 Badonkadonk—an 1,100-pound armored vehicle with roomy plush interior, killer hot-rod lighting, and a state-of-the-art sound system. Although normally focused on graphics and furniture design, NAO Design put together the prototype Badonkadonk as a publicity gimmick, formally launching it at the August 2002 Burning Man Festival after several trial runs around the Stanford party scene. More productive uses have since been discovered; the "Donk" is used by the Stanford Band drum section to transport heavy equipment (and intimidate rival teams) on game days and in 2005, the designers added a pyrotechnical system—including flamethrowers (which we assume to be very useful). Sadly, the vehicle isn't street-legal. And while it can pull 40 mph, NAO Design has yet to sell one of these bad boys, meaning there's still a chance to be the first kid in your block (nay, hemisphere) to own one. A single Badonkadonk will set you back $20,000 on Amazon.com, shipping and handling not included.

Be an Army of One

YOU WILL NEED

- A weapon

A truly effective singleton soldier would need some sort of weaponry that would allow him or her to take out/effectively control large numbers of enemy combatants. And sure, while you could get this effect from one guy, a big red button, and a Patriot missile, we're thinking of something a little more nuanced. Perhaps, even, a little less inherently deadly. Luckily, the Pentagon is already on top of this one. In late 2006, they unveiled the Active Denial System, a weapon that looks like a small vehicle-mounted radar dish but packs a big crowd-control wallop. Essentially, anyone in the path of the ADS will end up feeling like their skin is on fire. The result: one quickly dispersed group of potential assailants. The device works thanks to millimeter waves, the less dangerous, easier-to-control cousins of the microwaves you use in your house every day. Like microwaves, milliwaves heat things up. Unlike microwaves, however, they can't penetrate the skin, so there won't be any awkward cooking of internal organs. Instead, milliwaves just make your skin hurt and, thus, make you want to get away from the ADS very quickly.

◆ **Some fancy togs**

In the future, a soldier's uniform will have more useful functions than just being a great way to pick up dates. The Defense Advanced Research Projects Agency, sort of the American military's equivalent of Q from *James Bond,* is currently working on several different technologies that could be incorporated into clothing while simultaneously cutting down on the sherpalike loads (between 60 to 70 pounds) that soldiers in the field currently have to haul around. Among the many upgrades in the works are:

- Cloth that can stop bleeding, either by tightening like an insta-tourniquet or sending directed heat to cauterize blood vessels
- Solar power cells, sewn or laminated right into tents or bags, that can cut down on the number of batteries soldiers have to tote around for their ever-expanding electrical arsenal
- Armor made from nanotechnology fibers that have the same weight as cloth. When hit by something, however, (a bullet, let's say) it becomes instantly impenetrable.

◆ **A medical mascot**

Specifically, the squirrel. According to *Wired* magazine blogs editor Noah Shachtman, DARPA also has it's eye on adapting the hibernation techniques of everybody's favorite furry little tree dwellers into technology that could allow severely wounded soldiers to survive longer—giving medical crews a better chance of treating them in time. Turns out, when squirrels hibernate their heart rates slow to no more than 10 beats per minute; their breathing slows dramatically, and their bodies become so coid that they feel dead. If an injured human could do the same thing, she'd stop bleeding and would basically become a soldier-scicle, ready to be shipped back to better-equipped hospitals well behind the front lines.

Survive an Asteroid Impact

Oh, this isn't something you worry about, tough guy? It should be. In 1992, NASA scientists used data gathered from astronomical surveys and analysis of old impact craters around the globe to calculate the chances of Earth being hit by an asteroid at least .62 of a mile wide (i.e., big enough to cause mass mortality and threaten civilization as we know it). Turns out, one of these puppies smashes into us every 500,000 years or so, meaning that every year there's a 1-in-500,000 chance of being hit. Not intimidating enough? Think of it this way: Assuming a 70-year lifespan, every person (and that means you) has a 1-in-7000 chance of a major impact event happening in their lifetime. In comparison, the chances of you dying in an airplane crash are only 1 in 20,000. Now that we've got you sweating, let's talk survival.

Step 1: *SPOT THE HARBINGER OF DOOM*

You'll no doubt be pleased to discover that we're already paying people to do this. Yes, as you sit here reading (and growing increasingly paranoid), scientists around the world are scanning the heavens for the asteroid that could wipe us out. Heading up this effort is Spacewatch, an American program based at the Kitt Peak National Observatory near Tucson, Arizona. Since 1980, the scientists at Kitt Peak have been discovering, tagging, and tracking Near Earth Objects (NEOs), the common term for any asteroid or comet whose path brings it uncomfortably close to Earth. Then, in the early 90s, the system became highly automated, as the observatory's powerful telescope was fitted with a giant camera that snapped up pictures of anything moving through the sky. Once spotted, an object's orbit is calculated, essentially giving us an early warning detection system. Spacewatch really got to flex its muscles in April 1999, when preliminary calculations of a new asteroid's orbit placed it smack in the middle of Earth by the late 2020s.

Unfortunately, the asteroid immediately moved right into the glare of the Sun, making it difficult to do a more accurate study for a number of months. When the object finally came back into view, the Spacewatch team was able to determine that the asteroid wasn't going to hit Earth after all. Instead, it's expected to pass within 19,000 miles of us on August 7, 2027. That doesn't sound too worrisome, until you realize that the Moon is about 238,000 miles away. In space, 19,000 miles may as well be grazing distance.

Step 2: *NEUTRALIZE IT*

So what's our plan for stopping an asteroid once we spot it? Um, have you seen *Armageddon*? Yeah, that's about it. No, really. Since 1967, the official government-approved method for asteroid stoppage has involved detonating nuclear warheads alongside the offending space rock in hopes of scooching it over and out of our way. According to computer modeling, this plan—farfetched as it may sound—has a 90-percent estimated success rate. The only real problem is making sure we know enough about the asteroid's composition and size that we don't go overkill on the nukes and end up exploding one big deadly asteroid into thousands of small, still-not-so-great asteroids. There is one other idea floating around, however. Dr. David Williams, from London's University College, has proposed a plan to move an asteroid by landing solar powered engines on its surface. Light from the sun would charge up the engines, powering an ion gun that would slowly and steadily push the offending asteroid out of Earth's path.

SUCCESS! Proceed to Step 3a: *CELEBRATE*

At this point (per Steve Martin's Christmas wish) all the children of the world join hands and sing together in the spirit of harmony and peace.

FAILURE! Proceed to Step 3b: *PANIC*

At this point all humanity freaks the heck out and civilization disintegrates beneath a pile of sweating, clawing masses desperate for their own survival. We, on the other hand, would be down in the *mental_floss* emergency bunker, reading up on the dinosaurs and our ancient mammalian ancestors—both of which survived cataclysmic asteroid impacts and went on to flourish. Scientists now think that the massive extinction event that occurred about 210 million years ago was caused by an asteroid, possibly the one that landed around that same time near Manicouagan, Quebec, Canada. Roughly 90 percent of the Earth's life forms died out at that time, but out of the ashes came the dinosaurs, which then went on to rule the world (in their own sloppy way) for the next 140 million years. Then, around 65 million years ago, at the end of the Cretaceous Period, another die-off took down the dinos, along with 60 percent of their contemporary species. This, too, was likely caused by asteroid impact, probably at Chicxulub in Mexico's Yucatan Peninsula, where a massive crater suggests that the Earth was hit by an asteroid nearly 10 miles wide. Among the survivors of Chicxulub were the tiny varmints that made up the first mammal populations. And we know how successful they've been. Unfortunately, nobody really knows how either dinosaurs or mammals survived when all the species around them were being wiped out. But that, our friend, is what research is for.

Dodge Bullets

According to the Boxers

YOU WILL NEED

- **To learn kung fu**
- **To believe in your invincibility**
- **To not be white (sorry, David Carradine)**

Never let another person tell you that *Crouching Tiger, Hidden Dragon* is totally unrealistic. They've obviously never come face-to-face with the members of I-he Chuan, the Society of the Righteous and Harmonious Fists. Around the end of the 19th century, China was going through some serious social and cultural upheaval as Western influence and power began to disrupt traditional life. In 1900, several small secret societies banded together to fight back against foreigners and foreign culture. Unfortunately, they chose to take that "fight" thing literally instead of symbolically, touching off a wave of horrific violence against missionaries, colonialists, and any Western sympathizers. The British called these revolutionaries "Boxers," after a glaring Western misinterpretation of the kung fu fighting style. But they were more than just a bunch of angry martial artists. The secret societies that made up the Boxer Rebellion also

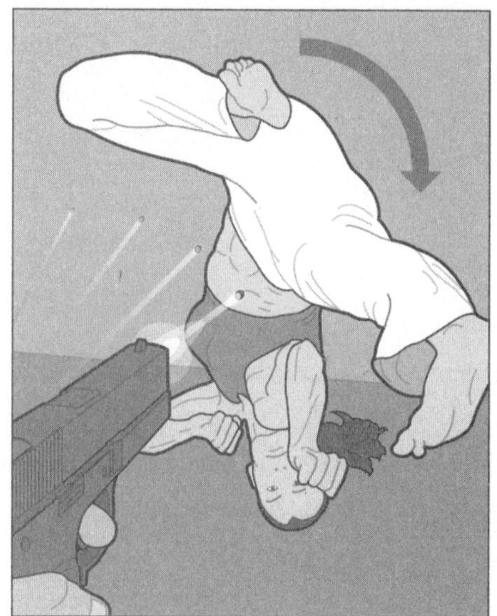

had a highly charismatic religious element—involving public ceremonies full of ecstatic dancing and spirit possession. Through these displays, the Boxers hoped to acquire special powers, including flight and the ability to breathe fire. And, when the firearm-less Boxers managed to push the British army to retreat behind the walls of Peking, many Chinese attributed their success to their "iron shirt" power, the ability to withstand and evade bullets. These magic claims were bolstered by real-life incidents during the conflict, such as the time an Austrian machine-gun regiment opened fire on a group of Boxers and failed to kill a single one. Of course, Boxers did get shot during other battles. But since the supposed strength of an iron shirt depended on the fighter's technique and belief, any Boxer who was killed could be written off as being unworthy. Unfortunately, this staunch belief in supernatural powers came back to bite the Boxers in their, uh, boxers when an international army of reinforcements showed up to defend the British. Faced with an even larger hail of bullets, the iron shirt ability failed to withstand the assault.

Be a Spy

According to Daniel Defoe, inventor of the novel and father of journalism

YOU WILL NEED

- Flexible loyalties
- A good cover story
- To spend some time in prison

Step 1: *GET RECRUITED*

In 1702, Defoe published a little pamphlet called "Shortest Way with the Dissenters," a satirical tract in which he suggested that hanging was probably the best way to deal with religious odd-ducks. The catch: Defoe himself was a dissenter, being a Presbyterian in Anglican England. Blissfully unaware of the irony, many religious conservatives (known as Tories) initially welcomed Defoe's ideas. As you might expect, the bliss turned to rage when they realized they'd been had. In keeping with the then-lack of freedom of speech, Defoe was arrested, pilloried, and thrown into prison—where he probably would have spent a good long while had it not been for the intervention of Robert Harley, Earl of Oxford. Sort of the M to Defoe's Bond, Harley arranged for the writer's release—provided he went to work as an informant and propagandist for the Tory government. Although Defoe clearly opposed the Tories, he opposed staying in prison more and quickly agreed.

Step 2: *KEEP UP A GOOD FRONT*

Defoe spied for the Tories for the next 20 years, but his writing was so prolific that few suspected his seedier activities. While on Her Majesty's secret service, Defoe managed to simultaneously run eight different newspapers—most of the contents of which he wrote himself. Along the way, he invented or perfected just about every recognizable aspect of the modern newspaper: from investigative reporting, to candid obituaries, to the gossip column. And, as if he weren't busy enough, in 1719, Defoe invented the modern novel when he published *Robinson Crusoe.* Of course, he also wrote plenty of Tory propaganda, both in *The Review*, one of his many papers, and in numerous pseudonymous tracts. He also apparently spent a great deal of time buddying up to England's Catholic community and reporting on their activities to Robert Harley. However, his public writing career overshadowed his private cloak-and-dagger work to such a degree that it wasn't until the 19th century that anyone was able to prove he was a spy.

Step 3: *DON'T BE AFRAID TO SWITCH SIDES*

During his career as a Tory spy, Defoe managed to royally tick off the opposing Whig party plenty of times. In fact, once, the Whigs actually sued him over a series of libelous pamphlets—and won—resulting in another prison term for Defoe. Amazingly, however, this second stint in the pokey also led to a job offer. For a period of time, Defoe worked as a double agent, writing (we assume poorly) for the Tory journals while secretly working for the Whigs. Then, when the Tories lost power, he spied for the Whigs exclusively.

Break out of Prison

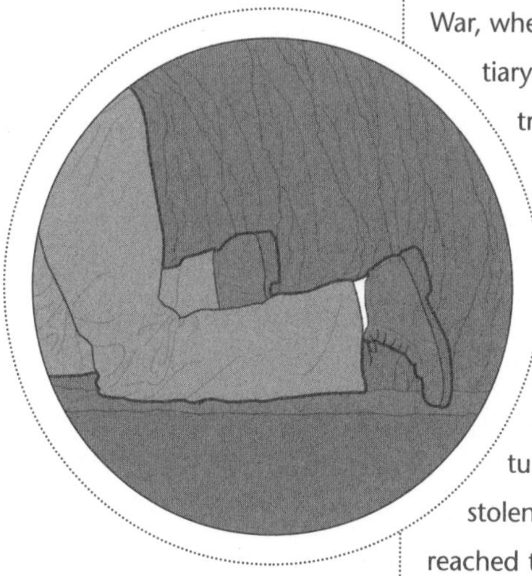

Method 1: *BY TUNNEL*

You can get as fancy as you want, but a good, solid tunnel is still the most reliable method of prison escape. It's tradition, the kind of thing you'd learn from your grandpappy—provided you came from that sort of family. In fact, the most successful tunnel escape in American history dates back to the Civil War, when 109 Yankee officers dug their way out of a Confederate penitentiary. To be fair, Libby Prison in Richmond, Virginia, wasn't exactly Alcatraz. A former warehouse, Libby didn't have actual cells. Instead, hundreds of prisoners were kept in squalor in eight 103-x-42-foot rooms. And while the yard around the prison was heavily guarded, the rooms, apparently, weren't so much. In 1863, a group of officers realized that they could access an abandoned basement by prying through the brick wall of the kitchen room. Over a series of months, they spent their nights digging a narrow tunnel into the basement wall using their hands, clamshells, and stolen tools. By February of 1864, they'd dug enough that the tunnel reached to the far side of a board fence, across the street from the prison. On February 9, the original 14 conspirators, plus one friend each, crawled out of the tunnel and walked off as casually as possible into the night. An hour later, an associate began spreading the word to the rest of the inmates. Things went pretty well at first, but as dawn crept near, the prisoners bum-rushed the tunnel and Confederate guards realized something was amiss. Of the 109 who escaped, 48 were recaptured. The rest hiked through more than 50 miles of frozen swamp to cross Union lines at Williamsburg.

Method 2: *IN DISGUISE*

Disguises were also a favorite tactic of Civil War prisoners. In July 2003, National Geographic News reported that it was common for Confederate prisoners housed at Illinois's Camp Douglas to escape by dressing up as members of the camp's black staff. Given that they were just darkening their faces with charcoal, the similarity sounds a little implausible today, but apparently the plan worked well (and often) enough that Camp Douglas officials stopped hiring African-American laborers. Some of the boldest disguise escapes come from another P.O.W. facility—Germany's Colditz Castle. A former fortress-turned-mental asylum, the Castle was first commandeered by the Nazis to house political prisoners, then treasonous German officers, then Allied prisoners—the "difficult cases" who kept escaping from other prisons. In hindsight, putting them all together maybe wasn't the best idea. Within a year of its 1939 opening, there were so many escapes brewing simultaneously that the inmates appointed "escape officers," men who sacrificed their own chance at freedom in the name of ensuring that everyone else's plans succeeded. Their key job: Making sure that disparate escape attempts didn't fatally intersect. Using costumes from the camp's theater (the prisoners' 1941 spectacular "Ballet Nonsense" was supposedly excellent), various individuals attempted escapes dressed as the Castle's electrician, guards, and even the camp Kommandant. In June 1941, a French Lieutenant named Boule nearly made it out dressed as a woman. Boule's drag act was apparently so good that when he dropped his watch on the way out, a British officer attempted to return it to "her." Unfortunately, this got the attention of the guards who then noticed Boule's unlady-like 5-o'clock shadow.

Method 3: *THE WAY YOU CAME IN*

In the 1970s, white anti-apartheid activists Tim Jenkin, Alex Moumbaris, and Stephen Lee were sent to prison for their political activism. And not just any prison. At the time, South Africa's Pretoria Local Prison was the sort of place Alcatraz wished it could be. And yet, from the moment they got in, the three men were looking for a way out. In 1979, they finally found it. Over the course of two years, the men taught themselves lockpicking and made replicas of several of the keys they'd need to escape. They also fashioned street clothes by retailoring their own prison pants into khaki bellbottoms and using spare prison gloves and shirts to make casual hats. On the night of December 11, 1979, they put their planning to work and—without any violence or even a single confrontation with a guard—unlocked the ten doors between themselves and freedom, then simply walked out.

Survive the Witness Protection Program

YOU WILL NEED:

- Assistance finding housing in your new community
- $60,000 a year in subsistence payments
- 1 reasonable job opportunity
- Identity documents
- Counseling (naturally)

Don't worry, all this comes standard with the Witness Protection Program

Created by the Organized Crime Control Act of 1970, the Witness Protection Program does exactly what the movies say—hide witnesses from vengeful thugs by giving them new identities. Since its inception, some 17,000 people have used the program—and no witness who followed the program guidelines has ever been harmed. In that spirit, we've provided this helpful list of "don'ts" guaranteed to make any government-funded moving adventure a little more pleasant.

Don't: *HIDE OUT IN ENGLAND*

Actually, the chances are pretty slim. To be in the Witness protection program, you have to be, well, under protection, in this case by federal marshals, who don't travel abroad. Even so, you should take our advice to heart because, unlike America's federally organized system, Great Britain's version of the Witness Protection Program is handled by individual police forces—and, apparently, this does not always work out for the best. In 2000, Alan Decabral, a witness to a gangland murder, was shot in a parking lot after living under Kent police protection for less than a year. And another witness, Thomas McCartney, charged police in Northern Ireland with failing to even give him his promised identity papers. Part of the problem is that most British police forces don't require witnesses to sever ties with former friends—let that be a lesson to you.

Don't: *COMMIT YOUR OWN CRIMES*

Seventeen percent of all protected witnesses commit a crime while under protection—including the first one. Joseph "The Animal" Barboza became the first person to use the WPP after testifying against the mafia in 1968. Given the name "Joe Bentley," he was moved to California where the FBI enrolled him in cooking school. But, in 1971, he ended up on trial for first-degree murder. The trial, and the ensuing conviction, blew Barboza's cover and he was shot in 1976, shortly after being paroled.

Don't: *INVITE YOUR "OLD FRIENDS" TO VISIT*

Life in a new city can be lonely sometimes, but it's probably best not to call up the old buds you left behind. Unfortunately, Brenda Paz, a 17-year-old witness against a notorious nationwide gang called MS-13, did just that in 2003. According to a 2005 article in *Newsweek*, Pas was hiding under a new identity in a Minnesota Embassy Suites hotel room when she invited two-carloads worth of MS-13 members to come check out the hotel's hot tub. Within days, she was dead.

Blow Stuff Up

Oh, sure, you could just go buy some fireworks, but where's the fun in that? To really leave your smoking, blackened mark on history there are two things you've just got to have.

---

1) *A DEDICATED STAFF*

Don't make the mistake of thinking you can do this alone. There's a reason James Bond's archenemies always have hordes of minions. Or, on a less intentionally evil note, think of the Manhattan Project. To build the world's first nuclear bomb, the U.S. government eventually ended up employing more than 130,000 people over the course of 5 years. And you wouldn't catch a single one of them slacking off on the job—not even for legitimate health concerns. For instance, Elizabeth Riddle Graves, who worked at Los Alamos, New Mexico, developing key parts of the bomb's core, didn't let her pregnancy stand in the way of science. In fact, when she went into labor at the lab, she first finished the series of experiments she was working on before heading to the hospital. In retrospect the whole "baby + Los Alamos" thing doesn't seem like such a great idea, but those were simpler times and the point is, she cared. Almost as important are the staff members who will stick by you, and your vision, long after things go boom. Alfred Nobel invented dynamite and then assuaged his conscience by setting up a fund for peace awards—but had it not been for his youngest engineering assistant and executor Ragnar Sohlman, the name "Nobel" would still be synonymous with destruction. When the inventor died in 1898, his vast estate was stored in numerous bank accounts sprinkled through eight different countries. And while his will called for the money to go toward the Nobel Prize, some members of his family had other ideas of how it might be spent. To fulfill his boss's last request, young Ragnar armed himself with a gun and sped (relatively, this was the 19th century) from city to city collecting the dough, with Nobel's greedy relatives in hot pursuit. Then, after managing to withdraw all the funds and put them in a single Swiss bank vault, he spent the next 3 years fighting legal disputes before the first Nobel Prizes could finally be awarded in 1901. His descendant, Michael Sohlman, is the current executive director of the Nobel Foundation. You can't put a price on employees like that.

2) *CREATIVE INNOVATION*

Innovation can take many forms. Sometimes, you build off the work of others—like in the development of the car bomb. The first vehicle-based bombardment, according to Mike Davis, author of *Buda's Wagon: A Brief History of the Car Bomb,* actually involved a horse cart and was the creation of an Italian-American Anarchist named Mario Buda. In September of 1920, Buda took his horse-cart bomb to the streets of New York City, leaving the contraptions across the street from the J. P. Morgan Company. Just after noon, his vehicle exploded, taking 40 bystanders (and the poor horse) along with it. More than 200 people were injured, but the real target of the attack—J. P. "Robber Baron" Morgan himself—was completely unharmed. It would be another 27 years before the concept he developed really took off, however. Davis believes that the first modern car bomb exploded on January 12, 1947, when a fascist paramilitary Jewish organization known as the Stern Gang drove a truck full of explosives into a British police station in what was then Palestine. Other times, however, innovation requires a little more imagination. During World War II, armchair generals often sent their "great" combat ideas to the U.S. military—and most were filed in the wastebasket. But one concept, the brainchild of Pennsylvania dental surgeon Lytle S. Adams, did make it into production. Dr. Adams big idea: bats. On January 12, 1942 (we don't know what the deal is with January 12 and explosions), the doctor sent a letter to the White House proposing a system of bat bombs. According to records, the plan was to fill a bomblike canister with hibernating bats and then drop the canister from a plane. Slowed by a parachute, the canister would open and the bats (somehow awakened) would fly out—each one carrying a tiny time-delayed napalm explosive. Impressively, the military spent 2 years and $2 million on "Project X-Ray" before deciding it was unfeasible.

Wrestle an Alligator

YOU WILL NEED

- **1 alligator, unsedated and unbowed**
- **1 person, just a little bit crazy**
- **1 rope, preferably strong**

Step 1: *CHECK THE CLASSIFIEDS*

In 2000, members of the Seminole tribe near Hollywood, Florida, put an ad in a local paper. They were looking for a new alligator wrestler. While mano-y-gator conflict is nothing new to the Seminoles (the leathery beasts were once a valuable—and traditionally hand-caught—food source), it's only recently that the tribe has had such hard luck finding people willing to jump in there (i.e., the swamp) and go for it (i.e., pin several-hundred-pound, sharp-toothed creatures to the ground with only their soft and presumably tasty bodies). However, this isn't necessarily a bad thing. Wrestling alligators for the benefit of white tourists used to be one of the few Seminole-friendly job markets in Florida, but that's changed. Seminoles now have improved access to higher education and better paying (and significantly less lethal) jobs. They also tend to own their own tourist attractions now, instead of working for outsiders. All of this adds up to fewer Seminoles willing to meet the continued tourist demand for alligator wrestling. And, thus, the need for a classified ad.

Step 2: *DON'T EXPECT A GREAT PAY SCALE*

Answering the ad, and ultimately winning the gig, was 32-year-old Greg Long. By November 10, 2000, Long was wrestling alligators for $8 an hour. Yes, believe it or not, this dangerous job pays only a little better than a nice, safe McDonalds' burger-flipper position. Tips are recommended.

Step 3: *EXPECT TO GET BIT*

The "wrestling" in alligator wrestling is something of a misnomer. Rather than thrashing about Greco-Roman (or even WWF) style, an alligator wrestler's main goal is to catch an alligator from a pool or pit and then bind its jaws shut with a rope. Along the way, they might perform a few tricks, such as carefully setting their chin on the gator's upturned maw, all while explaining a few interesting tidbits about the animals' habits and biology to the crowd. Despite not being nearly as violent as it sounds, all alligator wrestlers will most likely be bitten at some point. Capturing and pinning a 'gator requires a significant amount of strength and timing. One wrong move, and your arm or leg could become lunch. In 2006, an alligator took a real-estate baron down a peg. Florida land-developer Ronald Bergeron suffered several shattered finger bones after he tried to wrestle an alligator during a party. The gator actually dragged Bergeron underwater briefly before party guests were able free him.

Be MacGyver

Object: *PAPERCLIP*

Use it to: *FIGHT THE NAZIS*

After the Nazis took over Norway during World War II, there was only one way to tell a Norwegian freedom fighter from a Norwegian Hitler sympathizer: Look to the lapel. If the Norseman was staunchly standing by his king and country, rest assured he'd have a paperclip fastened to his collar. In fact, accessorizing with a paperclip was how underground resistance fighters were able to identify each other. While Norway is definitely a quirky place, the choice of "paperclip equating patriotism" wasn't made just to be silly. The device's inventor, Johan Vaaler, had become a Norwegian cultural icon ever since he'd obtained the first paperclip patent back in 1899. It's no wonder then that the paperclip became a symbol of Norwegian pride, similar to the American bald eagle, only more easy to fit inside an office desk.

Object: ***PEZ DISPENSER***

Use It To: ***STOP SMOKING***

You may remember it as the Darth Vader–headed dispenser of all things chalky and fruit flavored, but the history of PEZ actually goes quite a ways back. Originally a candy without a plastic home, PEZ was invented in 1927 by Austrian Eduard Haas as the first cold-pressed hard candy. Mint-flavored and wrapped in waxed paper, they bore little resemblance to today's PEZ other than the name, "PfeffErminZe" (the German word for peppermints). Rather than targeting children, Haas created PEZ as a stop-smoking aide, sort of the Neanderthal Nicorette. In fact, when the dispensers first appeared a couple of decades later, they were designed to mimic the slim style and flip top of a Zippo lighter. When everyone else was having a smoke, PEZ users could flick their own "lighter" and pop peppermints instead.

Object: ***LIQUID PAPER***

Use It To: ***PULL YOURSELF AND YOUR SON OUT OF POVERTY***

In 1951, Bette Nesmith Graham was a recently divorced single mom—not exactly the best position to be in 1951. Desperately in need of work, she took a job in one of the few careers open to her, as a secretary in a typing pool. Unfortunately for Bette, those XX chromosomes failed to magically make her a gifted typist. After several months of error upon error, she was worried that she'd soon be fired. And then . . . inspiration!

One day, Nesmith filled a nail polish bottle with white tempera paint and took it to work. Whenever she made a mistake, she simply painted over it. Before long, her coworkers wanted in on the trick and word spread. Soon she started getting orders from typists at other companies. By 1962, demand for Nesmith's "Mistake Out" was so high that it got her fired—in a rush one day at the office, she managed to write her own company's name on one of her boss's letters. But that layoff turned out to be just the push Nesmith needed. Within 6 years, the fortunately renamed Liquid Paper company was a million-dollar business.

Bend the Laws of Science

Time Travel

YOU WILL NEED:

- To be a whole lot smarter than us. Seriously. As Barbie once said, "Science is hard."

First, the Bad News: Time travel to the past is unlikely. Scientists think that our best chance of time travel is to produce some way of reaching the speed of light, where time slows down. But that would only take us to the future. To go back in time, we'd need to go faster than the speed of light. And therein lies the problem. The closer an object gets to the speed of light, the more its mass increases until, at the speed of light, the mass actually becomes infinite. (We told you this was confusing.) An infinite mass can't speed up, so traveling faster than the speed of light is impossible. Or, at least, that's the theory.

Then, the Good News: Travel to the future just might work, but you probably won't be doing it in a machine. Most current theories of time travel rely on theoretical natural phenomena, such as rotating black holes. All currently observable black holes do not rotate. Made from stars that have imploded under their own weight, black holes have a singularity at their center—a place where the laws of physics cease to exist and all matter is smushed in a cosmic trash compactor. But, since 1963, scientists have believed that, if a black hole were rotating, it wouldn't necessarily form a singularity. Instead, a spaceship could pass through the hole in the center and pop out some other place, or time. No one's found a rotating black hole yet, but that doesn't mean they don't exist.

And Then, Some More Bad News: Time travel theory is fraught with begged questions no one knows the answer to: If you can travel forward in time, but not back, would you be stuck in the future? Could you ever preplan where or when a rotating black hole would spit you out? And what would happen if you became your own grandpa? It's all a mystery.

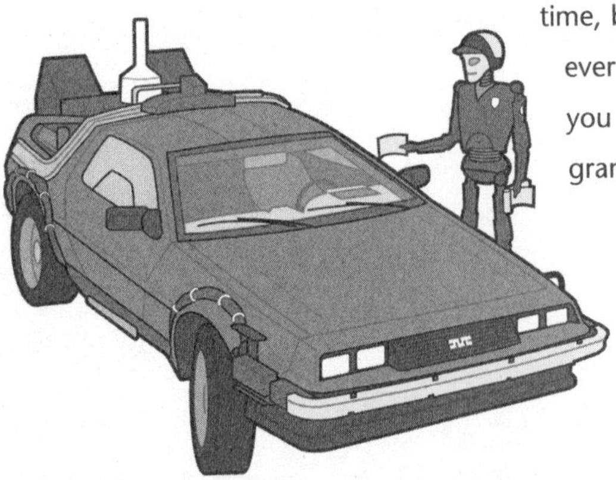

One Man Who Might Know the Truth: John Titor. Between November 2, 2000, and March 21, 2001, Titor, a man claiming to be a soldier from the year 2036, began making posts to Internet forums. Titor claimed that, in his future, the Y2K computer error had caused a worldwide crisis and that a new American civil war would begin in 2005. Clearly, neither happened, but apologists suggest that Titor's intervention—particularly a top-secret mission to 1975—stopped the Y2K bug and changed the course of history, making our present and future different from the one he'd experienced.

One Party Not to Be Missed: On May 7, 2005, a group of students at M.I.T. threw a Time Traveler Convention party, complete with bands, lectures, and a DeLorean. But just because you weren't there doesn't mean you have to miss it. In fact, organizers planned the party as the only time travel convention the world would ever need, because the guests of honor could always make it eventually. To that end, they heavily publicized the party, hoping that the date and geographic coordinates would be sufficiently preserved through history so that future time-machine inventors could find it. But the convention came and went without any futuristic V.I.P.s. The students reasoned that time travelers might have been there, just incognito . . . but, of course, if travel to the past is impossible, the guests of honor might have been forced to miss their own shindig.

Live on Mars

With the folks at NASA tentatively planning on putting a person on the Red Planet by 2018, it's high time we on Earth started thinking about the basic elements of Martian survival. Leave the rocket science to the rocket scientists (trust us, they've got it covered). Instead, turn your attention to mastering the art of daily Martian life. These tips should help:

MAKE FRIENDS WITH BACTERIA

Diamonds may be an Earth girl's best friend, but in space she's better off relying on *Deinococcus radiodurans*. Known to its friends as *D. radiodurans*, the bacteria is quite possibly one of the toughest organisms on planet Earth, surpassing the staying power lumberjacks, Chuck Norris, and even all other bacteria (according to the Guinness Book). After all, when was the last time those weaklings survived a dose of sterilizing radiation—one of *D. radiodurans*'s most famous accomplishments. The bacteria can also survive

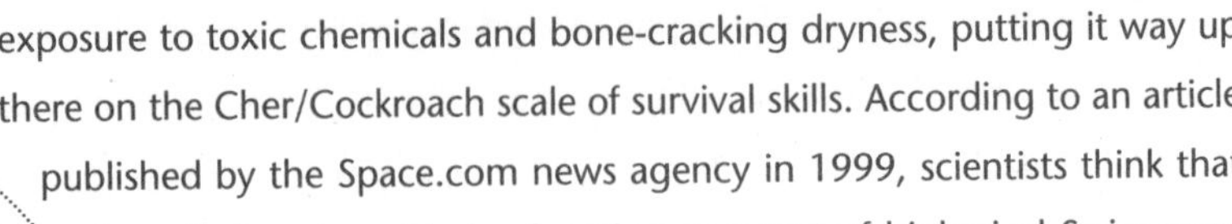

exposure to toxic chemicals and bone-cracking dryness, putting it way up there on the Cher/Cockroach scale of survival skills. According to an article published by the Space.com news agency in 1999, scientists think that *D. radiodurans* could also function as a sort of biological Swiss army knife. Gentically altered strains of *D. radiodurans* will one day function as nuclear janitors, capable of cleaning up radiation around former weapons testing sites. Meanwhile, on Mars, this ability would make *D. radiodurans* capable of turning the highly corrosive Martian soil into a kinder, gentler landscape, less likely to eat through a spacesuit. And the bacteria may also be used to develop drugs that can withstand harsh conditions in space and on Mars and that could even be made on-colony.

GET A NEW WATCH

In space, no one can hear your alarm clock beep. In fact, at this point, nobody's really sure what alarm clock you ought to be using anyway. Twenty-four-hour days, after all, are an Earth invention. It takes Mars 24 hours and 37 minutes to revolve once on its axis. And while that may not sound like much of a difference, it really adds up over time—a "year" on the Red Planet is equal to 669 Martian days, or 687 Earth days. As for Martian months, nobody's even remotely sure of where to draw the line for a planet with two moons. Not that plenty of people haven't weighed in on the issue of the Martian calendar—according to NASA researcher Dr. Michael Allison there are more than 50 versions floating around. In the meantime, the NASA scientists who monitor Martian rovers Spirit and Opportunity had to find a short-term practical solution in 2004. With their work revolving around when it was daylight on Mars, many of these workers found it difficult to keep their schedules straight. Enter Garo Anserlian, a California watchmaker who spent 2 months and more than $1,000 designing a mechanical wristwatch that would keep Mars time. It was harder than it sounds. Because watch gears are obviously made to tell time on Earth, creating a Mars watch basically meant reinventing the wheel. Anserlian ended up having to hand-attach lead weights to preexisting watch gears in just the right pattern to slow time down by 37 minutes a day.

LEARN TO LOVE TOFU

One thing's for sure, a spaceship is no place for a cow. And, when you're talking about trips to Mars, there probably won't be room for a big stockpile of astronaut ice cream, either. In fact, the only thing standing between Martian colonists and two years of dinner-in-a-tube are the researchers at Cornell University who are developing a space menu based around 15 to 30 crops that could be grown on Mars. Because of the cost of transportation, only about 15 percent of the calories each Mars colonist consumes could come from Earth-made food. The rest would have to come from wheat, potatoes, rice, soy, peanuts, and other fruits and veggies grown in hydroponic greenhouses in space. Working with these restrictions, the food scientists have developed dishes like "chicken drumsticks" made out of carrots, sweeteners made from potato starch, and cheesecakes made from tofu.

Find a Unicorn

You don't have to be a virginal princess to get your very own sort-of-equine symbol of purity and beauty. (Phew!) In fact, if you know where to look, finding a unicorn (or, at least, a handy facsimile) is pretty darn easy.

"Unicorn": ***NARWHAL***

Actually: ***A MID-SIZED WHALE WITH A BAD CASE OF BUCKTOOTH.***

Still Worth Finding: Because their tooth is something of a dentological anomaly. Biologists estimate that there are only about 50,000 narwhals in the entire world. But humans hardly ever see them, partly because they spend up to 6 months of the year in the coldest, most desolate part of the Arctic. However, in 2005, researchers were able to track down a few. That year, a team lead by a Harvard University professor/dentist named Martin Nweeia conducted the first major study of the narwhal's big tooth. Often passed off as a unicorn horn in medieval European markets, the tooth of the male narwhal is the only known tooth in the world to grow in a spiral

shape. It's also constructed very differently from other animals' teeth. Instead of having the hard material on the outside and the soft material inside, the narwhal's tooth structure is completely reversed. Weirder still, each of these tooth-tusks, which can reach up to 8 feet long, has more than 10 million exposed nerve endings. Just sipping a cold soda with an exposed nerve in your mouth can be agony, and yet the icy Arctic waters don't seem to bother the narwhal. So far, nobody knows what advantage, if any, the animal gets from all those exposed nerves or whether it feels any pain. But Nweeia has speculated that the tooth might help the narwhal navigate by sensing minute changes in water chemistry, pressure, and temperature.

"Unicorn": *ELASMOTHERIUM*

Actually: *AN OVERGROWN, HIRSUTE RHINOCEROS*

Still Worth Finding: Because it's extinct. Seriously, if you find one of these, give us a call. We'll quit this gig and come be your booking agent. Also known as the Giant Unicorn, the elasmotherium was an ancestor of the modern rhino that lived in Siberia and Europe *waaay* back during the Pleistocene Age (think 1.6 million to 10,000 years ago). So how did this heavy hitter (height: 6 feet, length: 20 feet) end up being mistaken for the unicorn? Depends on what unicorn you're looking for. The single horned beasties of Chinese legend, for instance, bear little resemblance to the delicate, virgin-loving ponies of Europe, and a lot of resemblance to, yes, elasmotheriums. This goes a long way to explaining why the unicorn horn was a symbol of virility in China: Elasmotherium horns were huge—reaching up to 6 feet in length.

Believe in Fairies

Step 1: *IGNORE OCCAM'S RAZOR*

In 1917, two young girls did the impossible, capturing dancing, cavorting fairies on film. Like a fluffy, pink version of the Zapruder Film, the fairy photographs taken in Cottingley, England, became a cause célèbre on both sides of the Atlantic, drawing famous characters like Sherlock Holmes's creator Sir Arthur Conan Doyle into an improbable debate about what, exactly, the girls had photographed and whether fairies really did exist. Doyle was greatly caught up by the brouhaha, writing two major magazine articles and a book (*The Coming of the Fairies*) proclaiming the girls' veracity, and arranging for expert studies, which concluded that the pictures were not double exposures and had not been retouched. Amid all the hubbub, however, no one seemed to have noticed that the "fairies" in question were clearly two-dimensional paper cutouts pinned to the shrubbery. People were certainly more innocent and/or naïve before the advent of Photoshop.

YOU WILL NEED

- A low threshold of belief
- A camera
- Some decent drawing skills
- To clap your hands, naturally

Step 2: *DENY, DENY, DENY*

Even more amazingly, the perpetrators of the hoax (cousins Elsie Wright and Frances Griffiths) maintained that the fairies were, indeed, real far into adulthood. Even after an art historian discovered a 1915 children's book containing illustrations that the fairies had quite obviously been cribbed from, Wright and Griffiths stuck to their story. It wasn't until 1982, by which point Wright was in her 80s and Griffiths a septuagenarian, that the women finally cracked, admitting the fairies had begun as a prank on their parents and had simply gotten out of hand. Unfortunately, the confession didn't stick. Over the following years, both women would occasionally claim that there had really been fairies, but that they hadn't been able to photograph them and Griffiths went to her grave in 1986, still claiming that one of the five photos was real.

Find a New Planet (or Lose an Old One)

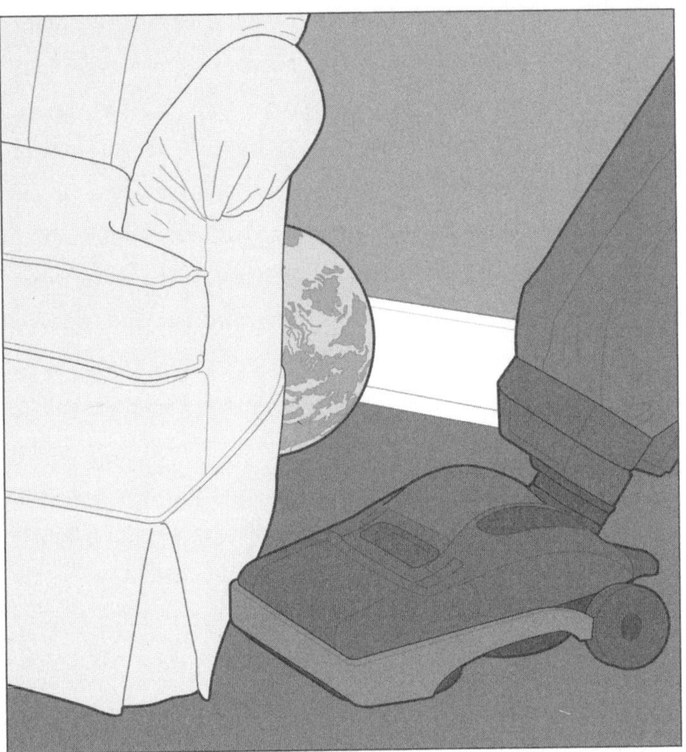

Step 1: *SPOT A NEW CELESTIAL OBJECT*

In 2005, a team of astronomers announced that they'd found a new addition to our solar system: An object floating around in the distant reaches beyond Pluto. Poetically named 2003 UB313, the object was discovered when Michael Brown of Caltech, Chad Trujillo of the Gemini Observatory in Hawaii, and David Rabinowitz of Yale University set out to review some telescope footage they'd taken almost two years previously. The trio had been looking for Kuiper Belt objects—large, often planet-sized masses that run in a ganglike pack on the edge of our solar system. To find these, they set up their telescopes to automatically take several images of the same section of night sky over the course of several hours. Then, the researchers went through the images and looked for things that moved. Needless to say, it was a really long and tedious process made doubly frustrating by the fact that they often missed things. Hence the reason they were reviewing old footage. Spotting 2003 UB313 was a major victory. But its discovery was about to cause a major scientific showdown.

YOU WILL NEED

- **High-powered telescopes**
- **A copy of the International Astronomical Union's definition of a "planet" (just to be on the safe side)**

Step 2: *FIGURE OUT JUST EXACTLY WHAT THAT OBJECT IS*

Not long after UB313's discovery, photos taken from the Hubble Space Telescope showed that it was just a little larger than Pluto, as its discoverers had suspected. That figure led to a flurry of excitement and the announcement that UB313 was, in fact, the 10th planet in our solar system. But this happy ending didn't last. Instead, it fed into the decades-old astronomical argument about what exactly constitutes a legitimate planet. Sure, in school they were quick to tell us that a planet is a big sphere made of dust and gas, but that definition describes a lot of things in space, including several other Kuiper Belt objects around the same size as Pluto and a large, spherical asteroid called Ceres. So were those all planets, too? The discovery of UB313 basically forced astronomers to finally sit down and hash out what a planet actually is.

Step 3: *BRAVE THE WRATH OF YOUR COLLEAUGES*

The definition of planet turned out to be only slightly less controversial than, say, the definition of marriage—to the astronomy world anyway. Over the next year, a team from the International Astronomical Union researched the issue and came up with some hotly contested proposals. At one point, a definition that reached the international voting stage would have expanded the number of planets to upwards of 53 and set the stage for the introduction of hundreds more, Michael Brown told Space.com in August 2006. Finally, on August 24, the proposals were put to a vote. The winning definition dismissed any celestial body that didn't have enough gravity to clear its orbit of other bodies as a mere "dwarf planet"—including 2003 UB313. But the controversy was far from over because, as you've probably heard, that definition also demoted Pluto. Officially, the former 9th planet is now just one of dozens of dwarf planets hanging out in the Kuiper Belt. But, although the definition is now in stone, it's still got the power to start scientific fist fights. For one thing, it means that NASA's New Horizons probe, launched toward Pluto only 8 months before the vote, is now on its way to visit a non-planet, making it somewhat ridiculous. Even touchier is the set up of the vote. Of the 10,000 astronomers who belong to the IAU, only 424, less than 5 percent, were available for the vote. Because of this, it's likely that the world hasn't heard the last of Pluto and its supporters.

Become a Mom . . . and a Dad

YOU WILL NEED

- **Nobody's help. You're doing this yourself, dag nabbit**
- **To be a girl**

Step 1: *SWEAR OFF THE OPPOSITE SEX*

Whatever, right? Men are stupid anyway. And, if you happen to belong to one of several lucky species of lizards or insects, you can happily live the rest of your life without ever having to put the toilet seat down again—all while catering to the needs of your biological clock. Parthenogenesis is a natural biological process by which female animals can reproduce without the help of a guy. In some cases, as with the Desert Grassland "whiptail" lizard, parthenogenesis is the only reproductive outlet available. While they started out as a sterile hybrid species (like mules), whiptail lizards have amazingly been reproducing by parthenogenesis for so long that there aren't any males of the species left. Other species, like the Komodo Dragon, have turned to all-female reproduction in situations where no males were available.

Step 2: *KNOCK YOURSELF UP*

All you have to do is contribute two sets of chromosomes, instead of the usual one. The egg, now containing the correct number of chromosomes, acts as if it had been fertilized. Komodo dragons apparently just do this without prompting, but whiptail lizards still require the, er, stimulation of mating behavior. In order to get the reproductive juices flowing, two female whiptails have to get together and, essentially, reenact a late-night Cinemax flick.

Step 3: *LIVE WITH THE CONSEQUENCES*

Not everything about parthenogenesis is peaches and sunshine. The practice severely limits genetic diversity. And in species like the whiptail, where virgin birth has been the norm for generations, the babies end up being exact genetic replicas of the mother—meaning whiptails are essentially frozen in their evolution. Komodos have it a little better because of the way their sex chromosomes work. Komodos don't share our familiar "X" and

"Y" system. Their sex chromosomes have completely different designations (WZ makes a girl) and when they have a parthenogenic birth all the offspring are male. Once those babies are grown, the mom can simply mate with them. Scientists think it's this ability that allowed the Komodo to populate island chains—all it took to create a fully functional colony was one female making it to shore.

Change Your Child's DNA

When Willie Nelson admonished mamas everywhere to not let their babies grow up to be cowboys, he had no idea how accurate his assessment of a mother's power really was. Turns out, moms have a lot of control over what their babies become, both before and after birth.

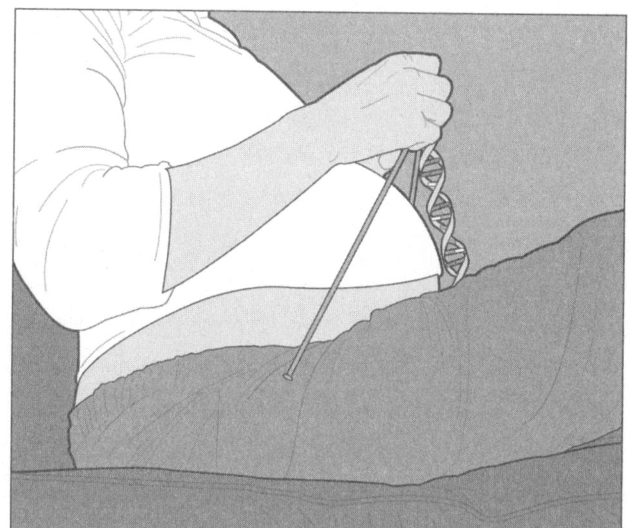

YOU WILL NEED

- To be a mom (sorry, guys)

USING YOUR DINNER

For instance, research done at Duke University Medical Center in 2003 revealed that what a mother eats before and during pregnancy can actually switch certain genes on and off in her child. The study took a group of obese, yellow mice and fed them diets that were rich in the nutrients vitamin B12, folic acid, betaine, and choline. Despite still carrying their mother's genes for yellow fur and obesity, the baby mice born from this test were brown and remained svelte throughout their lives. This worked because the gene that controls both coat color and appetite is affected by methyl groups, of which vitamin B12, folic acid, betaine, and choline are chock full. Methyl groups can switch genes on or off or, in some cases, just increase or decrease their impact. Unfortunately, while this might be a great thing sometimes, like say if it cut out the gene that might give your kid diabetes, methyl groups might also turn off "good" genes, like the ones that inhibit certain types of cancers. Right now, nobody has a good enough idea of how methyl groups work to know how to target in on specific "bad" genes without impacting good ones. We do, however, have plenty of evidence that what pregnant moms eat affects gene expression and can have surprising consequences a long way into their children's lives. For instance, according to an October 2003 *New York Times* article on the subject, famines in Holland after World War II left many fetuses (and their mothers) malnourished. Years later, Holland saw a big increase in the number of adults with schizophrenia, an increase directly linked to what nutrients those adults had (or, rather, hadn't) gotten in the womb.

USING YOUR LOVE

Just because your child has left your womb doesn't mean you no longer have power over its DNA expression. Two separate studies done by neurobiologists at Columbia University and Canada's McGill University have shown that maternal behavior after birth can also lead to a child's genes being turned on and off—in this case, genes that will eventually determine how that child parents his or her own offspring. According to a May 2006 *Discover* magazine article, the American neurobiologists studied two groups of rats, those that spent a lot of time grooming and licking their babies and those that didn't. It turned out that, if a female baby rat didn't get licked enough then her body turned off a series of genes that should have produced certain "mothering" and "love" hormones, like estrogen and oxytocin. Deprived of those, the female rat grew up to exhibit the exact same insufficiently nurturing behavior her mother had shown her—thus continuing the cycle for another generation. On the other hand, when a baby girl rat got an extraordinary amount of lick-based attention from her mommy, she went on to actually have higher-than-average levels of estrogen and oxytocin. Again, the expression of genes and the production of hormones caused her to display maternal behaviors that were similar to her own mother's.

Slow Down Time

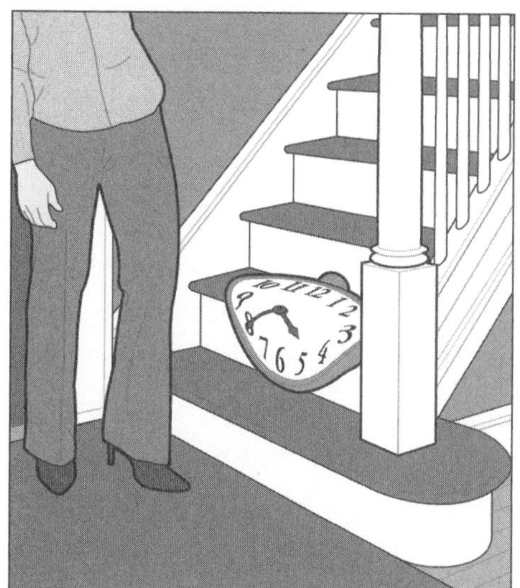

YOU WILL NEED

- To go downstairs

First, you'll need to know the truth about gravity. When he published the General Theory of Relativity in 1916, Albert Einstein also pointed out a small discrepancy in Newtonian physics—gravity isn't a force. Instead, according to Einstein, what we call gravity is essentially a curving or warping of spacetime itself, caused by a massive object, like, say, the Earth. Invisible to our eye, but clear as day to anyone with the mathematical chops to understand it, our home planet makes a dent in spacetime sort of the same way a bowling ball would curve a stretched rubber sheet. This is what we perceive as a gravitational field.

Now you're ready to take it slow. One of the key elements of Einstein's explanation of gravity is the fact that gravitational fields affect time. The General Theory of Relativity predicts that within a gravitational field, time will run more slowly than outside the field. On Earth, the power of the gravity field decreases as you move further away from the planet's core. So, to slow down time, you simply need to move closer to the core. According to a November 2006 National Public Radio story, even a change as seemingly meaningless as leaving the top floor of a building and going to the basement will make a difference, albeit an infinitesimally small one. You won't, for instance, notice time moving any differently, but certain highly sophisticated clocks will reflect the discrepancy. Take, for example the clock the Smithsonian Astrophysical Observatory launched in 1976. They sent the thing 6,000 miles high on a Scout rocket to test the theory. And while researchers estimated that the clock that went to space would run 4.5 parts in 1010 faster than its Earth-bound counterpart—they were actually right, within .01 percent accuracy! The Earth's gravitational field doesn't make a very big time discrepancy, but that's because the Earth itself doesn't make much of a dent in spacetime. A larger, heavier object, like a black hole, would create a gravitational field big enough to slow time in a much more meaningful way. Of course, going to the center of a black hole is also a lot more risky than hanging out the basement of your apartment building.

Fly

According to aeronautical pioneer (and Wright Brothers' arch-nemesis) Glenn Hammond Curtiss

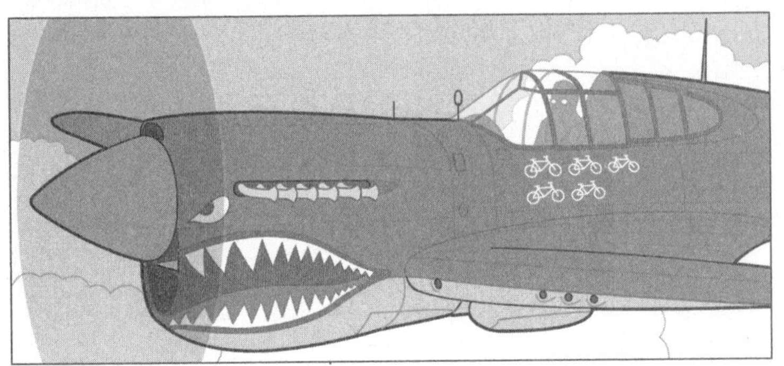

Do: *GET INTO BICYCLE REPAIR*

It's easy to forget, but biking was a high-tech, geeky hobby around the turn of the 20th century. Chains, gears, and rotors formed the backbone of a brand-new field of motor engine development. Meanwhile, adaptations in lighter, more aerodynamic bike construction gave a boost to would-be flyboys. In fact, you might say that bike repair was to airplane invention what hacking would one day be to the creation of the home computer. In that train of thought, the Bill Gates of biking was definitely New Yorker Glenn Hammond Curtiss—a champion cyclist and self-taught mechanic. Curtiss spent the first few years of the 20th century designing the world's best racing bikes and light, powerful motorcycle engines. Then he went into the airplane business and ended up the most praised and simultaneously reviled figure in the history of flight. He also ended up filthy rich.

Don't: *BE AFRAID TO BE THE BAD GUY*

Curtiss's moustache-twirling reputation began in 1906 with a fateful (some might say, mercenary) visit to the Wright Brothers' Dayton, Ohio, workshop. Technically, Curtiss was just in Dayton for the state fair where he was helping a friend demonstrate some dirigibles. But after the Wrights helped corral a particularly feisty airship, the three bonded over their mutual interest in flying machines and headed back to the Wrights' place for a guided tour. Although they'd flown at Kitty Hawk three years previous, the Wrights were still knee-deep in the patent process and wouldn't show off their plane. However, they did discuss the flier's mechanics in enough detail that when Curtiss suddenly became an airplane entrepreneur a year later, the brothers Wright sued him.

Do: *JUSTIFY BAD BEHAVIOR WITH GOOD TECHNOLOGY*

A lot of historical accounts begin and end with Curtiss's bad-boy side. But, here at *mental_floss*, we're willing to point out that, whether or not he stole his ideas from the Wrights, Curtiss was hands-down the better innovator. Case in point: the first flight. The Wrights' 1903 jaunt at Kitty Hawk was a success, as we all know. But just barely. Only a couple of feet off the ground, the Wrights managed to cover just a few hundred feet in distance and couldn't stay airborne longer than a minute before crash-landing. In comparison, Curtiss made the first public flight in U.S. history in 1908, behind the controls of his *June Bug* plane. He flew for over a mile and won the Scientific American Trophy. The next year, his plane went up against the Wrights' creations at the first international aviation exposition in France. Althought they didn't attend the event, several Wright planes were at the exposition and were expected to dominate the event, but Curtiss's one plane ended up besting them. He went on to start the first airplane manufacturing company, design the first hydroplane, and create the first airplane capable of taking off and landing on water.

Don't: *LET OLD FEUDS STAND IN THE WAY OF FUTURE PROFITS*

Shortly after his public success with the *June Bug*, Curtiss got a letter from the Wrights "reminding" him that if he were going to commercially manufacture airplanes, he'd need to pay them a cut. Curtiss apparently filed the letter in the waste bin, thus touching off nine years of increasingly hostile litigation. Curtiss's legal battles with the Wright Company even outlasted the Wrights themselves; after Wilbur's early death, Orville Wright sold his share of their company in 1915. The Curtiss/Wright conflict wasn't resolved until 1917, when the U.S. government simplified their World War I manufacturing by pooling all aircraft patents into one, thus nullifying the Wright Company's claims for restitution. With this forced peace, Curtiss and the Wright Company joined forces. Today, Curtiss-Wright still designs engines and components for air and spacecraft.

Grow Meat

Besides his more famous roles as stalwart defender of freedom and hilariously drunk dinner guest, Winston Churchill can also count "scientific visionary" among his many wearable hats. In "Fifty Years Hence," an essay he wrote in 1924 and which was published in *Popular Mechanics* in 1932, Churchill envisioned a world where, "We shall escape the absurdity of growing a whole chicken in order to eat the breast or wing by growing these parts separately under a suitable medium." Granted, he didn't quite hit the mark timeline-wise (unless you know something about 1982 that we don't), but his prediction is finally inching closer to reality. Beginning around the turn of the millennia, scientists (and, more important, their financial backers) gained a new enthusiasm for figuring out how to grow meat without growing an animal. Part of the motivation is NASA-related. With the Moon and Mars both on the horizon, the space agency wants to figure out a way to provide renewable sources of nutritious food for astronauts on long missions without actually having to tote a whole cow along on the shuttle. But health and a humane outlook are also big motivators. Researchers at the University of Maryland and Holland's Utrecht University both point out that lab-grown meat would provide a way to eat steak without hurting a cow. Better yet, the meat could be modified in the Petri dish to produce burgers that contain the überhealthy Omega-3 fatty acid (usually found in such delicacies as fish oil), rather than the artery-clogging Omega-6 fatty acids that meat usually hides. And, we're not even sure we need to mention this, but, so you know, lab conditions are a lot more sanitary than your average feed lot—a fact that could mean the end of mad cow, salmonella, and bird flu.

So far, it seems like science is moving pretty smoothly down the road to better meat eating. In 2001, a scientist at New York's Touro College succeeded in taking fillets o' naturally grown fish and artificially growing them a little bit longer in the lab. Then, in a rather unorthodox experiment, the fish was also successfully coated it in olive oil and fried. The result smelled like fish sticks, but apparently no one had the gumption to taste it. Braver are the artistic souls from the University of Western Australia, who grew frog "steaks" on a flexible membrane in 2003, and served them up for dinner. According to reports of the meal, the sauce was good, but the meat ended up as a slimy mass attached to a fabric-textured backing. Mmmm. So far, the biggest advances in the field seem to be those made by the teams in Maryland and Holland, which have managed to work out the reasonable, repeatable meat-growing process described here.

YOU WILL NEED

- A biopsy from a pig, chicken, cow, or fish
- A bioreactor
- Growth liquid
- A good exercise program
- A love of sausage

Step 1: *GROW, GROW, GROW YOUR COW*

In a Petri dish, combine a few cells from your biopsied tissue and some sort of nutritious growth serum. This step is crucial and, unfortunately, also the one that makes this process really, really expensive. Currently, nutrient-rich growth liquids are high-tech mixes used by research labs and are priced accordingly. The result: Growing a pound of meat can cost anywhere from $1,000, to $10,000, to an astronomical $45,000, depending on who you ask. However, there is light on the horizon. Maryland researchers are on the trail of a new, infinitely cheaper growth matrix made from plant or fungal sources that could cut the cost to a far more palatable $1 per pound.

Step 2: *BAKE*

After your two or three cells have divided into several million, the next step is to spread those across a thin, flexible sheet and place it in the bioreactor to grow. However, you can't just leave this meal to sit. Meat and fat cells, left to grow on their own, will produce a result that looks more like a blob of tapioca pudding than any steak. To avoid this unappetizing fate, you have to artificially replicate what happens when live animals exercise their muscles. The easiest way to do this is by stretching and flexing the sheets every few minutes.

Step 3: *PROCESSING*

Sadly, for all your trouble, the meat you end up with will be more like a piece of paper than a juicy porterhouse. While this lab meat is perfect for grinding into sausage, chicken nuggets, and fish sticks, any of which may be on your grocery shelves within 5–7 years, large, three-dimensional "cuts" are still a very long way off. The main problem: Nobody's figured out how to grow blood vessels, fat, and meat in a way that makes lifelike tissue yet.

Teleport

Step 1: *SET ASIDE YOUR* STAR TREK *DREAMS*

The good news: Teleportation is possible. The bad news: It might not be possible (or, at least, advisable) for you. In 1993, after decades of dreaming and scheming, science finally figured out that the laws of physics did allow for possible teleportation of objects from one place to another, instantly, across time and space—which, we gotta say, sounds pretty great. Unfortunately, this announcement, the result of a major physics research project at IBM, included a very important caveat. Teleportation is possible—but anything teleported would first have to be destroyed before it could be recreated. Turns out, when physicists talk teleportation, what they really mean is less the movement of an object and more the transfer of that object's salient characteristics. The popular analogy is to compare it to a fax machine. You don't actually send your document, you send all the relevant information about your document, which is then reconstructed into a different, but similar, piece of paper. That's not really Kirk up there. That's a copy of a copy of a copy of Kirk. Creepy.

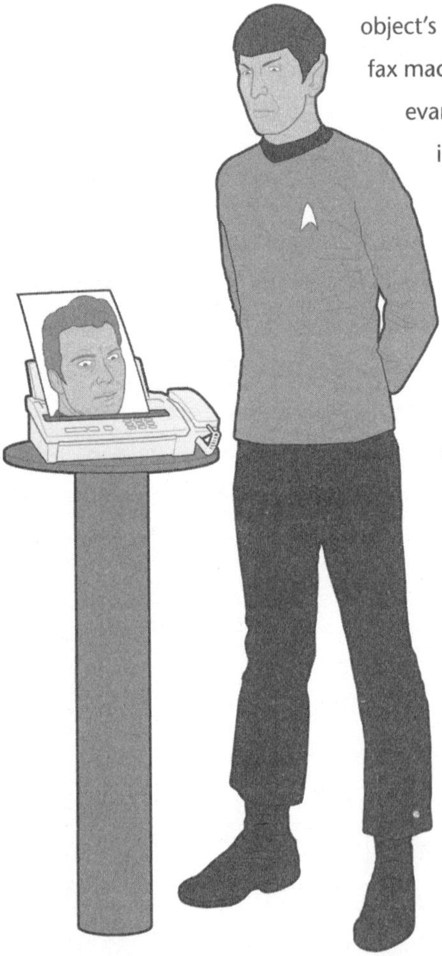

Step 2: *WAIT*

Despite this crushing blow to the imagination of science dorks and airplane-phobics everywhere, research on teleportation has continued. And it's been successful. In 1998, physicists at the California Institute of Technology managed to teleport a single teeny, tiny photon (aka a particle of light) across a distance of a little more than three feet. Although one small step for the photon (or, rather, for its duplicate), this was one giant leap for the development of transporters. Mainly, the experiment demonstrated that it's possible to get around Heisenberg Uncertainty Principle, which states that you can't know both the location and the speed of a particle simultaneously. The researchers bucked this by "entangling" a couple of particles and using the information they could gather about one to keep themselves abreast on what was going on with the other. Since then, other teams of researchers have succeeded in teleporting whole atoms and, in 2006, small groups of atoms. Unfortunately, it'll probably be years and years before we get to see anything useful—like a much-needed cup of coffee—instantly appear where we want it.

Power Your Interstellar Spacecraft

WITH NUCLEAR BOMBS

It's 1958, and the United States government wants to travel to, as they say, "infinity and beyond!" What's their solution? H-Bombs, of course. Nicknamed Project Orion, a crack team of scientists decided that the best way to soar between stars would be to load up a spacecraft with several small hydrogen bombs, which could then be spit out and detonated at preset times. A system of metal plates and springs on the back of the craft would absorb the impact and push the rocket forward, enabling it to reach fantastic, Buck Rogers-worthy speeds. The plan sounds crazy today (not to mention environmentally disastrous), but at one point, the team had the backing of "Father of Modern Rocketry" Werner von Braun and had even successfully tested a small model using dynamite. However, all research on this method of travel ground to a halt in 1963, when the United States signed the nuclear test ban treaty. Thank goodness.

WITH SPACE HYDROGEN

The Bussard Ramjet, another child of the 1960s, hoped to be more practical than the Project Orion ships (not that you could get too much more impractical). Unlike Orion, the Ramjet didn't require you to carry fuel onboard. Instead, the ship, proposed by physicist Robert W. Bussard in 1960, would have collected the hydrogen atoms that float around free in space. Once pulled into the ship's drive system, the atoms were to be subjected to laser heat and the resulting nuclear fusion blast would power the ship. Unfortunately, in order to actually be able to suck up enough space mass to get the hydrogen it needed, the Ramjet would already have to be booking along at 6 percent of the speed of light—a rather daunting 59,014,263 feet per second. So far, this poses too much of a problem to make the Ramjet very useful.

WITH LIGHT

Turns out, light does more than just warm things up. It also pushes on them. Based on this principle, many scientists think we might one day be able to "sail" through space using giant lenses that would collect the light thrust either from the sun or an on-board laser. In 2000, NASA's Jet Propulsion Laboratory actually demonstrated that this method does work—on a small scale. However, in order to make the system work for real, we need to figure out how to make bigger, more powerful lasers than have ever before been constructed (on the order of 10 million gigawatts of energy). Otherwise, space sailing could end up dead in the water.

Develop Multiple Personalities

YOU WILL NEED

- The help of a professional (possibly)

That Way: ***VIA TRAUMATIC CHILDHOOD ABUSE THAT LEADS TO DISSOCIATION FROM YOURSELF***

As far as popular culture is concerned, Multiple Personality Disorder is the Grand Prix of crazy. How else to you describe a mental illness that causes anywhere from three to 300 different personalities to take up residence in one single body? Western culture is so dang fascinated by MPD that we'll gladly shell out cash to see any movie, read any book, and learn more about any court trial that involves the disorder. Amazingly, despite all that popularity, most of us still have no idea that the name of the disorder was officially changed way back in 1994. It's now known as Dissociative Identity Disorder, a name which better reflects the modern understanding that the extra personalities are broken off from the original rather than grown out of the ether. The most famous of all DID patients is, of course, Sybil (aka Shirley Mason) a woman who's story of experiencing 16 personalities (including 2 men and a baby) became a best-selling book and hit movie in the 1970s. "Sybil" was identified as Mason after her death in 1998 and her case is indicative of the classic explanation for how and why DID develops. Dissociation is believed by many to be a type of post-traumatic stress disorder, where horribly abused children separate parts of their personality so they can deal with what happened to them. In effect, the abuse "happens" to someone else. In many cases, alternate personalities are emotionally tough or deeply protective of the base personality. The disorder is also characterized by bouts of amnesia, where events may be remembered by one personality, but not all. Often, the specific memories of abuse and the personalities guarding them have to be teased out under hypnosis . . . and that's where the controversy comes in.

OR

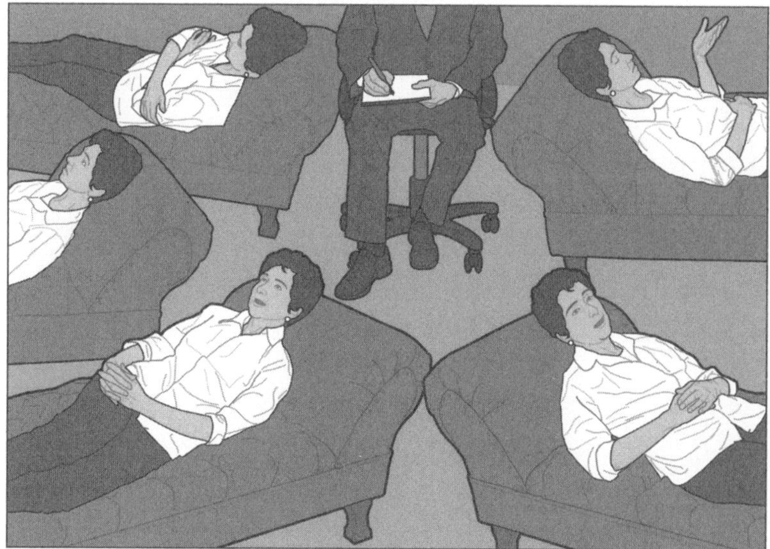

This Way: ***VIA A DAMAGING CYCLE OF SUGGESTIONS AND REWARDS FROM YOUR THERAPIST***

Since the 1980s, the psychology community has been sharply divided over whether DID actually exists. Case in point: Sybil, again. Tapes unearthed in 1998 seemed to indicate that when Mason originally went in for psychiatric care she wasn't experiencing multiple personalities. In fact, those other "people" apparently emerged as Mason's psychiatrist encouraged her to name different sets of emotions, usually while under the influence of hypnotism and/or sodium pentothal (i.e., truth serum)—facts another psychiatrist, who worked with Mason when her regular shrink was out of town, has confirmed. So are psychologists actually causing this psychological disorder? Not intentionally, says Dr. Paul McHugh, a Johns Hopkins professor who's one of the most well-known critics of DID. He cites an incident in the

1880s, where a French doctor believed he'd discovered a new disorder that combined hysteria and epilepsy. In fact, the hospital had just been housing both types of patients together and, when the hysterics had displayed epileptic behavior, they had been "rewarded" with attention and interest from the doctor and his staff. McHugh thinks that most DID patients are actually probably severely depressed individuals who want a reason and cure as much as their therapists want a rare encounter with DID. The combination is then encouraged by the patients' tendency toward higher-than-average susceptibility to hypnotism and the proliferation of multiple personalities in pop culture. For instance, before *Sybil* came out, only 75 cases had ever been reported. Since the book's release, there have been more than 40,000.

Master the Super-Natural

Start Your Own Religion

According to John Humphrey Noyes, spiritual entrepreneur

YOU WILL NEED

- A message
- Incentives for joining (Toaster ovens? Maybe!)
- Some nifty outfits (optional)
- A big ol' spiritual goal

Step 1: *GET INSPIRED*

John Humphrey Noyes was hardly the guy you'd expect to end up an influential minister. Born in 1811, he resisted all attempts to understand religion, first fending off his deeply pious mother and then New England culture as a whole during the revival craze of the 1820s. But in 1831, Noyes made the fateful decision to attend a four-day revival meeting in Vermont, at his mother's request. He was no more moved by this meeting than any other he'd been to—that is, until a couple of days later when he developed a raging fever and, fearing death, decided that maybe there was something to this "God" thing after all. Within months, the college student had dropped out of Dartmouth and enrolled in the Andover, and later the Yale, divinity school. But despite his on-a-dime conversion, there were a few doctrinal details of which Noyes remained unconvinced. Like sin, for instance. Noyes didn't get that one. He couldn't conceive of himself as a sinner and claimed to feel no guilt. Because of this, he quickly began preaching Perfectionism, the doctrine that Jesus not only forgives new converts to Christianity; he also makes them sinless.

Step 2: *GET SOME FOLLOWERS*

As if a clean slate wasn't enough to motivate people, Noyes's burgeoning denomination offered some other weighty incentives. For instance, in Noyes's church, women and men were equals—no small change to the 1830's status quo. Another bonus Noyes offered was a whole new family. In 1844, the growing group of believers adopted a biblically based communism, moving to a farm in upstate New

York. Here, they shared everything from possessions, to food, to each other. Yes, each other. Noyes's communal church practiced a doctrine called "complex marriage," where all the members were considered to be married to each other. And though there's some evidence that Noyes may have coined the term "free love" to describe this situation, he also made it clear that there were some rules. Before any canoodling could happen, the separate parties had to get each other's approval through an objective liaison. And, once they did get together they couldn't stay there very long—Noyerites believed that going steady was a sign of sin and lack of commitment to group welfare. Of course, the commune wasn't just giggles and naked Twister. Residents were also expected to give up caffeine and tobacco, limit their intake of "luxuries" like meat, and turn over their reproductive rights to a committee that decided which couples were fit enough to breed and which were to practice a birth control technique, evocatively dubbed "male continence." In short, the upsides and downsides to membership pretty much balanced each other out, and the commune was never larger than 300 people strong.

Step 3: *GET A NEW DIRECTION*

Surprisingly, this arrangement worked out really well for more than 30 years. Compare that to the lifespan of your average 1960s-era free love commune, and the record isn't too shabby. Part of why Noyes' community worked, however, was that it had a reliable income, thanks to farming and several small, artisan industries that all the members faithfully worked on. When opposition from nearby communities and internal rebellion by the younger generation of Noyerites finally doomed the commune, many former members stuck around and stuck together. They incorporated the old artisan industries, particularly a silver shop, into an honest-to-Adam Smith capitalist corporation, which they named after their former commune—Oneida. Yes, just like your grandma's flatware.

Weigh the Human Soul

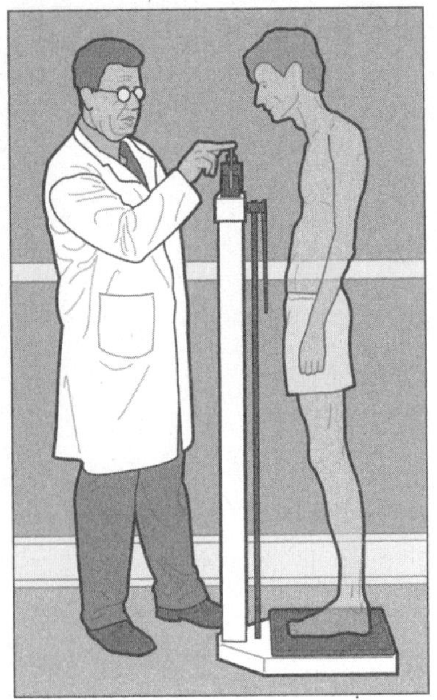

YOU WILL NEED

- 1 live, but soon-to-be-dead, guy
- 1 large scale
- A willingness to be just a little tacky
- Something nice for the deceased's family—flowers, maybe?

Step 1: ***GET YOURSELF SOME CONSUMPTIVES***

Before the advent of tuberculosis vaccinations, the Cullis Consumptives' Home in Dorchester, Massachusetts, might as well have been called Dead Guys 'R' Us. Or, rather, Dying Guys 'R' Us. Either way, it wasn't a place most normal people wanted to end up. But, then, history has shown that Dr. Duncan MacDougall wasn't exactly normal. After all, what normal respected surgeon would forgo his lucrative practice and instead dedicate his life to discovering the true weight of the human soul? In 1907, after four years of planning, MacDougall arrived at the Consumptives' Home and set up his unusual laboratory—an oversized commercial scale fitted with a cot. Somehow (sadly, we have no account of his conversations with the patients), MacDougall managed to convince 6 dying men into dying on his scale for the benefit of science. He carefully recorded their weight as they progressed toward death and noted the exact moment of demise, as well as any weight loss that followed. The first test subject was an astounding success: "suddenly coincident with death," MacDougall reported a 3/4 of an ounce drop in weight. The number would later be famously metricized to 21 grams.

Step 2: ***PISS OFF P.E.T.A.***

Following his Dorchester experiments, MacDougall's scientific method took a decidedly odd turn. He chose to follow up his human trials with tests on animals—setting up his scale in the barn and bringing in a batch of dogs. Of course, consumptive canines were harder to come by. "The ideal tests on dogs would be obtained in those dying from some disease that rendered them much exhausted and incapable of struggle," MacDougall said. But "it was not my fortune to get dogs dying from such sickness." Translation: the good doctor poisoned the dogs. Sure, the People for the Ethical Treatment of Animals weren't around at the time, but trust us, they're retroactively furious. In the end, the dogs didn't actually lose weight after death, an inconvenient discrepancy for which MacDougall found a theological answer—dogs, like other animals, don't have souls to measure.

Step 3: *CROSS YOUR FINGERS AND CALL A PRESS CONFERENCE*

In March 1907, the results of MacDougall's experiments appeared in the *New York Times*, which was apparently suffering from a slow news day. But while this publicity is probably why he's remembered, the news story also inadvertently pointed out a few glaring holes in MacDougall's research. The first subject had ostensibly lost 21 grams. But two other subjects were thrown out of the results for problems with the scale, and the last three lost weight after death . . . and then kept losing it for minutes afterward! In the end, none of the subjects lost the same amount. MacDougall explained this as simple tenacity, i.e., some people's souls hang on longer. Nevertheless, he admitted that more research would need to be done to get some conclusive answers. Sadly, further volunteers must have been harder to find. When the *Times* checked back with MacDougall four years later, he'd moved on to a new experiment—taking pictures of the soul.

Shapeshift

Don't listen to those naysaying physicists; it's easier than you think! Just ask . . .

NASA ROBOTS

Sure, it was one small contortion for a robot, but it ended up being one giant leap for space travel. In 2005, NASA successfully tested its first Tetrahedral Walker (TET walker), a pyramidal robot with motors at each corner. The design allows the robot to move over a wide variety of rough terrain. Because the motors can shrink and expand, the pyramid's legs allow the robot to basically roll over the top of large obstacles. Tested at McMurdo Station in Antarctica, the robot is expected to be most useful on space missions to other planets, such as Mars. But before it can really start changing the shape of space travel, the Tet walkers will need to shrink. NASA's goal is to eventually manufacture the walkers on a nano level and then bond thousands of tiny Tets into a swarm that can adapt itself to a huge variety of interstellar needs. The organization claims that a cloud of nanotechnology, Tet walkers wouldbe able to work together, combining to turn themselves into multiple pieces of equipment, including transport ships and communications systems—sort of like a cross between Transformers and the Wonder Twins. A single swarm could supply any number of needed systems for a space colony. Even better, if the swarm is damaged by a meteor or a dust storm, it will reconfigure itself to "heal" the holes without draining much-needed resources from the colony.

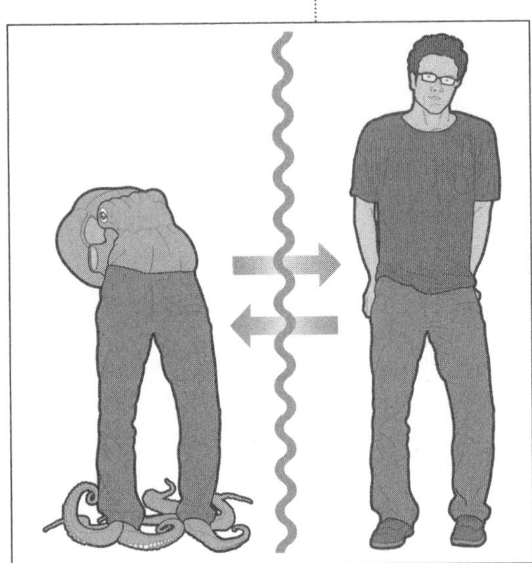

THE MIMIC OCTOPUS

Who needs dark glasses? The mimic octopus, a species discovered off the coast of Indonesia in 2001, has a better way to disguise itself. While most octopi can change their color and pattern to blend in with rocks and the sea floor, the mimic can actually take on the shape of other, more dangerous, animals. When threatened by predators, the mimic octopus can impersonate poisonous deep-sea dwellers, like the lion fish. Beyond being the first shape-shifting octopus, however, the mimic is also the first species ever discovered that can fake the look of more than just one animal. For instance, while certain flies have yellow and black stripes that make them look like bees, the mimic can shift form to pick up traits of the aforementioned lionfish, as well as banded sea snakes, sole fish, anemonies, jelly fish, and stingrays.

ANCIENT PLASTIC SURGEONS

Lost in time? Need a new nose? No problem! As long as you're in India, that is. The swingin' subcontinent has been home to remarkably advanced plastic-surgery techniques since at least 600 B.C.E., when the surgeon Sushruta first wrote down the technique for rebuilding a schnoz. Rhinoplasty was a pretty popular procedure at the time, but not because the ancient Indians were overwhelmed with self-loathing. Rather, plastic surgery tended to be the result of a run-in with the criminal justice system. Several crimes, including adultery, were punishable by nose removal. But, luckily for philandering spouses everywhere, there was no law that said you couldn't get that nose replaced. Surgeons like Sushruta used the leaf of a creeper vine to measure out a chunk of replacement flesh, which they cut off a cheek. That flesh was attached to where the nose had been and was fitted with small pipes to create the effect of nostrils. After the nose was packed in cotton and left to heal for a few weeks, the surgeon would return to trim away excess flesh. The result was something that looked almost like it might have been a nose at one point. But, hey, progress is progress.

Walk on Fire

YOU WILL NEED:

- **1 large open fire**
- **1 helping of basic physics knowledge**

The secret to a successful fire-walk: Don't walk on fire. Hey, we're not being glib—we're being technical. Firewalkers actually walk on a bed of hot coals and ash. Anyone who walked on actual flames would end up with third-degree burns, but coals, being nonvolatile lumps of carbon, are not very good conductors of heat. Ashes, meanwhile, are great insulators . . . further slowing the heat transfer to the point that, if you walk quickly, your feet won't get fried. To make up for these safety precautions, most firewalks happen at dusk or at night, when the glowing coals look more dangerous than they actually are.

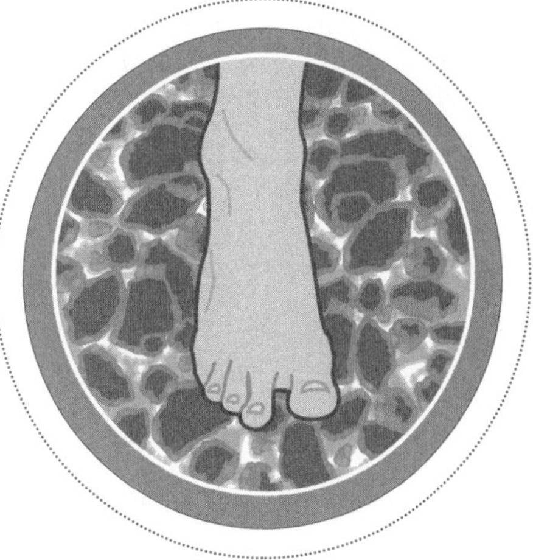

Revive the Really, Really Dead*

Ever since things went horribly wrong in Jurassic Park, mankind has carefully pondered the ethical and biological dilemmas of reviving extinct species and thought, "Hey, I could do better than that." And, sure enough, over the past 10 years, Michael Crichton-esque cloning experiments have popped up all around the world. Currently, teams of researchers are attempting to replicate the Tasmanian Thylacine (a doglike marsupial) and the Spanish Bucardo Mountain Goat (the last of which was smushed by a falling tree in 2000). There was even a failed attempt to resurrect the Woolly Mammoth.

However, there are several problems with these experiments. For one thing, ancient (read: cool) animals like the mammoth don't have enough intact DNA to clone, so you're pretty much limited to saving the Bucardo goats of the world. For another, clones are notoriously unstable. In 2000, an Iowan cow successfully gave birth to the clone of an endangered Asian Guar—only to see the calf die from illness a few days later. And clones, being clones, can't breed with themselves; so you can't really revive a whole species, just an individual. But, a group of dedicated scientists in South Africa may have found a way around these dead ends—at least for one long-gone subspecies.

YOU WILL NEED

- 1 extinct species, preferably herbivorous
- Its modern, surviving relatives
- 20-odd years of careful breeding

The quagga—an animal resembling a cross between a zebra and a horse—died out in the late 1800s after several decades of overzealous hunting. Long thought to be a distinct species, the quagga was outed as a cousin of the Plains Zebra by taxidermist Reinhold Rau, who tested fragments of quagga DNA in the early 1980s. Rau realized that if the quagga had originally evolved from the Plains Zebra, he might be able to replicate the subspecies through selective breeding. In 1987, he launched the Quagga Project, an organization that tracked down Plains Zebras with quaggalike traits and began cultivating the animals in the Karoo National Park, the quagga's ancestral home. By 2005, the project had succeeded in producing Henry, a light-brown baby zebra whose stripes fade out around the middle of his body.

* As in "extinct."

Get Excommunicated

According to Joe DiMaggio

The legally divorced baseball legend was shut out of the Church in 1954, after marrying the also divorced, non-Catholic, and thoroughly provocative Marilyn Monroe . . . and of course, for still being married to his ex-wife, in eyes of the Church. Both the marriage and the excommunication eventually ended but, of the two, the excommunication lasted longer. DiMaggio and Monroe divorced after only nine months, but "Joltin' Joe" wasn't brought back to the fold until 1962, when the progressive Second Vatican Council revoked his excommunication.

According to a Saint

Turns out, personality conflicts with the boss aren't a problem that's limited to secular business. Today, Mary MacKillop is remembered as a pioneering philanthropist; a nun who went beyond the call of duty by establishing a well-connected and well-organized network of schools and orphanages in the 19th-century Australian wilds. She's also been beatified—meaning that she's one confirmed miracle away from becoming Australia's first native-born saint. In other words, not exactly the sort of gal you'd expect to be in trouble with her superiors. But in 1871, Sister Mary was excommunicated by her local bishop. To better manage the order of nuns that she'd founded, Mary had formed her own internal central governance system, taking it upon herself to send nuns and teachers where they were needed—regardless of official bureaucracy. Her actions were effective, but arguably out of step with her vow of obedience. Enraged by what he thought was a heretical power grab, Bishop Laurence Sheil came to Mary's house while she was sick in bed and excommunicated her then and there. But, as any Catholic kid will tell you, guilt is a powerful force. Shortly before he died in February of 1872, the bishop repealed Mary's excommunication. By the next year, she was back in good enough standing to personally visit the Vatican.

According to Non-Catholics

Don't worry, you can be excommunicated, too! 3 easy tricks:

PRESENT THE WRONG FINGER

It takes a lot to aggravate the Episcopalians. In fact, the Director of Archives for the Episcopal Church USA says he can think of only three excommunications. But, if anything's going to get you thrown out of one of America's most laid-back denominations, it's flipping off the rest of your congregation—which is exactly what 68-year-old North Carolinian Lewis Green did in 2000. It wasn't just a randomly passing bird, however. Green had spent years criticizing and badgering the rest of his church, largely through a self-published newsletter. The issue came to a head, however, when Green directed his obscene gesture at the congregation during a December mass. Green, for his part, accused the church of trampling his right to free speech. When the church agreed to reinstate Green if he'd study a Bible passage about how to treat fellow Christians and apologize for the offending finger, Green declared it would be "a cold day in hell" before he'd apologize.

ASK THE WRONG QUESTION

In September of 1993, a small group of Mormon intellectuals were simultaneously kicked out of the church. The September Six, as they were called, were largely made up of authors and professors. And while they weren't connected to each other, they did share a common bond—an inconvenient tendency to publicly question the church's teachings on history and women. While the crimes seem rather tame, they came at a tense time for the Mormon hierarchy. Critics outside the church were increasingly questioning the behavior of historical Mormon leaders and doctrines such as the exclusively male priesthood. The excommunications came as Mormon leadership moved to stamp out interchurch dissent. Surprisingly, however, most of the September Six aren't exactly what you'd call anti-Mormon. One of them was rebaptized back into the church in 1996 and several others still attend services as nonmembers.

WRITE THE WRONG BEST SELLER

Takfir is the Muslim equivalent of excommunication; basically, it's what happens when somebody (preferably a religious leader) declares a person to be non-Muslim. It isn't often used, mostly because Sunni Muslims, the members of Islam's largest denomination, aren't real fond of the idea. To them, *takfir* spreads *fitna* (dissention or backbiting) and gets uncomfortably close to preempting the divine judgment of Allah. This calm, rational argument, however, doesn't seem to stop the more radical clerics from *takfir*-ing whoever they darn well please. Which is precisely what happened on February 15, 1989, when Iran's Ayatollah Ruhollah Khomeini declared author Salman Rushdie a non-Muslim and issued an order for his execution. The point of discord: Rushdie's new book, *The Satanic Verses*, featured a less-than-favorable, fictionalized version of the Prophet Muhammad as a minor character. The death sentence forced Rushdie into hiding until Iran's Foreign Minister revoked it in 1998. But, as of February 2006, the fatwa was back on—with an Iranian foundation offering a $2.8 million bounty for writer's head.

Perform an Exorcism

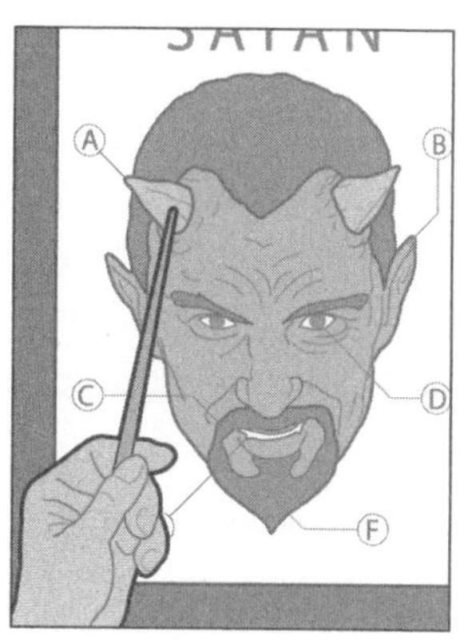

Good Idea: *GET A PROPER EDUCATION*

It's not a likely offering at your local state school, but if you're willing to head to a university in Rome you can take classes in exorcism for college credit. Since 2005, the Vatican-recognized Regina Apostolorum Pontifical Academy has offered a class on combating the works of the Devil. Participants—mostly priests with a few theology students thrown in—learn about the history of Satan worship and the legal and medical issues associated with combating it. The class winds up at the end of the year with a big finale: testimonies of true exorcisms given by two of Italy's 400 practicing exorcists. Lesson #1: Don't get cocky. Priests who get too proud of their abilities risk spiritual failure. Instead, students are advised to stick to the papally-approved exorcism guidelines, last revised in 1999.

Bad Idea: ***ASK YOUR BEST SIKH BUDDY FOR HELP***

Why? Because it might get him thrown out of his religion. Native to India, Sikhism places a heavy emphasis on distancing itself, spiritually speaking, from the local Hindu majority. Sikh deny the polytheistic Hindu pantheon and discriminatory caste system, and refuse to participate in what they call "blind ritual and superstition"—including exorcism. These rules are laid out in the *Rehat Maryada*, the Sikh guide to ethics and good behavior. More than a simple etiquette manual, the *Rehat Maryada* is an enforceable code—violators risk being ostracized by the religion's governing body.

Good Idea: ***DON'T ASSUME THE SPIRIT IS ALWAYS EVIL***

It might just want your help, not your soul. In Jewish tradition, possession usually takes the form of a *dybbuk*, a human soul that wasn't allowed into the afterlife. In order for the *dybbuk* to leave this world, they often have to finish some important act. To get that closure, they need a body—your body. People possessed by a *dybbuk* display a different personality, but unlike demon possession, the *dybbuk* usually leaves when its work is done and it doesn't actually mean its host any harm. In fact, the best way to exorcise a *dybbuk* is to simply help it out.

Make a Zombie

The word "zombie" can be traced back to an African word for powerful ancestral spirits. In America, it's immediately associated with brains-loving undead eating machines. But in Haiti, people don't fear the zombie itself. Instead, they fear becoming one. According to the research of anthropologist Wade Davis, zombies are actually the victims of an extremely rare—but very real—form of capital punishment. Haiti was founded as a farming colony with an economy based on the African slave trade. Over the years, individually and sometimes in large groups, slaves would escape from the plantations. Being on an island, you'd think that there weren't a lot of places to escape to; but Haiti's interior, covered with mountainous jungles, actually provided the perfect environment for runaway slaves to not only escape their tormentors, but also set up underground societies of their own. Known as the Maroons, the free men formed their own religions and government based on African ones. One of those systems, which, according to Davis, survives to the present day, is a secret society of elders called the Bizango who make

and enforce community rules. Under this system, zombification is the equivalent of a death sentence, with the offending criminal having his soul sucked out and being forced to work for the Bizango for the rest of his physical life. Think of it like the Dementors in the *Harry Potter* series. Few cases of zombification have actually been documented. But one person who's former zombie status is pretty well a sure thing is Clairvius Narcisse, who was legally declared dead by medical professionals at a hospital in 1962. Eighteen years after his burial, Narcisse inexplicably ran into his sister at a local market. Turns out, after he'd refused to cooperate with his brothers in their plan to divide the family inheritance, he'd ended up zombified. He was only able to escape after the man holding him prisoner had died and the effects of the drugs he was given had worn off.

YOU WILL NEED

- Drugs
- A victim with a culturally influenced psychological predisposition

Step 1: *THE KNOCK-OUT DRUG*

According to Davis, this is a mixture of several different naturally occurring chemicals, including biogenic amines, bufogenine and bufotoxins (all derived from the skin of a local toad), and tetrodotoxin (found in the flesh of puffer fish). The combination of chemicals can be absorbed through the skin, particularly through an open wound, and make the victim appear to be dead. Their breathing slows, their blood pressure lowers, and they become cold. Meanwhile, however, their mental faculties are still largely intact, creating a pretty terrifying scenario where a victim can watch, but do nothing to prevent, their own premature burial. Zombies, by the way, aren't the only people who've experienced this. In Japan, puffer fish sushi is a delicacy. And, even though it can only be prepared by a licensed chef, accidents have occasionally happened, leaving some sushi gourmands dead and others in a days-long state of suspended animation.

Step 2: *THE ZOMBIE DRUG*

After burial, whoever created the zombie has to dig them up within eight hours before they suffocate and die for real. Then, the zombie is fed a paste made of datura, a strong, disorienting hallucinogen made from Haitian plants. But, while the drugs are certainly powerful, they aren't the only thing keeping zombies as zombies. Davis thinks that the same combination of chemicals might not produce the zombie effects were it not for the fact that Haitians have already been culturally prepped to fear becoming a zombie and to know what it would be like if it were to happen to them.

Commune with the Dead

Given that most *mental_floss*ers are blessed with a skeptical and scientific nature, this guide probably seems very silly. After all, what person of vast intellect (such as yourself) would actually believe in ghosts? Um, well, about that . . . turns out, Thomas Edison—arguably America's greatest scientist—spent the last 11 years of his life attempting to perfect a device that would allow him to speak to the dead, which he wrote about in an October 1920 issue of *Scientific American*. Granted, he failed to come up with anything useful, but the point stands—science can mingle with the things that go bump in the night. The following tips should aid any future experimentation:

DON'T CALL A PSYCHIC

Scientifically speaking, mediums don't seem to work. A recent study at the University of Arizona, described in Mary Roach's book *Spook*, tested a psychic's abilities by putting her on the phone with 6 unidentified people. The phone system was set up so that the psychic and her subjects couldn't speak to one another. Instead, she felt their presence (and the presence of their dead loved ones) through the airwaves and privately recorded the impressions she received. Then, the 6 subjects were sent 2 unidentified psychic readings—one that was theirs and one that wasn't. They were asked to highlight the parts that they thought applied to them and their family. The results: Subjects found just as much "correct information" in the control readings as they did in their own—not exactly good news for an industry that claims to pass on accurate messages from the Passed On.

DON'T EXPECT THE DEAD TO BE REAL SHARP

Sadly, even if our consciousness does survive longer than our bodies, it may not survive intact. In 1946, Robert H. Thouless, then-President of the Society for Psychical Research, concocted a sure-fire test for life after death. An avid cryptology hobbyist, Thouless composed two encrypted paragraphs and, after ensuring that they were unbreakable, published them in the SPR magazine, instructing the members that, after his death, he would try to communicate the solutions to a medium. When he died in 1984, the University of Virginia took up the Thouless Project—a scientific effort to get accurate keys to Thouless's codes from beyond the grave. So far, they haven't been successful. But this failure may not be the mediums' fault. In 1986, A.T. Oram, the SPR secretary, reported that eight different psychics had made contact with Thouless—only to discover that the dead man no longer remembered his own codes.

IF ALL ELSE FAILS . . . TAKE A NAP

As you fall asleep, the brain shifts from your voluntary nervous system—the one that allows you to consciously decide to hold your breath or move your arm—to the involuntary nervous system—the thing that keeps you breathing even when you're out cold. During this transition, your mental wires can sometimes end up just wee bit crossed, producing visions, sounds, and even a false sense of touch known as hypnagogic hallucinations. Unsurprisingly, this falling-asleep phenomenon is widely blamed for bedroom-based hauntings—but it may also be responsible for phantom hitchhikers. On long, late-night car trips, drivers will often get mesmerized by the highway or briefly doze off and then jerk back awake. In situations like this, the probability of hypnagogic hallucinations increases—making people believe they've seen a deer in the middle of the road or picked up a hitchhiker who disappeared.

Don't Get Left out of the Bible

According to books that missed being immortalized as scripture

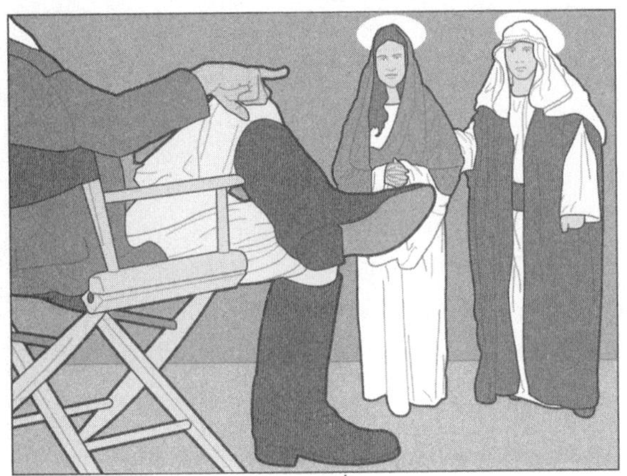

Book: *THE INFANCY GOSPEL OF JAMES*

Didn't Make the Cut: Because prequels are never as popular as the original story (we're looking at you, Mr. Lucas).

The Infancy Gospel of James focuses on the early life of the Virgin Mary and is the source of most extrabiblical traditions about her. Here, Mary is a miracle baby, born to aging parents and sent to live with priests. And Joseph isn't her husband but a widower who agrees to be her guardian after the priests decide that she's a bit too, well, female to stay at the temple. When Mary turns up pregnant, the priests have her and Joseph pass an honesty test by drinking blessed water that will make them sick if they lie. Most odd, though, is the author's decision to have Salome, best known for asking for the head of John the Baptist on a platter, improbably fill the roll of Holy midwife.

Book: *THE GOSPEL OF THE EGYPTIANS*

Didn't Make the Cut: For being a little too ascetic.

Only parts of this Gospel survive, but these bits advocate self-denial and celibacy in order to kill ties to the body, break the cycle of birth, and theoretically return man to a sinless, androgynous state. Sounds like fun. Thankfully, early church leaders weren't too fond of the idea either; many gospels left out of the Bible share these beliefs. Another thing apocryphal gospels share: Salome. She appears here as one of the women who finds Jesus' tomb empty on Easter morning.

The Book: *TRANSITUS MARIAE*

Didn't Make the Cut: Because reunion specials are even less popular than prequels.

Supposedly an account of the death of the Virgin Mary, the *Transitus Mariae,* is only one of many works that tell roughly the same story. Here, the death of Mary leads to an Apostle reunion, as all 12 are transported to her deathbed from around the globe and even from beyond the grave. Jesus, too, puts in an appearance, leading a train of angels from Heaven to receive both his mother's soul and body. Before the body can be taken up, however, the author fits in a bit of anti-Semitism, having a Jew who dares to touch Mary lose both his hands. Mercifully, the Apostles intervene (possibly remembering that they, themselves, are Jewish) and restore the man's appendages.

Know Everything

According to the Makers of the First Encyclopedia Britannica

YOU WILL NEED

- Lots of facts
- A good editor
- A few editions before you really get it right

TIP: *DON'T CUT CORNERS*

The original volume was the work of a gang of Edinburgh, Scotland, printers who, inspired by the ideals of the Scottish Enlightenment (and the prospect of owning a potentially best-selling reference guide), set about putting together the end all and be all of encyclopedias between 1768 and 1771. They meant the book to be a compendium of all the useful knowledge collected by man over the 6,000-year history of classical civilization. It was a large and daunting burden, which they put entirely on the shoulders of exactly one editor, a cash-strapped university student by the socially awkward name of William Smellie. And while they did pay him the equivalent of $38,000, they also demanded he produce the encyclopedia's 100 parts in weekly installments. So you'll have to cut old Smellie a bit of slack if the text he produced isn't quite up to our modern standards.

TIP: *DON'T BE AFRAID TO ADMIT YOUR ERRORS; YOU CAN ALWAYS UPDATE LATER*

The first edition, published in completed form in 1771, summed up the entirety of the fairer sex in three words ("Woman: Female of man") and openly admitted that its writer was a little unclear on whether California was an island or a peninsula. On the other hand, it did contain some incredibly useful advice, such as how to cure a toothache. (With "laxatives of manna or cassia dissolved in whey or asses' milk." OK, so maybe not so useful.) Fed up with his editors' demands, Smellie declined to write the 2nd edition and, by the 1820s, Britannica's owners had begun farming out the writing work to actual experts.

Identify a Witch

YOU WILL NEED

- **1 potentially evil old biddy**
- **Standardized tests to determine guilt or innocence**

FIND THE WITCHES' MARK

One surefire way to pinpoint a witch was, well, by pinpoint. Between the 12th and 17th centuries, when witch-finding was at its most popular, Europeans believed that witches, as part of their Satanic initiation rituals, received a marking on their flesh that was supposed to be invulnerable to cold, pain, or any feeling at all. What's more, the spot wasn't supposed to bleed if pricked. Although the usefulness of this so-called "gift" of the Devil is debatable, it was considered a sure-fire witch ID badge. When an outbreak of witch accusations hit a town, the city officials would often hire a "prodder" to figure out whether the accused had witches' marks. Prodders were often paid for each witch they removed from town. A successful prodder might make up to 15 times more than the average worker. This fact led to some dishonest business practices; for instance, retractable pins which were incapable of causing pain or drawing blood.

GET ONE WITCH TO TURN STATES' WITNESS

In many trials, one woman accused of witchcraft would agree to identify other witches in exchange for her own safety. When the Scottish village of Forfar had an outbreak of witchcraft around 1661, for example, accused witch Helen Guthrie kept herself and her 13-year-old daughter alive by claiming to be able to ID a fellow witch on sight. Guthrie also offered her captors fantastical (and somewhat titillating) stories about what she and her fellow witches had done during their religious festivals. Unfortunately, this tactic didn't work for very long. Guthrie was executed along with 8 other women in late 1662.

TEST THEM WITH WATER

Symbolically purifying and representative of the baptismal font, water was a popular means of witch identification. Following a religious service, which might last as long as 3 days, the accused was tied up so that her left thumb was connected to her right toe. Then she was lowered into the water. If she floated: witch. If not: hopefully she was fished out in time to enjoy her innocence. Although the water trial is one of the most famous witch-finding teststoday, trial by ordeal in general was actually outlawed by a Papal ban in 1215, suggesting that perhaps the religious authorities in Rome were equally aware of its, er, possible problems.

Live Forever

According to Science

One sure fire way to live longer is to just keep doing what we've been doing for the last 100 years, i.e., going around vaccinating more people, eating better food, and improving preventative health care in general. Granted, we're no Methuselahs, but we're certainly doing better than our ancestors. But, if you're really going to insist on that "forever" part, your best bet, scientifically speaking, is probably on sirtuins—naturally occurring body chemicals that can actually increase your lifespan. Of course, you should be aware that there's a price to pay for this sort of longevity: namely, your dinner. Back in the 1930s, researchers discovered that if mice ate 1/3 less food, but still got all the nutrients and vitamins they needed from supplements, they'd live 1/3 longer than mice that ate normally. Even more amazingly, the mice were just as energetic as their gluttonous counterparts. More recently, research done by MIT biology professor Leonard Guarente has shown that a serious drop in caloric intake kicks on sirtuin production, and those chemicals, in turn, protect your DNA from damage . . . thus increasing the lifespan of your cells and your whole body in general. We'd sign up to be a human test subject for this; but frankly, a life without second helpings is not a life worth living.

According to Fame!

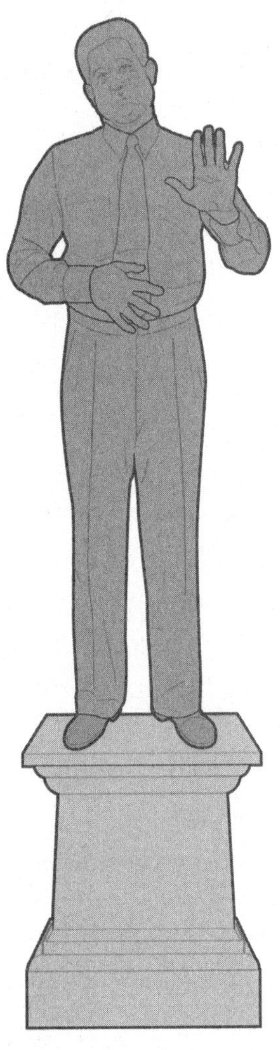

The problem: How do you get people to remember your name after you've left this mortal coil? The solution: statuary. A little bronze, a little marble, and suddenly, your everlasting recognition is secure. Of course, the trick here is that you have to do something that will make it worth folks' while to carve your likeness—like, say, dramatically and heroically saving your uppercrust city from being annexed by its less-classy neighbor. In 1923, the city of Los Angeles was growing rapidly and gobbling up just about every outlying community in its path—eventually threatening the enclave of Beverly Hills. On the one side were proponents of the annexation, who argued that Beverly Hills' water supply was lacking and everyone would be better off if they joined forces with L.A. On the other side, patriots like silent film stars Mary Pickford, Will Rogers, and Rudolph Valentino valiantly fought for Beverly Hills' continued independence. It was a difficult battle that pitted neighbor against fabulously wealthy neighbor and prompted dirty tactics—at one point pro-annexationists left bottles of fetid water, ostensibly drawn from the Beverly Hills' wells, on peoples' doorsteps along with a note warning that the liquid had "laxative qualities." Nevertheless, freedom prevailed. The final vote was 507 to 333 against annexation. Lest this bravely fought battle be forgotten, the citizens of Beverly Hills memorialized their local heroes in a bronze "Monument to the Stars" erected in 1959. Built one block north of their hard-won city limits, at the intersection of South Beverly Drive and Olympic Boulevard, the monument features bas-reliefs of Pickford, Rogers, and Valentino (along with otherwise forgotten stars like Fred Niblo and Conrad Nagel), all of whom served in their city in its time of need.

Flirt with the Dark Side

Become a Cyborg

According to Kevin Warwick, who's already done it

YOU WILL NEED

- **Academic status that allows you to get your expensive neurosurgery comped**
- **A swell media nickname—Captain Cyborg should do just fine**

START SIMPLE

In 1998, Kevin Warwick, then a cybernetics professor from England's Oxford University, made history and headlines by having a small electronic transmitter implanted in the skin of his arm. The goal of the experiment: to see if the glass-enclosed silicon chip was safe and whether it could successfully send signals to computer chips that weren't in Warwick's body. The results: 100 percent nifty. Alerted by the chip in his arm, computers in Warwick's campus office knew when to open the door for him, turn on lights, and even greet him by name. (According to Warwick, the computers used to call him "Professor." Their relationship has grown since—now they know him as "Kevin.") Sure, it wasn't exactly a moonwalk, but it was a small step toward what Warwick believes will be a bright future for mankind. Or, should we say, robomankind.

UP THE ANTE

In 2002, Warwick took his experiment a step further, this time having a crack team of neurosurgeons connect a transmitter to the nerves of his left arm. This time he proved humans have the potential to communicate with computers and each other via digitally transmitted impulses from the nervous system. In one experiment, Warwick controlled a robot arm 3,000 miles away using only his mind. In another, he exchanged sensory information with similar implants in his wife and a colleague—essentially the first scientifically proven instance of human telepathy.

GO NUTS—YOU'VE EARNED IT

Next up for this nutty professor: an implanted cell phone. In previous experiments, Warwick was able to pick up a radio signal on his implanted electronics and he thinks it's only a matter of time before someone makes a "handset" that's really a part of your hand.

Destroy the Earth

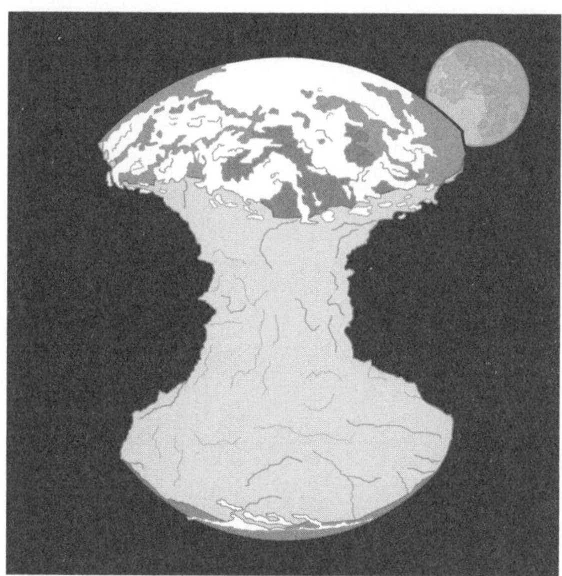

YOU WILL NEED

- A rather twisted sense of malevolence against your own planet
- Additionally, access to vast reserves of cash couldn't hurt

BY LARGE HADRON COLLIDER

When the EU's Large Hadron Collider goes live sometime in 2007, it will be the fastest, most powerful particle accelerator/collider ever built. The project is so important to the field of particle physics that nearly two-thirds of all the particle physicists in the entire world are involved with it. Of it's many important functions, researchers hope that the Large Hadron Collider will give them the most accurate glimpse yet into the conditions that were prevalent immediately after the Big Bang. Essentially, this thing is going to help us better understand the universe. So why is it dangerous? Recently, some physicists have begun building a theory that black holes, which we normally think of as vast, dark entities hiding in the vast reaches of space, are actually forming regularly in our own atmosphere—prompted by the collision of certain particles at high speeds. You know, like what happens in a particle accelerator. Now, according to the theory, those tiny atmospheric black holes vanish almost as soon as they form. But some people worry that, in the environment of the LHC, a black hole might form and then fail to disappear, which, obviously, would mean big trouble for planet Earth. Most particle physicists agree that this doomsday scenario is unlikely, but whether it's impossible—well, that remains to be seen.

BY SITTING AROUND AND WAITING

Destruction is all a matter probability, according to astrophysicist J. Richard Gott. In 1969, Gott happened to visit the Berlin Wall on a holiday and started pondering how much longer it could be expected to exist. But, instead of researching Cold War politics, he pulled out the laws of probability—working out a formula that led him to declare, with a 50 percent certainty, that the wall would be gone by 1993. You might be willing to dismiss the fact that the wall fell in 1989 as a lucky guess, but Gott, who has since refined the formula to give estimates that are 95 percent accurate, has also correctly estimated the closing of several Broadway shows. Less frivolous was his prediction, in a November 1997 article in *New Scientist*, for the duration of the entire human race. According to Gott, humanity has at least another 5,100 years, but certainly less than 7.8 million. Although hard to accept as an imminent death sentence, it is, none the less, a highly probable limit to our existence and one that any forward-thinking speciescidal lunatic should take into account.

Get out of Jury Duty

The Easy Way: *BE FAMOUS*

Hey, we didn't say anything about this being the easily accessible way. But, if you're blessed with the sort of fame that leads media types to follow your every move, chances are, you won't ever get chosen for jury duty. Why? Frankly, your presence (and that of your posse) would be distracting in the courtroom. In 2003, for instance, Bill Clinton was called in as Prospective Juror No. 142 on a New York City murder trial, but was eliminated only a couple of days into the jury selection process. The judge on the trial felt that President Clinton and the Secret Service Agents who follow him at all times would sensationalize the atmosphere in the courtroom.

The Illegal Way: *LIE*

Whether you say you're "prejudiced against all the races," as per Homer Simpson, or simply claim that your grandma died, lying is a time-honored way to both get out of jury duty AND get thrown in jail for contempt of court. Just ask Benjamin Ratliffe, an anti-death-penalty activist from Columbus, Ohio. In June 2006, Ratliffe was called in for jury selection on a capital murder trial. Unwilling to risk being on a jury that might want to hand down a death sentence, Ratliffe decided to take matters into his own hands. When he was given a questionnaire to fill out, he intentionally flubbed a couple of key questions. At one point in the questionnaire, Ratliffe claimed he was "bad jonesin' for heroin." When asked if he'd ever fired a weapon, he responded, "Yes. I killed someone with it, of course." The result was a sort of be-careful-what-you-wish-for moral lesson. Ratliffe did get out of jury duty, but he also spent 24 hours in jail for obstruction of justice before he finally agreed to apologize to the judge.

The Smart Way: *KNOW A BIT OF LEGAL TRIVIA*

The next time you're in the jury selection process and really want out, just inform the court that you know all about jury nullification . . . and you aren't afraid to use it. A little-known facet of common law dating back to Elizabethan England, jury nullification happens when a jury hands down a "not guilty" verdict—but not because they think the defendant is innocent. Instead, they're making a statement about the law itself. The first jury nullification happened in 1670, when William Penn (of Pennsylvania fame) and William Mead (you don't know him) were charged with unlawful assembly—a crime basically created to prevent unsanctioned religious groups from getting together to worship. Clearly, both men were guilty, but the jury refused to convict them on the grounds that the law was unjust. The practice continued in America. Throughout the mid-1800s, Northern juries would frequently nullify prosecutions against people who violated the Fugitive Slave Laws. And, during Prohibition, juries around the country nullified numerous alcohol control violations. Prior to the 20th century, nullification was accepted as common practice, but around the late 1800s, judges started taking a harsher view of it. In 1895, the Supreme Court even handed down a ruling saying that judges don't have to inform juries of their right to nullify. Today, most judges take advantage of this. Many will even tell you that you can't legally nullify a law. Of course, there's some debate over whether that's true or not. (At any rate, jurors can't be punished for the verdict they return and not-guilty defendants can't be retried—so we figure, what the heck.) Either way, most judges don't want to deal with a juror who might pull the nullification card, so if you bring it up, you'll likely be eliminated from the jury pool.

Shrink a Human Head

If you've always wanted to triumphantly carry the head of a telemarketer around on your belt there's only one way to achieve your goal—the Jivaro way. The only culture known to shrink human heads, the Jivaro live in the Amazon rainforest in Ecuador and Peru. Their religious beliefs place a heavy emphasis on appeasing the angry spirits of dead relatives, so anything that could calm down the late Great-great Aunt Sophie was highly valuable. Enter tsantsa, shrunken heads used as talismans to appease the dead and bring good luck. Made from the heads of powerful enemies, tsantsa were the key component in days-long religious festivals. But, once the festival was over, the tsantsa lost its value and was usually thrown out, fed to dogs, or traded to tchotchke-hunting Europeans for guns and machetes.

YOU WILL NEED

- 1 head of vanquished foe
- 1 high-quality fillet knife
- 1 small fire
- Hot pebbles
- 1 large pot of water
- Charcoal
- Needle and thread

Step 1: Cut a line in your enemy's skin from the top of the head to the back of the neck. Carefully peel the skin away from the skull, turn it inside out, and scrape it clean.

Step 2: Sew eyes and mouth shut—this will keep the spirit of your enemy from coming back for revenge.

Step 3: Simmer skin in pot of water until it has shrunk by a third (about 2 hours). You can use this time to sacrifice your enemy's skull and brain to the Anaconda god.

Step 4: Fill neck cavity with hot pebbles (sand works, too) and shake. Skin will become like leather.

Step 5: Moisturize, moisturize, moisturize!—polish leathery skin using charcoal and wild berries.

Step 6: Finally, smoke over fire for one night. Then you're ready to attach your very own shrunken head to a necklace and hit the village.

Be a Hacker (Without a Computer)

YOU WILL NEED

- Information
- Ingenuity
- A phone
- A somewhat flexible moral code

Step 1: ***EAT A BALANCED BREAKFAST***

Breakfast cereal is to hacking what the opposable thumb is to human evolution. In 1972, a Vietnam Vet and named John Draper found a toy whistle in a box of Captain Crunch. It was to be a momentous meeting. Acting on the advice of a friend, Draper tinkered with the whistle until, rather than just a random hum, it produced a 2,600-hertz tone. But this was more than just some musical experiment. Draper's friend knew, and the world would soon learn, that that tone was very important to the workings of the Bell Telephone system. In those pre-fiber-optics days, Bell used certain tones like codes; the right note could "unlock" features such as calling collect or, in the case of the 2,600-hertz tone, long distance. As those of you born after 1990 may not remember, calling outside of your home area code used to be a pretty pricey venture. With his special tone in tote, Draper managed to bypass the whole "paying for services rendered" thing and skipped right to the reaching out and touching. Although he didn't discover the trick, Draper did popularize it. He also greatly improved upon it, inventing a device—which he called "the blue box"—that was capable of playing many different phone-company-exploiting notes. From this point on, telephone manipulation was just a push of a button away. A generation of illicit pleasure/free-phone-call seekers fell in love with the blue box and came to regard Draper as the father of their hacker culture.

Step 2: ***TELEGRAPH, TELEPHONE, TELL A SUBCULTURE***

News of (and plans for) Draper's blue box quickly spread across the nation, helped along by an article in *Esquire* and an anarcho-hippie newsletter called the Youth International Party Line. Founded as the voice of Abbie Hoffman's performance art group/ political organization, the Youth International Party's newsletter quickly became a source of semilegal useful information, covering everything from lock-picking to vending-machine manipulation to hacking. Strangely enough, the newsletter inspired like-minded troublemakers to come together and share ideas in person—which is how John Draper met future Apple Computer CEO Steve Wozniak. The two crossed paths not long after the invention of the blue box at a potluck dinner thrown by the People's Computer Club of Menlo Park, California. Most of the details of this great meeting of the computing minds have been lost to history, but one fact does remain. Apparently, during the dinner, Draper explained how the blue box was made and Wozniak (not yet the upright corporate citizen he would one day become) immediately went home and built one. Legend has it that, among other things, Wozniak used his blue box to perpetrate a spree of crank calls—including one to the Pope. Yeah, that Pope.

Some of the information for this entry came from an article, written by John Brandon, which appeared in the May–June 2006 issue of mental_floss.

Destroy Tokyo

It's certainly a lofty goal, if somewhat unneighborly. But if that's what you really want to do, well, we suppose it's still our job to help. These three tried-and-true methods are sure to get the job done—and, as a note to our Japanese readers, we promise a guide to destroying New York in any possible sequels to this book.

Method 1: *BY GODZILLA*

Since his cinematic debut in 1954, Godzilla has been everybody's favorite Tokyo destroyer—not that they'd say anything if he wasn't. After all, how do you argue with a guy whose Japanese name Gojira roughly translates as Gorilla-Whale (*gorira-kojira*). Of course, you could always counter with a bigger gorilla. In 2005, *National Geographic* reported that paleontologists in southern Argentina had discovered a new ancient species of gigantic crocodiles that they nicknamed "Godzilla." More than 135 million years old, creature, *Dakosaurus andiniensis*, had a head like a carnivorous land dinosaur and a tail like a fish. From one end to the other, it measured 13 feet. And yet, it wasn't the largest of its contemporaries. Swimming through the same stretch of area, were 20-foot-long, Loch Ness-esque plesiosaurs and 75-foot ichthyosaur monsters. Eat that, Mothra.

Method 2: *BY EARTHQUAKE*

Destroying Tokyo via earthquake might actually be easier than shaking down any other city in the world. Part of the problem is that the Japanese capital sits on top of not one, not two, but three tectonic plates—the Eurasian, the Pacific, and Philippine Sea plates. Together, they form what's known as a subduction fault, where one plate dips down below the other. The earthquakes that form here are stronger and happen more often than those that occur along slip-shift faults, like America's San Andreas, where two side-by-side plates rub against each other. In fact, little tremors rattle Tokyo on a weekly basis. Worse yet, scientists discovered in 2005 that the plates are thinner than anyone previously thought. Thinner tectonic plates equal (you guessed it) a more dangerous fault line. The last time this fault really got to moving, back in 1923, it hit a 7.9 on the Richter scale, leveled half the city, and claimed 105,000 lives.

Method 3: *BY FIREBOMB*

Even more unfortunate than the immediate damage the 1923 earthquake inflicted, was the future damage it inspired. People around the world saw how the fires that broke out in the aftermath of the quake were able to burn through the dense wood-and-paper landscape of Tokyo. And, when America entered World War II against the Japanese, those lessons didn't go forgotten. Around 1942, the U.S. military began developing incendiary bombs, designed to instantly replicate the effects of the earthquake. Actually clusters of smaller bomblets, these firebombs separated as they fell. On contact, each minibomb exploded in a blaze of superhot gas and napalm-like burning jelly, and everything the jelly touched burst into flames that were almost impossible to put out. On March 10, 1945, America dropped thousands of these bombs on Tokyo. The resulting fires burned for days and completely destroyed 16 square miles of the city. In one night about 100,000 people died and 2 million were left homeless—a devastation worse than that of the later nuclear bomb attack on Nagasaki and nearly as extensive as the destruction at Hiroshima. One of the attack's planners, Robert McNamara, would later reflect that after the firebombing of Tokyo, if the U.S. had lost the war, he and many others would have been tried as war criminals.

Be a Ladies' Man

YOU WILL NEED

- A way with women
- A flexible moral compass
- An architecture license (seriously, it's a sexy profession)

ONE AT A TIME

Frank Lloyd Wright, the man who revolutionized American architecture, was equally, uh, revolutionary when it came to his love life. In 1889, he married Catherine Lee Clark Tobin and set about raising a family of 6 with her. However, that version of his personal life came to an abrupt end in 1909, when Wright went on an extended vacation to Berlin, Germany—with Margaret Cheney, the wife of a client, in tow. The pair spent more than 2 years in Europe before returning to Chicago and starting a new life as man and wife (though not legally, as Catherine refused to grant him a divorce). That second coupling would only last until 1914, but, to be fair, its end wasn't Wright's fault. That year, a disgruntled member of the family's hired help set the Wrights' house on fire after locking all but one door. As the former Mrs. Cheney, her two children, and two other guests fled the fire, the workman axed them to death. The freak incident plunged Wright into depression bad enough to distract him from his work, but not bad enough to keep him from hooking up with another woman less than a year later. He spent 7 years with that woman, Miriam Noel, before finally getting his divorce from Catherine in 1922. He married Miriam the next year. But, by 1924, Miriam left him, an event from which Wright quickly recovered by falling in love with a Yugoslavian ballerina named Olga Hinzenberg. Amazingly, this relationship managed to last to the end of the architect's life in 1959.

SIMULTANEOUSLY

While Wright cornered the market on serial sort-of monogamy, Louis Kahn kept a slightly busier schedule. Beginning around the early 1950s and until he died in 1974, Kahn was keeping three different sets of women and children, only one of which he was actually legally wed to. Despite the fact that this was pretty much an open secret in architecture circles, his *New York Times* obituary famously listed only his wife and her daughter as survivors, leaving out his other two children entirely.

Escape from Death Row

BY SHEER LUCK

Accused of brutally murdering his elderly employer, Englishman John Lee was quickly convicted and sentenced to hang. On February 23, 1885, he climbed the gallows at Exeter Prison for what should have been the last few moments of his life. Should have been, but wasn't. Although the trapdoor that Lee was to fall through had been previously tested, it failed to open when he was standing above it in a noose. A little more testing proved it worked and Lee was brought back up and the noose replaced around his neck. Again, the trapdoor refused to open. After yet more successful testing, the officials attempted to kill Lee for the third time and that, too, failed. By this point, the crowd of observers was getting mutinous, so Lee was taken back inside the prison. A few days later, a judge commuted his sentence to life in prison. To this day, no one knows exactly why the trapdoor wouldn't budge whenever Lee—who became known as The Man They Could Not Hang—stood on it.

ON FOOT

Notorious both for its toughness and fondness for capital punishment, the Texas penal system isn't the sort of place that death row inmates frequently leave in any way but a body bag. In fact, nobody on death row had escaped from a Texas correctional facility since a member of the Bonnie and Clyde gang hoofed it in 1934. But statistics did little to dissuade a team of 7 inmates who attempted to bust out of the maximum-security penitentiary near Huntsville, Texas, on Thanksgiving Day 1998. Their plan wasn't exactly the stuff of *The Shawshank Redemption* and 6 of the men gave themselves up inside the prison grounds, to prevent being killed by a hail of gunfire. But one, Martin Gurule, made it over the razor wire fence and into the woods, becoming the first death row inmate in more than 60 years to achieve such a feat. Unfortunately for Mr. Gurule, his success was short lived. Seven days after defying odds, dogs, and bullets, Gurule's body was discovered in a nearby creek by a couple of off-duty police officers on a fishing trip. Apparently, Gurule had drowned in the swollen creek no more than a few hours after his escape, probably because of the weight of the supplies he'd strapped to himself.

BY LAST-MINUTE STAY OF EXECUTION

Forget dead man walking phone calls from the governor, 18th century Englishman John Smith (not be confused with that other John Smith) definitely holds the record for most last-minute reprieve. In December 1705, Smith, a soldier, was convicted of also being a part-time cat burglar. At the time, this conviction carried the penalty of death and, later the same month, Smith was brought to the gallows. Throughout his imprisonment, Smith had claimed that his powerful friends would get him a stay of execution, and, sure enough, they did. However, the news of the stay came after Smith had been swinging from the noose for a full 15 minutes. Amazingly, "Half-Hanged Smith" lived to tell his own tale. After being cut down, he was revived by a physician and went on to have a fine career as both public curiosity and (yes, still) a part-time cat burglar.

Travel to the Center of the Earth

No villain is complete without a ludicrous plan. Yours: Journey to the center of our planet. Unfortunately, this is easier said then done. Fortunately, someone already came up with a helpful plan for the doing part. In 2003, CalTech planetary scientist David J. Stevenson proposed a way to send a probe into deep Earth. Published in the journal *Nature*, "Modest Proposal: Mission to Earth's Core" laid out a step-by-step plan for inter-Earth travel—it was brilliant, theoretically possible, and only briefly mistaken for an April Fool's joke.

YOU WILL NEED

- $10 billion
- 1 thermonuclear device, small
- 1 probe, heavy duty
- Molten iron to taste (100,000 to several million tons)
- Gravity

Step 1: Get $10 billion. Surprisingly, this is not the hardest part.

Step 2: Find a nation willing to take one for the team, by letting you blast a 984-foot deep hole in their country. This is where the nuclear bomb comes in handy.

Step 3: Pour in enough molten iron to fill your new crevasse. Hopefully, gravity should now kick in, pulling the heavy metal toward the center of the earth and lengthening your original hole at a rate of about 10 miles per hour. At that speed, your iron river should reach the earth's core in a week. And naysayers never fear, according to Dr. Stevenson's calculations, high pressures below ground would reseal the earth after the iron passed by—preventing any awkward uncloseable chasms.

Step 4: Before the flow gets moving too fast, toss in a probe. For maximum effectiveness, said probe should be able to withstand temperatures surpassing 3,000° Fahrenheit and pressures 1,000 times greater than the bottom of the deepest ocean. It also has to be strong enough that it can reach the center of the Earth and transmit some data back to you. Given those manufacturing standards, this may be a time to go union. Remember, you get what you pay for. And, just in case Detroit has lost its edge, let's go with an unmanned probe. Better safe than sorry.

Control the Weather

Step 1: *CONVINCE PEOPLE YOU AREN'T A NUTJOB*

This will be tough, but you'll need to do it successfully if you're going to have any hope of procuring some funding. The problem is that when most people think of weather-control devices, they think of quacks like George Ambrosius Immanuel Morrison Sykes, who traveled the country promoting his weather machine in the late 1920s and early 1930s. According to *Boston Globe* reporter Drake Bennett, who wrote an article on weather control in 2005, Sykes's big break (and even larger crack up) came in the summer of 1930, when the innovative owners of New York's Belmont Park horse racing track decided to ensure gambling satisfaction by keeping that years' racing season rain-free. To do this, they hired Sykes. And, by all accounts, they got a pretty good deal—the would-be weather god agreed to be paid only for the days he actually succeeded in keeping the storm clouds away and, in fact, actually promised to pay the Belmont owners double for days he failed. Surprisingly, Sykes first week on the job went so well that his contract was extended. As irony would have it, this was when the deluge began. From this point, the weather thoroughly failed to obey Mr. Sykes's command; even when he promised rain, the sun shown. But, while his machine probably lacked scientific merit, it turned out tha the concept of making rain wasn't entirely unrealistic. Sixteen years later, a General Electric research chemist managed to actually do what Sykes had faked. In 1946, Vincent J. Schaefer flew over a mountain in Massachusetts, sprinkling three pounds of crushed dry ice along the way. The result: a man-made snowfall. And, later that year, Kurt Vonnegut's meteorologist brother, Bernard, discovered that silver iodide would also prompt precipitation. By 1951, "cloud seeding" was being used to dampen 10 percent of the United States.

Step 2: *RETAIN A GOOD LAWYER*

Technically, what you are about to do is illegal. Hey, don't look at us. Blame the government! Back in 1966, the U.S. military began a massive cloud-seeding experiment in Vietnam. Called Project Popeye, it was meant to soak the Ho Chi Minh trail to the point of being impassible, hopefully bogging down the North Vietnamese forces in the muck. And in 1972, the last year of Project Popeye, a state-funded cloud-seeding operation in South Dakota got a little overzealous and ended up creating a flood that killed more than 200 people. When both these incidents hit the news wire, they created a sensation of fear and, yes, loathing. Antiweather-control sentiment eventually culminated in a United Nations treaty that forbade using weather control for military purposes or for any violent reason. America ratified the treaty back in 1979. But this shouldn't necessarily block you from pursuing your dream of benevolently tampering with nature. It certainly didn't stop U.S. Senator Kay Bailey Hutchison and Representative Mark Udall from sponsoring pro-weather-control bills in 2005. Both bills would have created a Weather Modification Advisory and Research Board tied both to the White House and the Pentagon. Practical or practically hilarious? We aren't sure, but Congress seems to be mulling it over. Both bills ended up in committee where they've been growing moss and assorted lichens for more than a year.

Step 3: *GET DOWN TO THE SCIENCE*

Cloud-seeding is definitely the most popular form of weather control—namely because we know for sure that it works. Grains of silver iodide dropped into a cloud work as a sort of irritant, causing droplets of water vapor to form around them. When the cloud gets heavy enough, it rains. But scientists are working on new and improved methods. Ross Hoffman, a researcher with Massachusetts-based Atmospheric and Environmental Research, has used computer models to demonstrate how a deadly hurricane could be stopped or moved away from a city. Ironically, Hoffman's method actually involves making the hurricane stronger—even a slight change in wind speed can drastically alter the direction and duration of a storm. Heating up the storm would work, too. Unfortunately, in order to make either small change happen, we'd have to be able to produce, store, and transfer a massive quantity of energy—far more massive than any ever before controlled by humanity. Translation: Don't expect this any time soon. However, in a decade or two, the story may be very different. By then, its possible that we might have technology capable of harnessing energy from the sun and beaming it to Earth, where it can warm up the offending hurricanes.

Rule with an Iron Fist

YOU WILL NEED

- Fear
- Awe
- Loyal minions

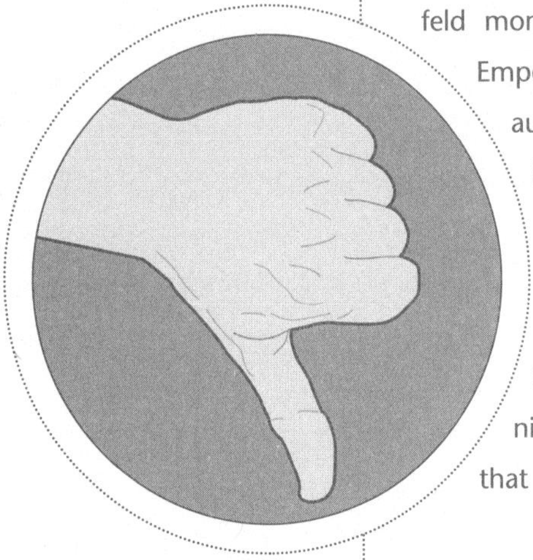

Step 1: ***MAKE ARBITRARY, SELF-SERVING LAWS—AND ENFORCE THEM BRUTALLY***

This is really half the fun of being a supreme ruler; what annoys you should also annoy the nation. Tired of boring conversation? Can't stand close talkers? Outlaw 'em. (And the people who accuse you of governing by Seinfeld monologue? Well, might as well ban 'em, too!) The Roman Emperors were big fans of this tactic, according to Michael Powell, author of *The Lowbrow Guide to World History*. Gaius Caligula, for instance, who ruled Rome from 12 to 41 C.E., was super sensitive about his slowly spreading bald spot. To help combat his low self-esteem, Caligula first made it a capital crime for anyone to look down at him (and his patch) from a high place. Eventually, he took to shaving anyone seen flaunting a head of nice hair. Mullets were punishable by death. (Here, we concede that Caligula may have had a point.)

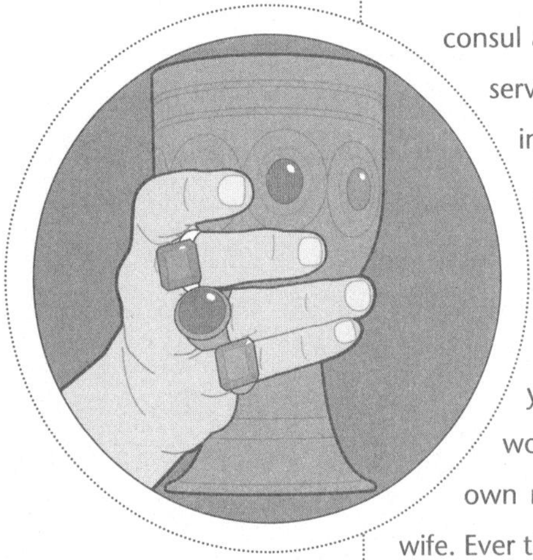

Step 2: ***LIVE LAVISHLY***

Naturally, Roman Emperors excelled at this, too. When not worrying about his hairline, Caligula found time to appoint his horse, Incitatus, a consul and shower the animal with jewels, furs, statues, and its own servants. Other rulers tend to take "living lavishly" to mean "living with lots of hot chicks." Take Mswati III of Swaziland. Arguably the last absolute monarch in Africa, Mswati has at least 13 current wives and seems to take a new teenage fiancé every year or so—even when doing so conflicts with his own royal decrees. In 2001, Mswati declared a national 4-year period of celibacy for all Swaziland's virgins, hoping it would stop the spread of AIDS. But in 2005 Mswati broke his own rule when he took a 17-year-old schoolgirl to be his eighth wife. Ever the fair ruler, Mswati fined himself a cow. Meanwhile, everyone else was forced to go on living chastely.

Step 3: ***KEEP YOUR FRIENDS CLOSE, AND YOUR ENEMIES IN GULAGS***

Nothing intimidates quite as effectively as a good set of secret police. Russia's Ivan the Terrible figured that out pretty quickly into his career as a despot. Between 1565 and 1572, Ivan amassed as many as 6000 members for his Oprichniki and, along the way, he taught them a thing or two about style. Realizing early that uniforms add to the mythos, Ivan dressed the oprichniks in black-colored monk's robes. Their coat of arms bore the signs of the broom (for "sweeping away traitors") and severed dog's head (for "snapping at the enemies' heels")—and there's some evidence that, when the Oprichniki really wanted to make an entrance, they'd bring both mascots with them in the flesh. Answering only to the Tsar, the oprichniks were authorized to take out anyone Ivan saw as a threat: from minor members of the aristocracy to entire towns. But, efficient though they were, the oprichniks eventually got too big for their britches and were, themselves, accused of treachery.

Fight a Land War in Asia

YOU WILL NEED

- Swords
- Sex appeal
- Little fur hats

Step 1: ***FOCUS ON YOUR FIRST IMPRESSION***

In the early 13th century, a guy named Temujin built up an army that eventually conquered most of Asia and large swaths of Europe, creating the largest contiguous empire ever made. Never heard of him? Of course you haven't. Temujin, whose name likely referred to his family's history in the blacksmithing business, was smart enough to know that you can't lead an army into global warfare with a moniker that makes your followers think "guy who makes horseshoes." Around 1206, he took on a new, more appropriate name and would eventually be known to history as Genghis Khan. While "Khan" was the Mongolian word for "ruler," there's some debate over what the "Genghis" part was attempting to get across. Most likely it was meant to be read as something along the lines of "Universal Ruler." Apt, wouldn't you say?

Step 2: *WIN THE LOVE OF THE PEOPLE*

If your name alone isn't enough to make potential subjects bow down, you might try being a genuinely decent guy. Although associated, particularly in Europe, with a lot of bloodshed and maiming, Genghis was actually pretty progressive, as far as 13th century warlords go, and should be remembered for his brain as well as his brawn. Among other things, he outlawed the practice of kidnapping already married women or selling them into marriage/slavery. Additionally, he also regulated the food supply to make sure that everyone had enough to eat in winter, and organized a legal system that was actually, well, organized, appointing official judges and introducing the use of record keeping.

Step 3: *IF YOU CAN'T BEAT 'EM, JOIN 'EM*

Regardless of whether he won his subjects hearts and minds, Genghis Khan certainly won over their gene pool. A prolific father of several other prolific fathers, Khan and his descendants had their pick of women. Many, many women. Essentially, their power and prestige managed to turn the evolutionary survival of the fittest in their favor. Today, within the boundaries of the former Mongolian Empire some 8 percent of all men carry a Y-chromosome that directly links them to Genghis. And while that's only .5 percent of all men worldwide, that's still a pretty impressive achievement for the genes of one man.

Build a Nuclear Bomb

YOU WILL NEED

- Radioactive materials
- Some highly classified know-how

HOP ON THE WEB

Besides providing you with up-to-the-minute reports on the state of Britney Spears's panties, the Internet is also very useful for tracking down instructions for building a nuclear bomb. (In fact, we're pretty sure that the Internet only does these two things . . . well, that and giving you access to all sorts of exciting workday distractions via mentalfloss.com. But we digress . . .) However, buried in the pile of Google results for "how to build a nuclear bomb" you probably didn't expect to see a site run by the U.S.

government. In a report published in November 2006, the *New York Times* revealed that a Web site set up by the United States was inadvertently providing sensitive information that might be able to help the wrong people build their own nuclear bomb. Oops! The Web site was set up in Spring 2006 as a way to give intelligence agencies a hand sorting through the 48,000 boxes of documents taken from the prewar Iraqi military, many of which hadn't yet been translated. But, in late fall, several pages of Iraq's late-80s/early-90s nuclear research were posted. According to nuclear experts, those pages contained the Web's most detailed instructions for nuclear weapons manufacture, including helpful hints for getting around tough spots that held up Iraqi progress. The whole Web site was quickly taken down once the error was discovered. Unfortunately for you, experts said that the instructions wouldn't have been very useful for individuals.

FIND SOME RADIOACTIVE MATERIALS

This can be difficult, particularly for a solitary enthusiast/nutcase like yourself. However, it's easier in Russia and the former Soviet Republics, where there have been many, many incidents of poorly guarded radioactive materials being stolen, both by average Josefs who wanted to sell it to make a quick buck for their families. It's also been traced back to the Russian mafia who, technically, also wanted to sell it to make a quick buck for their "families." In fact, misplaced nuclear something-or-others are so common in the region that civilians will occasionally stumble upon them accidentally, without any nefarious intent. In 2001, near Lja, Georgia, for instance, a group of men gathering wood in a remote rural area found a couple of strange containers that produced heat. This being the former Soviet Union in winter, you can imagine how welcome the hot boxes were back at camp. Unfortunately, after less than an hour of cozy warmth, all of the men became violently ill and developed severe radiation burns. When concerned officials reached the men's camp, they found that those would-be camp stoves were actually thermonuclear generators that had been releasing radiation levels equivalent to the immediate aftermath of Chernobyl.

REMEMBER, SIZE DOES MATTER

Miniaturization is a major issue for any nuclear program, let alone one that's meant to be carried out by one person. The United States began its nuclear history with Fat Man and Little Boy, the bombs dropped on Nagasaki and Hiroshima, which weighed, respectively, 10,300 and 8,900 pounds. Both bombs were over 10 feet in length. That definitely limited where and how you could use them. As large scale bombers gave way to slim, sexy missiles as a means of deployment, the size of the nuclear device had to get smaller, too. By the early 1990s, America had reduced the size of a nuclear bomb to about 780 pounds.

Build a Dynasty

According to Irna Phillips, creator of the soap opera

YOU WILL NEED

- **Leadership skills**
- **Innovative ideas**
- **Worshipful subjects**
- **Descendants to carry on your dream**

First: *FOUND YOUR EMPIRE*

Irna Phillips wanted to be a Hollywood star, but her acting coaches felt she had a face meant for radio. Fortunately for Irna, this was 1930, back when radio-acting jobs were plentiful and didn't necessarily involve the words "prairie," "home," or "companion." She went to work for Chicago's WGN station, where, less than a year later, she was asked to develop a 15-minute daily program about a family. The result was *Painted Dreams*, which followed the loves and adventures of a wise Irish matriarch, her grown daughter and a young, female boarder. Still trying to break into showbiz, Phillips provided the voice for the mother and several other minor characters, but her skill at concocting elaborate stories and tortured love lives would quickly eclipse her acting credentials. Within a few years, Phillips was in demand throughout the radio world. By 1943, she had five programs on the air, was pulling in a salary equivalent to more than $2 million today, and was writing more than 2 million words a year. Her melodramas, later sponsored by cleaning product companies like Proctor & Gamble and aimed at housewives ages 18–49, became known as "soap operas."

Second: *SOLIDIFY YOUR POWER*

Beyond simply creating daytime entertainment's longest-lasting genre, Phillips also pioneered nearly every convention and cliché that went along with it. Her soap operas featured organ music to punctuate dramatic moments, she pioneered the open-ended serialized style and weekly cliffhanger ending that kept listeners coming back for more. She even created the first medical drama—inspired by her own chronic hypochondria, which prompted near daily visits to doctors and hospitals. And, in 1937, she created a particular drama that would go on to become the world's longest running entertainment program and the world's longest continuous story—*The Guiding Light*. Originally, the "guiding light" in question was the lamp in the study of a small-town reverend, which served as a beacon to his frequently emotionally beleaguered parishioners. On *The Guiding Light*, Phillips pioneered what was to become another standard part of soap opera fare, plots that tied directly to pressing (and salacious) social concerns. Phillips wrote to the leaders of organizations like the Red Cross, Child Welfare, and the American Legion to find out what social problems they wanted to educate her audience about. Often, the organizations actually sent her individual case histories, which she wove into the plots. In fact, during the 1940s, *The Guiding Light* featured radio's first (and soap history's first of many) illegitimate pregnancy. When soap operas made the jump to television, Irna Phillips went with them. *The Guiding Light* hit the boob tube in 1952.

Third: ***HAND THE REIGNS TO A NEW GENERATION***

Despite her success, Phillips wasn't completely at home in the television genre. According to Gerard J. Waggett's *The Soap Opera Encyclopedia*, NBC attempted to run the first color TV broadcast of *The Guiding Light* in 1953. But Phillips, for unknown reasons, deliberately set the entire episode in a surgical ward, where nearly everything—from props, to costumes, to the walls—was either black or white. The episode was a flop and Phillips ended up single-handedly pushing back the adoption of regular color broadcasting by almost a decade. But while she may not have been totally comfortable in the television world, her heirs certainly were. Throughout her career, Phillips employed various assistant writers who later went on to create famous and long-running soaps of their own. In fact, nearly every soap on daytime TV today was created by Phillips or by one of her disciples.

Convince Others to Do Your Bidding

Method #1: ***BY REMOTE CONTROL***

It's every despot's dream: tiny electrodes, implanted into the brains of your subjects, compelling them to follow your command. Of course, the technology has more "ethical" applications as well. Currently, scientists are experimenting with electrodes that can make several different species of animals perform useful work, including protecting humans. In several different studies, fish, primates, rodents, and even pigeons have been fitted with small electrical implants that allow scientists to tap in and take control. Once that's done, the researchers simply manipulate skills and habits that the animals would be using anyway. One of the most successful studies was conducted on rats, taking advantage of the creatures' heightened sense of smell. Researchers at the State University of New York Science Center taught the rats to expect a reward (via artificial stimulation of their brains' pleasure centers) every time they caught of whiff of the material used to make plastic explosives. Thanks to that positive motivation, the animals now seek out the scent, thus becoming an extremely effective (and cute!) tool for bomb detection squads.

Method #2: *BY PARASITE*

Toxoplasma gondii is a small creature, but it wields enormous power. Mice ingest this parasite from eating cat feces and, once in their brains, toxoplasma prompts the mice into risky behavior. Amazingly, this behavior actually makes the mice more likely to be eaten by the cats. What can we say, it's a mutually beneficial cycle. Of course, people also come into frequent contact with cat feces via the dreaded litterbox. Scientists estimate that nearly 40 percent of humans worldwide carry *Toxoplasma gondii* but, other than being a potential danger to unborn babies, we always thought the parasite was no problem for us. Turns out, we were wrong. In 2006, a researcher at Australia's Sydney Institute of Technology discovered that toxoplasma can control human behavior as well. In men, this control manifests similarly to mice, causing guys to be more reckless, more violent, and less intelligent. For women, however, toxoplasma has a different effect, leading them to the sort of behavior that's best suited to, say, a *Girls Gone Wild* video. So why does the parasite make women act sexy and men act dumb? Nobody knows—yet. But humans beware, a different study showed that toxoplasma victims of both sexes are more likely to cause car crashes and have higher rates of schizophrenia than the unaffected population.

Method #3: *BY PSYCHOLOGICAL MIND CONTROL*

Put on your tin hats and get ready to be shocked. From 1950 to 1965, the CIA and the Canadian government funded mind control experiments run by Dr. Ewen Cameron, the second president of the World Psychiatric Association. Seriously. Cameron's research centered on a technique he called "psychic driving," which involved breaking down a mentally ill patient's damaged personality. In exchange for the equivalent of $500,000, he agreed to apply the same techniques to more stable minds. Unwitting patients at Montreal's Allan Memorial Institute (many suffering from nothing more than mild depression) were subjected to such "treatments" as months-long drug-induced comas, surprise LSD trips, and extra-strength electroshock—all while a series of statements played over and over in their headphones. The effects were profound. One woman, who had been a college honors student, spent the rest of her life suffering from recurring bouts of incontinence and thumb sucking. In the 1970s, many victims got together to seek legal action. In 1994, the CIA and the Canadian government settled out of court, paying the defendants thousands of dollars in damages. A few people, whose psychological damage was less severe, had to wait even longer. In 2004, the Canadian government agreed to pay reparations to them as well, in one case as much as $100,000.

Feed an Army

YOU WILL NEED

- **To do a better job than your historical counterparts**

First: ***KEEP A TIGHT REIN ON YOUR SUPPLY CHAIN***

Military contractors might seem like big, old, loveable teddy bears, but the truth is, some of them can be bad apples. That's why, to make it big in the army-feeding business, you'll need to throw away your wide-eyed ideals and learn how to be a cynic. And who better to teach you than the United States military, which has been dealing with corrupt suppliers for more than 150 years. Uncle Sam learned his hardest lessons during the Civil War, when love for the Union did nothing to stop contractors from ripping their troops off—at the expense of soldiers' stomachs. The ration situation was already dire, due to a lack of helpful (and tasty!) artificial preservatives. The average soldier subsisted, grudgingly, on salted meat, rock-hard cracker, sugar, salt, and coffee. So it didn't help matters (or morale) much when four out of five of those foodstuffs arrived rotten, stale, or insect-ridden. Meanwhile, the contractors were charging the government top dollar for these "quality" "goods." Eventually, it got to the point where even the coffee was ruined. In 1861, the army switched from whole coffee beans to a concentrated proto-instant coffee solution that, while being easier to prepare in the field, left much to be desired in the way of flavor. Worse, the "essence of coffee" was made from a thick glop of prepared coffee, sugar, and milk—milk that had been purchased from corrupt dairymen and was, more often than not, spoiled. The result: a pot of brown sludge that left your bowels feeling as foul as your tongue.

Second: *DON'T FORGET THE ROUGHAGE*

This is more serious than you think. Besides making you the butt (heh) of sophomoric jokes, not getting enough fruits and veggies could actually contribute to your demise. In 2007, new research showed that France's famed Emperor Napoleon was felled not by homicidal English poisoners, but by his own diet. Comparing Napoleon's medical history and autopsy documents with data from 135 modern victims of gastrointestinal cancer, scientists were able to determine that the little conqueror died of a cancerous stomach. In fact, the doctors who performed Napoleon's autopsy reported finding a massive tumor, at least 4 inches long, on the side of his stomach. As it turns out, the salty, rich, largely veggie-free diet Napoleon spent decades eating with the rest of the French military helped to provide the perfect tummy conditions to let the bacteria and the ulcers run rampant.

Third: *FIND CREATIVE SOLUTIONS FOR ALL-TERRAIN MEALS*

The U.S. military menu has definitely improved since the Civil War. Today's soldier can whip him or herself up a batch of veggie primavera, home-style tuna casserole, or even beef pot roast—just heat and serve. But what happens when you're stranded in some remote location, where more than 7 pounds of MREs per day starts to seem a little too heavy? For those situations, the army has a handy suggestion: dehydrated meals reconstituted with pee. The newest development in military eating technology is a high-tech filter capable reducing most toxins by 99.9 percent. Thanks to the feature, ultra-lightweight field rations (think less than a pound for a day's supply of food) can now be prepared with dirty water . . . or even urine. Filtered through a cellulose membrane just .5 nanometers wide, the liquid comes out clean enough to cook up a packet of chicken and rice—but only temporarily. Small as it is, the membrane can't remove urea, so using pee to make your food in the long term will still give even the heartiest soldier a bad case of kidney damage.

Go Insane

YOU WILL NEED

- 1 (or more) chemical imbalances
- 1 (or more) vendettas against a public figure
- 1 gun

First: ***REALIZE THAT "THEY" REALLY ARE OUT TO GET YOU***

Although a sure-fire way to become crazy, adopting this tactic can also get you into some serious trouble. Just ask Daniel M'Naughten, a Scottish carpenter who, in 1843, decided that a recent streak of financial bad luck was actually the result of a multilevel conspiracy dedicated to destroying him. Among the perpetrators of this heinous plot, M'Naughten fingered the Pope and British Prime Minister Robert Peel. Doing what anyone caught in an inescapable web of lies and deceit would do, M'Naughten chose to confront his tormenter, showing up outside 10 Downing Street late one night. Words were exchanged. Shots were fired. And when the smoke cleared, M'Naughten had killed not PM Peel, but his personal secretary—just another brick in the conspiracy's wall, no doubt.

Then: ***CONVINCE EVERYONE ELSE THAT YOU'RE JUST AS CRAZY AS YOU SAY YOU ARE***

This is easier said than done. Nowadays, anyway. Back in the 19th century, M'Naughten had very little trouble convincing a jury of his peers that he was loonier than a barrel full of monkeys. Declared "innocent by reason of insanity," his trial marked what is widely accepted as the first successful use of the insanity plea. However, then, as now, the idea of letting a killer go free wasn't a particularly popular decision. No less an irate citizen than Queen Victoria complained to Parliament and the case was eventually reviewed by a high court panel of judges. Their decision: Defendants cannot be held responsible for their actions if, at the time, they didn't know what they were doing was wrong. Known as the "right/wrong test," it influenced legal theory for generations to come. As for M'Naughten, his "not guilty" verdict was overturned and he spent the rest of his life in a mental institution.

Let Life
Hand You Some
Lemons...

Get Stranded on a Desert Island

YOU WILL NEED

- 1 career that places you in frequent contact with tropical islands
- 1 unhappy superior
- Fresh water
- Ingenuity

Step 1: *ROYALLY TICK OFF YOUR BOSS*

Just ask Christopher Columbus. The so-called discoverer of America was down on his luck by the time he'd made his fourth trip to the New World in 1502. He'd never found the vast quantities of gold needed to repay his investors (i.e., the Spanish Royal Court) and, as if to add insult to injury, he managed to get caught in a hurricane that sunk his boats and stranded him and 120 crewmen on the coast of what is now Jamaica. In fact, his crew was only 150 miles away from the Spanish fort on the island of Hispaniola but, because of that whole not-paying-back-Royal-loans thing, nobody came looking for them.

Another brilliant example of interoffice relations gone wrong is the story of Scottish privateer Alexander Selkirk, who got into a fight with his captain over some routine ship repair back in 1704. Selkirk, the second-in-command and ship's navigator, thought the repairs needed to be made before the boat took off on another raid. The captain disagreed, so Selkirk cleverly announced that he'd rather stay on the deserted island where they'd anchored than get back on an unsafe ship. Unfortunately, he chose to end this speech with a Jerry Magiure-esque "Who's comin' with me . . . ?" and nobody stood up. Worse, the captain then decided to take Selkirk at his word and literally left him, marooned, on the island.

Step 2: *PASS TIME CONTEMPLATING WHAT YOU MIGHT HAVE DONE TO DESERVE THIS*

We hate to be a Debbie Downer but, for Columbus, some prestranding public relations might have gone a long way toward a timely rescue. As it was, the captain had so stridently alienated the Spanish government that, when he sent two crewmen by canoe to the Hispaniola colony for help, the men were promptly thrown into prison. Then the Governor of Hispaniola sent a messenger (by boat) to Jamaica to inform Columbus that no boat could be spared to rescue him. Ouch. All told, Columbus was marooned on Jamaica for almost a year before his imprisoned crewmen were released and managed to charter a ship to rescue their Captain.

Step 3: *THINK: WHAT WOULD MARTHA DO?*

As for Selkirk, he ended up living alone for more than four years, but it wasn't all bad. The island had been the location of a failed Spanish colony, which had left behind feral goats and a veritable all-you-can-eat salad bar of semi-wild produce, including oats, plums, pumpkins, radishes, figs, and parsnips. There were even cats, which Selkirk tamed by the truckload, eventually sharing his cozy hut, cat-lady-like, with more than a dozen. Frankly, it was a better life than you'd find on board a boat. In fact, when a British ship showed up to rescue Selkirk in 1709, he declared their worm-eaten biscuits and salted beef to be inedible. Instead, he invited the crew up to the hut for a healthy, home-cooked meal, simultaneously awing them with his kitchen skills and saving most of them from dying of scurvy. Selkirk's ability to turn lemons into lemon soufflés was such a good thing that his story was later fictionalized into a rather famous novel—*Robinson Crusoe.*

Drive an Animal to Extinction

Method 1: *THROUGH GLUTTONY*

There used to be hundreds of thousands of giant tortoises roaming South America's Galapagos Islands. Today, there are roughly 15,000. What can we say? Turtles are tasty. In the 16th and 17th centuries, the Galapagos were the swashbuckler's equivalent of a 7-Eleven—the last chance to stock up on food before hitting the vast emptiness of the Pacific. Besides being slow and docile (i.e., easy to catch) the tortoises could also survive for up to a year without food and water. Sailors often captured hundreds at a time, stacked them on their backs, and thus had fresh meat all the way to India.

Method 2: *OUT OF SHEER HATRED*

Passenger pigeons once traveled in flocks so large, they could block out the sun over a town for eight hours. In the process, they gobbled down all the fruits and grains they could get their beaks on and left the "remains" for farmers to step in. All this made them rather . . . unpopular. Throughout the 19th century, killing passenger pigeons was a favorite frontier pastime. Baited with alcohol-soaked grain, gassed with sulfur fires, and loaded live into trapshooting launchers (they were later replaced by clay "pigeons"), the passenger pigeon population quickly petered out. The last one died in the Cincinnati Zoo on Sept. 1, 1914.

Method 3: *VIA TRAGICOMIC IRONY*

Collector and proto-environmentalist Rollo Beck visited the island of Guadalupe, off Baja California, on December 1, 1900. During the trip, he sighted a flock of nine Caracaras, a rare bird he wished to study (and stuff), and so shot down all but two of them. Those two turned out to be the last Caracaras ever seen alive.

Plagiarize

According to H.G. Wells

Turns out, the man who foresaw submarines and space travel was probably as much a plagiarist as a prophet. In 1920, after less than a year of research and writing and with no previous experience in the subject, Wells published *The Outline of History*, a two-volume set that attempted to cover everything from the formation of the universe to World War I. Despite those shaky foundations, it was an instant best seller, which is how a Canadian woman named Florence Deeks heard about it. Wells's book turned out to be very familiar to Deeks. Nearly two years previously, she'd written a remarkably similar work, titled *The Web of the World's Romance*, with which Wells's tome shared the same outline, the same anecdotes, and even the same factual errors. More damning, Deeks had sent her manuscript to Wells's publisher, who'd kept it for a year before rejecting it. And, according to historian A. B. McKillop, the returned manuscript was more dog-eared than a frustrated freshman's copy of *Lady Chatterly's Lover*. In her 2002 book *The Spinster and the Prophet*, McKillop told the story of Deeks's attempt to sue the vaunted Wells for plagiarism, a suit she ultimately lost several times over, despite said pile of evidence. In fact, according to McKillop's research, it's very likely that Wells did indeed use Deeks's book as a sort of crib sheet for his own.

According to Madonna

No virgin to plagiarism accusations, Madonna has settled out of court for one offense and lost a lawsuit over another. In 2004, the singer/dancer/sex object reportedly paid off the son of a famous French photographer (to the tune of more than $600,000) after he claimed that her video for the song "Hollywood" had blatantly ripped off several of his late father's photographs. Less than a year later, Madonna was back in court, this time over allegations that her song "Frozen" incorporated the melody from an earlier song recorded by Belgian singer Salvatore Acquaviva. The song had appeared on the 1998 album *Ray of Light* and bore striking resemblance to Acquaviva's 1993 ditty "Ma Vie Fout L'camp (My Life's Getting Nowhere)" Ultimately, Madonna lost the suit, resulting in all remaining copies of *Ray of Light* being pulled from store shelves.

According to Martin Luther King Jr.

Before he became famous as the leader of the American Civil Rights Movement, Martin Luther King spent several years as a relatively anonymous graduate theology student at Boston University. Although considered a model student at the time, it later turned out that King's academic career wasn't as glossy as it appeared. In 1990, archivists with the Martin Luther King Papers Project publicly released findings showing that King's 1955 doctoral thesis, *A Comparison of the Conception of God in the Thinking of Paul Tillich and Henry Nelson Weiman*, was riddled with underattributed (and a few completely unattributed) quotes, as well as some cribbed conclusions.

Given that King (and his faculty advisor) were both dead by the time anyone noticed the faux pas, we'll probably never know exactly what happened. In the end, the University opted not to posthumously undoctor Dr. King, but the incident remains a smudge on the great man's legacy.

According to Johnny Cash

Although the "Man in Black" never actually went to prison himself, he certainly did do his share of thievin'. In *Johnny Cash at Folsom Prison: The Making of a Masterpiece*, author Michael Streissguth shows that Cash's most famous song, "Folsom Prison Blues," was actually ripped off from the work of big band conductor and music arranger Gordon Jenkins. In 1952, Jenkins released the song "Crescent City Blues" as part of a concept album called *Seven Dreams*. Other than a change of venue, achieved via the addition of a few undeniably superior lyrics, Cash's 1956 "Folsom Prison Blues" is the exact same song. Nonetheless, it took Jenkins more than a decade to file a suit, after which Cash settled with him, out of court, for an undisclosed sum.

Sell a Kidney on the Black Market

YOU WILL NEED

- **1 good and/or cheap surgeon**
- **1 remaining kidney in good working order**
- **1 empty bank account (for motivation)**

First: *YOU'VE GOT TO REALLY, REALLY NEED THE MONEY.* Sure, humans have two kidneys and you can live without one, but most black-market kidney dealers don't provide quality medical care for their donors—often sloppily pulling out kidneys without any regard to other organs or broken ribs. Some extractions aren't even done by doctors. This is probably why the majority of live kidney donors come from undeveloped countries where $1,500 American is considered a good trade for a bodily organ. In fact, in one single village in Moldova, the *Washington Post* found that nearly half of all the local men had sold a body part, mostly kidneys. Some local governments have tried to crack down on organ trade, but without much success. In India, a 1994 law criminalized organ sales—but inexplicably left a loophole for "unrelated kidney sales." More than 2,000 Indians sell a kidney each year and there is a growing trend toward selling half a liver as well.

Second: *YOU NEED TO FIND A BUYER.* Fortunately, this is not at all difficult. Unfortunately, you're probably going to get ripped off. In India, local dealers pay villagers $1,000 U.S.D. for a kidney, which they turn around and sell to wealthy clients for upwards of $150,000. Those clients, usually from Israel and countries in Europe and North America, are willing to pay so much because kidneys (and other organs) are harder to come by then you'd think. In the United States, kidney patients wait an average of three years for a new organ. In Israel, where religious considerations prevent organ harvesting from brain-dead patients, the wait is even longer. It's illegal to buy organs in both the U.S. and Israel, so many patients seeking blackmarket kidneys travel to countries where the laws are more lax. Brazil is a hot spot for this "transplant tourism." In fact, many would-be donors there offer their organs for sale in local newspapers.

KIDNEYS: A BUYER'S GUIDE

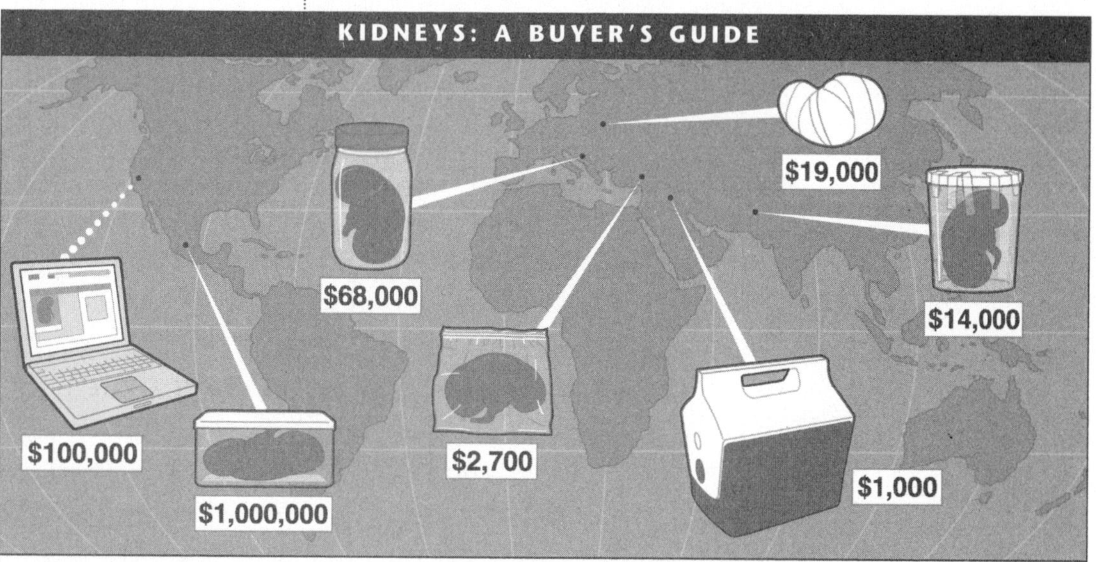

The price for a kidney from a live donor varies—so be sure to shop around.

Turkey: $2,700
Iraq: $1,000
Pakistan: $14,000
Ukraine: $19,000
Bosnia-Herzegovina: $68,000
Ebay: A February 2000 auction reached $100,000 before eBay stopped the sale.

Mexico: $1 million (A priest, working as a middleman for a corrupt doctor, tried to charge an undercover news crew this amount in 2004.)

USA: no record on live donors, but families have been offered free funerals, reduced telephone rates, and up to $1 million for their deceased loved one's body parts

Write a Really Bad Book

Bad writing is, of course, in the eye of the beholder, but Bruce Felton and Mark Fowler have a better claim to the title of beholder than most. In the 1970s, they conducted a thorough survey of critics, experts, and media and came up with some of the world's most reviled writing. From their book, *The Best, Worst & Most Unusual*, we take the following tips:

USE RHYME IN A NONFICTION WORK

And you thought high school history class couldn't have possibly gotten any worse. You're just lucky that your district opted not to teach with Major Frederick Howe's 1882 opus *A Condensed History of the United States of America in Rhyme*. Yes, in rhyme. We'll let that sink in. Worse, Major Howe, as his title implies, wasn't a professional poet or even a professional writer but a military man with a penchant for history and overwrought purple literature. Surprisingly, he wasn't the only person to attempt the poetic textbook. In 1886, one Adrian Hitt published a 381-page presidential epic entitled *The Grant Poem, Containing Grant's Public Career and Private Life from the Cradle to the Grave*. Look for it at your local poetry slam.

TRAUMATIZE CHILDREN

Growing up, as we did, reading life- and self-esteem-affirming picture books, it's a little creepy to realize that the earliest children's lit wasn't nearly so happy-go-lucky. When the genre first popped up in colonial times, one of the major themes was death—both the horrid deaths of bad little children who didn't obey their parents and the blessed, saintly deaths of those who did. In fact, when good children died, their deaths were often lionized and presented as an example to follow in such works as George Hendley's *A Memorial for Children, Being an Authentic Account of the Conversion, Experience* and *Happy Deaths of Eighteen Children*. Bad children, on the other hand, were depicted speaking such bedtime-ready lines as "My days will quickly end, and I must lie/Broyling in flames to All Eternity." Sleep tight!

RUIN SEX FOR EVERYBODY

The award for worst love scene definitely goes to the Marquis de Sade, who in his 1791 novel *Justine* depicted his heroine and her lover exchanging both kisses and (horrors) vomit.

Sell Your Younger Siblings

Oh, admit it. You've been tempted. Relax, it's okay. Everyone has had to deal with sibling rivalry at some point or another, even:

MICHAEL DUKAKIS

There's no worse time to have a brother who hates you than when you're running for public office. Just ask this would-be president of the United States who, during his 1988 campaign, had to contend with not only the slings and arrows of average political debate, but also with more personal allegations involving his troubled (and by then, deceased) older brother Stelian. The two had always had a somewhat contentious relationship. Interviews with their mother in *Time* magazine during the campaign reflect an "anything you can do, I can do better" type situation. In high school, Stelian made the honor society. Michael became its president. Stelian joined the tennis team. Michael was named captain. So it's little wonder that, when the elder brother developed severe depression that forced him to drop out of college, he took to blaming Michael for his troubles. In fact, when Michael Dukakis ran for Massachussetts state representative, Stelian campaigned against him. Although Stelian was killed by a hit-and-run driver in 1973, his mental health became an issue in Michael's presidential campaign. Political opponents suggested that the candidate might be prone to mental illness and President Ronald Reagan even made a joke referring to Dukakis as "an invalid." The issue ended up forcing Michael to disclose his entire medical history and became a major factor in his eventual loss. Whether somewhere Stelian was smiling, we'll never know.

KOOKABURRAS

Thanks to the indoctrination provided by Girl Scout camp sing-a-longs, we were always under the impression that the kookaburra was a friendly, funny little bird. And they may well be . . . but definitely not to their siblings. In 2000, a study published in the journal *Behavioral Ecology and Sociobiology* revealed that kookaburras, as a whole, tend to kill (or at least, slowly starve) the youngest sibling in their nest. The birds almost always lay sets of three eggs and these arrangements turn foul pretty quickly for the last to hatch. The birds are actually born armed with a hooked end to their beaks that seems to be used solely for killing their brothers and sisters (a few days after birth, the hook falls off). So what's the point of all this kookaburra-on-kookaburra violence? Survival. Biologists believe that the larger chicks in the nest kill off the smaller ones in an effort to keep more food and more resources for themselves. Sort of like when your brother used to punch you in the arm for a candy bar, only more gruesome.

MATHEMATICIANS

You'd think that with their dedication to logic and unemotional thinking, math-men would have an easier time getting along with their siblings. Sadly, not true. At least not for the Bernoulli brothers, Johann and Jacob. The Bernoullis were a Swiss family famous for their mathematical prowess (Johann's son Daniel is widely known for having a physics principle named after him) and for their tendency to hold long-standing grudges. What exactly prompted the feud between the brothers is unclear but, according to historian Jeanne Peiffer and mathematician Douglas Quinney, the two routinely schemed against one another during their lives. Some of the lowlights: repeated attempts to professionally embarrass one another, usually involving Johann dissing Jacob's inability to quickly solve difficult problems while Jacob flaunted Johann's computational errors; at least one accusation of shameless intellectual theft on the part of Jacob; Jacob's successful blackballing of Johann's application for a professorship at the University of Basel; and Johann's subsequent delight when Jacob later died, leaving an open professorship which Johann quickly (and successfully) campaigned for. Who'd have guessed that math could be so Jerry Springer?

Cause an International Crisis

First: ***DON'T READ YOUR MAIL***

That way, you can remain blissfully uninformed about important events that you (and your staff) are likely to misinterpret. Case in point: On the night of January 25, 1995, Boris Yeltsin found himself dusting off the old Cold War–era nuclear command briefcase when an early warning radar station detected a missile rising out of the Norwegian Sea and heading for Russia. Several tense, finger-on-the-trigger minutes later, Yeltsin received word that the rocket, though real, was actually part of a Norwegian scientific mission to study the northern lights—a mission Moscow had been informed of months previously. Turns out, bureaucratic error had stalled the message before it could reach the folks over at the early warning defense system. Worse, this wasn't the first time simple mistakes have pushed the world close to mutually assured destruction.

YOU WILL NEED

- A perilous (and paranoid) diplomatic climate
- Weapons of mass destruction
- Human error

Second: ***PUT OFF THAT EYE APPOINTMENT***

Things are not always what they seem. And, if history is any indication, if what you see seems to be a Russian nuclear threat, you probably ought to look closer. On November 5, 1956, the American military received four disturbing security warnings: Unidentified planes were flying over Turkey, 100 Soviet fighter planes were spotted over Syria, a British bomber had been shot down over Syria, and the Soviet naval fleet was moving into an attack position. Taken together, those reports looked like a prelude to a Russian attack on American allies. In fact, they almost triggered N.A.T.O. nuclear air strikes against Russia, until further study revealed that the Soviet fleet was just doing routine exercises, the bomber had had a mechanical failure, and the "Soviet fighter jets" were actually a large flock of swans. The lesson here, by the way, went unlearned. Six years later, in the midst of the Cuban Missile Crisis, the United States sent several nuclear-armed jets taxiing down the runway in response to an alarm triggered by a foreign intruder. The assailant had set off sirens climbing the fence at a defense station in Duluth, Minnesota. Luckily, officials noticed something awry and drove out onto the tarmac to flag the planes down just in time to stop a takeoff. Hardly a communist spy, the mysterious intruder was revealed to have been a bear.

Third: *MIX WORK AND PLAY*

War games can be useful tools and certainly have their place—but that place probably ought to be somewhere where they aren't mistaken for the real thing. At 8:50 a.m. on November 9, 1979, hardened warriors at 4 of the U.S. military's top command centers were plunged into a blind panic when their computer systems started showing a full-scale Soviet nuclear attack on the United States. Immediately, a retaliation to end all retaliations was prepped for launch. Luckily, before we fired anything, somebody decided it might be a good idea to make sure those hostile enemy missiles actually existed and made a couple of quick calls to Pacific radar stations. The result: nada. There wasn't so much as a cloud in the sky. Turns out, a computer tape loaded with a Soviet first strike scenario war game had been accidentally inserted into a computer that was being used for real-life surveillance.

Fourth: *DON'T RELAX*

To cause a really good international crisis, you'll need to be as edgy and paranoid as possible. In 1983, that's how the Soviet Union ended up closer to the brink of nuclear war than it had been since the 1962 Cuban Missile Crisis. To be fair, 1983 was a really tense year. The United States had invaded Grenada, putting it within spitting distance of Cuba; a bombing in Beirut that killed 146 Americans was being blamed on Soviet forces; and the Ruskies themselves had recently mistaken a passenger airliner for a spy plane and shot it down—killing hundreds of civilians. In between the hard-line rhetoric coming from the States and their own monstrous screw up, the Soviets were expecting some kind of show down. On November 2, N.A.T.O. command posts around the world began moving nuclear weapons into attack positions. The Soviets knew it was time for the annual N.A.T.O. training exercise, but feared it wasn't a test. After all, they'd seriously considered using war games as a cover for a first strike themselves.

For the next 9 days, the U.S.S.R. was on high alert. According to some sources, nuclear-armed jet fighters were waiting on the tarmac, engines primed and ready to go, until November 11, when N.A.T.O. ended what had been just a training exercise after all.

Host a Roman Bacchanalia

YOU WILL NEED

- A toga
- A favorite Fellini movie to emulate
- An MP3 of "Shout!" (to play on loop)

BRING THE WIFE

While not exactly paragons of female equality, the Romans also certainly weren't at the bottom of the patriarchy pole either (that spot probably goes to the Greeks, who believed that ladies shouldn't be seen or heard and basically kept them locked up in the house). Unmarried Roman women, particularly those who were engaged via arranged marriage, didn't have a whole lot of freedom, but that changed once the marriage was validated. At that point, wives were regarded more as their husband's helpers than his property. They had power within their home, could go out of it when they wanted, and were usually invited along with their husbands to dinner parties. (Any of which would have caused a minor social crisis and possibly forced intervention had it been tried in ancient Greece.) However, unlike their husbands, women were generally expected to stay sober for these parties and were almost never invited to the booziest shindigs.

GET CREATIVE WITH THE MENU

The original Roman dinner probably isn't at all like what you'd imagine. Up until the later years of the Republic, almost everybody in Rome, from wealthy to slave, based their diet around a fat-and-wheat gruel called *puls*, into which various vegetables (and, if you were rich, meat, cheese, fish or eggs) might be added. Yum. By the time of the Empire, however, this relatively Spartan diet had blossomed into a full-on decadent cuisine. Dinner, called the *cena,* would often begin around 3 p.m. and last for hours. With guests, you might be up until late in the night. There were 3 courses, with any number of dishes involved in each and, for the better sort of parties it was generally understood that the more whimsical the menu, the better. Thus, you got dishes like the "Trojan Pig," a whole roasted porker stuffed with sausages and fruit meant to spill out like entrails when the stomach was cut open; creative cuts of meat like uterus or marinated lark's tongues; and exotic additions like stuffed whole dormice, whole ostrich, or peacock.

DON'T FORGET THE ROTTEN FISH

Of course, no Roman dinner party was complete without *liquamen*, ancient Rome's rather disgusting answer to ketchup. The sauce was made by taking the guts of several different kinds of fish, mashing them into a liquid, and letting them stew in the sun for weeks, even months, before straining off the solids and bottling (tightly) the rest. Romans put this stuff on everything, from meat to veggies . . . even some desserts. Nevertheless, they weren't immune to the sauce's gross nature. Reportedly, the smell put off by fermenting liquamen was so rancid, even to Roman noses, that production of the condiment was banned within city limits.

KEEP IT ALL DOWN

Much has been made of the vomitorium, the room distinguished Romans supposedly retired to in order to, uh, "make room for another course." But, sadly, history has burned us all on this one. According to Cecil Adams, author of *The Straight Dope* books, vomitoriums weren't rooms to vomit in at all. Rather, they were an architectural feature added onto the entrances of stadiums to help keep the flow of human traffic moving. Apparently, the mix up can be blamed on Aldous Huxley, who first used the term incorrectly back in 1923. That's not to say, however, that Romans weren't doing some seriously nasty things during dinner. Ancient texts describe tableside bedpan service and ralphing that was, apparently, rampant. They just didn't have a special room for it.

Join the Amish

YOU WILL NEED

- Fortitude
- A strong desire to get out of the rat race
- A beard (guys only!)

Step 1: *LEARN THE DIFFERENCE BETWEEN AMISH AND MENNONITE*

You're never going to endear yourself to your new neighbors if you can't tell one apart from their theological cousins down the road. Historically the older of the two sects, Mennonites believed in plain, unadorned living and adult baptism, making them not all that different from the other Christian groups that popped up in Germany and Switzerland in the 17th century. But, around 1693, one of their members, a guy named Jakob Amman, started to get a little rowdy. Amman traveled around the countryside preaching a more hard-line version of Mennonism that called for, among other things, a return to traditional clothing, avoidance of worldly grooming trends like moustaches, mandatory uncut beards, and the public shunning of excommunicated church members. Taking their name from Amman's, his new followers called themselves "Amish." Over the next few hundred years, both groups did their fair share of theological off-shooting. Today, there are numerous sub-groups of both Mennonite and Amish, making it difficult to pin them down with generalities. However, in most cases, the easiest way to tell the two apart is to look for a family car—most Mennonites drive them, most Amish don't. But, just because they enjoy a faster mode of travel doesn't mean the Mennonites are ostentatious about their automobiles. In fact, it's common practice to cover any Detroit-installed chrome with black paint, just to let the world know they aren't trying to be flashy.

Step 2: *MOVE TO OHIO*

Contrary to popular belief, the geographic epicenter of Amish life is not Lancaster County, Pennsylvania. Turns out, several counties in east-central Ohio are actually home to the largest Amish community in the world—population 29,000, and growing. Each Amish family has an average of 7 children, so their numbers have seemingly doubled every 20 years since outsiders started keeping records in the 1940s.

Step 3: *SHOP AT SPECTOR'S*

This department store in Middlefield, Ohio, caters to Amish customers. Since 1937, they've dealt in things like quilting supplies, fabric, and the other necessities of Amish life that can't be easily made on the farm. And with several locations around the state, it may well be the world's first Amish-centric chain store.

Step 4: *GET A FARM*

Believe it or now, it's harder than it sounds. There are two things working against you. First, that whole population growth issue means that every generation sees even more young men in need of a farm of their own. The other problem, however, comes from the outside. Across the country, the rural areas the Amish inhabit are rapidly becoming exurbs, and what was once farmland is being sold to make way for subdivisions and Wal-Marts—making raw land, even when it is available, prohibitively expensive. In Lancaster County, for instance, 100 acres can now cost as much as $1 million. If, however, you can get your hands on some good farmland, get ready to build a lot of barns. You probably already know that Amish construct their own, and their neighbors', in massive 24-hour barn raising parties. But, because many Amish groups don't believe in using "worldly" devices like lightning rods, those hand-built barns often end up getting re-hand-built.

Destroy History

YOU WILL NEED

- Questionable content
- A way to keep it out of the public eye

HIDE IT

Although widely beloved as a sort of satirical Santa Claus today, any rational look at the biography of Mark Twain would reveal a very different man. The real Mark Twain was more often depressed than jolly, more bitter curmudgeon than wacky old coot. Then there was the atheism, the temper, and, oh yeah, the fact that he spent his later years surrounded by a flock of adoring underage girls. That last bit wasn't as bad as it sounds. The girls were always chaperoned and, apparently, the whole thing was on the up and up. But the pictures still look sufficiently suspicious that Twain's daughter, Clara Clemens Samossoud, kept them out of the public eye as long as she was alive. And that wasn't all she censored. Clemens Samossoud also forbade the publication of two of Twain's later books—*Letters from the Earth* and *The Autobiography of Mark Twain*. The former, a novel written as a series of letters from Satan to various Archangels, wasn't published until 1962. Around the same time, Clemens Samossoud approved the publication of five never-before-seen chapters she'd had cut from the autobiography when it was originally published in the 1930s. What brought on the sudden change of heart? A *New York Times* story from that fateful year reported that Twain's daughter was probably attempting to silence Soviet literary critics, who'd attacked her (in particular) and American society (in general) for censoring the books.

BURN IT

Really, few historical figures were above leaving behind written material their modern fans might term objectionable. Case in point, George Washington. In *George Washington Slept Here*, author Karal Ann Marling describes how, in 1925, one of J. P. Morgan's sons used some of his vast inherited wealth to buy up and then destroy several "smutty" letters attributed to our nation's founding father.

Start a Riot

YOU WILL NEED:

- A mob
- A way to make them angry
- Pitchforks?

Step 1: ***FIND A GOOD CAUSE***

May we suggest "the poll tax"? Basically a tax based on the number of people in your household rather than on the amount of income you bring in ("poll" in this case is derived from an English word for "head"), poll taxes were, up until the late 19th century, an extremely common and extremely lucrative source of income for most governments. However, they were (unsurprisingly) unpopular with the masses—you know, those people with the torches and pitchforks? In England alone, dissatisfaction with the poll tax has lead to more than a dozen riots over the centuries, the most famous and widespread ones occurring in 1381 and 1990. Yes, 1990. Up until that year, local community taxes had been paid based on the value of the home you owned. If you didn't own a home, you didn't have to pay. In an attempt to make the system more fair, the British government changed the community tax so that it was, instead, a set amount that had to be paid by every adult in town. However, given income disparities between those adults, the new system wasn't particularly fair, either, a fact the citizenry made clear during a series of protests-turned-riots in March. In London, cars were overturned and lit on fire, police and firefighters were attacked with bricks, and many stores were looted—adding up to the worst riot the city had seen in a century. In fact, the whole system was so unpopular nationwide that it helped take down a prime minister. In November 1990, among calls for the poll tax's repeal, Margaret Thatcher stepped down after leading the United Kingdom for 11 years. Her replacements reverted to the old taxation system the next year. But, by 1993, yet another new PM had instituted a different plan—a tax that applied to everyone in town, but on a sliding scale based onthe value of your home or apartment and on the number of adults living there.

Step 2: *FIND A CONVENIENT LOCALE*

Constantinople used to be quite good for this sort of thing, with regular riots breaking out every few years before 1000 C.E. The worst of these was the Nika riots that swept the city in January of 532 C.E. The city burned for five days and, in a clash between the military and civilian protesters, a reported 30,000 people were killed. The cause was a caustic mix of politics and sports hooliganism. Roman society during this period was divided by a pair of warring chariot-race teams: the greens and the blues. Beyond being simply sports teams, these were also civic organizations charged with the responsibility of organizing public displays honoring the emperor. The trouble was, at the time, most people weren't too happy with His Majesty Justinian. The animosity came to a head when the unpopular emperor passed an even more unpopular law requiring that all sports fans be prosecuted equally for wanton public violence—thus breaking down a centuries old tradition of looking the other way. Then, provocatively, he went on to enforce the law, ordering the execution of several men, both greens and blues, who'd started a previous riot. Although Justinian commuted their sentences to imprisonment, the two teams banded together, demanding a full pardon and launching a rebellion halfway through an annual chariot race festival. The ensuing violence came to be known by the code word used by the conspirators—"nika" or "conquer." Unfortunately for them, however, the proposed conquering didn't really pan out. Although rioters managed to free the condemned men, burn the chariot racetrack, and cause days of disorder, they were eventually beaten down by the Roman army. Worse, the riots prompted Justinian to cancel all chariot races for several years after.

Build an Inland Sea

When Life Gives You Massive Flooding, Make Lemonade

According to the State of California

In a fit of early 1900s nature-subduing enthusiasm, the good people of California decided to turn Imperial Valley (a desert) into a vast agricultural paradise (not a desert). To do so, they started cutting irrigation channels from the Colorado River. When those filled up with silt, they cut a little deeper, digging out a large gap in the river's bank to increase flow. Then, in 1905, the floods came, washing out the engineered canal and pouring thousands of gallons of water directly from the river into a previously dry below-sea-level basin. It took two years to get the flooding under control, by which point the basin had become a lake—the Salton Sea. In 1907, the first sport fish were imported and a tourist attraction was born.

STRUGGLE WITH NATURE, AND WIN (AT LEAST TEMPORARILY)

With the broken canals now repaired, the Salton Sea had no inlet or outlet. Instead, all it's water came from farm irrigation runoff. At first, nobody saw this as a problem. Then the sea's salinity (and pollution levels) started to increase. Turns out, farmers were pulling water from the sea, putting it on their crops, and letting it flow back in. Each time, the water picked up a little more salt and a few more pesticide chemicals. Eventually, this led to outbreaks of algae, massive fish die-offs, and a salinity level greater than the Pacific Ocean.

ASSUME YOU WON'T HAVE TO DEAL WITH MORE FLOODING IN THE FUTURE

By the 1960s, regardless of its increasingly salty nature, the Salton Sea had become one of California's busiest tourist attractions and it's most popular state park. Investors built swanky resorts, but, unfortunately, nobody thought to build flood control systems. Then came 1976, when a tropical storm hit the area, marking the beginning of seven years of extra-heavy rains. Most of the new developments ended up under water or bankrupt as investors bailed. Worse, increased runoff meant that even more chemicals and salt poured into the sea. By the 1980s, there was little left of the once-thriving fishing and boating industries. Today, the sea is home to several half-flooded trailer-park communities and one thriving bird sanctuary. Still ever saltier, it's expected to lose most of its fish population in the next few years.

Perform Your Own Surgery

YOU WILL NEED

- Fortitude
- A pocket knife

Step 1: *BREAK THE CARDINAL RULE OF MOUNTAINEERING*

Think the first rule of "Fight Club," only opposite. Whenever you go out into the mountains to hike or climb in a little-traveled area, you're always supposed to make sure that someone knows where you are and when you're supposed to be back. But when Aron Ralston went out to climb a canyon wall near Moab, Utah, on a Saturday afternoon in April 2003, he forgot to tell a single person about his plans. He also brought only a day's worth of water and very little food.

Step 2: *GET IN AN ACCIDENT*

While Ralston was attempting to climb around a boulder on the canyon wall, the boulder fell, knocking him to the ground and pinning his arm underneath its 800-pound mass. An experienced outdoorsman, Ralston tried several different methods of leveraging his weight against the boulder to get it to move. None of them was successful. Worse, the canyon was only three feet wide and about 100 feet deep, so he knew that, in the unlikely event someone missed him and sent out a search party, it was even more unlikely that said searchers would be able to spot him. This is what you'd call an "Oh, crap" moment.

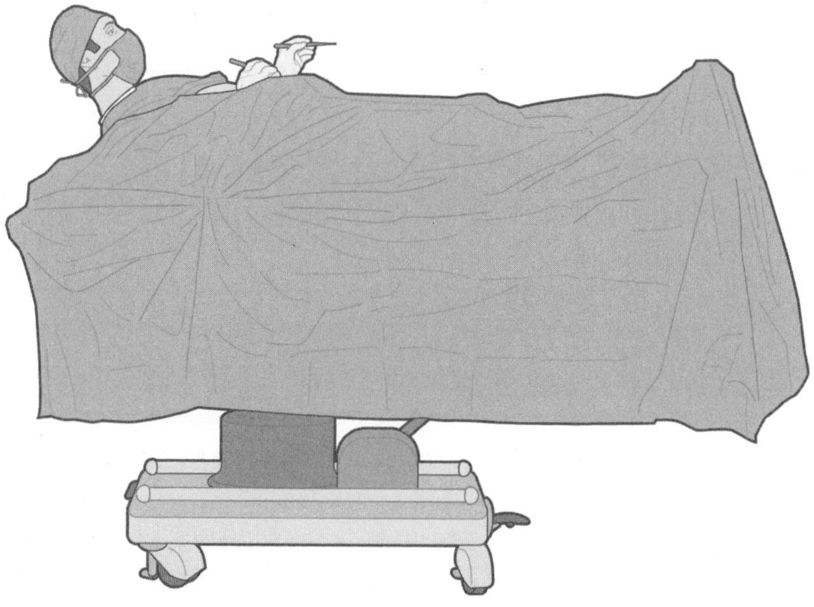

Step 3: ***LEAVE A WILL***

Ralston was pinned under the boulder for more than 4 days. According to an interview he gave to Tom Brokaw a few months later, he gave up all hope of being found. Instead, he recorded final messages to his family on his video camera and carved himself an epitaph/body identification aide on the canyon wall:

RIP
OCT 75
ARON
APR 03

Step 4: ***TAKE DRASTIC MEASURES***

But Ralston wasn't quite ready to give up. On Thursday, 5 days after his fall and more than a day since he'd run out of water, Ralston decided to take an extreme step. Bracing his arm against the boulder, he broke his arm bone below the elbow, hacked through most of the muscle with a dull pocketknife, and pulled apart the rest with the pliers attached to the knife. Thus freed, he hiked seven miles back to his truck, where, luckily, rescue crews happened to be gathered.

Marry Your Cousin

The good news: That hot guy you met last weekend likes-likes you as much as you like-like him. The bad news: The place you met him at was the family reunion. Now what?

YOU WILL NEED

- **Understanding parents**
- **A working knowledge of marriage law**
- **A fallback list of philosophical questions to stump anti-cousin-marriage crusaders**

Step 1: ***KNOW YOUR BIOLOGICAL SCIENCE***

According to a recent study by the National Society of Genetic Counselors, the chances of two first cousins having a child who suffers from birth defects or mental retardation is only about 2 or 3 percent higher than the chance of a similarly afflicted child being born to an unrelated couple. Overall, you and your cuz have about a 93 percent chance of having a perfectly normal baby. However, there is a catch. If your parents were also getting "friendly" with close family members, those comfy, low-risk statistics don't apply to you. The chances of inheriting two recessive genes that cause a defect increase considerably in small populations who've been

marrying cousins for several generations. Take England's Pakistani population, for example. Within the group, an estimated 55 percent of all marriages are between cousins. The immigrants have attempted to retain their culture and connections from their old homeland, but in the process, a lack of new genetic input has led to some serious problems. Today, Pakistanis in Britain are 13 times more likely than the rest of the population to have a child with a genetic defect. In one case, a woman whose parents and grandparents were both first cousins now suffers from a very rare condition called Epidermolysis Bullosa, which makes her skin extremely fragile and prone to blistering.

Step 2: *KNOW WHAT STATES WILL HAVE YOU*

You can't just go live any old place. Despite being legal in Canada, Europe, and just about every place else (about 20 percent of marriages worldwide are between cousins), cousins aren't allowed to marry in 24 states. And, in another 5, you can only marry your cousin if at least one of you is sterile. Of course, the law is different everywhere, and a lot of the states base your ability to wed on how closely related you really are. For instance, 6 states ban marriage between first cousins once-removed (i.e., the child of your first cousin), but marrying your second cousin (all the people with the same great-grandparents as you—this is tough, we know) is perfectly legal anywhere. There are also exceptions to be found. For instance, in Minnesota, people who's "aboriginal cultures" encourage uncle-niece marriage can go ahead and enter those unions A-OK, even though they're technically illegal for everyone else. We might call it a grandfather clause, but that joke would be too easy.

Step 3: *KNOW WHAT YOU'RE TALKING ABOUT WHEN YOU SAY "COUSIN"*

This really isn't as easy as it sounds. While nearly every cultural group in world has some sort of rules for whom you can and can't marry, those rules differ greatly and often depend on how that society defines the concept of family. In America, nobody would see a difference between you marrying your mother's sister's son or your mother's brother's son (stay with us here!). Either way, you'd have hooked up with a first cousin and that would be bad. Or, at least, mockable. In parts of South America, however, that distinction makes a huge difference. The Yanomamo, natives of the Brazilian and Ecuadorian rainforest, are more than willing to marry the children of either their mother's brother or their father's sister. On the other hand, the children of a mother's sister, or a father's brother are forbidden. That's partially because the Yanomamo words for a "mother's sister" and a "father's brother" are the same as the words for "mother" and "father". Likewise, the children of those relations are referred to as your "brother" and "sister." And there's no way you'd marry them!

Get Electrocuted

Step 1: ***GET INTO A PERSISTENT VEGETATIVE STATE***

This is actually fairly simple to do, you just have to be really, really unlucky. Blunt force trauma that leads to a serious and prolonged swelling of the brain should do the job nicely. Be careful though. You don't want to cut off oxygen to your brain. If you do, that will make the next part much less likely to work.

Step 2: ***FIND SOMEONE WHO WILL SHOCK YOU OUT OF YOUR PERSISTENT VEGETATIVE STATE***

According to a September 2006 article in *Wired* magazine, the best (and frankly, only) people to turn to are either the Japanese or an American orthopedic surgeon named Edwin Cooper. Why? Because both independently came up with a theory that small electric shocks can knock coma victims back into wakefulness.

In America

Cooper, currently the only American doctor practicing the technique, hit on the idea in the mid-1980s while working with quadriplegics and microcephalics (people born with unusually small skulls). Both groups tend to loose muscle mass and so Cooper was helping them "exercise" by running small electric currents through their immobile limbs to stimulate and artificially "grow" the muscles. Along the way, he realized that the shocks were having unintended, but welcome, side effects. Sometimes, during electrical therapy, some unresponsive patients would become, briefly, much more with-it. That's a lot of qualifiers, but it was enough to get Cooper curious. Over the past 15 years, he's tested electrical-stimulation therapy on about 60 people who were considered brain dead. Of those patients, 38 have had their progress rigorously tracked through formal research studies conducted by the University of Virginia and East Carolina University. The group is still too small to give certain results, but Cooper's research seems to show that the patients he's treated emerge from comas sooner, regain function more quickly, and are more likely to leave the hospital under their own steam.

In Japan

Electronic stimulation is pretty standard procedure in the Land of the Rising Sun and has been for about 20 years, since Dr. Tetsuo Kanno discovered it. Like Cooper, he stumbled on the idea accidentally, while attempting to help stroke victims regain muscle movement. Unlike Cooper, who delivers shocks through a wristband, Kanno actually implants electrodes directly onto patients' spines. He and his staff have also treated many more people than Cooper. In one study done on 149 of his patients, 42 percent showed significant improvement. And that's patients who'd been in a persistent vegetative state for more than 19 months—states which are normally considered permanent after 12 months.

Step 3: *DEAL WITH THE AFTERSHOCKS*

Unfortunately, waking up is harder to do that the statistics make it sound. Often, a "significant improvement" might mean that a patient who was completely passive and unresponsive can now blink or focus their eyes and vaguely acknowledge what's going on around them. It's known as a minimally conscious state and while it's definitely a step up from being a vegetable, it's not exactly a full recovery. And, considering that the Japanese version of the treatment can cost upwards of $30,000, it's a big buy in for a small pay off. Even Dr. Cooper's most successful patient, a woman who was hit by a logging truck as a teenager and spent two months in a persistent coma before Cooper revived her, isn't back to normal. Although it's remarkable that she can speak, move, and take care of herself, her speech and walking are both slurry and awkward. And while she's graduated from college and has a job as a recreational therapist, the brain damage she suffered also appears to have turned off her internal self-control, making it difficult for her to keep friends.

Spontaneously Combust

One of the Western world's favorite irrational beliefs, reports of human bodies that randomly caught fire and burnt from the inside out have been cropping up since at least 1673, reaching something of a literary apex when the diagnosis found its way into Charles Dickens's 1852 novel, *Bleak House*. But despite all the shout-outs, there's still no hard evidence. So, to our regret, you'll have to settle for just going up in flames and hoping that, afterward, some paranormal researcher will misattribute your death to SHC, spontaneous human combustion.

SMOKE, SMOKE, AND BE FEEBLE

Not coincidentally, most of the people who have ostensibly died from SHC were old, often ill, smokers. In at least two of the most commonly cited cases, old burns from dropped cigarettes dotted the house, providing a likely scenario for how the deceased ended up on fire to begin with. Other factors that also go a long way toward explaining the phenomenon: bathrobes made of flammable cloth, an inability to walk (let alone stop, drop, and roll) unaided, and (in one case) two pockets full of matches. Really, debunking this is almost too easy.

PUT ON WEIGHT AND SIT UP STRAIGHT

Of course, proponents of SHC say that all these things don't explain how a person could be burnt to ashes, leaving nothing but a stray foot and a completely intact apartment. And they're right. There's a different explanation for that. Heat, as you may have learned in grade school science class, rises. Which means that fires tend to burn up, rather than down or side-to-side. If you were sitting upright in a chair and a fire started around your midsection, it's completely plausible that everything above your waist could burn while your feet stayed safe. Add to that an unhealthy amount of body fat and you've got a fuel source that could quickly create a very hot fire.

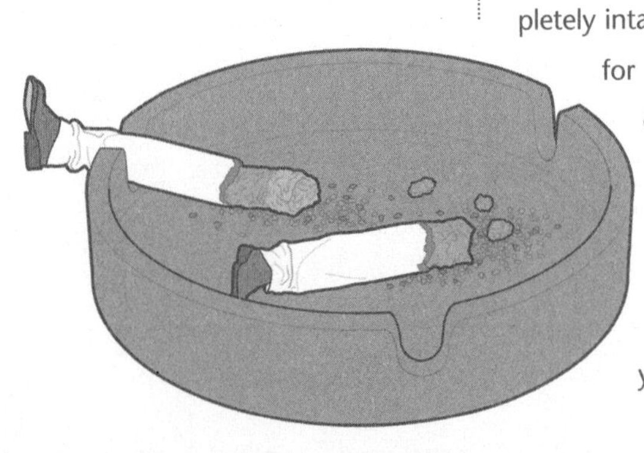

In fact, in the late 1980s and early 1990s, scientists at Edinburgh University were able to recreate a typical SHC death scene using pigs (which have a body fat ratio similar to humans), flammable bathrobes, and a small spark. In these experiments, the clothing acted as a wick for a candle, melting the pig's internal fat and then feeding off it, reducing the porker's upper body to nothingness while leaving the surrounding room untouched.

Speak Your Mind

According to fans of Singlish

BE CREATIVE

A hybrid language made up of English, several obscure Chinese dialects, and a little bit of Malay and Tamil thrown in, Singlish is popular with young working-class Singaporeans. Spoken at lighting speed and often unintelligible to English speakers from other countries, Singlish is often stereotyped as a simplified, dumbed-down language. But this couldn't be further from the truth. Instead, it's a melting pot with its own, unique set of grammar rules. In Singlish, long and short vowels all sound the same and consonant clusters on the ends of words are often chopped off—turning "act" into "ac" and "stopped" into "stop." Another feature that leaves confused outsiders crying for their dictionaries is Singlish's tendency to regard verb tense—and, really, all verbs in general—as purely optional. "She so pretty" is grammatically correct here. Singlish slang and idioms are derived from southern Chinese dialects and tend toward a Maxim-like crudeness. A person with high expectations might be described as "ai pee, ai chee, ai tua liap nee,"—meaning "want cheap, want pretty, want big breasts." Also, there's the matter of attitude. If a Singlish speaker wants you to know they're serious, they'll verbally express their strong feelings by adding "lah" to the end of the sentence, as in "his price too high for me, lah."

THEN, BE REBELLIOUS

Unfortunately for Singlish speakers, the Singaporean government doesn't hold a very high opinion of this sort of creative expression. Concerned about public image overseas, the government stipulates that each citizen be fluent in English and one other national language—of which Singlish isn't an option. In addition, since 1965, the northern Mandarin Chinese dialect has been the officially preferred secondary language, leaving the southern-dialect speakers out in the cold. As an unapproved language that incorporates many other unapproved languages, Singlish has a special place on bureaucratic hate lists. In fact, the government recently launched a public campaign called the Speak Good English Movement, in hopes of stamping out Singlish once and for all. But the masses are fighting back. In 2002, the first all-Singlish film, *Talking Cock: The Movie,* hit theaters and became an instant hit—despite having the dubious honor of being the first movie to earn an NC-16 rating for bad grammar.

Ask a Lady Her Age

Gasp! Not the ultimate society faux pas! True, it's tacky. But even a perfect gentleperson feels the need to be a little base now and again.

YOU WILL NEED

- **One lady, preferably dead**
- **Archaeological dating tools**

REMEMBER, IT'S ALL RELATIVE

The earliest dating methods available to archeologists were what're known as relative techniques, methods that involve comparing your bones or artifacts to the full body of archeological knowledge in order to get a general idea of how old your stuff might be, usually as compared to other nearby remains. There are several different relative techniques, all based on analyzing and comparing different aspects of the find. For instance, say there was another body buried close to your lady. If you wanted to figure out whether the two had been buried at the same time, you might test them using fluorine dating. This technique analyzes the amount of fluorides in each skeleton. As minerals leach out of soil and into bones, fluoride levels increase the longer a body has been underground. The rate of accumulation differs based on the area's geography, but if you have two bone artifacts from the same place, fluorine dating will tell you whether or not they were buried at the same time. In fact, this is the technique that scientists used to debunk the Piltdown Man fake back in 1949. Ostensibly the skull of a prehistoric human with apelike characteristics, Piltdown Man turned out have way lower levels of fluorine than any of the bones and artifacts it had been buried with. In fact, the jaw of the skull had no more fluorine than a living animal. Which makes sense, considering that the skull turned out to be a fake made from an Ice Age-era human head and a modern orangutan jaw, buried where hoaxers knew archaeologists would find it. Besides fluoride levels, relative dating techniques might also analyze: an object's location in layers of earth; the object's relation to a known timeline of pottery styles; or its relation to obsidian artifacts, which accumulate moisture as they age.

EXCEPT WHEN IT'S NOT

In 1947, a chemist named Willard Frank Libby figured out that the decay of carbon 14, a radioactive isotope that begins breaking down with the death of a living creature, can be used to date that creature back to the time it died. This was the beginning of absolute dating techniques, most of which use measurements of radiation, electromagnetism, and other factors to determine precise ages. Carbon 14 dating, for instance, has given accurate ages for artifacts whose ages were already known—such as beams of wood from an Egyptian temple. It works this way: Nitrogen 14 floats around in the Earth's atmosphere, where it's exposed to radiation from the sun and becomes carbon 14. The carbon 14 then falls down to the ground where it's absorbed out of the air by plants. Herbivores get a load of carbon14 when they eat the plants. Carnivores get theirs from eating herbivores. Omnivores, like us, absorb carbon 14 from both plants and animals. But, when a woman (or a fish, or a plant) dies, she stops eating and, thus, stops absorbing carbon 14. And, slowly, the stuff that was already inside her begins to break down. From studying radioactive isotopes, we know that carbon 14 has a half-life of 5,730 years. Put simply: 5,730 years after your lady died, half the carbon 14 she'd absorbed in life would be gone. Another 5,730 years later, she'd be down to a quarter of her original amount and so on, until you hit about 50,000 years. At this point, the levels of carbon 14 remaining are so minute that you couldn't get a very accurate date. Libby's method, with some modern improvements, is still the most commonly used of all absolute dating techniques. Unfortunately, our great-great-grandchildren might not be able to use this method if they become archeologists. The invention of the atomic bomb in the 1940s, which also happen to give off carbon 14, seriously screwed with the levels of the isotope that modern plants and animals absorb. Anything born after 1940 would be much harder to date accurately.

Be Unlucky

According to the number 13

Step 1: *GET A REPUTATION AS A POOR DINNER GUEST*

Nobody knows exactly why western culture has come to regard the number 13 as indicative of death and misfortune. However, some of the problem might lie in the number's persistence in ruining perfectly good dinner parties. For instance, many references cite the story of the Last Supper as the source of the superstition, since the guests at that event numbered 13—Jesus plus his 12 apostles. In this version, the 13th guest is supposed to be Judas Iscariot, who reportedly left the dinner first and went on to sell Jesus out to the Romans. But the Norse gods also had a rough time with 13. In one story, 12 of the lords of Valhalla throw a banquet, specifically not inviting the troublemaker, Loki. And with good reason. When Loki later crashed the festivities, his arrival led to the death of Baldur, a much more friendly god. Given this history, it's no wonder that 19th century hostesses worked feverishly to ensure that no party had exactly 13 guests, or, if that couldn't be helped, that at least they weren't all seated at the same table. If such a situation occurred, according to the superstition of the times, either the first person to leave the table or the last to arrive was sure to die in a year or less.

Step 2: *BE UNFAIRLY MALIGNED*

Of course, number 13's bad reputation hasn't carried over to every culture. The Maya, for instance, weren't prone to *triskaidekaphobia* (fear of the number 13). In fact, they held it as lucky, thanks to the fact that there were 13 months in their year. Meanwhile, ancient Greeks also looked favorably on the number, associating it with Zeus, king of the gods.

...Then Make
Lemonade

Be a Loveable Eccentric

According to Joshua A. Norton; aka Norton I, Emperor of the United States and Protector of Mexico

Step 1: ***HAVE A GOOD BACKSTORY***

Joshua Norton certainly did. Originally from England, he'd immigrated to San Francisco in 1849, and set about becoming a rich man—primarily through real estate wheeling and dealing. But that life came to a screeching halt less than 10 years later when Norton attempted to corner the rice market . . . and lost his shirt. He ended up destitute and working in a factory. Somewhere along the way, he also appears to have lost his mind, becoming obsessed with United States politics and slowly coming to the conclusion that a democracy couldn't possibly govern America's diverse interests and complicated economy. What we needed, Norton thought, was an emperor.

YOU WILL NEED

- **A unique gimmick to help you stand out from the rest of the "crazies"**
- **A certain amount of chutzpah**

Step 2: ***ARRANGE A PUBLIC INTRODUCTION***

It's the unambitious eccentric who comes up with the idea of an imperial America and fails to act on it himself. And Norton was nothing if not ambitious. Eager to make his intentions publicly known, Norton wrote a declaration, naming himself absolute ruler of the United States, then sent it to the *San Francisco Bulletin*. Maybe it was a slow news day, or maybe the editors of the city's largest newspaper just had a sick sense of humor—whatever the reason, they went ahead and published it. On September 17, 1859, the beginning of Norton's reign was noted without any other commentary in the paper.

Step 3: ***MAKE YOURSELF RECOGNIZABLE***

Immediately, it became clear that San Franciscans had a soft spot for creativity unburdened by sanity. Local newspapers began to print every Norton I announcement they could get their hands on—from his December 1859 dismissal of the Governor of Virginia for hanging John Brown to his July 1860 dissolution of the United States of America. In some cases, papers invented fraudulent imperial decrees as editorial satires of real-life politics. Yet, the venerable man himself was still often mistaken for a common vagrant. In 1867, a city patrol officer arrested His Majesty and sent him off on an involuntary stay in a mental institution. The decision was widely panned by the public and the press. Eventually, pressure built to the point that the Chief of Police was forced to release Norton with full public apology. After that the incident, all San Francisco police officers were made to recognize the emperor and saluted when he passed them on the street. But something was still missing. Something, like a uniform. Luckily, one was quickly supplied by the local U.S. Army base. Norton wore the blue uniform (with gold-plated epaulets) until it became shamefully worn, at which point the city Board of Supervisors appropriated money for a new one. In thanks, Norton raised them all to the rank of nobility.

Step 4: *REMAIN IN-CHARACTER, NO MATTER WHAT*

Norton would have hardly been fit to rule if he only believed he was Emperor of the United States some of the time. So, for the remainder of his life, the former busted real-estate magnate walked around San Francisco as if he owned the place—and the locals, by all accounts, happily indulged him. Norton ate for free just about anywhere he wanted and wasn't shy about reaming waiters who didn't live up to imperial standards. He also received free lodging. In September 1870, under the threat of banishment, Norton issued a decree demanding that the palatial Grand Hotel furnish him with rooms. Apparently, the management complied. The state legislature was equally accommodating. Norton attended all public functions and had a reserved seat at the state senate, where he never missed a session. In the rare moments where he did need to pay for something, Norton was never short of cash, thanks to San Franciscans willingness to purchase 50-cent bonds from him on sight. When he died in 1880, on his way to a lecture at the Academy of Natural Sciences, Norton was given a sendoff befitting his imaginary station. The *San Francisco Chronicle* ran a banner headline—"*Le Roi Est Mort*"—and a group of wealthy San Franciscans picked up the tab for a lavish funeral with over 10,000 mourners.

Information for this article came from the San Francisco Museum and Carl Sifakis's American Eccentrics.

Eat Cannon Fodder

Although just as plentiful in stores as their equally puffy cousin popcorn, puffed wheat and rice aren't something you ever hear your friends and neighbors making at home. Obviously, this is partly a cultural thing—nobody is conditioned to want hot, buttered wheat at the movies. But part of the problem is also scientific. Popcorn, after all, is a pretty easy thing to produce. All you have to do is heat a particular breed of corn kernel until the moisture inside begins to release steam. Pressure builds up and the hard exterior casing explodes, instantly releasing the popped interior like a buttery drop of sunshine. Grains like wheat and rice, on the other hand, don't have hard shells to build steam inside, so puffing them takes a little more creativity. The modern method used by your favorite breakfast cereal company today was invented in 1902 by botanist and businessman Alexander Anderson.

YOU WILL NEED

- Some form of grainy starch
- A penchant for wanton (but largely harmless) violence

Step 1: *PROCURE A PRESSURE CHAMBER*

Anderson used test tubes in his first experiments and later upgraded to carefully constructed sealed tubes. But, by the time his company debuted puffed rice at the 1904 St. Louis World's Fair, the inventor had switched to something a bit more show-boaty—specifically, a re-engineered cannon left over from the Spanish-American War.

Step 2: *TURN UP THE HEAT*

No matter what type of contraption you use, the method is always the same. Grains are sealed into a container and quickly heated so that the pressure builds up to nearly 200 pounds per square inch and the starch contained in the grains begins to turn to jelly.

Step 3: *OPEN THE HATCH*

Now all you have to do is unseal your containment system, instantly lowering the pressure and causing the now semiliquid grains to expand outward. Away from the heat source, they quickly cool and harden, creating the puff we all know and love from various sugar-frosted breakfast bombs. If the process sounds similar to a gun going off, that's because it is. For many years, Quaker even marketed its puffed rice and wheat as being "shot from guns."

Don't Mow Your Grass

Step 1: *KNOW WHAT YOU WANT*

Owning a lawn is a deeply conflicting experience. On the one hand, it's your outside living room, your pride and joy, and the heart and hearth of the American dream. Yet, none of those warm, fuzzy associations is enough to cover up the fact that doing yard work just plain stinks. Wouldn't it be great if the grass on your lawn never grew tall enough to need mowing, never turned brown, and was entirely sterile, thus producing no nose-afflicting pollen? Thanks to a group of researchers working with the Howard Hughes Medical Institute of the Salk Institute, this miracle grass might one day be possible. In 2006, the scientists announced that they had discovered the hormone signaling pathway in plants that could control such growth.

YOU WILL NEED

- A degree in chemistry
- A degree in biology
- A connection with the meatheads down at the local gym

Step 2: *SAY "YES" TO DRUGS*

Or rather, say "yes" hormone manipulation. Much like the muscle-bound hulklings lifting weights on the beach, plants control their growth through the use of steroids. Specifically, a type known as "brassinosteroids." These chemicals travel through a plant's entire body, sending messages from the DNA to the cells. In fact, they might be one of the oldest courier services in the world, outpacing UPS by at least several million years. Researchers claim that these messengers date back more than a billion years, dating them back to the time before plants and animals became separate entities.

Step 3: *SIT BACK AND ENJOY YOUR MOWING-FREE LAWN*

When plants detect traces of brassinosteroids moving through their molecular message system it sets off a chain reaction, turning on some genes and turning off others. Subtract the brassinosteroids and the plants not only refuse to grow, they cease aging and reproducing as well—meaning plants that are perpetually green, short, and pollen-free. Better yet, researchers believe this same principle could be applied to food plants as well, leading to more productive rice paddies and berry bushes that are a more convenient height for picking.

Avoid a Fate Worse than Death

What's worse than death? How about being buried *before* you're actually dead?

YOU WILL NEED

- A "healthy" level of paranoia

Tip 1: *LIVE IN THE PRESENT*

Rest easy. Here, in good old 2008, we don't have a lot to worry about when it comes to premature burial. Heck, even if your doctor were to make an inaccurate diagnosis and you weren't really dead, you most certainly would be by the time modern mortuary methods got through with you. (Embalming fluid, anyone?) However, back before the advent of the stethoscope in the 1850s (and the advent of the licensed medical professional around the same general time period) death by burial wasn't an entirely ridiculous fear. In fact, it inspired enough terror during the 19th century that some people took to leaving their deceased loved above ground until rotting set in. Just to be on the safe side. Today, of course, most of us assume that "dead" is dead. Of course, there are always exceptions. According to Snopes.com, in 1994, a woman named Mildred C. Clarke was put, alive, into a body bag at the Albany (New York) Medical Center Hospital and remained there for 90 minutes before an attendant noticed the bag "breathing" in and out.

Tip 2: *EMPLOY THE SPHINCTER TEST*

Exactly what it sounds like, but not as bad as you might think, the Sphincter Test was a method of detecting death ostensibly employed by Turkish doctors. Michael Largo's book *Final Exits* cites *The Thesaurus of Horror*, an 1817 book that promised to give readers the real scoop behind premature burial and other terrifying bits of tombstone trivia. According to the thesaurus, the Turks had mastered a highly advanced proof-of-death test that involved inserting a tube into the mouth of the presumably expired and forcing air through it while blocking the lips and nose. If the body uncontrollably farted, it was determined that the person was truly dead, as a living body was expected (perhaps unreasonably for some people . . . you know who you are) to have greater sphincter control.

Tip 3: *INVEST IN APPROPRIATE TECHNOLOGY*

Inventor George Bateson turned his case of taphephobia (from "taphos," the Greek word for grave) into a profitable business, inventing a device that promised to give those who feared being buried alive a way out should their worst nightmares ever be confirmed. The Bateson Revival Device consisted of a bell, which was attached to the outside of a casket. A cord ran from the bell through the length of the coffin's interior, so that, were there any movement at all inside, the bell would ring. Bateson apparently lived well off his creation until 1886, when he guaranteed that his own burial would be timely via self-immolation.

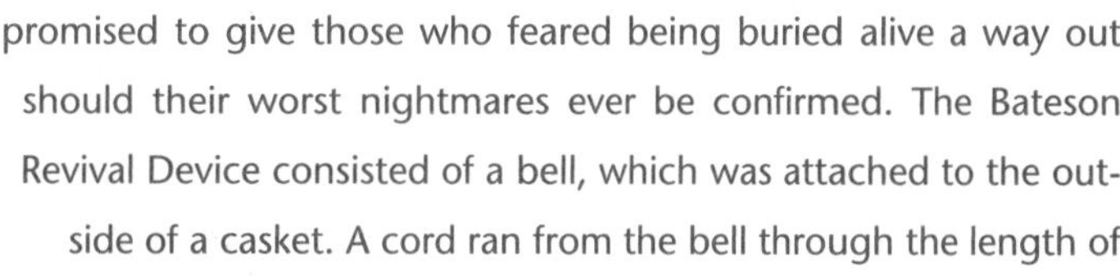

Get by with a Little Help from Your Friends

Whether it's moving into a new apartment, watching your cat while your gone for the weekend, or helping you bury that inconveniently dead body . . . people who need people are the luckiest people we know. Still tempted to discount the value of relationships, Grizzly Hermit? Consider this: Even reptiles need their buds . . .

YOU WILL NEED

- Friends . . . with benefits
- The ability to make new friends when your old ones disappear

Step 1: *PICK THE RIGHT CROWD*

The tiger keelback snake is native to Japan and several other nearby islands, where it's known for defending itself by spraying a toxin called bufadienolides into the eyes of its attackers. The toxins prevent proper heart function and give the snake a great getaway plan, but for years, scientists suspected that the tiger keelback wasn't capable of producing bufadienolides inside its own body. The chemical mystery was solved in 2007, when scientists started to take notice of the snakes' roommates. According to a January 2007 article in *Cosmos* magazine, almost all the islands where tiger keelbacks live are also home to several species of bufadienolides-secreting toads.

Step 2: *INVITE YOUR NEW FRIENDS TO DINNER*

That discovery, of course, still left scientists with the question of how the toxins were getting from the toads' skin into the snakes. Assuming that there probably wasn't a bunch of teenage hippy keelbacks slithering around licking the toads, researchers figured the toxin was getting transferred when the snakes ate their amphibious neighbors. It's a plausible solution, but an odd one. There are plenty of other animals that reuse the venom of another species, but those are almost exclusively invertebrates. It's not very often that you find backbone-blessed animals engaging in this sort of thing. But, researchers studied the spit of snakes from toad-ed and toad-free islands and found that, amazingly, they were right. In environments where no toads could be found, the snakes completely lacked the bufadienolides toxin. Poisonous toad: It's what's for dinner.

Don't Let it Get You Down

According to Richard Milhous Nixon

YOU WILL NEED

- **To face adversity, and plow on through it. Repeat, multiple times**
- **To keep your pride, even when you caused the adversity yourself**

UP Unlike many of the men who went on to become president of the United States, Dick Nixon didn't come from a privileged background. In fact, far from it. His dad was a grocer and, although middle class, he grew up in a poor area of Yorba Linda, California. A striver from an early age, Nixon fought (in the symbolic sense) his way to the academic top of every school he attended, eventually getting a scholarship to Duke University Law School. Ironically, the young Nixon had dreams of being a lawyer who prosecuted political villains without remorse.

UP The future president had a solid career in law and in 1946, won a seat as a congressional delegate for the state of California. Once elected, he sat on the

House Un-American Activities Committee and started rooting out communists. In a famous incident, he accompanied confessed Soviet spy Whittaker Chambers to Chamber's garden where (in front of a cadre of photographers) Chambers revealed a strip of top secret microfilm he had hidden in a pumpkin. Nixon made headlines nationwide and his career took off. He later used his persona as a staunch anticommunist to tar and feather his opponent in a race for senate, branding the incumbent as "pink right down to her underwear." Coincidentally, this was also the campaign where he picked up his famous nickname, "Tricky Dick." But, nonetheless, the gamble worked. Nixon was voted into the Senate in 1950.

DOWN By all rights, it should have been an up. In 1952, Nixon was tapped to be Dwight Eisenhower's vice presidential running mate. Good stuff, right? Well, sorta. In the midst of the campaign, news reports surfaced accusing Nixon of accepting inappropriate gifts of cash and valuables. Eisenhower almost dropped him from the ticket, with Nixon saving himself via an 11th-hour televised defense speech. He ended up becoming vice president, but the speech has gone on to be regarded as a prime example of low-life, rhetoric-heavy politicking. Nixon made sure viewers knew that his wife wore not mink but a "respectable Republican cloth coat." He also downplayed his acceptance of gifts by focusing on the one he was "gonna keep"—a puppy named Checkers.

DOWN Although he went on to have a pretty good two-term vice presidency under Eisenhower, Nixon didn't get assistance from Ike when he really needed it. During the 1960 presidential campaign, Nixon ran against John F. Kennedy, largely promoting himself as having more experience than the charming junior senator. Unfortunately, when reporters asked Eisenhower about whether Nixon had made any major contributions to foreign policy, Eisenhower replied, "If you give me a week, I might think of one." Ouch.

DOWN Having lost the presidential election, Nixon attempted to make a small-scale comeback in 1962, running for governor of California. Unfortunately, he decided to run against a popular incumbent, losing by a landslide. Worse, during his post-election concession speech, a stressed Nixon flipped out just a little, accusing the media of plotting his downfall and claiming he was quitting politics with the famous line, "You won't have Dick Nixon to kick around anymore."

UP Nixon's retirement lasted about as long as one of Cher's. By 1968, he was back in a presidential campaign, this time claiming to be "tanned, rested, and ready" and touting a plan to win the war in Vietnam (a plan which was both secret and, as it turned out later, nonexistent). He won. But knowing what came next, we'll finish up on that high note.

Get out of the Frying Pan and into the Fire

YOU WILL NEED

- A problem
- A solution
- A way to solve the problem caused by the first solution

According to the Welsh

Problem #1: Wales was not a good place to be Welsh in the mid-19th century. Cultural assimilation was rampant, spurred on by concerted British efforts to literally stamp out the use of Welsh language. Desperate to hang on to their cultural traditions, groups of Welsh began looking for a place they could move to that would allow them to live as they wished.

Solution #1: Options brought for consideration included the United States, New Zealand, and, oddly, Palestine. But, while small groups of Welsh did end up going to these places, they didn't find any of those locals much more hospitable. Eventually, Welsh leaders decided that, if they didn't want to be assimilated by force or laziness, they were going to have to find a sparsely populated land outside the cultural reach of the British Empire. By these standards, the wind-swept, barren plains of Argentine Patagonia must have looked pretty promising. Located near the very bottom of the Southern Hemisphere, Patagonia had so few Western settlers that the Argentine government was literally giving land away to anyone who would promise allegiance. Their emotional attachment to the British all but withered, the Welsh jumped at the opportunity.

Problem #2: Arriving in 1865, the Welsh settled in and got ready for the farming season. Unfortunately, it turned out that none of them had realized that the seasons were flipped south of the Equator. They arrived for what they thought would be summer and instead found themselves plunged into the depths of winter. Not so good, considering the fact that they had expected to be farmers.

Solution #2: Make friends with the locals. In the end, the Patagonian Welsh owe their survival to two groups of people: the Argentine government, which financially bailed them out a couple of times; and the local native population, which, after convincing the Welsh that they weren't out for blood, managed to teach the new immigrants proper farming technique.

According to the lady who wrote The Joy of Cooking

Problem #1: A life that didn't turn out according to plan. In *Stand Facing the Stove*, a biography of cookbook entrepreneur Irma Rombauer, author Anne Mendelson tells how Rombauer, a wealthy doctor's daughter, married a promising young lawyer. Unfortunately, her storybook life quickly took a turn into Dickensian bleakness when her husband started having nervous breakdowns that affected his ability to work and, in 1930, led to his suicide. Rombauer was left a financially unsecure widow.

Solution #1: Become an author. Rombauer's husband left the family $6,000, which, she decided would be best put to use writing and publishing a cookbook. In turn, she hoped, the book would help her recoup her investment and then some, providing her family with a stable future.

Problem #2: Irma Rombauer really didn't know how to cook. Raised in an era where almost all middle-class housewives had servants and cooks, she really didn't know how to do much of anything—other than be a gracious hostess. Her relatives' opinion of her cookbook-writing plan was "Worst idea I've ever heard of." Worse, because of her lack of experience, Rombauer couldn't find a publisher and ended up spending half of her inheritance getting the manuscript vanity-published.

Solution #2: Turns out, Rombauer's friends and family underestimated both her abilities as a writer and the need for extremely basic cooking tomes. Tightened immigration laws had recently dried up much of the cheap household labor population, so Rombauer wasn't the only housewife learning to cook for the first time. And her cookbook, which she published in 1931, with its extremely detailed instructions and conversational, witty tone, was essentially the first of its kind. Republished by Bobbs-Merrill in 1935, *The Joy of Cooking* sold almost 7,000 copies in 6 months and made Rombauer very famous and very rich.

Get Detained at Customs

Dangerous Item: *COMEDIANS*

Don't Bring 'Em to: *MYANMAR*

The citizens of this country just want to avoid trouble—the kind that starts with a capital "T" and that rhymes with "C" and that stands for "comedy." Once known as Burma, Myanmar has a long tradition of stand-up comedy, usually in conjunction with traditional dance and theater. But, since the rise of the military government nearly 20 years ago, comedy and comedians are increasingly unwelcome because of their propensity to make jokes at the junta's expense. Jokesters have even spent time in jail. Two members of an act known as the Moustache Brothers were imprisoned, with hard labor for five years after they cracked some antiregime jokes at a 1996 rally. A letter campaign by American comedians eventually got the two freed in 2001, but they're now banned from performing their act in Burmese.

Dangerous Item: *CAMERA PHONES*
Don't Bring 'Em to: *SAUDI ARABIA*

These trendy little devices were banned in 2002, amid concerns that the tiny cameras were being used to secretly photograph women in family or all-female environments where they might not be dressed as modestly as they would in public. In fact, according to news reports, accusations of camera-phone use had led to fights at weddings and pat-down searches of students at all girls' schools. But, after the ban incited a thriving black-market business, the phones were relegalized in 2004.

Dangerous Item: *VEGEMITE*
Don't Bring It to: *THE UNITED STATES*

In 2006, rumors (fueled by breathless reports by the Australian and New Zealand press) began circulating that the United States had banned the yeast-based, salty spread Vegemite from its shores. Popular (for some strange reason) with folks from down under, the spread contains large quantities of folate, a chemical whose artificial form, folic acid, is tightly regulated by the FDA. Natural folate doesn't fall under the laws, so Vegemite isn't actually in danger of being banned, but the FDA does limit the types and amount of products that can contain folic acid. Why? Because while small amounts of folate are important (particularly for fetuses and pregnant women), nobody knows what side effects it could produce if you were to start eating it in larger doses.

Run around like a Chicken with Its Head Cut Off

It should have been your average chicken dinner. On September 10, 1945, in Fruita, Colorado, Clara Olsen sent her husband Lloyd out to the barnyard to pick a fryer for chow. Lloyd chose a plump, delicious-looking 5-and-a-half-month-old Wyandotte Rooster and killed it in the usual way. But from that point, nothing about that rooster was ever usual again. Most of the time, a decapitated chicken will, indeed, go running around for a minute or two. But, instead, this rooster simply shook himself and then picked up life where he'd left off; strutting around the barnyard, preening his feathers, and making some pathetically adorable attempts at pecking for food. He was still alive the next day, and thus a legend was born: Mike, the Headless Chicken. Mike's tenacious spirit is still celebrated in Fruita each May at the "Mike the Headless Chicken Festival," but if you want a brainless beastie of your own, here are three things you'll need.

YOU WILL NEED

- **A picky mother-in-law:** After a week of Mike wandering around the barnyard like avian zombie, Lloyd Olsen took the chicken in to see the scientists the University of Utah in Salt Lake City. There it was discovered that Mike's survival had less to do with an unstoppable will to live and more to do with Lloyd's mother-in-law. She was the dinner guest Mike had been picked out for and, knowing how much she liked chicken neck, Lloyd had been careful to lop off Mike's head as close to the chin as possible—missing the jugular and leaving most of Mike's brain stem and one ear still attached to his body. The scientists determined that a blood clot had prevented the chicken from bleeding to death, while his brain stem continued to control his reflex actions. The result: a headless chicken without a care in the world.

- **An eyedropper:** Without a mouth, Mike couldn't really be expected to feed himself. But the Olsen's quickly realized that there was still a way to keep him fed—his exposed esophagus. Using an eyedropper, they were able to place feed and water directly into Mike's throat for the rest of his life. Over the next year, he grew from 2.5 pounds to nearly 8 pounds. Fat, happy, and headless—that was Mike.

- **A publicist:** Naturally, you don't keep this kind of news buried out back. Dubbed Miracle Mike, the chicken, the Olsens, and the chicken's business manager hit the road on a nationwide tour that took the headless chicken from San Diego and L.A. to New York and Atlantic City. At every stop, huge crowds paid 25 cents a head to catch a glimpse of Mike's greatness. At the height of his fame, Mike was insured for $10,000 and featured in *Time* and *Life* magazines. But, tragedy eventually struck, as it so often does, at a motel in Arizona. In the middle of the night, 18 months after his decapitation, something blocked Mike's esophagus and he choked to death before the Olsen's could find his life-saving eyedropper. Like any real star, Mike had fun, died young, and left a beautiful corpse.

Be Close, But Get No Cigar

YOU WILL NEED

- One technicality, ripe for the misinterpreting

Step 1: *QUESTION EVERYTHING*

Your history teachers always said that George Washington was the first president of the United States, but your college buddies begged to differ. According to them, the first guy to hold the title was John Hanson.

Step 2: *EXAMINE THE EVIDENCE*

So who's right? Turns out, your history teacher—by one coiffed white wig hair. Hanson (who, coincidentally, grew up on a plantation only about 30 miles downstream from Washington's Mount Vernon) was a big player in the run up to the revolution, using his position as a member of the Maryland Assembly to help stock the fledgling American military with arms and recruits. In 1779, he was appointed to the Continental Congress and, as such, ended up being rather influential in hashing out the murkier details of the Articles of Confederation—the document that served as the basis of American government before the Constitution. It's here that he had his brush with little-known-historical fame.

Step 3: *DISCOVER THE TRUTH*

In 1781, Hanson was elected "President of the United States in Congress Assembled." We put it in quotes because we're trying to make a careful distinction. This title was not the same thing as "President of the United States." For one thing, under the Articles of Confederation, the United States didn't really exist—at least, not as we know it. Instead, this system put all-important powers in the hands of individual states, gave Congress no power to enforce what few tasks they were permitted to perform, and generally shaped a union that was more analogous to the United Nations than to an actual country. (In fact, these are the same reasons that the articles were ultimately declared a failure and were replaced.) Hanson's role in that set up was not an executive one. He was just the guy who led Congress, not the technically nonexistent nation.

Shiver Your Way to Greatness

According to Lynne Cox, Champion Swimmer and Genetic Anomaly

YOU WILL NEED

- To get in water as cold as 32° Fahrenheit
- To stay there for up to an hour
- To not die while doing so

Step 1: *SHOW YOUR BLOOD VESSELS WHO'S BOSS*

Lynne Cox has swum through some of the coldest water in the world—from the English Channel, to the Bering Strait, to the ocean off the coast of Antarctica. Yes, that Antarctica. And, lest you write her off as some sort of weird daredevil who wouldn't know the breaststroke from an unwanted grope at a junior high dance, she also holds a ridiculous number of speed records for these and other swims. Occasionally, she even breaks men's records. But, despite her accomplishments, in the scientific world Cox is known for one thing: surviving the cold. Cox wrote about her talent in an autobiography called *Swimming to Antarctica*. Early on in her career, biologists realized that she was staying in colder water for longer than a human body ought to be able to manage. In 1976, and again in the early 1990s, Cox became a human guinea pig, allowing researchers to test out how her body responded to cold. The results were amazing. In the 1976 study, Cox and the other subjects sat in 50-degree water in their swimsuits for an hour. All the other participants quickly began shivering, and their core temperatures dropped. Cox, however, did neither. Researchers still aren't sure exactly how her body withstands the cold, but they think that Cox might somehow be better than most people at closing down blood flow to her extremities. This theory earned some credence when Cox swam across the 45-degree Strait of Magellan. When most people exercise in very cold water, they actually lose heat faster than if they are sitting still. This is because exercising opens your blood vessels wide as your body attempts to "feed" the muscles in your extremities. But, in cold water, this reflex means that your blood is getting significantly cooled before it's pumped back to the heart. And that's not a good thing. Most people's bodies will try to maintain core heat by constricting the blood vessels, but after a little while, the body will decide that getting oxygen to the legs is more important and the vessels will open back up. Usually, this is the point where they die of hypothermia. But not Cox. In fact, during the four-hour Magellan swim, Cox's core body temperature actually rose.

Step 2: *GET SOME BLUBBER ON YOUR BONES*

But well-constricted blood vessels don't entirely explain Cox's abilities. Scientists believe that she has another thing going for her as well: well-placed body fat. Like all healthy women, Cox has a relatively even layer of fat spread out all over her body—although her's seems to be a little thicker and more evenly spread than most. With those two powers combined, Cox becomes Captain Cold Water. In all the studies performed on her, there's only been one other test subject who even measured close: an Icelandic fisherman who'd once survived a shipwreck in the Arctic.

Crawl out of Quicksand

Bad Idea: *TRUST THE MOVIES*

Do this, and you're liable to end up thinking that quicksand is something that only happens in the jungle or the desert and that it's a one-way ticket to the center of the Earth. Neither of which could be farther from the truth. Quicksand, as it turns out, isn't some mysterious entity. It's just your average run-of-the-mill sand and clay that's gotten saturated with water, usually from an underground stream. Heck, technically, you don't even need sand—any old fine-grained soil will do. According to the United States Geological Survey, quicksand can pop up just about anywhere. On the plus side, though, you don't have to worry about it being bottomless. Most patches of quicksand would barely reach up to your waist, let alone be deep enough to cover your head.

Good Idea: *KNOW YOUR PHYSICS*

Getting unstuck from quicksand is really a Vulcan-esque endeavor, requiring rationality, intelligence, and emotional distance. Unfortunately, the most common response to sinking into what previously appeared to be solid ground is to freak out like Captain Kirk at an intergalactic bikini contest. In reality, however, there's really not that much to fear. In 2005, researchers from the University of Amsterdam announced the results of their research on quicksand. According to their report in the journal *Nature*, the human body is actually much less dense than quicksand. Meaning that, under normal circumstances, a person in quicksand should really just bob around like a buoy on the ocean. No heroic effort required. Problems only set in when you struggle, which stirs the sand and water mixture up, making it more liquid and you more likely to sink. But, while surviving the pit is easy, getting out is another story. Because quicksand is so viscous, it's difficult for air to penetrate it. Thus, when you move your arm or leg, air can't fill the spot where you once were and a partial vacuum forms. This makes it

YOU WILL NEED

- A calm, rational demeanor
- A day or two to recuperate afterward

extremely difficult to pull yourself out of quicksand, even if you are moving slowly and deliberately. In fact, one of the true dangers of quicksand is exhaustion. Even removing one leg from the muck might make you too tired to hike back to camp and might open you up to attacks from wild animals or bad weather.

Avoid Dangerous Animals

Step 1: ***NEVER, EVER, EVER GO TO AUSTRALIA ****

Although it frequently masquerades as some kind of outdoor enthusiast's paradise, the continent/island/nation known as Australia is actually a safe haven for some of the deadliest creatures on the face of the Earth. Just looking at the snake population alone, it's easy to see why any smart traveler would avoid this fiery hell-hole. Not only is Australia home to more than 140 distinct snake species—100 of them venomous—it's also the only place in the world where the poisonous snakes outnumber the relatively safe ones. Now surely, the propagandists will tell you that most snakes prefer to avoid humans. But even if you do believe that (and we don't . . . just look at their beady eyes), there's still an ocean teeming with dangerous life that Australia has to own up to. Among the off-shore dangers: the world's most poisonous jellyfish. Since the late 19th century, 70 people died from box jellyfish stings, most of them children who succumbed to the creature's killer poison in minutes. Box jellyfish venom shocks the heart, interferes with breathing, attacks red blood cells, and damages the skin—so even the people who do survive an encounter often end up with permanent scarring. If you don't believe us about the dangers of Australian waters, simply ask former Australian Prime

Minister Harold Holt. Oh, that's right, you can't! That's because the poor minister disappeared while taking an ocean swim back in 1967. And if that's not enough proof, consider this: Even Australia's cute, fuzzy animals have something to hide. The famous duckbilled platypus conceals two poisonous daggers on its back legs. When you least expect it, this undeniably adorable beast could clamp its legs together on your ankle or hand, driving the spurs into your flesh. Don't be fooled. Your life may depend on it.

** Notice how there is no Step 2? Yeah, that's intentional. Australia really is just a giant black hole of deadly.*

Be Wrong

If you don't think you've ever been wrong . . . chances are you just were. But the key is to handle it gracefully and to correct your mistakes as best you can. If you don't, something like this could happen:

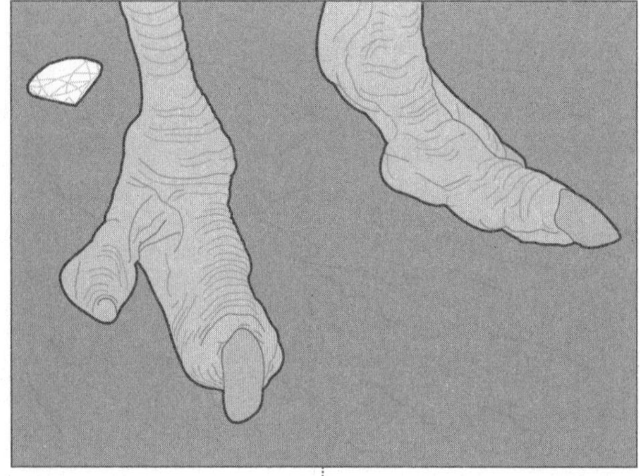

First: *DISMISS ANYTHING YOUR KIDS THINK IS COOL*

In his book, *The World's Greatest Mistakes*, Nigel Blundell relates an amazing story. In December of 1866, the children of a South African farmer brought home a colorful stone. Adding it to their collection of other interesting rocks, the kids thought their find was pretty special. Their mother, however, disagreed. When a neighbor (and amateur geologist) named Schalk Van Niekerk asked if he could buy the rock from them to take home and study, the children's mother told him he could just have it for free. After all, why bother paying for a pebble that was little more than a children's toy?

Second: *IGNORE THE OPINIONS OF YOKELS*

We certainly hope that woman's children never let her live that decision down. Van Niekerk, as it turned out, believed the pebble was valuable and took it to the Cape of Good Hope colony's foremost geologist William Atherstone. A year later, Atherstone announced that the "rock" was actually a 21-carat diamond, which was later sold to the governor of the colony for about 500 British Pounds. That's about $59,000 in today's currency. Ouch! An astute student of human nature might assume that a discovery like this would have set off a crazed, speculative diamond rush. But he'd have be wrong. (See, it's easy to do.) At the time, the Cape of Good Hope was considered a backwater—a far-flung colony from which nothing important came and to which no level of intelligence was assumed. Prominent Britons had long ago declared the geology of southern Africa to be unfit for diamond production and clearly Van Niekerk's paltry discovery was no reason to question that learned judgment. In fact, many English experts believed that Atherstone and Van Niekerk were part of a colonist plot to trick naïve would-be investors. With that in mind, *The London Illustrated News* refused to so much as publish a picture of the gemstone, for fear it would help dupe the unwary. And the British jeweler who confirmed Atherstone's report on the diamond declined to send anyone to the cape to look for more. Amazingly, while everyone in England was furiously denying the existence of South African diamonds, more and more of the precious gems were being found all the time.

Third: *STICK TO YOUR FIRST OPINION, ALL EVIDENCE TO THE CONTRARY*

Two years after Van Niekerk stumbled on the original "pebble," a British mineralogist finally deigned to actually visit the Cape of Good Hope and make a proper investigation. Of course, he came armed with a preconceived decision. Professor James Gregory arrived in South Africa in 1868, bound and determined to prove that there were no diamond deposits in the region. Supposedly, he traveled the length and breadth of the whole colony, examining every area where locals had found diamonds. We say "supposedly" because, in his final report, Gregory declared South Africa diamond-free—despite having traveled (or claiming to have traveled) through regions where other people were finding the gems just lying around in creeks and in the dirt. For all we know, he spent his time drinking mint juleps in Johannesburg. Gregory also devoted a great deal of time to coming up with a rational reason that could logically explain why so many diamonds had been found if the diamond deposits didn't exist. He failed. Instead, Gregory hypothesized that ostriches had accidentally swallowed diamonds in areas of Africa far, far away from the cape. Then, the ostriches traveled to southern Africa where they relieved themselves, thus dropping diamonds hither and non. By his theory, we can only assume that the Cape of Good Hope must have functioned as a giant, communal ostrich toilet. Unsurprisingly, Gregory's explanation turned out to be wrong. Shortly after he left the Cape, a massive 83-carat diamond was discovered. Known as the "Star of Africa," it inspired the colony's first mining investments. To this day, diamond-industry honchos still refer to bad judgments or mistakes as "pulling a Gregory."

Squander Your Genius

Method 1: *FADE AWAY*

For many years, William James Sidis was the quintessential stereotype of the child prodigy who couldn't make it in an adult world. The son of a renowned psychologist and one of the 19th century's few female doctors, Sidis was prepped to excel—his parents began teaching him English using wooden blocks shortly after he was born. He spoke his first word ("door") at 6 months. By age 5 he was typing his own letters to the Macy's toy department and had expanded his linguistic fluency to include Greek, Latin, Hebrew, Russian, French, and German. After breezing through grade school in a matter of months and high school in not much more time, he was accepted to Harvard at age 11 and made his first lecture to the school's math club one year later. Throughout all this, Sidis appeared repeatedly in the press and his parents actively encouraged public interest in their son. Unfortunately, all the attention made it difficult for Sidis to have a normal life. At Harvard, classmates threatened to beat him up, and when he took a teaching position at Rice University in Texas (at age 17) the media hounded him until his students' opinion of him was no better than his classmates' had been. In response, Sidis retreated from the public eye, devoting himself to a lifetime of seclusion and menial jobs, apparently in an attempt to preserve his own sanity. But he did continue working, using assumed names to write and (less frequently) publish treatises on Native American history, astrophysics, and his vast collection of streetcar transfers. When he died of a brain hemorrhage in 1944, the 46-year-old Sidis was penniless.

Method 2: *BURN OUT*

Like William Sidis, Philippa Schuyler was pushed into the public eye at an early age. However, Schuyler's life, it seems, was considerably worse. The daughter of a Harlem Renaissance journalist and a white Southern belle, Schuyler's life in mid-20th century America was already guaranteed to be complicated. Add to that a precocious intelligence, a pushy stage mother who exploited and manipulated that intelligence in the press, and a deeply weird childhood punctuated by beatings and a diet of raw, buttered meat (again, the work of her mom) and you've got a recipe for one severely troubled individual. Under her mother's direction, Schuyler gave her first radio-broadcast piano concert at age 5 and began touring a few years later. Disturbingly, mother promoted daughter as a curiosity, exploiting both Schuyler's talent and mixed-race parentage for public attention. But, as she grew up, Schuyler found that the white audiences that had clamored to see her as a "freak" child were decidedly less interested in her work as an adult. Schuyler's grown-up life quickly devolved into a string of attempts to pass for white and disastrous relationships further hampered by her mother's control-freak tendencies. Eventually, she gave up the piano altogether and turned her attention to journalism, a change which led to her death in 1967 while on assignment in Vietnam. Sadly, she might have lived had she been allowed more of a childhood. After the helicopter she was traveling in crashed in open water, Schuyler was still alive, but, never having learned to swim, she was unable to reach the nearby shore.

Method 3: *BOOZE IT UP*

Branwell Brontë was supposed to be famous. The talented only brother of Charlotte, Emily, and Anne, Branwell was privately tutored in classical arts and sciences by his father, while his sisters had to make due with a brief stint at a tuberculosis-ridden institute for the children of poor ministers. In adulthood, the girls stayed at home, while Branwell went out into the world to make a living as a painter and tutor. Unfortunately, this didn't go particularly well and he was fired from one job after another before returning to the family in 1845 and immersing himself in booze and (if 150-plus years of rumors are to be believed) laudanum. He basically remained in this state until his death 3 years later, quite possibly never having noticed that, in the meantime, his sisters had published some of the great works of English literature.

Be Misquoted

LIKE SHERLOCK HOLMES

"Elementary, my dear Watson." Famous words, but not ones Sir Arthur Conan Doyle would have recognized. Doyle never quoted his literary creation, Sherlock Holmes, saying the famous line. Instead, it came from a series of Sherlock Holmes movies starring Basil Rathbone. Which just proves what you learned in high school English class: watching the movie isn't the same as reading the book.

LIKE GEORGE WASHINGTON

"I cannot tell a lie." Except, of course, for that one. We've all heard the story about how young George Washington was bad enough to chop down a neighbor's cherry tree, but not bad (or, perhaps, smart) enough to lie about it . . . but it turns out that the story itself is a big, fat fabrication. Washington's first biographer, the questionable Anglican minister Parson Weems, cut the tale from whole cloth. It's the most famous story from Weems's saintly 1800 biography, conveniently published right after Washington died and could no longer defend himself.

LIKE THE BIBLE

"Spare the rod and spoil the child." You'll be happy to know that the maxim cited by your parents right before they turned you over their knees is not biblical in origin. In fact, its source is rather scandalous. Like a TV preacher caught in a seedy motel, "spare the rod" actually leapt from the brain of Samuel Butler, an English poet (not to be confused with the novelist Samuel Butler, author of *Erewhon*) who's also known for his long poem *Dildoides*—which holds the distinction of being the only book-length poem written about a shipment of French dildos. In the poem, the dildoides are destroyed by British customs, but not before Butler can describe them in somewhat painfully elaborate detail.

Become Obsolete

It sounds bad, but really, don't sweat it. It's just retirement, not an insult. So kick back, relax, and have your nurse bring another round of those fabulous prune juice martinis. We're going out in style!

LIKE THE STEAM-POWERED CAR

The first vehicles, from the one built and driven by mining engineer Richard Trevithick in 1801, to the famous Stanley Steamers of the Victorian Age, all ran on steam. And why not? Steam was the de rigeur technology of the day, promising to float everyone into the future on little white puffs. So what if steam cars took as long as 90 minutes to warm up and had to be refilled with water as frequently as every 30 miles? Of course, it helped that the fist internal combustion engines were louder and smellier than those of today and had the added bonus of needing to be started with a hand crank. If the car backfired, the hand crank could (and did) break drivers' arms. Unfortunately for steam-lovers, that golden age couldn't last forever. The broken bone problem was solved with the introduction of the electric starter in 1912 and it was pretty much downhill from there for the slower, fussier steam engine. It wasn't until 1924 that Doble Steam Motors introduced a car that matched the gasoline-powered versions in speed and convenience and, by that point, the war was already lost. Ironically, though, the Doble's car, called the Model E, turned out to be far ahead of its time. All the Model Es still running today are, without modification, clean enough to pass California emissions laws.

LIKE THE PLAYER PIANO

You probably think of them as a major feature of any respectable Wild West ghost town, but the basic gist of the player piano dates back to at least the 16th century, when the will of King Henry VIII listed him as owner of one such device. Essentially, player pianos were the oversized boom boxes of their day, enabling music lovers to listen to their favorite tunes even when there wasn't a trained performer around to pound the keys. Interestingly, the type of player piano we're most familiar with today knew how to play its songs the same way the first computers knew what operations to perform—via a series of holes punched in paper. The position of the hole and its length determined what note the piano played and for how long. To nobody's surprise, player pianos ultimately fell out of favor in the 20th century as more and more people chose instead to join the march of progress through phonographs, record players, tape decks, CD players, and on to the iPod.

Start Over Someplace New

According to immigrants to America

Do: ***TRAVEL IN GROUPS***

You hardly needed to tell this to immigrants to America in the late 19th and early 20th centuries. Political unrest, religious persecution, and drooping economies throughout Europe sent such a massive wave of newcomers flooding onto our shores that they overwhelmed the abilities of the old state-by-state immigration system. In 1890, the federal government standardized and streamlined the process. From that point on, there were only four ports through which an immigrant could enter: New York, Boston, Savannah, and San Francisco. Two years later, the most famous of these ports, Ellis Island in New York, was opened for business. The first person to pass through was a 15-year-old Irish girl. In commemoration of the event

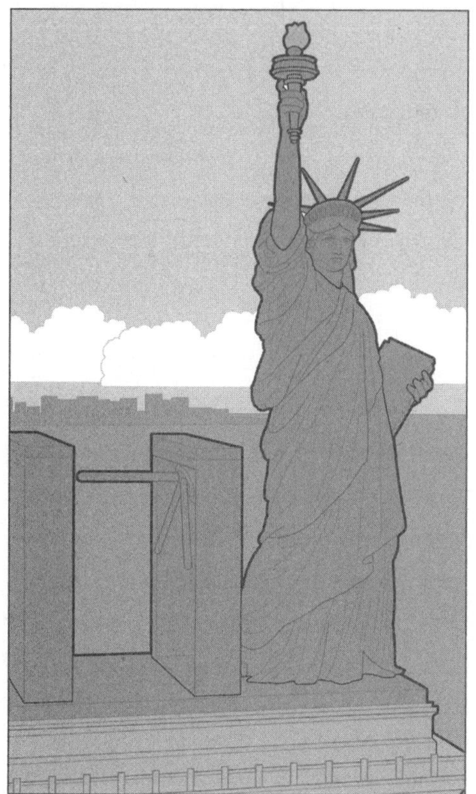

she was given a formal greeting by government officials and, more enviably, a $10 gold coin. (Back then, $10 was the equivalent of more than $200 today.)

Do: *BE IN GOOD HEALTH*

The first thing each and every immigrant did when they arrived in America was to get a medical examination. If you could afford first or second-class passage, this was usually as simple as a cursory glance-over. Immigrants who traveled in steerage, however, weren't assumed to have enough money to necessarily be in good health. These were the passengers who were shipped by ferry to Ellis Island before their boat docked in New York. There, a first, quick examination determined whether they needed to be more closely inspected. Those with apparent or suspected problems were marked by chalk letters scrawled onto their clothing. They received more thorough exams. If they turned out to really be deficient, they were detained until well and/or turned away from America completely. The most common illnesses were tuberculosis, an eye disease called trachoma, and mental illness or deficiency.

Don't: *WORRY ABOUT BECOMING "MRS. SMITH"*

Despite what you learned from watching *An American Tail*, immigrants with complicated last names weren't usually rechristened with Americanized versions by uncaring government bureaucrats. In fact, despite an abundance of urban legends to the contrary, it's unlikely that this happened to anyone at all. Immigrants came with documentation of their identity, which could be easily copied by any clerk. Besides that, Ellis Island employed numerous translators and was frequented by immigration advocates, largely ruling out the possibility of miscommunication. Based on known evidence, if anyone changed immigrants' names without their consent, it was the neighbors, teachers, and employers they met once they reached the mainland.

Die Laughing

YOU WILL NEED

- A sense of humor
- Poor health

Tip #1: *WATCH BRITISH COMEDIES*

In the last 30 years or so, at least 2 people have died while laughing at British-made comedies, which (and we're only guessing here) is probably at least twice the death rate attributable to American humor. The first incident happened in 1975 when a man named Alex Mitchell keeled over while watching a skit on the show *The Goodies*. (For the record, the skit was apparently about Scottish martial arts and involved a man in a kilt fighting off a blood pudding with a set of bagpipes. Maybe you had to be there.) While some people might have sued the television station for broadcasting such dangerous jokes, Mitchell's widow actually sent *The Goodies* a thank-you card—for making his last moments so pleasant. The second death came in 1989, when Danish audiologist Ole Bentzen got so into busting a gut over *A Fish Called Wanda* that his heart rate reached a speed of between 250 and 500 beats per minute (average heart rate: 70 bpm) and he went into cardiac arrest. When will someone stop this Britcom menace?

Tip #2: *GO CRAZY*

What's Laughing Psychosis? Picture the Joker from Batman and you're on the right track. A debilitating progressive neurological disorder, laughing psychosis is triggered by an excess of amino acids in the brain. As these amino acids coagulate into a big mass they cause various synapses to start misfiring, leading victims to start laughing for no reason. As the disease progresses, they'll often wake up in the middle of the night caught in fits of laughter. More than mere chuckles, victims begin to see things that aren't there and experience a break with reality not unlike what happens to schizophrenics. Naturally, such hallucinations increase the chance of death exponentially. The group most affected by the disorder: women ages 15 to 30, who have higher levels of estrogen that may help the amino acids to start getting out of control.

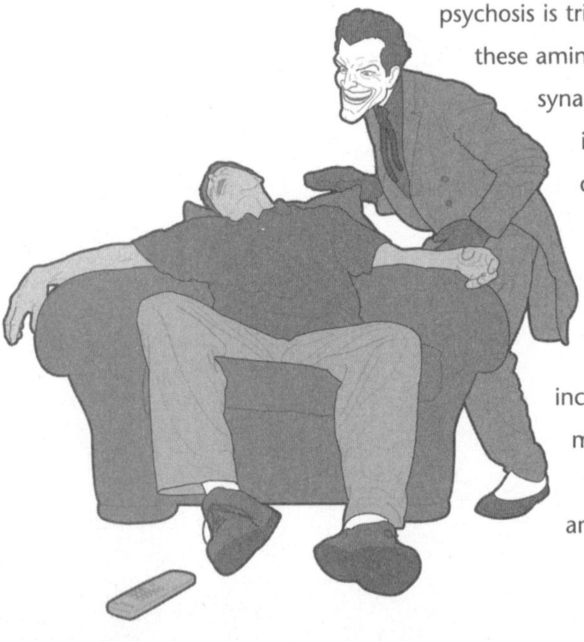

About the Author

MAGGIE KOERTH-BAKER is a freelance writer and contributing editor to *mental_floss* who balances her "serious ha-ha" writing for the Floss with "serious, no really" writing for national publications including the Associated Press, MSN.com, and *Health* magazine. In the line of journalistic duty, she has made international telephone calls to talk about heavy metal music, spent countless hours at the library, and bitten the head off a live fish. (See if you can guess which of those things wasn't done for *mental_floss*.) A contributor to several *mental_floss* tomes, *Be Amazing* is her first solo book project. That makes her feel pretty darn amazing. You can find more of Maggie's work online at www.maggiekb.com.

About the Editors

WILL PEARSON and **MANGESH HATTIKUDUR** met as freshmen at Duke University and in their senior year parlayed their cafeteria conversations into the first issue of *mental_floss* magazine. Seven years later, they're well on their way to creating a knowledge empire. In addition to the magazine, the award-winning mentalfloss.com and *mental_floss' Law School in a Box* (the number one boxed law school in the country!), the two have collaborated on nine *mental_floss* books.

A Genius for Every Occasion . . .

mental_floss Cocktail Party Cheat Sheets
978-0-06-088251-8 (paperback)
Don't be a wallflower at your next social outing, just fake your way through the conversation! These cheat sheets will have you equipped to handle the brainiest of topics in no time.

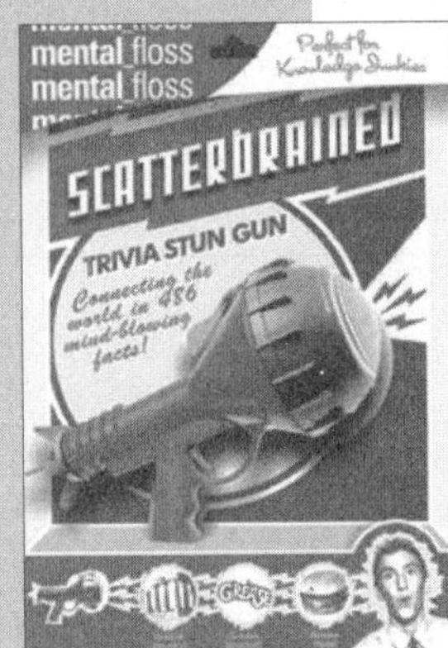

mental_floss Scatterbrained
978-0-06-088250-1 (paperback)
Based on *mental_floss* magazine's popular "Scatterbrained" section, this book features thousands of tantalizing bits of trivia that are connected—from Greece (the country) to *Grease* (the movie) to greasy foods and on and on.

mental_floss What's the Difference?
978-0-06-088249-5 (paperback)
Want to spot a Monet from a Manet, kung fu from karate, or Venus from Serena Williams? No matter who you're trying to impress, *mental_floss* has hundreds of quick tricks to make you sound like a genius.

mental_floss Genius Instruction Manual
978-0-06-088253-2 (paperback)
The ultimate crash course on how to talk, act, and even dress like a genius. Presented by the brainiac team at *mental_floss*, it's the one-stop shop for today's impossibly clever, cultured, and sophisticated person.

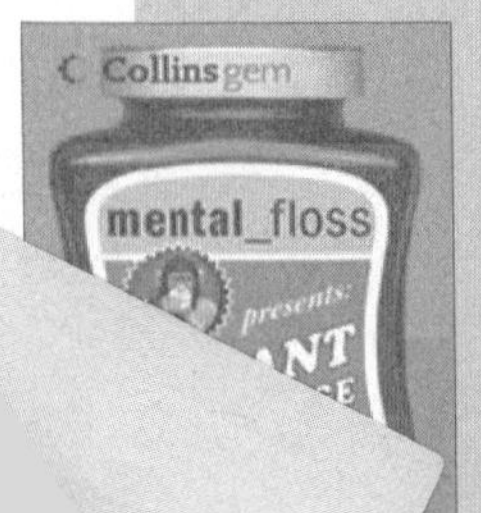

mental_floss presents Instant Knowledge
978-0-06-083461-6 (paperback)
This A to Z guide to tons of facts, trivia, and intellectual tidbits is a veritable Ace up your sleeve when attending cocktail parties, gallery openings, or dinner with the boss!

. . . also available from . . .

mental_floss

The Mental Floss History of the World
978-0-06-078477-5 (hardcover)
Go on an amazingly entertaining joyride through 60,000 years of human civilization, where you'll learn that just because it's true doesn't mean it's boring!

mental_floss presents Condensed Knowledge
978-0-06-056806-1 (paperback)
Nurture your inner smart aleck with this breezy, information-packed guide to what you should have learned in school, but probably didn't.

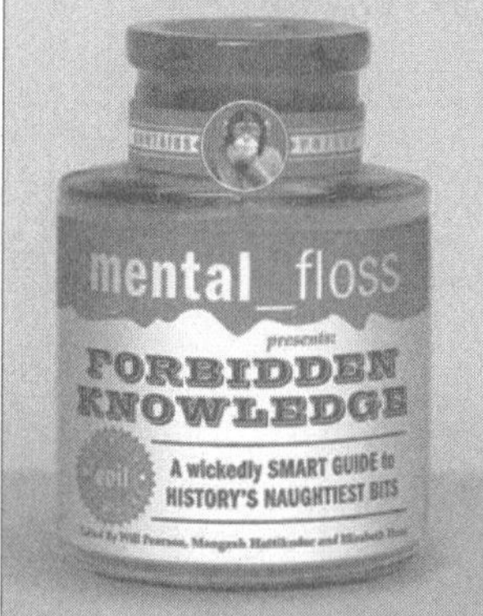

mental_floss presents Forbidden Knowledge
978-0-06-078475-1 (paperback)
An adorably naughty and delightfully mischievous romp through the dark side of human nature. It's the perfect way to add some spice to a dull conversation and proves that learning can be not only easy, but exquisitely sinful.

mental_floss presents In the Beginning
978-0-06-125147-4 (paperback)
Explore the origins of just about everything from countries to can openers, Champagne to Cheese Whiz, and Dixie Cups to "Dixie".